THE BASTARD LEGION

BOOK ONE

THE BASTARD LEGION

BOOK ONE

GAVIN G. SMITH

First published in Great Britain in 2017 by Gollancz
an imprint of the Orion Publishing Group Ltd
Carmelite House, 50 Victoria Embankment
London EC4Y 0DZ

An Hachette UK Company

1 3 5 7 9 10 8 6 4 2

A CIP catalogue record for this book
is available from the British Library.

ISBN 978 1 473 21725 6

Typeset by Deltatype Lt, Birkenhead, Merseyside

Printed in Great Britain by Clays Ltd, St Ives plc

www.gavingsmith.com
www.orionbooks.co.uk
www.gollancz.co.uk

For Dyanne

Every man thinks meanly of himself for not having been a soldier, or not having been at sea.

– Samuel Johnson, 1778

CHAPTER 1

Pounding drums and screaming guitars filled her lightweight spacesuit. It was supposed to be a stealth observation mission but Miska Corbin had grown bored as she closed with Faigroe Station. Her laser carbine became her air guitar as she wind-milled through space, trusting that the suit's reactive camouflage would render her invisible despite her frantic movement.

Far behind her the debris field around Tau Ceti made the small yellow sun appear as if it were caught in a pollution haze. It reminded her of the cities of Earth, not that she'd ever been there. Below, she could make out bands of red, brown and white clouds in the atmosphere of Tau Ceti G, the gas giant she was orbiting at some speed. A super-storm was forming among the clouds, slowly, like a huge whirlpool. It was beautiful, Miska supposed, but she'd been looking at it for a long time.

'Pumpkin?' The voice crackling over her comms link had become a low growl from years of shouting. It was a voice used to being obeyed – but somehow it was always soft when it spoke to her. She shut down the music.

'Dad!' Miska hissed. 'Don't call me that when we're running ops.' The assault team in the shuttle trailing her wouldn't have heard, but the pilot and co-pilot would have.

'What would you prefer? Agent, warden, general, *legatus legionis*?' he asked.

It was something she actually was going to have to think about, but perhaps not right now.

'What about a cool codename like Sabre, or Domino?' she suggested.

'Where's my targeting package?' her dad asked. Apparently he'd had enough of mucking around for one operation. The ugly, potato-shaped rock that was Faigroe Station was much closer now. From her slightly lower orbit Miska found herself looking up at the asteroid mine. She could see the underside weapon emplacements, mainly point defence lasers and railguns, but more significantly she could make out a missile battery as well.

'Working!' Miska sang over the comms link. She suspected her reply wasn't going to particularly reassure Gunnery Sergeant Jonathan Corbin, United States Marine Corps, retired. Her father. As she readied her carbine she noticed movement in the clouds far below her. Looking down she saw a number of bulky, though still aerodynamic, craft with wide, mouth-like fuel scoops rising out of the swirl. They were drone craft sent down by the station to harvest the gas giant's combustibles, to help fuel the mine. 'Interesting,' Miska mused as the craft rose up towards her, their manoeuvring engines burning hard.

'Miska?' Her dad's voice was sterner over the comms link this time. He had access to the lenses in her suit, he could see that she wasn't doing what she was supposed to be doing.

'All right, all right,' Miska said, though she chose not to say it across the link. She brought the laser carbine up to her shoulder, using the suit's compressed-air manoeuvring system to stabilise herself. Dialling down the carbine's destructive power but increasing its range through the smartlink, she used the laser to passively 'paint' each of the weapons emplacements. This allowed her spatial positioning system to work out the exact coordinates of the weapons, which she then transmitted to the *Hangman's Daughter*. The prison barge's own targeting systems would then adjust for the station's movement.

'Targeting packages sent,' she said over the comms link.

'Received,' her dad said. Then, after a few moments: 'Looks good.'

'Guys, come and pick me up,' she said to the shuttle pilots over the comms link.

'On our way,' the pilot replied. As it always did, a brief bio appeared in her Internal Visual Display. McMasters, Jon. Sentenced for thirty years in the ultramax prison barge for human trafficking.

Miska returned her carbine to its combat settings as she waited and magnified the rear-facing lens on her suit's helmet. She could just about make out the large, squat, ugly mass of the hundred-year-old surplus military assault shuttle, which had been repurposed as a prisoner transport. The shuttle was over the planetary horizon now, which meant that even the rudimentary scanners of the asteroid mine would be able to pick it up. Miska checked the civilian frequencies.

'Unidentified shuttle, this is Faigroe Station Co-operative's traffic control. We're going to have to ask you to cease your approach.' The woman's voice was calm but Miska could hear the tension in it, even over the comms.

'Faigroe Station traffic control, please be advised we are political prisoners who have escaped from the prison barge

Hangman's Daughter. We request sanctuary.' The voice belonged to the co-pilot. Gleave, Jeff. Ten years for fraud. He didn't really belong in an ultramax prison but had been sent there after a number of successful escapes from various planetary prisons. He had been chosen as co-pilot for two reasons: he had enough neuralware in his head that skillsofts, such as the ability to pilot a shuttle, could be uploaded into his brain; and he had been a conman. If he couldn't talk his way onto the asteroid mine then Miska and her dad hoped that he would at least get them a little closer.

'Faigroe Station to unidentified shuttle, we sympathise but we're going to have to ask you to stand off. As I'm sure you can imagine, we're a bit tense at the moment so unless we know you, you ain't getting on board.'

Miska checked the shuttle's position. It was directly below her and getting larger, the manoeuvring engines burning hard on the end of their arms.

'Faigroe Station, please! You're our only hope! We're low on fuel, we need food and medical supplies, we have a number of casualties in critical condition on board ... the guards ... during the mutiny ... they were brutal.' To give Gleave credit he was really selling the story. Maybe a little over the top.

Like all good lies, their cover story contained an element of truth. Although to be fair there hadn't been a mutiny; she had just stolen the prison barge and nobody had got hurt. Not during the theft, anyway.

When Miska glanced down at the shuttle it suddenly looked much bigger, and it didn't seem to be getting any slower.

'Guys, I don't mean to tell you how to fly but shouldn't you be slowing down now?' she asked. One of the problems of using smugglers to fly shuttles was that they all thought they were

4

still hotdog pilots running orbital blockades. She triggered the compressed-air propulsion system on the suit, shooting upwards as the shuttle caught up with her. It lessened the impact as she hit the top of it. It still felt like the bones in her legs were trying to get into her ribcage as the air was battered out of her. She bounced off the top of the shuttle but it came up to meet her again. Miska managed to twist and use the pads on her hands and knees, each covered in tiny molecular hooks, to adhere herself to the top of the shuttle.

'Ow!' she snapped over the comms link.

'Sorry, Pumpkin,' McMasters replied. She could hear the laughter in his voice. She couldn't really begrudge him petty acts of revenge after what she had done to him and all his fellow prisoners. Calling her Pumpkin, on the other hand …

'You know I can blow your head up with a thought, right?' Miska asked as she started crawling across the top of the shuttle even as it rose towards the underside of the asteroid. McMasters decided not to answer.

'Faigroe traffic control to unidentified shuttle, if you do not cease your approach and stand off we will open fire!' It sounded like Gleave's powers of persuasion hadn't done the trick. Miska increased her pace as she heard Gleave's reply. She didn't want to be outside when …

The darkness of space glowed bright red for a moment. The shot across their bows from the station's underside laser cannon had almost been close enough to toast her.

'Fuck's sake!' she said, not realising that the comms link was still open.

'Miska, language!' her dad snapped. She suspected it was an automatic parental reflex.

'Are you fucking kidding me?' Miska demanded. 'Someone's

5

shooting a fucking laser cannon at me!' She felt doubly aggrieved because part of the job description of a USMC gunnery sergeant was to take swearing to hitherto unexplored heights. Something her dad had excelled at, according to those he had trained.

It looked like a shower of falling stars was heading for the shuttle. Miska knew it was tracer fire from the station's railgun emplacements. She managed to make it to the airlock. Just.

'I'd really like to come inside now!' she shouted. She was caught in a silent rain of phosphorescent sparks as the rounds disintegrated against the shuttle's thick armour, leaving little pockmarks all over.

'With you in a moment,' McMasters said nonchalantly. It was largely luck that she hadn't been hit yet. There was another flash of light, this time coming from the planetary horizon. She was too far away to see the ship, but she knew that far behind the shuttle the huge prison barge, the *Hangman's Daughter*, had just heaved over the horizon and used the targeting information she had provided to fire on the asteroid mine. Light stabbed out high above the gas giant as Miska clung to the side of the moving shuttle, trying to make herself as small a target as possible. There were explosions on the asteroid, fountains of newly molten rock quickly cooling in the vacuum. The airlock opened.

It wasn't often that Miska got angry, but she was reasonably cross now. She also wasn't often frightened, but she didn't deal well with feeling helpless. She was self-aware enough to realise the irony of this as she pulled herself into the airlock and artificial gravity. The external hatch closed and the airlock started cycling air in.

'Gleave?' she asked the co-pilot over the comms link.

'Er, yes Pump ... Misk ... Miss?' he managed. He sounded shit-scared. She could hear the hard percussion of the railgun rain against the shuttle's armour. Outside the small porthole in the airlock, space glowed red again; moments later the railgun fire ceased.

'Miska's fine. I need you to take over piloting, understand me?' she said as the inner airlock hatch opened and she stepped into the corridor that led to the shuttle's prisoner bay. The laser-cutting torch that the Tau Ceti Company had given them was bolted to the ceiling on an extendable arm just outside the airlock.

'Erm ... don't you want me to speak to traffic control?' Gleave asked.

'Negotiations finish when they start shooting at you,' Miska told him. 'Do it now.'

'Hey, wait a second!' McMasters said. 'I was just messing around!' Miska opened the comms link so the assault squad waiting in the prisoner holding area could hear her.

'If I die then you kill everyone. Not just me, not just you, not just everyone on the shuttle, but all six thousand prisoners on board the *Hangman's Daughter*.'

'No wait, I'm sorr—'

Miska shut the link and sent the detonation code to McMaster's collar. He had been sorry too late. She didn't even hear the explosion. She was, however, slammed into the corridor wall as the shuttle veered suddenly before Gleave, presumably terrified by the explosive decapitation of the man who'd been sat next to him, managed to regain control of the shuttle.

All eyes were on Miska as she walked into the prisoner holding area. Her helmet visor slid over her head, collapsing into the suit's collar. Twenty faces stared at her as she ran her fingers through her unruly, almost spiky, dirty blonde hair. Some looked impassive, others frightened. A lot of them looked

1

angry, but no matter how well hidden it might be, she knew that the one thing the majority of the prisoners, her convict soldiers, had in common was their hatred of her and her dad.

Constructed from scuffed black metal and hard plastic composites, the prisoner holding bay contained four staggered rows of secure seating on each side. Each row had twenty-five seats. The twenty-four prisoners who formed the assault team were sat close to the thick blast door that led to the cockpit.

'Hello everyone,' Miska said cheerfully. 'It's very exciting outside at the moment!'

Nobody said anything, but forty-eight hard eyes belonging to criminals dangerous enough to be sent to an ultramax prison barge stared at her. She knew that the only things keeping her alive were the explosive collars around their necks.

'This is our first time out, so I'm going to go over the plan one more time. The miners on Faigroe Station, employees of the Tau Ceti Company, have illegally taken control of the asteroid. The company is paying us—' she thought about this for a moment, 'well, paying me, since you guys are doing it out of the goodness of your hearts and because of the collars round your necks – to get their property back. Our plan is terribly, terribly simple. We're going to dock with the station, cut our way through the airlock, and occupy the cargo bay long enough for me to trance into the net and use the command codes the Tau Ceti Company provided us with to take control of the station's systems and lock it down until company reinforcements can reach us.

'R.O.E!' Miska shouted. 'We're expecting spirited but weak resistance. These guys are miners. They've got next to no access to weapons other than the few they've taken from company security personnel. They do, however, have access to mining equipment. This includes cutting lasers. You answer force with

8

force. Someone gives you shit, give them shit back. They attack you, put them on the ground. They try to kill you, you kill them first. That said, I don't want a blood bath if we can avoid one, and I know the difference between a genuine threat and you trying to justify killing someone for the hell of it. I hope that the lesson McMasters just taught us all isn't lost on you.

'I'll be operating independently but you follow the drills we did in the run-up to this and you'll be fine. Any questions?'

'What does R.O.E mean?' Prola, Massimo. Consecutive life sentences for multiple counts of first-degree murder. There were some laughs at his question. An olive-skinned man in his early forties, he looked out of place in the repainted riot armour that had once belonged to one of the *Hangman's Daughter*'s guards. Once a button man, the Mafia term for a hitman, in the Cofino family on St Barnard's Prime, he would have been much more comfortable in a suit, wearing gold chains and rings. It had been the uniform of a lot of the La Cosa Nostra thugs she'd had to deal with in her life.

'Rules of Engagement, Mass. Wanna explain to Gunnery Sergeant Corbin why you weren't paying attention?'

Massimo chuckled. 'I'm just messing with you, Miska. Good to go ... or whatever.' He looked at her just a little bit too long. They'd called him the Fisherman back on Barney's Prime, because he liked to gut people with a hooked knife. It was kind of obvious what he'd like to do to Miska, given the chance.

'You going to kill the other pilot?' Torricone, Michael. Ten years for grand theft auto, then another thirty years and transferred to the *Hangman's Daughter* for the second-degree murder of a fellow inmate. He was an attractive Hispanic guy in his late twenties, dark eyes, tattoos crawling out from under his explosive lowjack collar and his helmet, a tear just below his left eye. Miska turned to look at him. He held her look. She saw no fear there, but more unusually if there was hatred then it was buried deep. He came across as very serious, maybe even sad.

'If need be, and anyone else,' she told him. 'But seriously, why don't we try and enjoy ourselves?'

Torricone's answering laugh was devoid of humour, and he turned away from her. There was something off in his expression. She wasn't sure if it was disgust or pity, but it left her discomfited for just a moment.

'I'm going to release the restraints. Weapons hot, so if you want to get it all over and done with then you can just shoot me in the back.' Miska turned and headed towards the corridor that led to the airlock. This was the most dangerous part of the mission. She heard the bars across the seats flip open. Heard the familiar shuffling of armoured soldiers as they grabbed their M-19 assault rifles from the clips next to the seats. Just as her dad had drilled them, they checked the weapons, albeit with varying degrees of clumsiness.

'Fuck you, bitch!' The scream didn't sound entirely sane. She heard answering insults from the other convicts. Miska stopped and sighed theatrically. Secretly, she was relieved. The assault team hadn't seen McMasters. It hadn't been immediate enough. An example still had to be made. Miska turned around. Not for the first time she realised that her five-foot-six-inches meant that the majority of prisoners were a lot taller than her.

'I'm not going! I'm not going to die for you!' Chaver, Brian. Serving a life sentence for some particularly brutal home invasions. He had gang tattoos and the emaciated frame of a habitual drug dealer, though her dad's physical training regime had been starting to bulk him out a little. The enforced cold turkey of prison hadn't got rid of his jitters, however. His M-19 slugthrower rifle was levelled at her.

'Put it down!' Mass shouted, his own M-19 up at his shoulder. Miska smiled at Chaver as she walked towards Mass.

'Rat motherfucker!' one of the other convicts snapped at Mass.

'You know who I am!' Mass snapped back but he didn't take his eyes off Chaver.

'Don't fucking move any closer, bitch!' Chaver screamed, the barrel of his weapon tracking her.

'Seriously. This won't help, *mano*,' Torricone said quietly. He was still standing quite close to Chaver, though other prisoners were shuffling away.

Miska reached up and pushed the barrel of Mass's weapon down.

'You're going to let us go or I will put this entire magazine into you. Do you understand me, bitch?' Chaver shouted.

'She'll kill us all, asshole!' Mass told him. A number of the other assault team members seemed to be in agreement.

'That's bullshit, man!' Chaver screamed. 'It's a bluff, she's not a monster.' Miska was taken aback, insulted even. And she hated home invaders.

'Yes I am,' she said and then smiled sweetly at the man holding a gun on her. 'Brian. Can I call you Brian?'

'Junior C to you, bitch!' Chaver screamed. The barrel of the M-19 was shaking.

'Fair enough. You see, Brian, I wouldn't hesitate to kill every last one of you. You need to believe that. Well, you don't. It's too late for you.'

'I'm going to give you to the count of three!' he screamed. 'Open the collars!'

11

'Don't do this, man,' Torricone said.

'Three!' Chaver shouted.

'Two,' Miska said, drawing her sidearm. Her augmented reflexes meant that she moved faster than Chaver's cheap cyber-ware could make him react. She pressed the barrel of the pistol to her own head. 'You see, Brian, if I'm going to be killed it won't be by someone like you.'

His eyes went wide as he stared at her. Torricone looked away, shaking his head. Even Mass looked surprised.

'One,' Miska said, and pulled the trigger on the pistol at the same time as she used her smartlink connection to safety the weapon and sent the detonation codes to Chaver's lowjack.

The gangbanger was just starting to squeeze his trigger. People dived out of the way as the collar blew with a muffled *crump*, and his head went tumbling into the air. Miska took the safety off her gauss pistol and then holstered it. Chaver's body rocked backwards and forwards for a moment and then fell. Blood spattered Torricone's face but he didn't move.

'Any more questions?' Miska asked cheerfully. Faces were appearing from behind the secure seating.

'Don't blow my head off or nothing,' Mass said, 'but I think there's something wrong with you.'

Miska grinned up at the Mafia hitman. 'Thank you!' she said and then leaned in close to him. 'I understand that this is a bit of a shitty situation for you guys but I promise you, you'll never be bored,' she whispered, loud enough to be heard by everyone.

'Right. C'mon guys, let's stack up!' Mass shouted, apparently having decided to take on a degree of command. Miska turned and walked up the corridor towards the airlock.

'We're about to dock,' a terrified Gleave said over the comms link.

'Miska,' her dad said, opening a private comms link to her. 'I don't want to see you ever put a loaded firearm to your head again, understand me?' He would have seen everything through the lenses in the prisoner holding area and those mounted on the assault team's helmet.

'Yes Daddy,' she said. 'I'm sorry.' But he didn't understand. It was just her here. She had to be the biggest psycho on board and there was a lot of competition. Chaver may have been a home-invading piece of shit but she was pretty sure he hadn't been one of the killers. He hadn't been capable, and they wouldn't have committed suicide like that. No, they'd be keeping a very low profile. As the assault team raced past her for the airlock she felt eyes on the back of her head. Somehow she knew it was Torricone.

CHAPTER 2

Miska watched Mass attach the hydraulic ram to one of Faigroe Station's cargo airlocks. The strobing beam of the cutting torch illuminated the convicts in harsh red light as they divided themselves into two squads.

Miska closed her eyes but the hellish glow still crept through her eyelids. Any computer and many electronic systems were accessible via the net. People like Miska who had an integral computer and a neural interface implanted in the meat of their brain were capable of complete sensory immersion within the electronic realm. Through their icons they could influence, manipulate and at times control their virtual surroundings, and through them the real-world systems the constructs represented. All she had to do was get into the station, connect to and enter the virtual reality representation of the asteroid mine's systems, and use the codes provided by the Tau Ceti Company. It sounded easy enough but Miska didn't like things that sounded easy. So she had checked out the codes, and they had seemed legit. She had researched Faigroe Station and what she had found out supported the intelligence that the company had provided. It had seemed like an ideal first mission for her fledgling mercenary penal legion.

The torch stopped cutting, molten metal running down the inside of the hatch.

'Remember, all you need to do is hold the space long enough for me to take control of the station's systems,' she said.

There were a few grunted affirmatives that were drowned out by the hammering of the ram. The laser-cut piece of hatch fell into the station's cargo bay. Miska glanced in through the hole, moving slowly so that her suit's reactive armour had time to blend in against the background. The cargo bay was dark and quiet but her modified eyes amplified the ambient light, making it look almost as bright as day. She saw crates of supplies stacked in haphazard rows. In the centre of the bay was the six-legged, beetle-like form of a mining mech. Its maw was a series of rock-crushing drills. There was no movement. Miska cursed the fact she had to wear a helmet for the reactive camouflage to work. The suit's audio sensors were good, but not as good as her enhanced hearing.

'So why is nobody waiting for us?' Torricone asked quietly over comms.

'They're just miners. Pickaxes against guns. I guess they didn't like the odds,' Mass said, though he didn't sound convinced.

Carbine at the ready, Miska moved slowly through the still-glowing hole in the hatch, half expecting to get shot the moment she showed herself. Nothing happened. She was on the asteroid now. Miska moved slowly to her right into a row of stacked pallets filled with ration packs.

'I am an awesome space ninja,' Miska said quietly to herself. She checked the row thoroughly and then moved back to a space between two of the stacked columns of pallets and climbed into it, letting the reactive camouflage do its work and render her effectively invisible.

'Deploy,' she said over the comms link. For a moment she had been tempted to leave them in the airlock, do the job without them and only use them if things went wrong, but part of the reason for taking this job was proof of concept. Could a penal mercenary legion, with its myriad of drawbacks, actually work? She checked the windows receiving the feeds from the assault teams' helmet lenses in her Internal Visual Display. They almost looked like a military unit as they came through the airlock and took up defensive positions in a semicircle around the hatch.

Miska closed her eyes and her neural interface went looking for net access. This was when she would be at her most helpless but the asteroid's rock was too good a shield for her to gain access from the outside. There were other ways she could have done this, snuck in through a comms connection perhaps, but such channels were heavily protected, and it would have meant a slight delay in her reactions. Given the speed at which things happened on the net, even an infinitesimal delay could spell disaster.

It went wrong quickly. The web architecture of the station was completely different to the simulation that the company had provided her with. It was supposed to look like some kind of retro, toxic theme park. Instead it looked like a high quality animation of a seventeenth century Caribbean pirate port. In parts she could see the old architecture underneath the pirate port. It looked as though it was corroding, being eaten away by the new code. The surrounding space was the black, glass-like ocean lapping at the white beach. There were tall ships in port, and other islands in the distance, presumably other stations orbiting Tau Ceti G. An angular fort sat atop a cliff overlooking the harbour. Behind her the shuttle was represented as a prison scow.

Miska was a tiny, spiky, cartoon version of herself that somehow managed to look cheerful, furious and very naughty all in one go. Her icon was carrying a huge club across one shoulder. The windows showing feed from the lenses on her suit and the assault teams' helmets orbited her. One of the squads was holding the airlock, the other had split into three fire teams and was sweeping the cargo bay.

'Well shit,' Miska said, not liking the new piratical net architecture at all because if the company intel was wrong about this, then what else were they wrong about? She glanced up at the fortress. All the secure systems would be up there. She pulled a handful of furry wriggling purple worms from the pocket of her polka-dot skirt. The worms were intrusion software and contained the control codes. She dropped them and they burrowed through the earth, heading up the hill towards the fort.

Miska watched them go. Then there was a figure standing in front of her on the beach. The icon was of a serious, attractive-looking young man with messy, shoulder-length dark hair and a stubbly beard. He was wearing a beret. He didn't fit the seventeenth century aesthetic. Miska was no history buff but she was pretty sure his clothes belonged to an era two or three hundred years after the golden age of piracy back on Earth.

'Well, you're a handsome devil,' Miska said. The icon held an ancient-looking pistol in his hand. He raised it and fired. Black lightning reached out from the barrel, hitting the worms as they burrowed through the earth, blowing them apart.

Miska's icon grimaced. 'This is a trap, isn't it?' she said. He nodded, almost apologetically. 'Abort! Fall back to the

17

shuttle!' she shouted over the comms link and then ejected her consciousness from the net.

There was just a moment of disorientation as her brain caught up with her physical body.

'Contact!' someone shouted over comms. She heard the unmistakable sound of M-19s firing long, undisciplined bursts as training gave way to adrenalin. Miska rolled out of her hiding place. The M-19 fire was answered by more automatic fire, which was followed by rapid small explosions. Miska didn't ask for a sitrep, a situation report; she suspected that the assault team would need to concentrate on just staying alive.

Checking the feed she saw armoured figures, carrying archaic-looking rifles, sweeping down through the rows of crates and firing at any intruders they found. The bullets were exploding when they hit their targets. Even if the bullets missed they exploded in the air close to her people. She heard screams and panicked shouting over the comms link. Her IVD showed that a number of the assault team's biometrics had flat-lined.

Through a gap in the pallets she saw more of the armoured figures in the next row running towards her. Miska brought the carbine up to her shoulder and fired a quick burst. The beams burned through the packing crates in a shower of sparks, setting one of the pallets on fire. She shifted her aim, fired again, and thought she heard an answering scream.

Miska moved quickly away from the airlock towards the end of the row and almost collided with another armoured figure coming around the corner. Miska dropped the carbine, letting it hang on its sling. She grabbed the barrel of the man's archaic slugthrower with her left hand, pushing it away from herself, and drew her fighting knife from the inverted sheath on her webbing with her other hand. The blade's synthetic diamond edge cut through the weapon's sling, then she rammed it into his throat up to the hilt. She kicked the man away, keeping hold of his weapon and hers. She touched the tip of her knife back to its scabbard and the smartgrip material sucked the blade up into it. There were more figures coming round the corner of one of the rows further up. She brought the slugthrower to her shoulder and fired. Airbursting explosions chased the figures back around the corner.

'Frag out,' Miska said over the comms link, though it was unlikely anyone was listening to her. She dropped the slugthrower and grabbed a frag grenade from the webbing on the front of her suit and threw it at the corner. She was already climbing the pallets as the frag exploded.

Miska reached the top of the column of pallets. There was a bright, strobing glow, accompanied by screaming from the airlock. From her elevated position she could see heads sliding off necks, torsos sliding off waists, bisected bodies tumbling to the ground in a red steam of boiled blood. The mining mech's cutting lasers. She heard the screaming buzz of the mech's drill bits start up, the clank of its heavy feet coming down on the rock floor as it moved towards the airlock.

Miska ran along the top of the pallets back towards the mech, relying on her reactive camouflage to keep her hidden. From up high she got a better view of the situation. It was all bad. She saw the flicker of muzzle flashes and explosions as her people were cut down. There were only five of them left alive, and two of those were in a bad way according to their biometrics. She watched as a one-armed convict, obviously in shock, walked into the drill-filled maw of the mining mech. His remaining limbs were shortly scattered around the cargo bay.

The mech's body sparked as someone laid fire down on it from inside the airlock.

'Shoot at the miners, shoot at the fucking miners!' Mass shouted over the comms link. As she sprinted across the pallets, Miska could make out Mass in the feed from his helmet lens, inside the shuttle's airlock. The Mafia button man was hitting the manual override on the external hatch. The airlock started to close, which wasn't ideal.

The insectile mech stepped forward. Heavy-duty forelimbs grabbed the closing airlock doors, holding them open. One of the injured convicts flat-lined, apparently having been stepped on. Miska reached the end of the row of pallets and jumped. The final member of her team still in the asteroid's cargo bay was running towards the airlock, coming up behind the mech. He got hit with so many explosive bullets that he was torn apart mid-stride. She couldn't worry about it now.

Miska landed on the back of the mining mech, hitting it hard, already starting to slide off. The hook pads on her knees and her left hand provided purchase and she crawled across the mech's back. She used her smartlink to the carbine to set timers on the four high-explosive armour-piercing grenades in its under-barrel launcher. The mining mech was heavily armoured, designed to withstand cave-ins, but it wasn't military and so had weak spots. An armoured hood covered the neck joint. Miska risked losing her fingers by holding onto the edge of the hood and firing the four grenades under it.

She finally had the attention of the asteroid's defenders. To them she must have looked like a flickering ghost riding the back of the bucking mech. Bullets exploded around her. The suit's inertial armour hardened but it still felt like she was being beaten by hammers and once again she was struggling to draw breath. Still holding the airlock doors open, the mech was pulling itself forward, trying to get its maw into the airlock so it could drill into the shuttle. Miska crouched, readying herself to jump. Something hit her in one of the hard armour plates on the back of her suit. Despite the kinetic padding distributing the force all around her body, it still felt like getting hit by a sledgehammer. She slid down the mech's head towards the spinning drill bits.

'Waah!' she screamed, eyes wide, heart trying to beat its way out of her chest. She straightened her legs out, throwing herself in a clumsy leap over the drills, landing in a heap just inside the airlock door, hard. She rolled over, the spinning drills bearing down on her. The timed warheads on the grenades exploded and the mech jumped backwards. She felt someone grab her helmet with both hands and drag her over the lip of the shuttle's airlock. The mech stopped, its head slumping down.

'Gleave, get us out of here!' Miska shouted over the comms link. The mech's heavy-duty clawed limbs were still holding onto the frame of the external hatch.

'The external—' Gleave's shaking voice started.

'Emergency override! Fuck health and safety!' The internal airlock door hissed shut, she heard the docking clamps release and the shuttle came away from the asteroid way too fast. It dragged the mech part of the way but it got jammed in the asteroid's airlock and was torn off the shuttle, buckling the external doors as it did so. The position of the mech would make it difficult to get the cargo bay's emergency depressurisation shield down, but that was not her problem.

Miska squeezed her eyes tight shut.

'Shit!' The word came out as a long exhalation. She resisted the urge to ball her hand into a fist and slam it into the bulkhead. She had not the slightest compunction about ordering the men under her command to their death. They were scum who had committed some of the worst crimes that humanity was capable of, but she did not want to waste life like this. And always at the back of her mind: what if one of the shooters was among the dead? It was unlikely, she hadn't seen much in the way of skills during the fight. Though Mass and Torricone were worth keeping an eye on. She opened her eyes and forced a smile back on to her face before taking the suit helmet off. She was covered in sweat.

'Well, that was exciting!' she finally managed when she was able to breathe again. Mass and Torricone were staring at her. They were the last two surviving members of the assault team. Mass was shaking. Miska was pretty sure it was fury and not fear. She hoped she wasn't going to have to blow his head up after all this. Torricone didn't look happy either.

Suddenly Mass grabbed Torricone and slammed him into the bulkhead next to the airlock door.

'You fucking coward!' he screamed in Torricone's face. Torricone slid to the side, breaking Mass's grip, putting him off balance and then pushing him away. Miska frowned. It was a slick move. Torricone must have been paying attention during her dad's hand-to-hand training.

'Don't touch me,' Torricone told Mass warily. Mass looked beyond furious.

'Are you out of your mind laying your hands on me?' Mass demanded. 'I'm a made man!'

'You think that matters here?' Torricone asked quietly. He might as well have slapped Mass.

Miska sighed and struggled to her feet. 'Gentlemen, while I applaud your commitment to violence, it's over. Mass?' Mass was ignoring her, just glaring at Torricone. 'Mass!'

His head snapped around to stare at her. All pretence of cooperation in his expression was gone. She could see what he really wanted to do to her in his eyes. Miska held out her hand for Mass's weapon.

'Give me your M-19 before you do something dumb,' she said quietly, holding his stare. Mass seemed to master himself and handed her the weapon. He was still angry, but the mask was down again. 'What's up?'

'This motherfucker wouldn't shoot any of the miners! Just wasted bullets on the mech and fired those bullshit baton rounds at the gunmen!'

The M-19, like most military rifles, had an underslung grenade launcher. The ones the convicts had inherited had come from the guard armoury on the prison barge. There were no military grenades like she carried, just non-lethal gel rounds and gas grenades.

Miska turned to Torricone. If he was frightened then he hid it well.

'Why didn't you fire on any of them?' Miska asked.

'I didn't want to kill anyone,' he told her. Mass shook his head, grunting in disgust.

'What about the tattooed tear?' she asked. Torricone didn't answer, he just walked away, making for the holding area.

'Mass, go and check the rest of the ship, make sure nobody managed to sneak on board,' she told the button man.

'Nobody got on—' he started. Miska just glared at him. He held up his hands, turned and walked away, heading in the opposite direction to Torricone. Miska slumped against the corridor's inner wall.

'Hey Dad,' she said over the comms link, suddenly tired. 'We're coming home.'

23

CHAPTER 3

Miska sent a data request to the *Hangman's Daughter*. The reply contained Torricone's file. She opened the file in her IVD as she walked slowly down the corridor towards the prisoner bay, assimilating the information quickly. He had been a car thief on Barney's Prime, or St Barnard's Prime, the main human inhabited planet in the St Barnard's Star system. He hadn't been just any old car thief, either. He had stolen top of the range automobiles and aircars to order. He had affiliations with a gang called the Disciples, and had some connections to organised crime, but he wasn't a member himself. He had been caught when the wrong warehouse had been raided on an unconnected matter. Someone had rolled on him as part of a plea bargain.

Car theft in itself wasn't enough to get you sent to an ultramax prison barge, no matter whose car you boosted. She checked his arrest images. He was covered in tattoos, many of them religious in nature, a crucifix across his back, the Virgin Mary over his heart – but the crown of thorns and the tear were prison tattoos. They had been done after his arrest. She checked

24

information on the prisoner he had killed: a gang-member, one of the Disciples he was supposed to have been affiliated with who was inside for 'chopping' – the illegal and bloody trade in stolen cyberware. Torricone's 'victim' had a lifetime of prior arrests and incarcerations. What interested Miska was Torricone's lack of arrests. He had obviously come up on the streets, and lived a life of crime, but other than a few juvenile misdemeanours he hadn't been caught. That meant he was smart, and the high-end vehicles he had stolen meant he was skilled.

'You've been hiding your light under a bushel,' Miska said to herself. Torricone should never have been on the assault team. She checked her father's assessment of him. It seemed that Gunnery Sergeant Corbin was of the opinion that Torricone was doing the bare minimum to get by. 'Because you don't want to draw attention to yourself,' Miska mused.

Miska reached the prisoner bay. Torricone had stowed his M-19 and sat back down in his seat.

'Why'd you kill him?' Miska called across the echoing bay as she stowed Mass's M-19.

'We're all innocent, remember?' he said. Turning towards him she could just about make out the ghost of a smile on his lips.

'This is your worst nightmare, isn't it?' Miska said. 'You wanted to keep your head down until I went away, not draw attention to yourself, didn't you?'

'Went away? Until the marshals catch up with you, you mean.'

Miska laughed. 'You know they'll be coming for me over a pile of your cellmates' bodies.'

Torricone sighed. 'You know what happens when you give people absolutely nothing to lose?' He pointed at Chaver's

25

headless corpse, still lying on the floor close by. Miska stopped just in front of Torricone, hands on her hips, studying him. 'See, I know I'm locked up with enough losers, enough no-hopers, enough morons and enough people who've just given up on life, that they'll keep trying, and one of them will succeed, kill you, then we all die.'

'But there's no reason why we can't enjoy ourselves before that happens. So why didn't you defend yourself?'

'You mean do your dirty work?'

Miska thought for a moment. 'I'd say those two positions were one and the same today.'

'They were just miners.'

'Armed hijackers and thieves. Possibly even terrorists, depending on your perspective.'

'Ever wonder what would make a group of people take up arms en masse like that? I recognise desperation when I see it.'

'So you'd have let them kill you?'

'I was hoping it would resolve itself in another way.'

'So it's better if I kill them, or Mass does? Your principles are more important than the other members of your team?'

'Whatever you try and make us, we're not military. I didn't owe them anything.'

Miska gave this some thought and then nodded. 'That's pretty cold.'

'You in a position to judge me?' he asked, taking off his helmet. She studied the crown of thorns tattooed around his shaved head.

Miska had to admit that he had a point. She pointed at the tear just under his left eye. 'Your principles didn't stop you from killing that chopper on Barney's Prime, though. Did they?'

'He wanted us to date. I didn't feel the same way about him.'

Torricone was looking at the worn metal floor of the holding area.

'That sounds suspiciously like self-defence to me,' Miska said. Torricone looked up at her but said nothing. 'Okay, sit back in your chair,' she told him. He did so. Miska sent a signal to the shuttle's systems via her neural interface. The seat restraints clunked down and locked Torricone in place. He was still looking at her.

'What'd it take for you to leave me asleep?' he asked. 'No training, nothing, just my dreams.'

'Wake you when it's over?' she asked. He nodded. 'Sorry,' she said with mock sincerity. 'I think you might be useful.'

'I won't do your dirty work.'

'Then I foresee rapid and sudden weight loss,' she said cheerfully as she bent down so they were face-to-face. 'But I think you'll come to like me!'

'I can't make up my mind if the mad thing is just an act, or there's actually something wrong with you.'

Miska straightened up, glancing back towards the corridor that led to the airlock. Mass was stood there, staring at Torricone.

'In your seat,' Miska told him. Grudgingly he walked over to his seat, never taking his eyes from Torricone. Miska ordered the shuttle's systems to lock the button man in place.

'We're going to be great friends. You'll see,' Miska whispered to Torricone before she almost skipped towards the cockpit. The day hadn't quite gone as planned but she was bouncing back, there was no point in letting it get her down. She had checked the external lens feed from the shuttle. They had dropped below the planetary horizon and were approaching the *Hangman's Daughter*'s hiding place. 'Play nicely, boys.'

The recently promoted pilot jumped as the door to the cockpit slid open. Gleave was covered in sweat and looked as if he might expire from sheer nerves at any moment. Just the sort of person you wanted flying a spacecraft.

'Oh God,' he managed.

'Hello,' Miska said brightly. The headless corpse of the previous pilot was still strapped into his seat. The entire front of the cockpit was transparent, with the shuttle's helm situated on a raised platform that allowed a panoramic view of local space – or, at least would have done, if it hadn't been for the red smear that ran down the windscreen.

'Where'd his head go?' Miska asked, looking around. She finally saw the pilot's head lying against the windscreen, underneath the raised helm. 'Wow, that's going to be a ball-ache to get.' She turned back to the pilot. 'I want you to know, I thought you did an excellent job under very trying circumstances.'

'Look, I'm not even really a pilot ...'

'I know you have just enough neuralware for us to upload skillsofts into your head,' she said tapping his temple.

He flinched at her touch. 'Oh God. Please don't kill me!'

Miska frowned. 'Why on earth would I kill you?' He didn't answer. 'But I do think you need to pay attention to what you're doing.'

The pilot turned back to the task in hand. There were quite a number of asteroids around Tau Ceti G. They came from the debris field that surrounded the G-Class star. Prospectors working for the Tau Ceti Company searched out the asteroids that were most likely to contain valuable minerals. Huge mass drivers were then used to fire the rocks further out of the system towards the gas giant. Tugs matched the asteroid velocity and then towed them into an orbit around the planet. There they were turned into mining camps, powered by helium and hydrogen harvested from Tau Ceti G. That meant there were a number of abandoned, hollow asteroids, which had just been left in orbit once they had been mined out. The shuttle was currently heading towards one of those.

Miska unclipped the straps holding the corpse of the pilot in place and strained as she heaved him out of the seat. He flopped to the floor. Gleave was studiously trying to ignore what was happening. With some effort, Miska dragged the body towards the door. It wasn't that she wasn't strong enough – despite her small frame she was mostly boosted, wiry muscle – it was that the floppy, dead weight of the body was somewhat awkward. She finally managed to throw it out of the cockpit and then sat down in the pilot seat.

'Ew! Sticky!'

'Erm ... do you want to take her in?' the pilot asked.

'You're doing just fine.' She glanced at his hands. He was shaking like a leaf. 'But I think you've spent too much time in prison. You seem uncomfortable around women.'

Gleave looked like he wanted to cry.

The shuttle was just coming round the edge of a huge hole in the asteroid. Jeff switched on the shuttle's searchlights and they played over the interior. Miska saw the edges of the huge prison barge, then the *Hangman's Daughter* turned on all her lights and illuminated the cavern. Miska looked up and around. There was something about the interior of the cored asteroid that reminded her of a cathedral. A sense of wonder.

'It's amazing, isn't it, Jeff? Can I call you Jeff?'

Jeff's only answer was a muffled sob.

The *Hangman's Daughter* was huge. It had been a

remarkable bit of flying from the ship's autopilot to get it into the hollowed-out asteroid. Though Miska had been forced to override the prison barge's particularly whiney safety protocols the first time they had hidden the ship.

Despite the diaspora, humanity had never quite managed to leave its criminality behind. The colonies suffered just as much from the social problems that had beset Earth throughout history, and as such incarceration and rehabilitation remained an issue wherever people went. Group 13, a private prison contractor, had come up with what they called the ultimate deterrent, or more accurately, what they thought was the ultimate dangerous-antisocial-individual storage facility: a prison barge. After all, it was difficult to escape from a ship in deep space, particularly one moving at superluminal speeds on the way to the next system to pick up the next piece of human cargo.

Group 13 had bought a number of ancient Tartarus Class troop carriers left over from the war with the alien Them, which had ended just over a hundred years before.

Refitting the troop transports had been a simple matter. After all, they had been designed to carry huge amounts of people in relative discomfort. They were still heavily armoured, which helped make them secure against people getting out, as well as hostile fire getting in. Although they had been significantly disarmed, they still had enough firepower to see off anything but the most committed attempt to free their human cargo. In fact, because the days of interstellar war were long gone and most modern conflicts were low intensity affairs, the *Hangman's Daughter* was probably a match for any ship that wasn't military. Though she was slow and couldn't manoeuvre for shit.

She was an ugly, roughly rectangular lump of industrial

superstructure with a tower at the stern that overlooked the rest of the ship.

Miska had purposefully had Gleave bring the shuttle in high. She didn't want the pilot to see her own ship clinging to the bottom of the prison barge.

It wasn't the smoothest of dockings but Jeff managed to get the shuttle in its plug-like bay on the forward edge of the barge. There were seven other shuttle-docking bays but only one other shuttle. That was another of the challenges Miska faced.

'Power her down,' Miska told Jeff, 'and then I'll have one of the droids escort you back.' Jeff looked as if he would relish returning to his pod. He almost jumped out of his skin when she slapped him on the shoulder. 'And good work, by the way.' She unstrapped herself and climbed out of the gory chair, though the stayclean finish on her suit meant that none of it stuck to her.

Jeff couldn't keep it together any longer. He burst into tears, head in his hands.

Miska walked out past Torricone and Mass. Torricone was sat upright, staring ahead. She flashed him a smile but he ignored her.

Miska walked out into the huge hangar deck, which ran for most of the length of the ship underneath the cellblocks. It had once been used to assemble troops and vehicles to load into assault shuttles, but now it was just a wide-open space that Miska was hoping to one day fill with power armour, mechs and vehicles of her own.

'Well, a girl can dream,' she said wistfully. The armoury was still down here but it was now a walled-in and secured area. The droid facilities were also on this deck.

Three of the droids were heading towards her. Guard droids that had come with the ship. They would escort Torricone, Mass and Jeff back to general population, or genpop. She had also sent a message to the ship to have the maintenance droids clean the shuttle, remove the bodies and return the remaining weapons and still-serviceable armour to the armoury, though there was very little left. She would also have them check out the shuttle, though she would do that herself as well before it was next used. She was heavily reliant on automation here, but even with her dad as overseer it didn't pay to get sloppy. What she could do herself, she did.

She ached and the spacesuit inner-suit was soaked through with her sweat. She made her excuses to her dad and went to shower and change.

She felt a lot better after the shower. She was standing in one of the empty washrooms just off genpop. She had put her earrings back in and was just in the process of carefully doing the same to her nose ring, even though she knew it meant another lecture about how she was just going to get it ripped out in a fight – though that had never happened once. She pushed her hair back, bunching it on top of her head, revealing the shaved sides of her undercut. Her hair was bothering her. Her natural colour was boring. She wanted to dye it purple again, but her elfin features already made her look even younger than her twenty-seven years, and according to her dad purple would make it even more difficult to be taken seriously as the leader of a mercenary regiment. Or, as she preferred to think of it, a legion. Her build, facial features and her bright green eyes were the reason she'd endured being described as cute by her fellow marines.

Most of them had only done it once, though.

She had left her suit and carbine outside the secure area and changed into the jumper, skirt, stripy leggings and the big boots she had brought in her daypack. She still had her gauss pistol riding her hip, as well as her knife. The only protection she had, however, was the implanted subcutaneous armour. Not that it would help if the inmates somehow got free.

She walked out of the shower room feeling refreshed but a little down as she made her way towards genpop. Her dad's face appeared on a nearby screen as she passed. The United States Marine Corps had always held their gunnery sergeants in a kind of religious awe. If they reached that rank then they were probably already legends in the Corps. Particularly if, like her dad, they had done so in the elite Marine Raider special forces regiment. He'd been dead for six months now. Murdered when two surprisingly capable home invaders broke into his house and managed to kill the experienced special forces soldier. Miska knew that the two murderers were somewhere on board.

The flinty eyes and chiselled, leathery face that filled the screens as she passed was just a VR simulation of her father; a recording, an electronic memory of who her father had been. A ghost.

'That operation you just ran,' her father started. 'We had a technical term for that kind of operation in the marines.'

'I was in the marines, Dad,' Miska said exasperatedly. It didn't seem to matter to him that she had just killed several people; she was always going to be his little girl.

'We'd call it a clusterflop!'

'Dad, not even the chaplain would call it a clusterflop, not even the colonel's wife at a formal dinner dance. It's called a clusterfuck. We knew it was a risk. I just didn't think it would go quite as bad as it did.'

She walked out onto one of the catwalks that surrounded genpop. She was on cellblock 6, the sixth of six levels, which overlooked a main exercise yard that she'd had the droids convert into a rudimentary assault course. Each level or cellblock was home to a thousand gel-filled pods. The internal lighting and the colour of the gel meant that the pods glowed blue. When all the prisoners were locked away and 'sleeping' in suspended animation, their bodily functions brought to a near halt, the whole of genpop had an eerie, almost ghostly glow to it. The majority of the pods were full, though twenty-three of them would be going empty today.

'Just enough for a legion,' Miska said to herself, not for the first time. She looked at the pod closest to her. The prisoner inside was a hugely built Maori, covered in *tā moko* tattoos and crude implant scars. She assumed that he was a member of the *Whānau*, which literally meant family in Maori. Originally a mine gang from Lalande 2, the *Whānau* had grown in size and power since the war and now were one of the six main gangs that made up the *Hangman's Daughter*'s prisoner population. The others were the Hard Luck Comancheros, originally a cyberbilly gang from Crawling Town on Earth; the pan-African Leopard Society and their brethren in the Crocodile Society; the Laughing Boys, who originally hailed from London, also on Earth; male members of the Crimson Sisterhood, belt pirates who operated out of the Dogs Teeth in the Sirius system; and the Bethlehem Milliners *bōsōzoku* gang. Then there was the criminal aristocracy, the Mafia and the Yakuza – though the *Hangman's Daughter* didn't hold a *capo di tutti capi* or an *oyabun*, just a *consigliere* who was the godfather in all but name, and a *shatei gashira*, or second lieutenant, with a breathtaking reputation for violence.

34

It wasn't just gangs and organised crime. They also had hit men, armed robbers, stand-over men, spree killers, serial killers, terrorists and cultists. Not all of them were killers, though most were violent; there were thieves, racketeers, extortionists, blackmailers, smugglers, choppers, black-clinic doctors, chemists and dealers. All the exciting ingredients of her own private, mercenary, penal legion. At least until the thought of her in control of close to six thousand dangerous criminals frightened someone enough to do something about it. Out among the colonies, however, among the crooked colonial administrations, mega-corp-run systems, independents and tinpot dictatorships – not to mention the criminal-controlled areas of space – she would have a lot of leeway.

Miska walked along the catwalk, glancing into the pods at members of her sleeping army, heading towards solitary, towards the Trinity. She passed one of the guard bots on its rounds. At least four of them were patrolling each cellblock at any one time, all armed with non-lethal weapons. The lethal weapons were in the watching gun turrets that tracked her movement, and in the now-empty armoured guard islands suspended in the centre of each cellblock. Each of the islands could be isolated from the catwalks in the case of a riot.

She might have had an army of six thousand under her nominal control, but what she didn't have was the resources to arm, equip and armour them. In fact, she was a little worried about feeding them when they were allowed out of sleep for exercise. In terms of equipment, all she had was what the guards had left behind, most of which was ancient surplus equipment, like the M-19s and the Wraith power armour suits. It was all serviceable, but no match for their modern equivalents. After today's loss of resources she could field maybe a hundred men at a push.

'So?' her father asked from a screen on one of the nearby support pillars.

'Well, the miners weren't quite the pushover that the company made them out to be.'

'Gobbin lied? You do surprise me.'

'They were organised; they deployed rudimentary infantry tactics. I'm guessing time-compressed virtual reality close quarter battle training.'

'Don't think they were mercenaries?'

Miska was shaking her head. 'No. Printed armour, printed weapons. You see the rifles they were using?' Her dad's face disappeared and lens footage of the fight appeared and then froze, the image of the rifle magnified. Her father's face reappeared on the screens.

'It's a replica of a twentieth century weapon called an AK-47, the weapon of choice for all discerning revolutionaries and malcontents of the era. Responsible for more deaths than any so-called weapon of mass destruction until the Final Human Conflict,' he said referring to the war between the US and Western Europe against the corporate-backed, wealthy equatorial states and their Chinese and Indian allies in the mid-twenty-first century.

'They were firing air-burst rounds.'

'I saw. I'm guessing repurposed mine explosives with printed circuitry for the sensors.'

'So someone is fomenting an insurgency against the company?'

'Looks that way.'

'Any idea who this guy is?' With a thought, she sent her father the picture of the beret-wearing icon she had seen in the mine's virtual construct.

'Yes,' her dad said. Miska stopped and stared at him.

'You do?' she asked, surprised. Her father might have spent a lifetime running black ops but that didn't make him an expert on hacker icons, which among the really experienced hackers tended to change with each job anyway.

'His name is Ernesto Guevara, aka Che Guevara, a Marxist revolutionary active in the mid-twentieth century. I'm guessing you didn't pay attention during your History of Insurgency classes?'

Miska grinned. 'No, I really didn't. So assuming that it's not really a four-hundred-and-fifty-year-old revolutionary, we're looking at a hacker who uses twentieth century revolutionary iconography to stir up anti-corporate sentiment?'

'Maybe.' Her dad looked unconvinced.

'Do you have another idea?' Miska asked as her dad's image jumped from one of the small screens to the huge screen that took up most of the wall that ran up through all six levels at the end of genpop. Miska came to a halt and looked up at him. Somehow this had become normal to her.

'Do you know what the *Anarchist's Cookbook* was?' he asked. She shook her head. 'It was a book published in the ...'

'Twentieth century?' Miska offered. Her dad was a massive retro freak. She had grown up watching and listening to the bizarre media of the era. She liked the music but she wasn't as big a fan of the war films as her dad was.

'This was covered in your insurgency training,' he said, somewhat peevishly. 'Basically, it provided information on making drugs, explosives, how to avoid surveillance, all sorts of tactics designed to undermine a government.'

'I think Che here is a bit more sophisticated than that ...' Then she caught on. 'You don't think he's a hacker at all. You think it's a virus.'

37

Her dad was smiling. 'That's right, a borderline-AI virus that teaches you how to make weapons, insurgency tactics, that kind of thing.'

'This sounds like something that HOC would do,' she mused. The Human Oversight Committee was a group of activists – or terrorists, depending on your point of view. They had grown out of the final days of the war with the alien Them. They had given themselves a mandate to protect people from corporate, governmental and military excesses. This insurgency-in-a-box virus sounded just like one of their tactics. 'Do they even still exist?'

'A lot of them were killed when they got into it with the Small Gods in the Sol System, but rumour has it that just drove them deep underground.'

The Small Gods were the powerful artificial intelligences who dominated parts of the Sol System and a few of the colonies. Originally information-forms, who had existed only as mysterious entities within the net, they had grown themselves powerful nano-form bodies out of the nanite-bombed wasteland areas of Earth.

'I don't suppose we have anybody on board who might know anything about the HOC?' Miska asked.

'If we do there's nothing overt in their jackets, but then that's the point of an underground organisation. It might also have been redacted by the arresting agency. I can search out a number of likely candidates who might be able to shine some light on this.'

Miska nodded. 'Okay, that's a start. I might put some feelers out in the TauNet.' Tau Ceti E was thirty light minutes away so it would have to be an autonomous program, and a very sneaky one, which could take some time.

'Careful, Pumpkin.' She could hear the concern in his voice.

'The US Colonial Administration is barely in control,' Miska told him. 'Everyone knows the system is run by the Tau Ceti Company.'

'That doesn't mean that the NSA aren't operating down there,' he said. 'Speaking of the TCC, did they set us up to fail?'

'Either that or their intelligence was sh— wasn't very good.'

'What are you going to do about it?'

'Renegotiate.'

Gunnery Sergeant Corbin smiled. 'That's my girl. What do you want done with Torricone?'

Miska shrugged.

'He refused to obey orders. It's a dangerous precedent, particularly with these scum.'

'Somehow I don't think he'll be boasting about it,' she said, though she was trying not to look up at her dad's six-storey-high face. She could practically feel his eyes narrowing.

'That's not the point.'

'Just put him back into rotation and keep an eye on him. If he starts shooting his mouth off, or acting up, then we'll deal with him.'

'Good-looking guy, isn't he?'

'And don't go too hard on him in training!'

'Aha! I knew it. You like him!' His index finger was pointing out of the huge screen at her like the barrel of gun. It was a relief that the image wasn't a holograph.

'Dad, I've told you that this is purely a commercial venture – not my own floating bad-boy harem.' Miska was getting irritated. She liked working with her dad but sometimes ...

'Young lady ...'

'And we probably need to make Massimo an NCO or

39

something,' she said, trying to change the subject, though she suspected that Torricone's future looked pretty bleak regardless of what she told her dad.

'You know that's the whole point. Part of Vido's power play.' Vido, or Uncle Vido as he insisted on being called, had been the *consigliere*, or adviser, to the Cofino family. He was the highest-ranking Mafioso on the *Hangman's Daughter*.

Miska shrugged again. 'He did the work, he deserves the reward, for what it's worth. Speaking of which, we're going to need an incentive scheme. I don't think just getting out and about and being really violent is going to be enough of a reward for them.'

'Well, we knew this would come – but we need to show them the stick before we offer some carrot.' She could tell by the tone in his voice that he still wasn't satisfied with the Torricone matter. 'We also need a name.'

'No,' Miska said. 'We need a brand.' She had been racking her brain about this but nothing quite sounded right. She realised it had suddenly gone quiet. She looked up at her father's face, his troubled expression huge on the screen. The silence had become awkward and she knew what was coming. His professionalism in their current undertaking was just him going through the motions.

'Miska ...' she could hear the hesitation in his voice.

'I don't want to hear it, Dad,' she told him.

'I don't think it's worth all this.'

'It? You mean you don't think you're worth all this?'

'I am an *it* now ...'

'Don't say that!' She was shouting at the screen now. Later she would be relieved that nobody could see her acting like a lunatic. Why did he always have to remind her? She knew, deep down, that this wasn't her dad, that this was just a recording. He didn't have to keep ramming it down her throat. 'You deserve justice!'

'This isn't justice. This is six thousand new victims.'

She stared at the screen for a moment. Felt herself hardening.

'Don't pretend these people are innocent, and if you don't want them to be victims teach them how to fight.' She turned and walked away from the screen. She was relieved when her dad took the hint and the screen went blank. She took a moment to look around at her sleeping army in the ghost light of their pods. The expressions on the faces of a number of them suggested they were each in the throes of a nightmare. She assumed this was because her dad was putting them through their paces.

She sent a message to the ship asking for solitary to be brought down. She wanted to see the Trinity. She wanted to see the weapons that she hadn't quite worked out how to wield yet. And, if she was honest, she wanted to look at the Ultra.

Solitary was three pods on the end of a heavy-duty robot arm. They were suspended high above the sixth level, the idea being that, in the unlikely event that any of them ever managed to get out of their pods, their choice was to jump or climb up the robot arm that ended at the ceiling. In theory it was supposed to give them nowhere to go.

The pods hung from the end of the arm like low-hanging fruit. Skirov was facing her. What was left of him, anyway. He had been seventh generation *Organizatsiya*, Russian organised crime or unofficial government, depending on who you asked. He had gone up in the ranks the hard way, by joining the army and then qualifying for the *Spetznaz*. On file his special forces training and experience should have made him the perfect recruit

41

for her penal legion, except he had taken his *Organizatsiya/Spetznaz* heritage a little too seriously.

Skirov had transformed himself into a cybrid warewolf. An armoured cybernetic killing machine designed to ape the werewolf myths and media of Earth, heavy on the plastic and the metal, light on the flesh and humanity. He had cut too far and too deep until he had turned psychotic. When he had finally been caught he was in an uncontrollable frenzy. The authorities' approach to this had been to remove much of his 'ware. There was little more than a spine, nervous system, ribcage, head and life support equipment in the pod.

Miska was of the opinion that it would have been kinder just to kill him. This thought, and the part of her that liked to play with dangerous things, made her want to rebuild the Russian. Like a project.

'We can rebuild him. We have the technology,' she said to herself, smiling at the memory of one of the ancient vizzes she used to watch with her dad, even though she was still angry with him. 'And then I can have a puppy.'

With a thought she revolved the pods so that Red was facing her. He was close to seven feet tall and hugely built in that kind of muscly fat way. His build had nothing to do with augmentations. He was mostly natural, according to his file. He was hairy all over, except for his bald head. He had a huge ginger beard and bushy eyebrows. Asleep he looked as peaceful as a baby. Miska had never seen him awake but apparently that was something to behold. Ironically he hadn't been sent down for that much. Aggravated assault in one of the tough ice-forming construction camps on Proxima E, but whatever he had found in prison he had seemed to like. Since being incarcerated, his sentence had just kept getting longer and longer until he started killing. He had never seen freedom again. He had killed more than seventy people, inmates and guards alike, and seriously injured and crippled many more. Even en route to the *Hangman's Daughter* he had managed to kill two other inmates and torn a guard's throat out with his teeth before he had been shot. Miska could see the puckered scar tissue from multiple bullet wounds. There were even a few bits of red, hairless flesh, regrown skin where he had been hit with laser fire. None of it had managed to kill him. To Miska he looked like some relic from humanity's barbaric past. Out of all the augmented criminals with fearsome reputations imprisoned on the *Hangman's Daughter*, Red was one of the few she really didn't want to tangle with.

Miska revolved solitary again and looked at the final prisoner. If Red was the past, then the Ultra was the future. If Red looked like he was a sleeping baby, then the Ultra was a beatific sleeping angel. And unlike Red, Miska did want to tangle with the Ultra. Never mind Torricone, this was what she couldn't tell her dad. He was the ultimate bad boy. Admittedly he was a serial killer thought to be responsible for the death of over a thousand people – but love, or at least lust, was blind, and she had never met anyone who didn't have their downsides. Besides, she had killed more than a few people herself; she had just been 'legally' employed to do so.

He had travelled from colony to colony, using various, nearly perfect, false identities. Always blending in with the wealthy elites everywhere he went. Then he would start to prey on humanity. During his arrest on Sirius 4, he had managed to kill six members of the exo-armour equipped C-SWAT team sent for him. He hadn't spoken a word since his arrest but under examination it was discovered that he had been augmented with unlicensed Small Gods' nanotech, though he had been human

43

originally, not grown. Nobody had ever managed to find out who he was. Nicknamed the Ultra, his profilers thought that he believed himself to be the next step in humanity's evolution. Miska could almost believe it.

He was physically perfect. Defined muscle, little or no fat, no body hair, pale skin like marble. He was about six and a half feet tall, with high cheekbones and shoulder-length pale blond hair. He looked like a sleeping god, which she guessed was the point. He was so pretty! She resisted the urge to bring the pod closer so she could run her hand across the front of it. He was an angel of death and she *so* wanted to see what he could do – but perhaps he was too dangerous even for her.

With a thought, she sent solitary back up towards the ceiling and turned to walk away. She needed to find a safe place to trance into the training construct. She had to address the troops. They still had an asteroid to take, money to earn.

CHAPTER 4

Miska sent a message to Laura Gobbin, her corporate contact with the TCC and then, with a thought, extended a drawbridge from the security island on cellblock 6. She wandered over the bridge, contracting it behind her. She let herself into the armoured booth and slumped into one of the seats to run through the helm-cam footage from the assault on Faigroe Station; she knew her Dad would be doing the same. When that was done she had her integral computer reach out for the *Hangman's Daughter*'s systems, allowing her neural interface to connect with the ship's virtual reality environment.

The VR training construct was called Camp Reisman. Her father, or rather the computer-generated ghost of her father, had named it. It was some kind of very private joke.

The construct had been the result of Group 13's contractual obligations. A series of automated routines and scenarios designed, in theory, to help rehabilitate the prisoners. Everyone – from prisoner, to guard, to warden – had known this to be a joke. Miska had replaced Group 13's construct with an adapted version of one used by the marines.

Now it looked like any one of the dozens of military bases she had been stationed at during her time in the service, albeit one with extensive top of the range training facilities. As a virtual construct it was limited only by the amount of processing power the *Hangman's Daughter* could provide, which was pretty extensive. Both Miska and her father could reconfigure it to provide almost any training environment. In practice they tried to keep it the same size and shape to encourage the convict soldiers to think of it as a real place. This tricked their minds into making the various training exercises more believable.

The virtual reality camp was a series of low, squat, ugly buildings designed to look as though they were made from printed regolith. There were barracks, an armoury, and a motor pool. There was no requirement for the prisoners to sleep, and weapons and vehicles could all be made to appear with a thought, but doing so broke the convict soldiers out of the construct's false reality. It was all about tricking their minds into accepting what was happening to them was real; programming what her dad called mental muscle memory.

There weren't any physical training facilities in the construct. The mind could be tricked into learning skills and tactics. Physical fitness came with real exercise so they had to make do with the sparse facilities they had on board the ship and a lot of running around while carrying a great deal of weight.

In the construct what they did have, however, was a training area that mimicked just about every conceivable combat environment. City blocks with high-rises, suburbs, the reconfigurable hulks of space and sea ships, a combat-driving track, various killing houses, a Zero-G simulation facility. Beyond the camp proper were forests, arctic wastes, mountains, an ocean, swamps, deserts, jungles and just about every other conceivable terrain – and all of it with a programmable atmosphere. Miska knew that out over the tundra a huge potato-shaped rock hung in the sky. A virtual replica of Faigroe Station created from the intel that the Tau Ceti Company had provided for them. And all of this was her dad's private domain.

Miska had entered the construct in the command post, or CP, a raised building in the centre of the camp. The top floor of the building had glass windows running all around it and reminded her of an interface/airport control tower. She looked over the camp just as a group of the convict soldiers began a joint vehicular/airborne assault in one of the urban areas. They would be facing a virtual enemy that could be programmed to replicate everything from an untrained gunman or gunwoman, to a regiment of veteran special forces. Getting shot, stabbed, blown up or beaten in here was designed to feel as real as possible. People got post-traumatic stress disorder from virtual training and the *Hangman's Daughter*'s training construct was tough, created, as it was, to mimic USMC basic training, followed by – for those who proved themselves good enough – Marine Raider special forces training.

Miska heard gunfire from behind her. She wandered around the tower. Various screens showed the different training exercises that were currently running. Here her virtual self was wearing the boots and trousers of her combat utility uniform with a drab, sleeveless olive T-shirt. Unlike the net, Camp Reisman was set up for verisimilitude. If she used her cartoon icon here it would just distract the convict soldiers, not to mention make them less afraid of her.

Below the CP, in one of the static ranges, one of the copies of her father was barking instructions at the prisoners' virtual reality icons as he marched up and down behind them. The prisoners' icons were all designed to look as much like their real selves as possible. She glanced at one of the monitors in the CP and the image switched to show her the static range. She checked the human-shaped targets. Their shooting was improving. Many of the prisoners aboard the ship had used guns before but even those with previous military experience had to unlearn bad habits.

The door at the bottom of the steps opened and one of her dad's copies strode up the stairs into the observation area. Despite the fact that he had been special forces, her father's combat utility uniform was immaculate. You could cut yourself on the creases. This was just one of multiple VR copies of her father that was overseeing the various training activities happening in the construct at the moment. In here Gunnery Sergeant Jonathan Corbin, USMC retired, was omniscient and omnipotent.

'Well?' she asked. The VR ghost of her dad regarded the icon of his still-living daughter with flinty eyes. At times like these it was easy to pretend that he was still alive. It was only the lack of visible cyberware that reminded her he wasn't. That and he looked younger. Marine Raiders, like most special forces, tended to back themselves up before running black ops, but her father hadn't been on active duty for years. After her mother had died on an operation, Gunnery Sergeant Corbin had come back to Sirius 4 to look after his daughters. There had been little to back up since then. This virtual copy of her father was missing something like nine years of memory. The best nine years. The nine years that she had really got to know her father, and, through his memories, her often-absent mother.

'Marines are motivated,' her dad said. 'Criminals aren't.'

'There have been penal legions before,' Miska pointed out.

'Frequently on the side of the bad guys.'

'Are they improving?'

'I'm not giving them any choice.' He went quiet for a moment, looking out over the camp. An explosion blossomed over by the landing field as a squad of prisoners conducted a simulated mobile raid in the six-wheeled light strike vehicles. 'They're going to realise that twenty-three of them aren't coming back.'

'No bullshit,' Miska said. 'Where'd we go wrong?' She was sure she knew the answer but it was always worth getting a second opinion on such things.

'Intel,' her dad said.

'Not my leadership?' she asked.

He turned to look at her. 'What leadership? You were tranced. You left them to it. Maybe it was too early but they were going to have to fly solo eventually. You've got a choice: either hack or lead, and if you want to hack then you need someone who knows what they're doing leading them, and I can't do it from in here.'

He was right of course; it was a conversation they'd had numerous times in the five months since she'd stolen the *Hangman's Daughter*. She still couldn't shake the feeling that she'd just been told off. At least he was keeping his opinions of the whole escapade to himself, this time. He turned back to watch the vehicular raid. The expression on his face suggested that he didn't like what he was seeing. Miska suspected that one of his copies was giving the convict soldiers conducting the raid hell at the moment.

'But first time out, ninety per cent mortality, you're going to have a morale problem,' he said, not looking at her. Miska nodded. 'So?'

'So take the new intel, assume that everyone over the age of fourteen is armed, armoured and has had at least rudimentary training, and add it to the simulation. I want you running power-armour assaults from stealth.'

Her father raised his eyebrows. 'From stealth? You think you've got a way in?'

'Mebbe.'

'What are you going to do about morale?'

Miska sighed theatrically. She was about to play a dirty trick on the convict prisoners, and scum though they might be, what she was about to do was a huge no-no in the special forces community. She felt bad about it. Well, as bad as she felt about anything.

'Make a deal with the devil,' she told her dad.

Miska jumped into a light strike vehicle parked outside the CP and sped across the base towards the urban combat environment. Several square blocks of city complete with its own realistically behaving population, or collateral damage as she'd come to think of them. Parts of the city block were burning. As she got closer she could see a semicircle of parked armoured personnel carriers and vectored thrust gunships. Within the semicircle were two platoons of convict soldier virtual icons, just a little under a hundred men, all in fatigues and armour, and carrying a variety of weapons. That was the thing about the VR construct – you didn't need real resources to buy all the toys. She could only dream of access to the weapons and vehicles they were training with.

'Four-man fire teams!' her dad was screaming at the company. 'One stays in the corridor. The rest enters the room.

First man takes the right corner, second the left. How fucking difficult is that to remember?'

The company looked surly and pissed off at the dressing down, the same as they almost always did when they were training. They were fingering weapons that they knew were useless against her dad and herself. He glanced at the light strike vehicle as it pulled up.

'Company ten-hut!' he screamed. Begrudgingly the convict soldiers climbed to their feet and stood to something approximating attention as her dad saluted in a way he probably hadn't had to since he had joined the Marine Raiders. It made her uncomfortable – she'd never got further than E-4 in the Corps – but it made sense here. Her father was trying to instil a sense of discipline in them, with varying degrees of success. Their icons were realistic enough that she could still see the hatred in their eyes. That wasn't a bad thing if it brought them together and they remained frightened of Miska and her father.

'At ease, gunny,' Miska said, using the slang term for gunnery sergeant. Even after two months of doing so in public, it still felt weird giving her father orders. 'I want to speak to Private Cofino, if I may.' Her father watched her for a moment or two. Clearly he could see what was coming and was less than pleased about it.

'Cofino, fall out!' the elder Corbin ordered.

Even more so than Massimo Prola, Vido Cofino, *consigliere* to the Cofino family, and distant cousin of the *capo di tutti capi* himself, Antonio Cofino, looked wrong in his combat utility uniform. He made his way over to Miska, trying to demonstrate every one of his sixty-plus years as he did so. As he approached, information on the mobster appeared in her vision: Cofino, Vido, life imprisonment under the RICO act for conspiracy to commit various crimes including illegal gambling, prostitution, drug distribution and murder. The salute Vido snapped out was almost up to standard. It must have cost him as well, Miska decided, particularly with the other convict soldiers watching. This man used to have the power of life and death over hundreds of people back on Barney's Prime, and now here he was taking orders from someone less than half his age.

'At ease, private,' Miska said. She suspected that in his youth Vido would have had the same hard lines in body and face as her father, but the *consigliere* had let himself go. His frame had run to fat, his face was soft, but despite all that there was a definite hardness to him. His smile was friendly enough, and looked genuine, but if you knew how to look you could see his predatory instincts, his understanding of human weakness.

'Walk with me,' Miska told him.

'How are you doing, Miska?' Vido asked when they were out of earshot of the other convict soldiers. A warm blast of air engulfed them as whining turbos pushed the gunships into the air.

'I'm good, Vido. Gunnery Sergeant Corbin passed on some of your ideas. I'm pleased to see you taking some initiative.'

The mobster shrugged as dust whipped around them, back blast from the gunships as they dipped their noses and headed back into the now mysteriously reconstructed city.

'Well, putting your flagrant disregard for our human rights aside, I learned a long time ago to try and make the best of a bad situation. Now, what are the chances of you calling an old man uncle? Y'know, like everyone else does?'

'That sounds really creepy, you get that, right?' Miska asked. Vido's eyes narrowed. The problem was she liked Vido. He was a likeable guy. She had to keep reminding herself of the things he'd done, and those were only what the FBI and New Verona cops had suspected. Who knew what remained unknown?

'We're a family. That's all,' he said, then his expression softened and he smiled again. He pointed back towards the city where the gunships were exchanging fire with gun emplacements in a number of the high rising buildings. She could hear the distant scream of hypersonic railgun fire.

'You know that's not for me, right?' he asked. 'I'm too old for this nonsense. I might be able to do it in here but out in the real world?' He patted his stomach. 'Too much *spiedini* and too many cigars.'

'I've read your physical, Vido, you're as fit as men half your age in here. Scared?'

Vido regarded her carefully for a moment or two.

'What do you think?' he asked.

'I think you know enough to not want to put your ass on the line unnecessarily, but I don't think you're scared of much.'

'I'm cautious.' He gestured at her. 'You know that I'll be of more use to you not serving in the front line, don't you?'

'Maybe,' Miska said, and then pointed towards the exercise. A firefight had broken out in the city. 'I also know that you've got to get your hands dirty before people will trust you to lead.'

'I was more thinking of an advisory position,' Vido said.

'We'll see.'

'How did Mass do?' he asked.

'Adequately,' Miska told him. Her father had been right; Massimo taking charge during the assault was due to Vido's empire-building.

'He's a good soldier,' Vido said. 'Was the mission a success?'

'No.'

They had reached the mess hall. Miska looked around to see

if she was in view of any of the other recruits and then leaned against the wall.

'Bad?' Vido asked, he even sounded like he meant it. Miska just nodded. 'What do you want from me?'

It felt like the steel jaws of a trap closing around her. She knew this first bit of corruption was just the top of a slippery slope but she needed to get *something* out of this clusterfuck.

'I need you to get Mass to toe the party line, get behind the official story.'

Vido gave this some thought and then nodded. 'And in return?' he asked.

'My undying gratitude and I don't try and launch your head into orbit,' Miska told him and smiled sweetly. Vido frowned and shook his head.

'That's beneath you,' Vido told her, and she knew he was right. This whole thing was still making her feel dirty.

'I make Mass a corporal, that helps you with your empire-building. Y'know, until you work out how to slip the collars and come looking for me.'

'Well, you have turned us all into slaves,' Vido pointed out. Miska couldn't help but laugh. At least he hadn't tried to deny it. 'Anyone else you want to toe the line?'

Miska spent a moment wondering just how much power Vido thought he had in the make-believe world of this virtual prison.

'No,' Miska told him. She guessed that Torricone would keep his own counsel and Gleave hadn't seen enough to dispute her version of events.

'That bad, huh?' Vido asked. It seemed that he had worked out that there weren't a lot of survivors. 'That could be put down to bad leadership.'

'Well I'm the only leadership you've got, so you'd better hope that's not the case,' she told him. 'Re-join your platoon.'

Vido headed back towards the urban training area.

'Vido?' she called after him. He turned to look back at her. 'Did you know Michael Torricone back on Barney Prime?' she asked.

Vido frowned and started to shake his head. 'I don't ... wait, Hispanic guy, tattoos?' Miska nodded. 'Yeah, Mikey-T, more knew of him. Went down because of some rat motherfucker, the way I hear it. Good thief but not a team player. Why'd you ask?'

Miska shrugged. *Good question,* she thought.

'You're being observed.' It was her father's voice over the comms link.

She looked up. One of the light strike vehicles was parked a little way off. Three of the four occupants were busying themselves with various tasks. The fourth, the front passenger-gunner, was watching Miska and Vido. A Japanese man in his mid-forties, the wiry-built man looked much more at home in combat dress than Vido did. His face was an expressionless mask with the ghost of a goatee on his chin. His hair was kept short and neat. Miska suspected that when he had been free, this particular man had been fastidious about his appearance.

As she looked at him his information scrawled down her vision. Shigeru, Teramoto, life imprisonment for multiple counts of extortion, and two murders. Shigeru was a *shatei gashira,* or second lieutenant, of the Scorpion Rain Society, a Lalande 4 Yakuza clan. He was watching Vido walk away. Vido glanced over at the Yakuza boss and nodded. Shigeru remained still. Miska would need to keep them apart, even though as far as she knew there was no enmity between the two men. Their spheres of influence were too far apart but they were the two biggest dogs on the block, in their own minds anyway, so sooner or later they were going to fight.

'Is he supposed to be there?' Miska subvocalised to her dad.

'He's not *not* supposed to be there,' her dad answered. 'Want him moved on?'

'No, the damage is done. Let them get to the end of their current exercise and then I want to see everyone in the amphi-theatre.'

'I can break them off now?' her father suggested over comms. The light strike vehicle with Shigeru in it turned around and headed back towards the landing pad.

'Maybe speed up the time a bit but don't interrupt their training any more than necessary.'

Six-thousand-plus hard stares, six-thousand-plus ultramax hard cases, all with a reason to hate her, and now there were twenty-three less. All of them looking at her. Torricone was right, even in uniform they didn't look like an army, they looked like a gang, a huge gang. They would tear her apart and worse if they had the opportunity. Even here, in this virtual world, if it wasn't for the inhibitor protocols in their icons they could do so and the biofeedback would probably kill her real body. She supposed she should be scared but frankly it was something of a rush.

They were sat in a poured concrete amphitheatre big enough to easily sit all six thousand of the prisoners. Miska stood on a stage facing them, her image projected onto a large screen directly behind her.

She let them grumble and curse. She could have threatened them with explosive decapitation if they weren't quiet, but she would devalue the threat if she kept on making it. She could even change the reality of the construct, have skin grow over their mouths, so they were silent, but it would get in the way of the verisimilitude of the construct, so she waited until their expectation overruled their urge to bullshit with each other.

'Hello everyone!' she said sunnily, to be greeted by a few half-hearted obscenities. A number of her dad's icons were patrolling the amphitheatre, occasionally glaring at the more belligerent prisoners. 'As you will know by now the operation to take back Faigroe Station did not go terribly well ...'

'You got them all killed!' someone yelled from the crowd.

'Murderer! You're no better than us!' another prisoner added.

'Examples?' her dad asked over the comms link. Miska just shook her head.

'Fair enough,' Miska said. 'Let's see.' And she moved to one side of the stage so the prisoners could see all of the screen as the footage played. It wasn't that the footage was faked, more that the way she had edited it changed the emphasis. The assault had failed because they had encountered far stiffer resistance than the intel had led them to believe. For the most part the two squads she had taken with her had crumbled in the face of said resistance. It was the latter that she emphasised. It was a shitty thing to do, effectively laying the blame on the dead. The deal she had made with Vido meant that Mass would back her version of events. As the prisoners watched the footage she scanned the crowd looking for Torricone, to see if she could gauge his reaction, but there were a lot of faces. It would take a moment for her to run a search for him but somehow she couldn't see him making a big effort to tell the real story, and for some reason she didn't want to see him while she was telling these lies. She let the footage finish and waited by the side of the stage for a few moments, letting the prisoners digest what they had seen. Then she walked to the centre stage.

'It doesn't matter what's fair, what's legal, whether I'm any better than anyone here. All that matters is this. I will put you in harm's way. You want to live, then you train and you learn to work together, or else we just keep doing this until you're all dead and I move on to something new.'

'Fuck you! We're dead anyway! Why bother?'

She managed to find the general area of the crowd that the voice was coming from but she had been too slow to pinpoint it. She could replay it from the construct's memory if she wanted to know. Grumbling sounds of agreement emanated from the crowd.

'Because it's a rush,' Miska said, smiling, and just from the prisoners closest to her she could see a few nods of understanding. 'And if you show me something other than bitching and whining, if you pull this off, then we can talk about rewards.'

The muttering picked up again.

'That's a pretty low trick,' her dad said over the comms link. She could tell by his tone that he didn't approve. He might have nothing but contempt for their scum army but at the end of the day he was training them and therefore, on some level, still thought of them as soldiers.

'Yes it is,' Miska admitted sub-vocally.

A flashing icon appeared superimposed across her vision. Gobbin had returned her message.

It looked like she was heading in-system.

58

CHAPTER 5

Miska looked around at the clutter in the cramped cabin of the *USSS Jimmy Carter*, or *Little Jimmy*, as she liked to think of the stolen ship. The spacecraft was a converted long-range system survey ship, extensively redesigned as a stealth-capable electronic warfare platform. Unusually for a faster-than-light ship, the *Little Jimmy* was capable of in-atmosphere operations. As such, the ship was sleek and aerodynamic. The exotic materials, some thought to be alien in origin, and the lack of right angles in the design, all helped to reduce the ship's sensor signature and made it more difficult to detect, particularly when powered down with its weapon pods retracted. The *Little Jimmy* was also Miska's home, which was why it was such a mess. It was mostly discarded clothes that covered the floor. She was professional enough that all her working gear was stowed away.

'I should still tidy this place up,' she mused, once again. On the other hand it wasn't like she was expecting company. The ship was big enough to support a crew of four within its cramped environs, and could probably carry triple that over short distances, but the cockpit and living quarters were all open plan to save on space.

Miska ambled into the cockpit. Subjectively above her was the interior rock wall of the mined-out asteroid, illuminated by the *Hangman's Daughter*'s running lights. Subjectively below her was the huge prison barge's hull. *Little Jimmy* was attached, limpet-like, to the underside of the *Hangman's Daughter*. Flexible tendrils grew out of the stealth craft and into the prison barge's hull. *Little Jimmy* had been designed to close with larger ships, attach itself to them, and then extrude the tendrils. They would then cut through the hull of the ship and look for secure systems to splice into.

Miska scratched at her hair before climbing into the pilot seat.

'Dad, I'm heading in-system, you've got the *Daughter*,' she told him over the comms link.

'Okay, Pumpkin, you get some rest as well, all right?'

She had to smile. Pumpkin might undermine her on an op, but it made her feel better, even though her real father had stopped calling her that after she'd signed up.

'Will do,' she told him and then cut the link. Her neural interface connected with *Little Jimmy*'s systems as the stealth ship came to life and her Internal Visual Display was suddenly flooded with telemetry and diagnostic information. She watched as the tendrils connecting the *Little Jimmy* to the *Hangman's Daughter* were sucked back into the smaller ship, the hard connection severed. With a thought, Miska switched off the electromagnetic clamps on the landing struts and a small burst of compressed gas separated the stealth ship from the prison barge. The *Hangman's Daughter*'s superstructure became a blur beneath her ship as she triggered the thrusters and shot out of the hollowed-out asteroid. Through the interface the sleek, sneaky ship became an extension of her body. She felt the burn of the thrusters, the flex of the hull, the cold vacuum all around her and, high above the swirling clouds of Tau Ceti G, she felt the tug of the huge gas giant's gravity. The ship's sensors became her senses, spread out across space as fast as light could carry them. She adjusted for the pull of the planet and, with a thought, hit the thrusters again, burning hard, leaving a long exhaust torch behind the *Little Jimmy* as she steered the ship coreward for open space. When the ship was finally free of the gas giant's gravity well she unfurled the sails, their gossamer light sprouting from the small, dark ship like faintly glowing butterfly wings.

'Pretty!' Miska announced to no one in particular as she felt the play of particle spray hitting the sails. Even through the artificial gravity she was vaguely aware of the tug of acceleration on her real body, but it was as much information as it was sensation. She would only be travelling at superluminal speeds for mere moments, but it would take a matter of hours to accelerate and then decelerate.

'Music ... something mellow.' Four-hundred-year-old music filled the cabin of the little ship and Miska put her boots up on the console and pushed the pilot's bucket seat back. It had been a pretty full-on day, she decided, and she wasn't particularly looking forward to having to deal with Laura Gobbin again.

TWO WEEKS AGO

Miska helped the guard through the executive's office's double doors with boosted leg muscles and the toe of her boot. He went sprawling across the blood-red carpet. She was pushing the second guard in front of her. He had his fingers laced together behind his head and Miska had a grip on both his hands, though she had to reach up high because he was so much taller than her. Her SIG gauss pistol was in her free hand.

The executive office was in one of the corners of the Tau Ceti Company's Main Arcology on Tau Ceti E. The city-sized building was hermetically sealed to protect against the howling winds and corrosive atmosphere of the planet. Two of the walls were panelled with wood, the other two were floor-to-ceiling windows looking out over the blasted, pitted surface of the company's mine works. Tau Ceti E may well have been in the system's 'Goldilocks Zone' for potentially habitable planets, but the floodlit landscape of tortured rock shaped by the winds looked more like Hell than Eden.

'Hiya!' Miska called. She was trying to remain cheerful but games like this were a waste of everybody's time. There were two more guards standing either side of a huge, polished, dark wood desk. One looked Japanese, the other one was of African descent. Other than their race they could have been bulky, bullet-headed twins. Both of them were bringing snubby gauss personnel defence weapons to bear on her. The bulk of the guard she had hold of would provide her with a degree of cover but the electromagnetically propelled darts would tear through him and probably get through her inertial and implanted subdermal armour. Unlike the two guards she had encountered in the outer office, she suspected that these two actually knew what they were doing.

Getting tired of having to reach up to keep a hold of the guard, she kicked him in the back of the legs and forced him to his knees, then levelled the pistol at the woman behind the

62

deck. The crosshairs from her smartlinked SIG settled over the cold, sculpted beauty of the human resources executive's face in Miska's Internal Visual Display.

'Hypothetically speaking, are you guys unemployed if I shoot her?' Miska asked.

Everything about Laura Gobbin's appearance suggested power: from the artificial eyes like chips of black ice coolly regarding Miska, to the long black hair tied back in a severe but complicated braid, to the tastefully understated power suit.

'They will still kill you,' Gobbin assured her. The voice was trained for command and manipulation. Miska wondered just how many self-help classes this woman had attended in her life. The final sign that Gobbin was trying too hard was the sheathed katana on the desk. In the bad old days executives used to duel for tenders and promotions, normally to first blood, though occasionally, it had been rumoured, to the death. Nowadays, although many executives practised kenjutsu, or some derivate of the art, and carried wooden bokken practice swords, few carried the real thing.

Out of the corner of her eye, Miska could make out the huge, worm-shaped mining robots, the size of high-rise buildings, chewing their way through the rock to create massive trenches, harvesting the planet's mineral wealth and shitting it out to be picked up by other industrial robots. A climber the size of an ocean-going super tanker was crawling up the nearby 'spoke', the huge elevator that carried the mineral wealth out of the corrosive atmosphere and into orbit.

The two guards hadn't fired, which Miska took as a good sign, but nor had they lowered their weapons. Gobbin was taking her time studying Miska.

'So are we having a gunfight?' Miska asked, trying to keep

the eagerness out of her voice. She knew she would have to shift aim and deal with the guards first, and she wouldn't be surprised if Gobbin had a gun within easy reach. She wasn't liking the odds much, particularly because as soon as it kicked off the rest of arcology's security was going to come running.

The guard she had kicked through the door was trying to get up. 'Ah-ah-ah,' Miska warned him. 'I will shoot you in the ass.' The guard lay face-down on the blood-red carpet.

A flicker of contempt passed over Gobbin's face. Miska suspected that there were hard times ahead for that particular guard. 'Why'd you make this so difficult?'

'I wanted to get an idea of your capabilities,' Gobbin finally told her. Miska laughed.

'I'm putting away my gun,' she told the two guards. Neither of them acknowledged her. 'You're big with the facial expressions, very emotive.' Still neither of them moved.

Miska sighed and holstered the SIG gauss pistol. 'They're like bookends,' she told Gobbin.

'Lower your weapons,' the HR executive told them. The two guards immediately slid their weapons back into their tailored suits.

'You guys are obedient, I bet she likes that. Do you ever get dressed up in little leather straps and let her spank your ass with a riding crop?' Neither of the guards said anything. Miska pointed at the guard on the left. 'You know what I'm talking about, don't you?'

'Miss Corbin, or is it corporal?'

'Miska's fine.' The guard lying face-down on the carpet was starting to get up again. 'Stay down,' she told him and he slumped back onto the red carpet. 'Wow, you really like doing what you're told. Well trained.'

'This kind of humour does not impress me ...'

Miska had let go of the guard she had been using as a human shield. He stood up, rubbing his fingers. Suddenly he spun round, swinging a hook straight for her face. The punch would have done some damage but his reactions were nowhere near as wired as Miska's. To her, he might as well have been moving in slow motion. She dropped into a crouch and the hook shot over her head. She slid her foot just behind the guard's and then dropped all her weight behind her elbow, hitting him just above the knee while sweeping her foot back. The guard fell awkwardly. Miska stamped on his knee, powdering it, and only just stopped herself from stamping on his groin as well. Both the guards on either side of the desk had their PDWs up again. Miska rolled her eyes and stepped away from the prone, howling guard, keeping her hands away from her own weapons.

'I didn't start it, boys,' she told them.

'Get him out of here,' Gobbin shouted over the agonised howls to the other guard who was still lying face-down on the carpet. He looked up at Miska, who nodded. The guard with the broken knee was dragged, unceremoniously, out of the office.

Miska looked around and realised there were no other chairs. It seemed that people were supposed to stand before Gobbin. Miska turned and walked back out through the double doors, returning a few moments later pushing a chair she'd found in the outer office, wheeling it just in front of Gobbin's desk. She was pretty sure Gobbin actually flinched when she jumped into the chair. She decided that putting her booted feet up on the desk might actually get her shot.

'So I've proven that I can move office furniture around,' Miska said. 'Any other hoops you want me to jump through?'

'I don't like buying things unseen,' Gobbin said.

65

'You're not buying anything, you're renting, and what do my capabilities at breaking and entering have to do with the mercenary force I command?'

It was clear it had been a power play. Gobbin had wanted to establish that she was in charge. Miska was of the opinion that there were easier ways. If Gobbin just paid up, then the customer would get what she wanted.

'I wished to see if you lived up to your reputation.'

Miska perked up. 'Didn't realise I had one of those yet. I thought I'd have to work at it.'

'A record of insubordination with Marine Force Recon.'

Miska shrugged. 'There's two sides to every story.'

'A data warfare specialist with the Marine Raider Regiment, special forces.'

'Allegedly,' Miska said.

'Presumably it was the Special Operation Group within the CIA Special Affairs Division that trained you as a pilot.'

Miska said nothing but the smile was gone from her face. She suspected that Gobbin was working hard to keep a smug expression off her own cold features. Miska was wondering how she knew so much, but then again everything was for sale out here. 'Deserter with a body full of military grade cyberware, thief, pirate, and finally slaver.' Even more than deserter this last rankled her, though it was hard to deny.

'Yeah, but my slaves are not very nice people,' she said.

'Indeed, and now you're wanted by the US government, its various colonial subsidiaries, and every other government that had a significant prisoner population on board the Hangman's Daughter.'

'This is an American colony,' Miska pointed out. Just for a moment she wondered if this was a trap. Was a Marshal's

66

rapid reaction force about to pour into the office and wrestle her down onto the blood-red carpet? She had to resist the urge to move her hand closer to her pistol.

'In name only. Things work differently out here. I wonder, would your father be proud of you?' The question felt like having a cold bucket of water thrown over her. Miska found herself staring at Gobbin. She suspected that the slight upturn of the lips was what passed for a smile with the HR exec.

'What's wrong?' Miska finally asked. 'Mommy and daddy didn't love you enough, no dates in high school, over-achieving older sibling, what?'

Now Gobbin's trace of a smile was gone.

'I was sorry to hear about your father. Home invasion, wasn't it? Odd that common criminals could take down someone with your father's military experience. Perhaps it was his advanced age?'

Miska swallowed and fantasised about leaping across the desk and snapping Gobbin's perfect neck.

'If what you think you know about me is true then why would you try and piss me off?'

'Do you think I'm in any danger here?' Gobbin asked.

'Yes, Laura. May I call you Laura? I do.' The guards shifted slightly. 'Easy, boys,' Miska told them. 'If we're so disreputable why not go with someone on your preferred supplier list?' she finally asked after a few more moments of uncomfortable silence.

'In a word: deniability. As I'm sure you can imagine, this terrorist takeover is a public relations—'

'Terrorist takeover?' Miska scoffed. 'The intel your security people texted over to me describes a sit-in, little more than a labour dispute.'

67

Gobbin's artificial eyes glittered. Miska suspected that the executive wasn't used to being interrupted. 'Ms Corbin, I would very much encourage you to think of them as terrorists. As I was saying, it is a PR nightmare. If you manage to successfully take Faigroe Station then all is well, if not ...'

'Then you blame us, disavow us, and say we acted independently ...'

'Indeed. Plus, to be honest, you are cheaper than your nearest competitor,' *Gobbin continued. Miska shrugged. Her mercenaries were, at the end of the day, untested.* 'Besides, I have a full prisoner manifest for the* Hangman's Daughter. *It makes for quite colourful reading. I know the kind of people you have on board. They would have little compunction about making an example of some of the miners. After all, we can't have this sort of thing catching on.'*

Miska decided to keep her thoughts on that to herself.

'How did you hear about us?' *she asked instead.*

'You were recommended.'

'Who by?'

Gobbin remained silent. It was enough for Miska. She stood up and made for the door.

'Ms Corbin.' *Gobbin had raised her voice just slightly.* 'I haven't decided if we will employ your services yet.' *Miska stopped by the door and turned to look at the executive.*

'Me hanging around is just going to decrease the chances of you hiring us and increase the chances of a serious assault on your person. If you want to hire us then send over all the intel you've got, including a full floor plan of the mine, with the contract.' *She left the office.*

The contract and intel had been waiting for her by the time she'd made it back to the Hangman's Daughter.

Except the intel had been wrong, Miska thought, way wrong. Though it was entirely possible that the Tau Ceti Company had no idea about the Che virus. If the virus's AI was capable enough, and the rebel miners thorough enough, then the TCC might not have any intelligence assets left on the station. Whether they knew of the AI or not, the increased capabilities of the miners meant that the job had changed significantly. Somehow Miska didn't think that Gobbin would see it that way.

Tau Ceti E looked like cloudy grey marble from her position. Magnifying the cockpit's windscreen she could make out the asteroid tether for the space elevator in geosynchronous high orbit, as well as a number of support satellites and various ships from bulk ore carriers to TCC security system cruisers.

Miska had deployed a number of micro satellites. She was using them as relays for the tight beam comms link. It would make it harder for them to trace the signal back to *Little Jimmy*. Some very serious, very competent, and very dangerous people were looking for her ... well, strictly speaking, for their ship. She sent a comms request to speak with Gobbin. Moments later the area of space surrounding the micro satellite she'd bounced the signal off was saturated with hard scans. Miska smiled. Eventually she received an invitation to a virtual conference hosted on the tethered high orbit station that was the final stop for the elevator. Miska closed her eyes, tranced, and sent her consciousness flying across the intervening space on beams of occulted light.

'Not happy,' Miska muttered. The icon she'd been assigned – rather rudely, to her mind – looked very much like her, but

69

was wearing a rather demure kimono and her hair was neatly combed. She checked her feet. She was wearing some kind of wooden sandals rather than boots.

She was stood in what looked like the reception area of a traditional Japanese tearoom, traditional except for the walls of poured concrete. The tearoom appeared to be on the upper floor of some high-rise building. There was an ornamental garden on a balcony, complete with rockery, complex patterns raked into sand, and a carp pond with a bamboo pump. Beyond the balcony was a veritable wasteland of Brutalist architecture and refineries, venting towers burning brightly in a twilight haze of smog.

'Weird,' Miska muttered, though years of retro action vizzes and *wuxia* sense games made her think it would be a cool place for a sword fight.

'Can I help you?' enquired a politely smiling automated icon that looked like a kimono-wearing *maître d'*. Miska didn't mean to but she ignored the polite question. Instead, she bunched her fists and scrunched up her face in concentration, in a way that she'd been told made her look like she was about to shit herself, as she hacked her assigned icon. Moments later she shook herself and the icon became her comically angry cartoon icon, thus ruining the decor of the whole construct. She looked at the *maître d'*. It was sufficiently well programmed to look appalled at this.

'It's okay, I see who I'm here to meet.'

Gobbin was sat at a low, lacquered wooden table on a raised area overlooking the pretend diners. As Miska crossed the tearoom she glanced around at the diner icons. She had no idea what era the tearoom was supposed to represent but she was sure she had seen similar in her dad's old vizzes and that it was pre-Final Human Conflict, so at least four hundred years old. There were a lot of flared trousers and floral print dresses.

As she approached Gobbin, the covert-ops human resources executive carefully laid her chopsticks down next to a nearly untouched dish of sushi. Her guards were standing either side of her. In the virtual environment they both had afros, and both wore brown, flared suits and carried medieval Japanese weaponry. It was weird that the guards would be here unless their skill set extended to electronic warfare, though perhaps the icons were just security programs designed to look like Gobbin's guards, so she could extend her *daimyo* fantasies into the virtual world.

Miska flopped down on a cushion on the other side of the low table and grabbed some sushi. It was well programmed. It tasted good.

'I'm not sure that such childish displays will sit you in good stead in the business world,' Gobbin told her, radiating disapproval.

On the other side of the window it had started raining. The rain was black. 'What's with all the pollution chic, anti-ecology stuff?' Miska asked around a mouthful of rice and fish.

'It reminds us that pollution is the natural result of commerce, something to be embraced, and often quite, quite beautiful,' Gobbin told her. Miska shrugged as she shovelled more raw fish into her mouth. Gobbin rolled her eyes. 'If you're calling me to tell me you've failed then spare me. I have better things to do than listen to excuses.'

I guess nobody ever told her that you get the best out of people when you're nice, Miska thought.

'Your codes were useless, and the miners were ready for us; they had been trained, and were much more heavily armed than

11

we had been led to believe. Your intel was way out.' *And killed twenty-three people*, she didn't add. She'd noticed a slight lag in reaction to her words. Miska was pretty sure that Gobbin was tranced-in down on the planet.

'It's a cold and imperfect universe, Ms Corbin. Why are you bothering me with this?'

'Because now it's not the job you hired us to do. It's a different job, more difficult, which means more manpower and more resources.' Miska wasn't looking at Gobbin as she ate.

'I do not appreciate you trying to renegotiate after we had already agreed terms.'

'Your shit intel was the renegotiation,' Miska explained. Gobbin seemed to be ignoring her. Miska shrugged. 'Okay, then let's go our separate ways, agree to never work together again and slag each other off in the net?'

Again the HR exec ignored her. She wondered if Gobbin was discussing the matter with her superiors down on Tau Ceti E. She glanced up at the HR exec's icon. It wasn't giving anything away, just staring at her.

'What do you want?' Gobbin demanded. Her image was a perfect mask of cold anger.

'Half as much again.'

'We will agree to pay another quarter of our originally agreed sum.' This last was through gritted teeth.

'Negotiation is for clients with competent intelligence,' Miska said, smiling, and then went back to her sushi. There was no denying that she needed the money if their penal mercenary legion was to be a going concern, but frankly Miska wasn't sure it was worth putting up with people like Gobbin. The HR exec made some of the mass murderers on board the *Hangman's*

Daughter seem like pleasant people. Miska was of the opinion that it took a lot to get under her skin but she suspected that if Gobbin had been wearing an explosive collar, it would have 'accidentally' gone off some time ago. Probably when they'd first met and she had mentioned Miska's dad.

'Very well,' Gobbin said.

Miska hadn't expected that. She almost replied with the word: Really? It was too easy. Miska opened an invisible window and surreptitiously replayed Gobbin's answer, running it through a program that analysed micro expressions. Many wealthy people went for top of the line icons that could pick up on that sort of thing. Miska had no doubt that Gobbin's icon was that good but the HR exec was smart enough to have dialled down the resolution. Even so, it was pretty clear that she was angry. Miska wondered if the HR exec had been told to agree with her demands by someone else. Even if that was the case, she couldn't figure out why. The TCC had all the power here. They could say no, refuse to pay and hire some other outfit. It didn't make any sense. So she decided to push her luck even further.

'I want something else,' Miska said.

'What?' Gobbin demanded.

Miska smiled. She was pretty sure she was getting under the HR exec's skin now. 'When we do this, and we will, you add us to your PSL.'

If there was a lag before the reply then it was minimal.

'Don't be ridiculous. Our preferred supplier list is an exclusive ...' then she went quiet.

Curiouser and curiouser, Miska thought.

'You never know when you might need a deniable army to do your dirty work,' she told Gobbin.

73

For several moments the HR exec's icon didn't say anything. Her lips pursed to the point of non-existence, eyes narrowed as though they could shoot black light.

'Very well,' she finally said.

Miska actually rocked back in the cushion. *They can't want us that bad*, Miska thought. The deal was too good, which meant something else was going on but if she cut and run on their first job they would just look flaky. Especially with a deal that, on the surface, looked so good. Miska knew she had to play this out, but just for a moment she wondered if the construct was a trap. Catch her tranced-in consciousness and then sweep local space until the original owners found the *Little Jimmy*. She was starting to think that the TCC had no intention of paying them when they succeeded, but even for a corporation as powerful as them there was only so often they could do that before people stopped dealing with them, and someone with six thousand convict mercenaries was actually a bad person to piss off. *Even if I can only arm a tiny percentage of them*, she thought grimly.

'You should know that we expect results, Ms Corbin. And we need a name for your organisation for accounts.'

'We're, er ... having branding issues at the moment.'

'There is something else you should be aware of, Miss Corbin.' Miska didn't like the predatory smile on Gobbin's normally cold features. *Here it comes*, Miska thought, *the stick to go with the carrot*. 'We have reason to believe that the National Security Agency have recently established a presence at the governor's house.'

Miska went cold. It was worse than she thought. Basically Gobbin was telling her that if the TCC weren't happy then they would turn her over to the NSA, the intelligence agency

74

responsible for electronic security, intelligence gathering and warfare for the US government. She suspected that they would very much like the *Little Jimmy* back.

CHAPTER 6

'I will PT you until you shit out your guts, spew up your lungs, and cough out your heart! You will love the pain! Breathing is for the weak!'

Miska had to smile as her father's voice echoed through the nearly empty hangar deck. You could train in virtual reality all you wanted but at the end of the day that wouldn't build up endurance and strength. It was one of their many problems. The *Hangman's Daughter* had been set up for all six thousand-plus prisoners to be regularly brought out of suspended animation and given the opportunity to exercise, and many of the prisoners were in good shape. They were only prison yard healthy, however; good for pumping iron and playing basketball. Miska needed them military healthy, where the emphasis was on endurance rather than making their prison yard tats look good. They had done what they could, rigging up obstacle courses, but much of it came down to running, circuit training and calisthenics.

Sweat-soaked and red-faced, a group of prisoners ran by her.

Each one took the time to cast a look of undisguised hatred her way. Miska smiled sweetly at them.

'What are you looking at her for!' her father screamed from the monitors affixed to the guard droids accompanying the joggers. 'Sprint, you human-shaped pieces of pus!' The prisoners picked up the pace as the four guard droids running with them extended their shock sticks.

The prisoners were woken up in groups of five hundred, which were then split up into smaller groups of a hundred. Each group was supervised by four of the guard droids. At all times they were in view of the security lenses and covered by the prison barge's automated turrets, not to mention they were all still wearing their collars. It didn't matter – the prisoners, not surprisingly, hated it. They'd lost quite a few of them in the initial weeks due to escape attempts, assaults on the droids and other prisoners, attempted assaults on herself, more than a few heart attacks and point-blank refusals to participate. Examples had to be made.

Each prisoner did three hours of PT three days out of every week. It wasn't nearly enough to get them as fit as Miska required, certainly not to Marine Raider standards, but it was the best they could do with what they had. Her dad already had concerns about the wear and tear on the guard droids and the drain on their sparse medical resources.

And more than anything else this is why they will tear me limb from limb if they ever get the collars off, Miska thought as she made her way across the echoing hangar deck listening to a hundred prisoners sing a Jody Call marching song. Her dad opened up a comms link.

'And don't think I haven't noticed that you've been neglecting PT,' he told her. She sighed and wondered once more about working with her dad. PT had started for her a long time before she'd joined the marines. She'd had a lot of excess energy that had required working off as a teenager.

'Yes Dad,' she subvocalised over the link.

'How was Gobbin?'

'By far the nicest HR professional I've ever spoken to.'

Her dad's image in the window looked stern for a moment and then a smile broke out across his face. The stern drill sergeant went away and he almost looked like another person entirely.

'Did you hurt her?' he asked.

'It was a virtual environment,' she told him. Then she gave the question some further thought. 'I messed up the decor. Corporations are weird, I don't think they get pretty.' He raised an eyebrow. 'She agreed to half as much cash again and a place on the PSL.'

'Get any of it upfront?'

'I don't think that's the way they work. We might have to invoice.' There was no guarantee of payment but if the TCC burned them on this her penal legion's second job would be particularly destructive debt collection.

'And?' he asked, apparently picking up on her uneasiness.

'And she's not calling the shots.' This wasn't a surprise. Gobbin handled HR for deniable black ops, but the loss of a profitable facility to internal insurrection would have gone all the way up to board level. 'It was too easy.'

'This is starting to sound like a burn to me,' her dad said as she reached the central elevator shaft intending to head up to the bridge. For some reason she didn't like the guards' quarters on the *Hangman's Daughter*, despite that being where the best facilities, such as they were, could be found. She liked the bridge, the security of *Little Jimmy*, and, oddly, being on the cellblocks among her sleeping army.

'Well, if it is a certain HR exec is getting thrown through her corner office window without the benefit of a hostile environment suit,' Miska muttered. If it was a burn she knew an abject example would have to be made. The prisoners had just about learned not to fuck with her, now the clients would have to learn the same.

'It's tough getting taken seriously as a twenty-seven-year-old general, huh?' her dad asked.

Sometimes people just have to learn the hard way, she mused. Another droid-escorted group of prisoners were running across the hangar as she reached the elevator.

'Oh, and I've found someone who might know about the Human Oversight Committee,' her father said. 'You want to speak to him at Camp Reisman?'

'No, decant him.' She'd had enough of virtual life for one day.

Hogg, Vernon, consecutive life sentences for conspiracy to commit kidnapping, aggravated vandalism, mayhem and assassination. The information scrawled down Miska's IVD as she wandered along the catwalk on one side of cellblock 5, past pod after pod of sleeping prisoners. Ahead of her, one pod opened and a gel-covered figure spilled out of it and onto the cold metal of the catwalk. The file said that Hogg was a similar age to Uncle Vido, but while the *Mafioso consigliere* was well upholstered, Hogg was rake-thin; where Vido's skin was soft, Hogg's was heavily weathered. It looked like old leather. Unlike many of the other prisoners Hogg didn't sport any tattoos, and according to his file he didn't have any cyberware.

'All conspiracy charges?' Miska called out as she walked towards him. Hogg was shaking and coughing up gel. He glanced her way at the sound of her voice. 'Sounds like you did a lot of talking and not much doing.'

He was looking around. She could tell he was checking for possible escape routes. This was a man who was used to living on the run. He'd spent five years evading the authorities and living rough after a property-damaging bombing campaign on his native Sirius 4.

He spat and used the railings to pull himself to his feet. He glanced down through the various levels of cellblock. Apparently deciding that there was no way out that way, he turned to face her and stood up straight. Miska stopped just in front of him. Everything about him suggested that he'd lived a hard life.

'Choices we make, huh?'

'They send you to prison for what they can prove,' Hogg told her. 'That's not the same as what happened.'

'You worked against the TCC in the Tau Ceti system, right?'

'I know that's where we are now, and I'm pretty sure that you're working for them. I also know you lost some people.'

'You know I need your cooperation ...'

'Or you'll kill me,' he said. Then sighed and turned away from her, leaning on the railings to look down at the other cellblock levels again. 'A lot of slaves.' He coughed some more and then spat down into the yard, the central court at the base of the cellblocks where the prisoners were allowed to congregate. 'I tried really hard not to exist here. I didn't want to be noticed.'

Miska leaned against the railings as well. She decided to let him talk. She wasn't sure why. There was something sad about him. Perhaps it was his surroundings. He looked like he belonged in the wilderness somehow.

'Didn't want any shit from the other cons?' she asked. He glanced over at her.

'Didn't want to do your bidding.'

'Mine?' Miska asked, a little surprised. Nobody went unnoticed in her regime.

'The government, the corporations, they've been at war with humanity since long before I was born.'

Miska laughed.

'That's not me. I'm a free spirit,' she told him cheerfully.

He nodded down towards the yard. 'I used to watch them down there. Petty arguments, pettier fights, false tribes, and I wanted to scream: can't you see you're just doing their work for them?' He straightened up and turned to face her. 'If you're going to war with the TCC, you need someone to blow up some colonial dictator, then I'm there. But I'm not going to kill some poor fucking miners.' Miska opened her mouth to tell him that he didn't have any choice. 'I don't want to die but I don't think I could live with myself afterwards, which makes your threats kind of redundant.'

Miska sighed, and wondered why nothing was easy.

'What if I said I'd let you go?' she asked. His head jerked around sharply and she saw it on his face, just for a moment, that most insidious of emotions: hope. Then he looked away and shook his head. In some ways Miska was almost glad that he'd stayed true to his convictions, even though it was a pain in the ass for her.

'What can you tell me?' she asked.

He shrugged. He was still shaking a little from the cold. 'What do you want to know?'

'You were part of the terrorist organisation called the New Weather Underground?'

81

'Funny, they didn't call me a terrorist when I was part of the resistance fighting the Cult of Ahriman during the occupation. But then they never do when you're killing for those with the money and power, right?' He looked over at her again. Miska just shrugged and he turned away. 'Yes, I was a Weatherman.'

'They were primarily based in the Sirius system?'

'If you say so.'

'Yet you operated in other systems?' she asked. Hogg just shrugged. 'Were you part of the Human Oversight Committee?'

He straightened up and turned to look at her again.

'The HOC don't exist any more.'

'Officially.'

'They really frighten people like you, don't they? An organisation, many of them ex-vets, prepared to protect people – with military force, if need be – from the excesses of the corporations and their puppet governments.'

Miska gave the question some thought.

'No, they don't frighten people "like me". And I've killed terrorists. They all think they're right and have the right to inflict what they believe on other people through violence. I've always thought it was just an excuse for guys like you to blow shit up.'

'Oh, I would have had another life, darlin', if I thought I could've, and terrorism is a perspective. I get pretty terrified when someone wraps an explosive collar around my neck and orders me to kill.'

Miska shrugged and then sent a message to the ship's systems. A picture of the Che virus appeared on the closest screen to their position.

'What's that?' she asked. Hogg glanced at the screen.

'Che Guevara,' he suggested. 'He was a ...'

'You guys have all got your heroes, huh? I know who he was. I want to know what that is.'

'It's a virus,' Hogg told her.

'A tool of the HOC?'

Miska turned to look out over the rails. Two levels below prisoners returning from the showers after their PT session, were being put back into suspended animation. One-by-one their pods were filling up with the blue gel. Something about it made Miska think of drowning men. She shook the thought off.

'No. It's sentient and the HOC didn't enslave things. An AI maybe.'

'Small Gods software?' Miska asked.

'Maybe, though it frequently works against the Small Gods as well. I guess there's a reason it models itself after a cultural icon rather than a religious one. It doesn't need to be worshipped, which at the end of the day is just another form of social control.'

Miska tried not to laugh at his earnestness. 'So it's not connected to the HOC?'

'The HOC might have worked with it from time to time but it's an independent operator. It infects a system when people really need help.'

'You say it's sentient. Can it be reasoned with?' Miska was trying not to think too much about how attractive the virus's net representation was.

'Yes, it's very reasonable,' Hogg told her, smiling. 'But if you mean can it be talked into helping oppress people so that already wealthy shareholders can get just that little bit richer, then no, it probably can't be reasoned with.' Miska sighed again.

'You seem happy enough to talk about it.'

'I only know how to work with Che, not attack it. The virus

83

is diffuse. You want to get rid of it you'd have to junk the entire system it's in and then another copy of it would just turn up again if things remain bad. I don't think you'll be able to do anything about it.'

'So how come it hasn't saved the colonies from the evils of oppression?' Miska asked.

'Maybe things would be a lot worse if it didn't exist? Maybe it sees itself as the very last resort.'

'Or it's controlled by someone or something?' she asked. Hogg remained quiet. She thought about explaining to him that she could compel him to answer but she'd never really liked torture.

'You got a conscience?' he asked.

Miska was stumped for a moment. The question had kind of come out of the blue. 'Kind of personal, isn't it?'

'Simple question for most people.'

'I don't know.'

Hogg laughed humourlessly. 'At least you don't try and rationalise the shit you do.' Miska shrugged again. 'Well then, this probably won't make much difference to you, but things have got to be pretty bad before the Che virus gets involved. The TCC must have been doing some pretty shitty things to those miners.'

'Help me,' she told him. Hogg just shook his head. 'With your help I could end this without killing anyone.'

'You're on the wrong side,' Hogg told her.

She thought about this as she sent another message to the ship. 'Yeah, but the oppressed don't pay very well.'

'Money, chains, explosive collars, it's all the same.'

'One more question. There were independent ships at Faigroe Station ...'

'Figures, the TCC are no friends to the indy ships. Got to be

84

a good little corporate citizen if you want to live under this sun. They'll be loving what the miners have done.'

'The indies are squeezed out of all the big contracts, robbed blind on harbour fees, that kind of thing.'

'Yeah, you're working for saints, so?'

'So they've gotta be recruiting crews from somewhere. There's a free port in-system, isn't there?'

Hogg didn't say anything. He didn't have to. He might have stuck to his principles but he was a terrible liar and he knew it. The stricken expression on his face told her that he thought he had betrayed his cause.

'Miss, I don't think you ever want to hand me a gun when you're around, understand me?'

'I'll bear it in mind.'

Hogg cocked his head to one side as he heard the sound of the guard droids Miska had tasked to put him back into his pod.

'Still sounds like jackboots.'

Miska was sat on the railings, her back to the long drop through the cellblocks into the yard, watching the droids put Hogg back in his pod. She could tell by the set of his shoulders that he was broken. That saddened her. She had quite liked him. It was something she had to guard against. She had found herself liking quite a few of them. She glanced up at the hanging fruit that was the solitary cells.

'Well?' her father asked, his image appearing on a nearby screen.

'You were listening?'

'Always.'

She frowned at that. 'Two teams. An infiltration team and an assault squad. Twelve of the Wraiths.'

'That's half our power armour and their Retributors have only got rubber bullets.'

'That's fine, I don't want a massacre.'

'Who leads the assault team?'

'Mass,' Miska told her dad. He frowned but didn't say anything, which suggested he couldn't think of anyone better.

'And the infiltration team?' he asked, though she assumed he knew the answer.

'That would be me. I need to speak to Vido again.'

Her father looked less than pleased.

Her father's virtual ghost strode into the windowless briefing room in the poured concrete bunker underneath the command tower in Camp Reisman. Uncle Vido was sat in one of the moulded plastic chairs arranged around the conference table. A holographic image of Faigroe Station shimmered in the air above the table. Part of Tau Ceti G could be seen in the image. The super-storm was still whipping up red, brown and white clouds far below the orbiting asteroid station. Massimo Prola was leaned against the wall, his large arms crossed in front of his chest.

'I'm not happy about this,' her dad surprised her by saying in front of the two *Mafiosi*.

'I asked them here as a courtesy,' Miska told her father.

Vido held his arms open. 'If I'm not wanted—' he started, and made to get up.

'Alcatraz,' her father said, and Vido, Mass and the holographic image, as well as everything and everyone in the VR training construct, froze in place.

'I thought we weren't going to do this too much?' Miska said. Her father crossed his arms.

'You're giving Vido too much influence,' he warned. 'You give a guy like that an inch and he takes a mile. If we treat him differently then it pisses off all the other prisoners and they become more difficult to handle.'

Miska sighed. 'I know how to handle these guys, Dad. The Company was practically in bed with them. Show them respect and it's easier to get their cooperation.'

'Respect? You've put a collar on him. He's still hoping to get out of here but he's got to make an example of you, or else he's going to look weak in front of his associates back in the world.'

'He's useful,' Miska insisted, though she knew he was right. Uncle Vido was charming, easy to get along with, and would have her tortured to death the moment he thought he could get away with it. 'He's looking for an advantage, and he knows that for the time being that means dealing with me. He pulls Mass's strings and Mass has earned a promotion.'

He looked unconvinced. 'This isn't going to work if we play by their rules. They have to play by ours.'

'It doesn't matter how often we hammer round-shaped pegs, Dad, they won't fit in square holes. They're not marines.'

'Then what are we doing here?' he demanded.

'Making do.' He still looked far from convinced. 'Let me do this my way and when it fucks up you can say you told me so.'

He narrowed his eyes at her foul language.

'Seriously, Dad, I was in the marines. I was a Devil Dog, yes?' Her father just crossed his arms. 'Leavenworth,' she said to the air.

'—I can go,' Vido finished as the rest of the room unfroze and he stood up. Mass and Vido spent a few moments looking around suspiciously but didn't say anything.

'It's okay, Uncle V, you can stay,' Miska told him. She caught

Mass frowning at her addressing the *consigliere* so familiarly.

Vido turned to look at her dad. He still had his arms crossed, he looked less than happy, but he nodded and Vido sat back down.

'So what's this about, crazy lady?' Mass asked. She could practically hear her father grinding his teeth.

'I'm promoting you,' Miska told him.

'Colonel?' Mass asked.

'He's been a captain before,' Vido pointed out. 'Admittedly not in a formal military.' Miska wasn't sure but she suspected that her dad had actually started growling, quietly, under his breath.

'Corporal,' Miska told him. Vido and Mass looked at each other; the *consigliere* shrugged.

'Cool,' Mass decided.

'I'm putting you in charge of the next assault on the station,' she told him.

Mass frowned. 'The last one didn't go so well. Where will you be?'

'Corporal, do you understand that anything that is discussed in here can't go any further?' her father asked.

'Sure,' Mass said. Her father leaned in close to Mass. Miska was impressed that despite her father being a VR ghost Mass shrank away from him. 'I mean yes, Gunny.'

'Respect, my leathery ass. What this camp needs is some Goddammed discipline,' her dad said, straightening up.

'I'll be inside,' Miska told Mass. 'And you'll be in Wraiths.'

Mass smiled at the thought of wearing the power armour suits.

'Outstanding,' Mass said. 'How many in the team?'

'One squad, twelve including the corporal,' her dad told them.

'We get to pick the team?' Vido asked.

'Jimmy Beans is down in cellblock 2,' Mass said.

'Two Times still here?' Vido asked Mass.

'Naw, he got out just before, did a full bid as well ... what about—'

'Ten-hut!'

Miska almost jumped as her dad screamed. Mass actually snapped to a pretty good impression of attention. Vido was looking around as if it was some kind of joke. Realising Gunnery Sergeant Corbin wasn't joking, the sexagenarian *consigliere* stood to attention. 'Are either of you generals?'

'No ...' Mass offered.

'I thought I asked both of you!'

'No,' Vido added. He seemed more surprised than angry.

'No what? Answer like you actually have testicles!' Mass's head shot round to glare at her dad. *Don't try it, little man,* Miska thought. *Ghost or not, he'll snap you like a twig.*

'No, Gunny!' Vido barked and elbowed Mass.

'No, Gunny!' Mass added.

'Are you, then, a pair of acid-bleeding, blood-drinking, bullet-shitting sergeant majors?'

'No, Gunny!' they both shouted.

'Pretend that you're men!'

'No, Gunny!' This time they practically screamed it. Miska suspected that her dad might be pushing them a little bit too hard but it was difficult not to smile.

'Do you make strategic decisions here?' he demanded.

'No, Gunny!'

Then they got to meet the real Gunnery Sergeant Corbin as he got right up in their faces.

'No, you do not! You do not because you know nothing!

Because you are nothing! You are effluence of less worth than the beer shits I take of a Sunday morning! Protoplasmic slime! You are living examples that evolution does not work! That God hates you! And your mother—'

'Woah!' Mass shouted and now Vido looked angry as well. Corbin turned on Mass.

'Do you think you are a hard man?' he demanded. 'A dangerous man! A killer!'

'Yes, Gunny!' Mass told him.

'Bullshit!' It may have been virtual saliva but it was still spraying Mass and Vido's faces. 'I've tried to scoop the guts back into men and women worth ten of you, a hundred of you.' It wasn't the words themselves, it was the contempt with which they were delivered. Training sergeants had to be tough and while they were frequently exasperated with those under their charge, they seldom, if ever, hated them. It was becoming clear, however, just how much her dad truly despised the men he was training. 'You're a punk playing at being a soldier.' He had stopped shouting now, and the quiet voice was almost worse. Mass was shaking with anger. He looked about ready to attack her dad.

'Mass,' Vido said.

'Did I give you permission to speak?' Gunny said, turning on Vido. 'Eyes front! You are still at attention!' Vido snapped back into attention.

'Do you both love discipline?' her father shouted.

'Yes, Gunny!' Vido shouted.

Mass was still seething. Her dad turned back towards the button man.

'Thank you, Gunnery Sergeant,' Miska said, before this escalated and Mass committed suicide with his mouth.

Her dad spent a few more moments glaring at them before stepping back and nodding to her. Mass was just about standing to attention, though still shaking with rage. Miska spent a moment wondering if there'd still be crime if all criminals had to meet her dad. 'Give me the room, Gunny.' Her dad snapped to attention and saluted before marching out of the briefing room.

'He's fucking—' Mass started.

'You finish that threat and I'll switch you off right here and now,' Miska told him. Any trace of her normal cheerful demeanour was gone.

It was probably because he was dead that she couldn't tolerate threats against her dad. Just for a moment she wondered if Mass had been one of the killers. If so then it had been a mob hit. She couldn't see the connection to her father, and as dangerous as Mass had undoubtedly been, he would have been no match for her father. Mass was glaring at her. She held his eyes and he looked away first.

'Do you know why we enforce discipline?' she asked.

'Because you're—' Mass started angrily.

'That's enough, Mass,' Vido said quietly, and then to Miska: 'The same reason we do. To keep people alive.'

'There is no "you", now. There is only us. Get used to it and you might live, maybe even thrive. Push against it and I guarantee you'll end up dead.'

'Oh, he's hard enough in here with his godlike powers—' Mass started.

'Shut up and listen, Mass,' Vido said. Mass looked as though he'd been slapped. He turned towards Vido.

'Something to say?' Vido asked. For a moment Mass looked as though he was about to attack the *consigliere*. Instead he swallowed and seemed to master himself.

'Did I make a mistake?' Miska asked the button man. Vido opened his mouth but Miska held her hand up. 'I asked the corporal.'

'No,' he managed.

'This isn't New Verona. You start from zero here. You want something? You earn it, okay?' Vido nodded. 'But you've got skills, you'll do fine. I've picked out a squad. They're from a diverse background, understand?' This time Mass nodded. 'So, if you can lead, lead. If not say so now.'

'I can do this,' Mass told her.

'They're not going to care what you were in a past life. You don't get their respect, you earn it.' He looked as though he was going to argue but decided against it. Miska hoped this meant he was learning. 'The railguns your power armour will be carrying have been modified to fire at a much lower velocity and they'll be loaded with rubber bullets. You are not to kill anyone when you take the station, do you understand me?' Mass frowned but nodded. 'Okay. I think you've got some hard times ahead of you. Gunny Corbin is probably going to torture you some during PT but he'll take you through the fine details of the plan and you'll be running simulated assaults here in the construct, okay?'

'Understood,' Mass said. Vido gripped his shoulder.

'Okay, dismissed.'

The two *Mafiosi* turned and almost marched as they made for the door. *A success for military conditioning?* Miska wondered. Mass left the briefing room but Vido stopped and turned to look at her.

'That was bracing,' he said and then left the room.

*

Miska followed out just behind Mass and Vido. One of her father's ghosts was waiting for them. As she watched them double-timing it across the camp, her dad shouting at them, she noticed another one of her dad's ghosts marching next to the double-timing VR icon of another prisoner. She recognised him as the Yakuza lieutenant Teramoto Shigeru.

'I told you so.' It was her father's voice over their private comms link. She already had a sinking feeling. Her dad's ghost and Teramoto came to a halt in front of her as both of them snapped to attention. She wanted to ask her dad what was going on over the comms link but she couldn't shake the feeling that she'd just be giving him the satisfaction.

'Prisoner Teramoto requests permission to speak with you,' her father told her. He turned to look at the man. With his neatness, there was something fussy about him, something of the pedantic accountant, but Miska had known enough truly dangerous people to recognise one when she met him. He bowed slightly towards her.

'Greeting Miska-*sama*, I wish to convey—' he started.

'Get to the point!' her dad shouted. He apparently wasn't in the best of moods today and he seemed determined to disrespect every high-ranking gangster he could find. Teramoto sighed and glanced at her father. On the other side of the camp she saw a VR simulation of one of the prison shuttles take off from the landing area. The sounds of engines and gunfire, comforting sounds from her childhood on various military bases, filled the air.

'I wish a seat at the table,' the Yakuza lieutenant told them. Her father gave her a rueful look.

'What table?' Miska asked, though she knew exactly what he was talking about. Teramoto did not answer, instead he just turned and looked in the direction that Mass and Vido had been taken.

'Funnily enough, the gunny and I have just finished explaining to two other people who thought they were something special that anything you get in here you've got to work for.'

Teramoto nodded.

'Of course my men and I have to—'

'You don't have any men,' her father growled. Teramoto turned to look at the gunnery sergeant. Her dad towered over him and effectively had godlike power in the training construct. The Yakuza lieutenant didn't seem the slightest bit intimidated.

'Begging the gunnery sergeant's pardon, but including the Bethlehem Milliners I command some three-hundred-and-seventy-five men within the bulkheads of the *Hangman's Daughter*.'

'You don't command shit,' her father snapped. Miska could see that her dad had had his fill of organised crime types for one day.

'They are willing to die but I understand we must prove ourselves, like anyone else,' Teramoto said. Miska noticed that he was missing two fingers from his left hand. Then red warning signs appeared in her IVD as a window opened showing lens feed from the hangar deck. A group of just under a hundred prisoners were all face-down on the deck, hands behind their heads, covered by two guard droids and a number of nearby automated turrets. Another two droids were covering a prisoner who was on his knees, hands held high, his young face an expressionless mask. Takeshi, Numa, serving ten years for manslaughter. He was the youngest member of the Bethlehem Milliners *bōsōzoku* biker gang. Where he held his hands up, the sleeves of his prison issue overalls had slipped down, revealing a small part of the detailed tattoo that ran up one arm. There was another prisoner lying on the deck close to Takeshi. Bennini, James, a combined twenty-seven-year sentence for aggravated assault, mayhem, possession of an illegal weapon and extortion. Also known as Jimmy Beans. With a thought Miska opened another window in her vision to check Bennini's biometrics. They were all flat-lined.

Miska cursed internally, glaring down at Teramoto. Her father was looking at the Yakuza lieutenant like he was something he had just stepped in.

'Is there something wrong, Miska-*sama*?' Teramoto asked.

Miska resisted the urge to break his nose. Instead, with a thought, she ran the lens footage back. The hundred-strong group of prisoners were running across the hangar deck as part of their PT routine. Takeshi had been running next to Bennini when he'd suddenly barged into the other prisoner, knocking him to the ground. Bennini, completely taken by surprise, didn't even see the open-handed strike that hit him – reinforced finger-tips powered by illegally boosted muscle crushing his throat. Takeshi then grabbed Bennini's head and managed to snap his neck before the guard droids reached him. The turrets hadn't taken a shot because there were too many of the prisoners in the way and it had happened too quickly for Miska, or her dad, to activate the collar in time.

With a thought Miska triggered Takeshi's collar anyway.

'Takeshi's dead,' she told Teramoto.

'I see. Did one of my men transgress in some way?'

'I need a terribly compelling reason not to switch you off right now,' Miska told him.

'Won't morale suffer further if it becomes known that you'll kill prisoners for no reason whatsoever?' he asked.

Now Miska was angry enough to grind her teeth. 'And I assume that's the story that will circulate if anything happens to you?' she asked.

'I've no idea what you're talking about,' he said.

'Not to mention discipline problems with your pet *bōsōzoku* gang?' she continued. Teramoto said nothing.

'Three-hundred-and-seventy-five men, huh?' her dad asked.

'Just so,' Teramoto said.

'That would make you an officer?' her dad continued. Teramoto just nodded. The gunnery sergeant leaned down and grabbed Teramoto by his collar. Just for a moment Miska saw a flicker of anger cross the Yakuza lieutenant's face, then it was an impassive mask again. 'Officers get fragged all the time.'

'Isolate him,' Miska said, and Teramoto disappeared. 'I'll deal with him later.'

'Slippery slope,' her father told her. It sounded like: I told you so. 'What about the other Yakuza and the Milliners?'

Miska thought for a moment.

'Leave them in play for the time being but change the rota so they're not on with any wise guys.'

'There could still be repercussions.'

'Oh, there will be repercussions, and I'm not sure that's a bad thing. Punish them accordingly.'

'A gang war in here would be a bloody zero sum game.'

Miska just nodded. They hadn't even completed their first job and already it was starting to feel like her precarious world was falling apart. She tranced out of the Camp Reisman VR construct.

And opened her eyes on her bunk aboard the *Little Jimmy*.

'Music,' she said and the harsh, strident opening chords of

late twentieth century rock music filled the ship's small cabin. She threw a few punches at the air, then a few kicks. She wanted to fight and wondered for a moment about beating Teramoto to death publicly. 'Aaaaaah!' The scream came out of nowhere, surprising her. Her fist cracked the tubular ceramic frame of her bunk. She dropped her hands down to her side, forcing herself to breathe, shaking her arms, rolling her head round, trying to release some of the tension in her body, trying to relax. Suddenly she spun around the cabin, whipping her hair around to the loud music. Her dad had been right about her neglecting her PT. She needed to do some training, get rid of all the pent-up energy, but for now she needed something to focus on.

Her weapons lay on one of the other bunks. She had stripped down, cleaned and run diagnostics on all of them. The plan was for the infiltration team to masquerade as a small group of down-at-heel mercenaries.

Possibly too close to the truth, Miska thought, before repressing the momentary negativity. Working on her weapons had gone some way to cheering her up. The cover story meant that she would have to be selective.

The Tyler Optics M-187 laser carbine with the underslung 30mm grenade launcher was out. The highly illegal military weapon was very expensive and tended to only be available to prestigious conventional units, officers and special forces. It would give her away.

Likewise, the compact SIG Sauer GP-992 gauss pistol was mostly used by special forces and covert operations types as the adjustable velocity meant that the weapon could be rendered almost completely silent.

Instead, she had decided on one of the guard's Winchester

semi-automatic police shotguns. She had adjusted the modular weapon, shortening the barrel, which in turn meant shortening the tubular magazine. The shotgun would now be easier to conceal but would only carry four rounds in the magazine and one in the chamber. She had removed much of the stock and reformed what remained into an ergonomic pistol grip. She had also reformed the slide on the auxiliary pump-action mechanism, used to clear jams, to add a fore grip.

Miska had also chosen one of the old Glock pistols that the human guards on the prison barge had carried. The ceramic sidearm held twenty 10mm caseless rounds in its magazine and was capable of semi- and fully automatic fire. Again, she had adjusted the ergonomic grip on the Glock to suit her.

She had lasered off the serial numbers and removed ID chips from both weapons. She would fire a lot of test rounds through both of them on the *Hangman's Daughter*'s range before she left.

She was still feeling hopelessly under-armed, but then she was banking on the rebel miners arming them. Besides, she still had her knife and everything was okay if she had her knife. She picked up the blade, careful not to cut the sheets on the bed. It was made from a solid piece of blackened belt-titanium. The nine-inch blade was fused with a synthetic diamond edge. The hilt was six inches long, wrapped in leather and ended in a ring. Although it was a functional fighting knife it was based on a weapon used by a character she had played in her favourite on-net game. Her dad, her real dad, not the digital copy on board, had given it to her when she passed special forces selection. The sad thing was that the VR ghost on board wouldn't remember. She slumped back into the pilot seat looking at the blade before sheathing it and returning to her last weapon.

A huge revolver, the .454 calibre Mastodon, a big game pistol that had been repurposed to hunt the alien Them more than a hundred years ago. The revolver was a family heirloom. She'd inherited it after her father had been killed. The cylinder contained six rounds. She didn't have any reloads. She wasn't taking the Mastodon either. That had a very specific purpose. It would be the weapon she used to execute her father's murderers.

CHAPTER 7

Miska had tasked the maintenance droids with repainting the prison shuttle. She'd taken a torch to any external markings that gave the shuttle's origins away and then, with some difficulty, hacked the secure transponder and given the shuttle a fake name and number. Now it looked just like any other repurposed hundred-plus-years-old piece of military surplus. Unless anyone looked inside, but that was the good thing about free ports, people respected your privacy. She couldn't use the *Little Jimmy* for a job like this. It would attract too much attention, besides which she didn't want the prisoners knowing about the stealth ship. It was her escape if things went bad.

Two members of the Hard Luck Comancheros gang were acting as pilot and co-pilot for the shuttle. They would drop the squad off and then return to the *Hangman's Daughter*. If anyone from the port paid them any attention then the shuttle would just appear to be some indy ship's interface vehicle.

Miska could have piloted it herself but she wanted some time to get to know the team. She'd brought Gleave along, both for his skillsoft-capable neuralware and his expertise as a confidence trickster. He was also capable of piloting the shuttle, albeit due to skillsofts rather than hard skills. Currently, however, he was spending a lot of time crying.

'Please no! Don't make me!'

Miska watched, a look of consternation on her face as he burst into tears yet again. They were in the prisoner transport area of the shuttle, though she hadn't locked down any of the prisoners.

'I shat myself! I'm a grown man and I had actual shit in my actual pants!' Miska frowned. The initial briefing wasn't going as well as she had hoped. 'I mean, his head just came off. *Pop!*' He made an exploding gesture with his hands and then whirled them around. 'And then it was just spinning around in the air! I was covered in his blood!'

Miska watched as the podgy, balding con man hunched over, sobbing into his hands. It wasn't the kind of resistance she was used to. Normally they swore, or threatened, and sometimes there was violence.

Torricone shifted uncomfortably. He seemed both embarrassed by, and a little bit sympathetic towards, Gleave. There'd been something of an argument with her dad about including Torricone in the team. Her dad had been suspicious of Miska's motivations, it seemed. Miska had told her father that she needed an intrusion expert, a thief. Her dad had pointed out that not only had Torricone been a car thief, and he couldn't see there being too many cars in the asteroid mine, but that he had already disobeyed orders and seemed reluctant to kill when the hammer came down. Torricone was leaning against the back of one of the seats, muscular, tattooed arms hanging down. He seemed reluctant to sit as well.

Merrill Lombard, the youngest member of the infiltration team, was sat in one of the seats, his legs over the arm, staring at Gleave as if he didn't quite know what he was looking at. Up until recently he had been a somewhat scrawny, gawky-looking kid in his late teens, but the relentless PT, while coming close to killing him on several occasions (according to her father), meant that he was starting to fill out. She knew from his medical file that he'd had corrective surgery on his eyes as a child, but somehow he still looked as though he needed a pair of glasses. Lombard had a near-genius level IQ and was something of a self-taught computer expert. He even had an integral computer and a neural interface illegally implanted into his brain. Miska could still make out the ugly implant scars on his skull through his short hair. The computer had been deactivated after he'd been arrested. He was serving consecutive life sentences for the biofeedback murders of fifteen of his virtual classmates. Lombard had been the victim of sustained cyber-bullying and had decided to deal with the perpetrators his way. Because the victims had included the children of some of the more influential members of his suburban community on Barney's Prime, he'd been tried and sentenced as an adult.

Miska intended on reactivating his computer and interface. This had caused another serious discussion with her dad. There were a number of hackers serving time for various crimes on board the prison barge. All of their implants had been de-activated. A hacker with access to a computer could prove to be the biggest threat to their operation thus far, but Miska's plan called for at least two hackers. Miska had chosen Lombard because she suspected that she could get him onside by treating him with a little bit of respect. It was kind of working but she kept on catching him looking at her breasts when he thought she wasn't paying attention.

'Please!' Gleave looked up at her through his fingers. 'Isn't there something else I can do, maybe a punishment duty? Don't you need someone to mop the cellblocks or something?' he begged.

'We've kinda got droids for that,' Miska told him. 'And there's really only one punishment around here.' She heard Torricone suck air through his teeth in disgust. Gleave was staring at her, appalled.

'Oh my God! You're going to blow my head off, aren't you?' He started wailing again.

'There is nothing to fear, none of this is real,' Nyukuti said.

He was of Australian Aboriginal descent, from a people called the Pintupi. He'd grown up in the asteroid mines of the Lalande system. He had served briefly in the Australian military but was discharged on psychological grounds. Apparently the powerfully built, scarred Nyukuti had gone on to work as a 'stand-over man'. As far as Miska could tell this meant that he tortured other criminals to get them to hand over their ill-gotten gains. It seemed a particularly Australian crime to her. There was a note in his file saying that members of the *Whānau* gang would kill him if they could.

'We are all living in the desert and dreaming of sharks,' he continued.

Gleave stared at Nyukuti. Miska found herself smiling. She had no idea what the man was talking about but she liked the sound of it. During his trial he had justified his crimes by claiming that this wasn't the real world, only dreams were real, and what happened outside of them didn't matter. Apparently he'd had an augmented reality feed inserted straight into his cerebellum, adding dreamlike sensory information right into his mind. He had been living in a quasi-fictional/mythological version of reality. Unfortunately for Nyukuti the AR feed had been disabled upon incarceration.

As a stand-over man, he had left his least fortunate victims physically unharmed, instead torturing their minds in custom-made VR constructs that had left them broken messes by the time he had finished.

Nyukuti was the only one who seemed enthusiastic about Miska's plan.

'I don't get you guys.' Miska said. 'I thought you'd be eager to be out and about.'

'I think it's the lack of free will that's the issue,' Torricone pointed out.

'I'm on board,' Merrill told her. He seemed eager to please. Torricone glanced at him and shook his head.

'I mean, what could be more fun than infiltrating a terrorist-held asteroid mine controlled by an evil computer virus?' Miska asked. She was oddly gratified that Nyukuti was nodding along with her. Gleave's sobbing grew louder.

'And that's the guy who's going to do the talking?' Torricone asked. Miska nodded. 'What's our cover?' If nothing else, he seemed resigned to being involved.

'Mercenaries,' Miska said, beaming. It seemed like an excellent cover to her, as it was so close to the truth. Torricone looked between Merrill and Gleave.

'Really?'

Gobbin had given them a deadline: a week. The corporations didn't like free ports and the indy ships that operated out of them. They turned a blind eye to the ports, however, because they could use such places to sell product that they didn't really want to pay taxes on. Most free ports were one big, grey economy with thick lines of black running through them. Miska had considered contacting the TCC's intelligence division for information on any free ports in the system but she was of the opinion that they had done enough damage for one mission.

She'd tranced in and had a good look around the local net in orbit above Tau Ceti G. She'd found lots of hints but nothing concrete, so she'd taken the chance and sent some of her more subtle programs into Tau Ceti E's net, some forty-five light minutes away, spread some of their very sparse money around, and finally got an answer.

The free port was called May '68 for reasons she didn't understand. There was no location, just a vast solar orbit. She was reasonably sure that the Faigroe Station miners would use the free port as a staging point for any recruiting efforts. The Che virus notwithstanding, the miners would need to recruit mercenaries if they wanted a hope of standing up to the TCC.

It took them the better part of a day to reach May '68 in the shuttle. They had gone over the plan, got used to their cover identities, and Miska had finally got some sleep. When she woke up they checked and rechecked their gear, and went over their plan and legends some more. Gleave seemed to come to terms with his pants-shitting terror and got into character. He was pretty much a different person by the time they saw the free port.

The pilot sent feed from the shuttle's external lens direct to Miska's IVD. She shared it with the rest of the team – all of them had enough 'ware to accept the feed, even Torricone. May '68 wasn't one station but rather a small convoy of ships. The core was an ancient and huge bulk carrier with a number of large freighters and smaller habitats attached to the stanchions that had once supported the carrier's huge engines.

Several smaller asteroids, presumably not so large that they caught the attention of the TCC, had been towed into place and were being mined by a number of ships that looked as though they were parasitically eating their way into the rocks' stone flesh. Bolt-on engine modules were attached to the asteroids to help keep them in place. There was a tethered ice asteroid with a scarily home-made-looking purification plant attached to it, huge pipes running from the plant into the core of the port. The whole thing was towed by several system tugs, each of them with huge engines for their size. It looked like a jury-rigged, unstable, glorious mess.

'Looks like a modern art masterpiece,' Gleave growled, and for a moment he reminded Miska of her dad. She wondered if that was who the confidence artist was basing his cover persona on.

There were a number of ships forming a screen around the free port. Most of them were small- to medium-sized freighters, as fast, armoured and heavily armed as their impoverished crews could afford to make them, designed for running system and planetary blockades; smugglers' ships. There were a few more heavily armed craft there as well. Ancient military surplus ships, but piracy was a zero sum game in a system so heavily corporate controlled, unless they wanted to prey on their own kind.

Miska zoomed in on some much smaller craft surrounding the free port. She saw Torricone frown. He was sitting on one of the collapsible beds they'd set up in the prisoner transport area.

'Fighters?' he asked. Miska studied one small craft, and then moved the lenses with a thought to focus on another. Each of the craft looked like an exercise in heavily armed, dangerous self-expression. Each of them was unique, and each of them looked like they'd been assembled from recycled junk.

'Drones,' Miska told him. The car thief nodded.

'Cool,' Merrill said. Nyukuti had his eyes closed. He had announced earlier on that he was going to attempt to use imagination to replace augmented reality in search of a dreamscape. He certainly gave no indication that he was paying attention to the external lens feed.

Miska heard the pilots hailing the free port.

'Unidentified shuttle, this is what passes for the May '68's traffic control. You're welcome to dock, everyone is, please have something to contribute, and if you try any shit, please be advised you'll probably get yourself dead.'

'At last!' Miska cried and everyone bar Nyukuti turned to look at her. 'Sorry. I just get excited when I hear people being reasonable.' Gleave narrowed his eyes. Merrill opened his mouth to say something and then seemed to think the better of it.

Concentrating on the lens feed window in her IVD again, Miska saw the shuttle pick its way through drones and indy ships towards a rickety-looking, bolted-on space dock facility.

'That may just be the most scary-assed thing I've ever seen,' Gleave muttered.

'Who are those dudes?' Merrill asked. It took a moment for Miska to realise who he was talking about. The shuttle was subjectively side-on to a ship that looked like some kind of industrial, open-topped barge, only one with large glowing engines. There was a complex telescope apparatus mounted on the barge and some other bits of tech that she didn't recognise.

The craft was crewed by what Miska thought were droids initially, a number of them lying prone on tech-heavy couches that presumably connected them to the craft.

'They're vacuum cleaners,' Nyukuti surprised her by answering. 'I've seen them among the asteroid communities in the Lalande system. They are some kind of cult of academics who wanted to get closer to their subject matter. Life as an Extra Vehicular Activity.'

'Those are people?' Torricone asked. 'Jesus.'

'Not so much any more,' Nyukuti told him. 'They have cut deep, they are mostly augmented brains in cybernetic bodies designed to protect them from the rigours of vacuum. There's little humanity left, I suspect.'

Miska wasn't sure if the stand-over man was sympathetic or fascinated.

'Brilliant, Zero-G,' Torricone muttered. Merrill looked unsure, and Gleave, with his born-again-hard legend in place, was looking pissed off. Only Nyukuti seemed unfazed by the free port's apparent lack of gravity, but then he'd grown up among asteroid communities and didn't seem fazed by much. Miska was starting to think she'd brought the wrong criminals with her: too many planet-bound types on the team.

They were pulling themselves along an unsteady docking arm towards the mushroom-shaped central area of the docking facility. Through the shuttle's lens feed in her IVD she saw the craft peel away from the free port and start on its way back to the *Hangman's Daughter*. As far as she could tell the two pilots were among the best shuttle pilots they still had on board the prison barge. They also weren't too whiny about the whole explosive collar thing. Miska appreciated that, and she wanted them to fly the assault team, which was going to be some tricky flying.

The May '68, like many free ports, was a collective built around shared wealth and, apparently, not being an asshole. Miska thought the second part of their ideology was yet to be established. Such collectives tended to attract people who wanted to reject certain aspects of society. As a space-based society one of the easiest aspects to reject was gravity. It also saved them on maintenance and energy costs.

They had adhered molecular hook strips to their boots. Those in turn adhered to the sparse carpet in the docking facility. They used the rails and handgrips where they had to as they made their way into the ore carrier core of the free port. Miska felt a moment of vertigo as she entered what was once the enormous ore carrier's cargo hold. The walls were covered in colourfully decorated containers and other structures that had been turned into homes and formed a tangled, multi-storied warren of tiny streets. A roughly cylindrical structure ran down the middle of the vast cargo bay. Miska magnified her vision. That looked like the commercial area, stalls, stores, warehouses made from containers; even restaurants and bars ran all the way around the central cylinder. The commercial area was connected to the living areas by a sprawling network of pipes and railings that looked like a vast and precarious climbing frame. The locals seemed adept at swinging around on the frame but Miska also saw people moving around on zip lines, or in freefall, and using gas propulsion systems to manoeuvre.

Everywhere she looked she saw vibrant self-expression of one sort or another, from the colourful and often abstract murals on the cargo container homes to bizarre, seemingly public sculptures. The self-expression seemed to stretch to the inhabitants themselves: everything from piercings to cosmetic grafts to significant cybernetic augmentation. Many had modified their bodies with multiple limbs configured to be of more use in Zero-G environments. Some of them looked as though they were trying to get as far as they possibly could from base humanity. Merrill and Torricone were both staring in a way that made Miska smile. Gleave was in character and looking around with what she suspected he thought was a steely-eyed gaze, and Nyukuti ... was clambering up a frame.

'Shit,' Miska muttered.

'You going to blow the top of his head off?' Merrill asked, watching Nyukuti expertly pulling himself up into the air towards the central hub. Miska narrowed her eyes and gave the question some serious thought. They were here undercover. All the collars were hidden. She suspected that triggering the explosive lowjack and publicly blowing his head off might draw attention to them.

'No,' she finally said.

'That doesn't seem fair,' Torricone said. It might have been the first time she'd really seen him smile.

'Yeah, why not?' Merrill demanded. She wasn't sure if he was annoyed about the apparent double standard, or just wanted to see someone's head fly off.

'Because Nyukuti's special,' Miska told him. 'Nyukuti, what do you think you're doing?' she subvocalised over a private comms link.

'I will be with you soon,' he replied. 'There is something I must attend to.'

'Okay, enough fucking around,' Gleave snapped. Miska wondered if he was taking his character a little too seriously. On the other hand, she thought she detected some genuine anxiety in his words. After all, they had just discussed blowing the top of people's heads off when they were supposed to be in character.

Miska had found the bar in the May '68's helpful but eclectically organised net. They had a wanted ad for mercenaries, and the bar seemed to be a clearinghouse for the local violent talent. It hadn't overtly mentioned Faigroe Station but there had been enough clues to suggest that was what the job would be.

They had made their way along the frame and onto the central hub. Miska was amused that Merrill finally seemed to have got the idea that they were supposed to be playing pretend, and had started acting like he thought mercenaries did. It had more to do with sense games and vizzes than anything else, and she'd had to ask him to dial it down a little.

The bar in question was called the Revolution Will Be Televised. Illuminated by steel-blue light, it was decorated in a retro graffiti style, and was projecting images from old films into the air, where floating clientele occasionally disrupted them. There were various dance platforms on all six of the walls, where dancers of various genders shook their bewildering array of thangs. The drinks were served from a complicated polyhedron-shaped structure, cleverly suspended in the centre of the room by air currents provided by fans in each of the walls. The barman had eight spindly cybernetic limbs, no apparent real arms or legs, and scuttled around inside of the polyhedron serving drinks.

They were sat at the bar, slowly spinning and drinking beer. Miska had provided each of them with a little pocket money before they left the shuttle. As the bar slowly spun they orbited over a table on one of the walls where it was obvious that a

111

mercenary audition was going on. *Well*, Miska thought, *if not mercenaries, then muscle*. There was a difference.

Sitting at the table was a thick-set, massively built man. Epicanthic folds suggested he came from Asian stock, Miska suspected Central Asia. He wore his hair in a crew cut. His enormous size meant significant muscle boosting. His eyes were artificial, and judging by the scars around them, cheap. His facial features had the blocky look that came with equally cheap subdermal armour – much of his skin was inflamed and flaking around the joins. The cheap-printed, supposedly durable work clothes he wore bunched up unnaturally in a number of places, suggesting that they covered an externally reinforced skeleton. Miska had seen people like him before. It was a cybernetic build designed for mining. Human flesh rebuilt to ape the ability of cheap droids. According to the personnel files provided by the TCC his name was Chanar Batsaikhan, and he was a shift boss on Faigroe Station.

There were a number of crews sitting at the tables surrounding Chanar's, waiting to speak to him. Miska spent some time looking at the other so-called mercenaries. She saw cheap ware, little indication of military experience, and a degree of desperation. They looked like bottom-feeding wannabes.

'We'll fit in, then,' she muttered to herself and then looked back to the table to find Torricone watching her carefully. Nyukuti still hadn't returned.

'Well?' Gleave asked. Miska was impressed with the confidence trickster. Simply by the way he carried himself she was starting to believe him to be a frosty-hearted life-taker, and not the frightened tub of lard that had wept for much of the flight over.

'Yeah, what do you think?' Merrill asked eagerly, staring at her.

'Well, I think they need our help,' Miska said smiling. She caught Torricone's face hardening in her periphery as she said it.

She heard some angry words as they rotated again. A muscle-bound merc-wannabe in a bikini top, torso covered in implant scars and tattoos, was on her feet. Chanar had been talking to her just before. Miska boosted her hearing in time to hear the wannabe accuse the miner of wasting her time. She pushed herself angrily away from the table. Her crew, who looked more like a gang than a mercenary unit, followed their boss.

'Okay, now,' Miska told Gleave, and then said to Torricone. 'Keep an eye on him.' She nodded towards Merrill.

'Hey!' Merrill protested but Miska had already pushed herself away from the bar. She tumbled in mid-air and landed a little way from Chanar's table in the path of another muscle-bound gun-hand making his way to speak to the rebel miner. She held her hand up.

'Ease up, playboy, we're next in line,' she told him. The guy looked down at Miska. He towered over her. *They always do*, she thought. He smiled, but it wasn't a mean smile, he seemed amused. His teeth had been replaced with pointed, stainless steel implants.

Gleave touched down surprisingly gracefully behind her. Miska wondered if he was running a Zero-G movement skill-soft in his neuralware.

'You know how this works,' she told the gun-hand apologetically. 'Nobody knows us here, so somebody's got to get backed down.' She was aware of Gleave sitting down. The gun-hand looked up at the bar. Merrill raised his beer to him. He looked back to Miska.

'You're quite little,' he said.

Miska frowned. 'Everything's relative.'

'And you haven't shown me the hardware yet.'

Miska slapped her head. 'I completely forgot. What must you think of me?' She opened her armoured leather jacket. Let him see the compact shotgun hanging down on its sling and the holstered Glock.

'Rocking the antiques, nice, whole retro thing going on. Not heard of electromagnetics where you're from?' Miska frowned again, though he did have a point. 'Down on your luck? No big deal, we're patient and we don't need to play these games. Good luck.'

Miska watched him return to his crew. A couple of them looked her way before leaning in to confer with the big man. Maybe they weren't all wannabes, she thought, before joining Gleave at the table with Chanar.

Up close the huge miner was sweating profusely and seemed jittery. The sweating she could understand – he had to move around a reasonable amount of bulk. The jitteriness looked wrong, somehow, out of place on someone his size.

'Problems?' Gleave asked as she sat down next to him. She looked around, checking the surroundings. As she did, Chanar twitched and glanced up at Torricone and Merrill at the bar. Miska was still having second thoughts about the wisdom of arming Merrill. To Chanar and the other crews, however, it looked like their backs were covered.

'Some confusion over the pecking order, nothing to worry about,' Miska told him.

'You backed them down?' Chanar asked, bemused. 'You're kind of little.' Miska turned back to stare at him.

'Five years, Marine Force Recon. Wanna see my skills up close and personal?' she demanded, sounding like someone who was fed up with being called small. It wasn't a difficult act. Chanar showed her the palms of two shaking hands in mock surrender.

'That's enough,' Gleave told her. Now he sounded like that pre-FHC cowboy actor that her dad had liked so much. 'You were saying?'

'Look, we're making this clear up front, we don't have much in the way of money ...' His voice was higher pitched than she had expected and he sounded a little shaky.

'So whatcha gonna pay us in, fucking good will?' Miska demanded. Gleave turned to look at her. She went quiet.

'Look, we had no choice but to rebel against the company, they were killing us with some kind of accelerated maximum yield program ...'

'I don't care,' Gleave told him. 'Get to the point.'

Chanar stared at him. Miska didn't think he was used to people talking to him like that. She was both surprised and relieved that Gleave didn't break down in the face of the stare.

'Okay, we've got some things in our favour: weapons, training. We've already fought off one attack from contractors,' he told them. *Mercenaries*, she corrected internally. Contractors had corporate tenure.

'Well, it sounds like you're doing fine on your own,' Gleave said. 'But if you want more gun-hands then you're going to have to pay. Now, if you don't tell us what with, we're gone.'

Miska thought Gleave was pushing just a little too hard. Just a little, like the macho way people thought military folks acted but rarely, in her experience, did.

'We're sitting on a lot of mineral wealth; very little of the asteroid has been exploited yet. We're offering shares. When this is over we're going to start limited terraforming on the asteroid, turn it into a habitat, see if we can make something sustainable out of it.'

Miska stared at him. *Wow!* she thought. She couldn't quite believe what she'd just heard. No wonder the muscle in the bikini top had looked angry. Chanar might as well have offered to pay them with dreams and fairy dust. Only the dangerously idealistic and truly desperate would take a job like this. She was shaking her head.

'Idealism always loses to corporate gold.' It was out of her mouth before she could stop it. She was aware of Gleave closing his eyes. She hated undercover work. She always had too much fun being herself.

'I've checked out your social media profiles,' he told her. *The false ones I slipped into the net earlier? Cool!* Miska thought. She'd laid an extensive false trail. Embedded it in such a way that someone moderately competent would have to put some work in to uncover it. 'We did a bit of digging. Seems to me you're not that much less desperate than we are.'

She'd had to choose between idealism and desperation as part of their cover to explain why they'd even consider taking such a ridiculous job. Miska had decided that they would have more luck pretending the latter.

'We? You don't look like the net-savvy type, who'd you get to do that?' Miska asked. *Might as well find out who the competition is*, she decided.

Chanar didn't answer but he did glance towards another table. A man, medium build, stunningly unremarkable, with dark hair parted in the middle, was sat at the table. He wore the kind of practical civilian clothes that mercenaries and contractors tended to repurpose. The clothes looked like they'd seen better days, however. There was something about him that didn't seem quite right, but Miska couldn't put her finger on what it was. She turned her attention back to the conversation.

'The hypercorps can't allow one insurrection of this nature to succeed,' Gleave told him. Chanar looked down at his shaking hands. He seemed more sad than exasperated.

'When you're fighting this sort of abuse you lose until you win. All we need to do is hold out long enough that it's more profitable for them to write us off than to keep fighting.' Something about the way he said it suggested to Miska that these were learned sentiments. He looked back up at Gleave. 'If somebody shows the way then maybe it will be like dominoes.' Miska actually laughed. Chanar was shaking his head. 'Look, I know how it sounds, I'm not some radical ...'

'You sound like one,' Miska said.

'I don't want to be a slave worked to death. I want a family, maybe some light at the end of the tunnel. But if I'm going to die young it may as well be on my terms, rather than for another tiny bit of profit squeezed into the quarterly forecast. There's room for profit, but not at the expense of life.'

'Good speech,' Gleave said. Miska wasn't so sure about that, but Chanar was certainly earnest. 'I can't buy pussy and booze with a speech.' Miska blinked.

'Then don't sign on with us,' Chanar said. Now he was getting irritated.

'You got projections on the shares? Your plans for the future of your rock?' Gleave asked. Chanar nodded.

'Boss, you can't be—' Miska started.

'You need some vision, young lady,' Gleave told her. Miska opened her mouth to retort.

'I'll fuck you up!' Merrill screamed, his voice only cracking a little. Miska looked up towards the rotating polyhedron bar. Some boosted muscle-bound thug had her hacker by the front of his shirt. Merrill was frantically trying to claw at the Glock that he'd pushed into his waistband; this was despite having been issued with a holster. In the unlikely event the boy lived, Miska saw a deeply unpleasant conversation with Gunnery Sergeant Corbin in the hacker's near future.

CHAPTER 8

Where's Torricone? was Miska's first thought as she sighed, stood up, and made her way across the wall ready to launch herself towards the bar. She'd always wondered about Zero-G bars; drinking heavily was messy enough in gravity. The bar had rotated away from her but she was pretty sure she could hear the sound of Merrill getting beaten on.

'Hi again.' The same gunman that she'd stared down before was in her way. His crew was at a nearby table watching her, hands close to weapons. 'I was hoping that we could just keep this a fight, y'know?' he said, smiling, showing her his mouthful of pointed, stainless steel teeth again.

'Who're you impressing by picking on the smallest guy on my crew?' Miska could see what was going on. She'd used him to put on a show and now he was repaying the favour. 'Why don't you and I dance?' she asked.

He laughed and nodded towards his table. An olive-skinned woman with long dark hair was sat on the back of one of the bench chairs. She had a long coat on. It was clear she had a gun underneath it and it was pointed at Miska. It was just disguised enough so the security lenses wouldn't pick it up.

'I'm pretty sure that I could take that off her and beat you unconscious with it,' said Miska.

'Maybe, but then the bar's got to get involved, maybe some of the locals. It's just a fight, let it happen,' Stainless – as Miska had started thinking of him – told her. Except it wasn't a fight, it was a beating. Merrill and his attacker, who was adhered to the floor of the bar, came back into view. Merrill was pressed down on a table getting punched and slapped. The Glock was hanging in the air a few feet away from them like an orbiting moon. Then Miska saw Torricone throw himself into the air from one of the walls. He grabbed the bar and clambered around towards Merrill and the merc who was beating on him. Then the bar spun out of view.

'I think your boy's about to get a 10 pointed at the back of his head,' Miska said, meaning the 10mm Glock. Stainless looked less than pleased. The bar spun round again. A bloodied and bruised Merrill was drifting away from the bar, and the merc had turned around to face Torricone who was now in a low stance, adhered to the floor by the stikpads on his boots, fists up. 'Or they could just box?'

'Your boy's fucked,' Stainless said, laughing.

'Yeah, 100 New Dollars says otherwise.' It was out of her mouth before she could stop it and she immediately regretted saying it. Stainless just smiled and nodded. She had no idea if Torricone could fight. She'd only really seen him not do it. Then she saw some poetry.

The merc that Torricone was facing towered over him. He swung a hook that looked like it could have felled an ox. Torricone ducked under it, delivered his own hook to the kidneys, then a cross to the side of the head that spun the merc's head around. A jab to the bridge of the nose broke it and the merc swayed back, before turning side-on to take another hook on a huge bicep, but it was clear the merc was unsteady on his feet.

Things changed when the merc lashed out blindly with a kick. His shin caught Torricone in the calf, just hard enough to tear the stikpads on his boots from the carpet and send him tumbling into the air.

'Your boy know how to fight in Zero-G?' Stainless asked. 'Because he looks like a slave to gravity to me.'

The merc pushed off after Torricone, angling his flight to come in behind the tumbling car thief and put him into a headlock, his legs wrapping around Torricone's torso. Stainless was smiling and Miska was pretty sure that it was all over. One of the dancers had to jump off his platform as the merc and Torricone crashed into it and bounced. Then Torricone slipped the head lock. Miska wasn't sure how he'd done it, it had happened too quickly. The car thief seemed to slither out between the merc's legs. Then somehow he scissor-locked his legs around the merc's arms and upper torso and hooked his ankles together. Miska could see his muscles bulging. Torricone looked angry. She chewed on her lip a little. Torricone punched the merc again and again, pulping his face, leaving trails of blood in the air until the merc stopped struggling. Then he let him go. The unconscious merc drifted away and bounced gently off another table.

'We kept it just a fight,' Miska said. Stainless turned away and made his way back towards the table. 'Hey, don't be that guy,' Miska called after him. 'My hundred bucks?' He ignored her.

121

'Fuck this!' The woman who'd been covering her with the shotgun flicked her coat open and lifted her weapon.

Miska was moving, her jacket open, her shotgun up, but the woman had frozen. There was what looked like a large and very sharp-looking steel boomerang held to her throat. The blade running on the inside of the curve was just pricking the woman's skin. There was a sword-like quality to the boomerang, and holding on to the weapon's grip was Nyukuti.

'It is all right to die now,' he told the woman. 'Look around, none of this matters.'

'You fucking bastard!' Merrill shouted.

What now? Miska wondered and then the gunfire started.

The young hacker, his bruised face streaked with tears, was firing at the merc Torricone had beaten unconscious. He'd recovered the Glock and was letting it rip on full auto, holding it sideways. The merc was spinning around in mid-air. Miska suspected Merrill was just flattening pistol ammo on armour but he was going to get lucky sooner or later, and the merc's friends were going for their weapons. Torricone pushed himself off the wall and straight into Merrill's line of fire. Merrill stopped shooting. Torricone reached the bar and disarmed the young hacker, who broke down in tears.

'What the fuck?' Stainless spat.

'It's just a ten mil,' Miska told him, 'man up.' She was surprised to see Gleave walk across the wall towards the table where Stainless and his crew were sat.

'He's not one of my crew,' Gleave told Stainless, his voice low and cold, just this side of menacing. 'He's my son.' Miska was pretty sure that Stainless blanched. Gleave turned to Miska. 'Do I need to get into this?'

'No, we're good,' Miska said. 'Though Jaws here owes me a hundred bucks.' Gleave turned to look at Stainless. Even Miska forgot for a moment that any one of the mercs on that table could have torn out his spine and beaten him to death with it. 'Is that true?'

'Well, er—' Stainless started.

'I asked you a question.' Stainless just nodded. 'You pay what you owe.' Gleave glanced up at the bar as it spun round to reveal an embarrassed Torricone hugging a weeping Merrill. Miska would have rolled her eyes if she hadn't been keeping an eye on Stainless's crew. Gleave looked back at Stainless. 'Understand me?' There seemed to be a lot of emphasis on those last two words. Stainless nodded again. Gleave turned towards Chanar, who was watching intently. 'We'll take your job, just keep the fucking amateurs out of our way.'

Chanar nodded but Gleave was walking towards the door. Miska backed out after him, keeping the shotgun levelled at Stainless and his crew. Torricone kicked off from the spinning bar, helping Merrill. Miska stopped by the door, waiting for Nyukuti. The stand-over man still had the bladed boomer-sword at the woman's neck. Finally he removed it and folded the two halves together like an enormous switchblade before tucking it into his armoured longcoat. He looked at the woman and shook his head as though disappointed before making for the door as well.

Miska nodded cheerfully at Stainless and backed out the door. She saw that a hundred new dollars had been transferred to her via her visible net social media presence.

She also noticed the guy watching her. Handsome, hair cropped short, green eyes, maybe early thirties, African-American heritage, his suede jacket just a little too nice for the

123

neighbourhood. She gave no indication of having recognised him, however.

Back at the hotel Gleave was shaking like a leaf and weeping. He'd managed to hold it together long enough for Miska to check their room for surveillance. The hotel room was actually a partitioned cargo container with several bunks, but still pretty nice for all that.

'I can't do this, I just can't. Did you see those guys ...? They would have murdered me.'

'I thought you were really good,' Miska said. 'I believed you.'

'I thought you behaved like a true warrior,' Nyukuti said, patting him on the back.

'Did you go out boomerang shopping?' Torricone asked the stand-over man. Nyukuti nodded. 'Okay.'

'We thought you'd abandoned us,' Merrill said. He was still snivelling a little bit. Miska made a mental note to try and remember that exposure to bullies made the hacker homicidal.

'Why would I do that? You are my tribe,' Nyukuti said, sounding genuinely confused. Gleave was staring at him, clearly terrified.

'Yep, nothing like explosive collars to encourage cama-raderie,' Torricone muttered.

'What are you talking about?' Nyukuti demanded. Torricone just stared at him and then shook his head.

'Jeff?' Miska said. He ignored her. 'Jeff!' He looked up at her, wiping off snot and tears with the back of his hand. 'What did you make of Chanar?'

'He was coming down off something,' Gleave composed himself enough to say. He'd pretty much confirmed what she'd suspected.

'He's a junkie?' Torricone asked. 'This gets better and better.'

Gleave shrugged. 'It looks like whatever it was he'd been off it for a while. I'm guessing withdrawal, cold turkey.' Miska nodded. Gleave was proving to be quite useful, it was just a shame he was such a coward. She turned on Torricone.

'Where the fuck were you?' Miska demanded.

'What? When?' Torricone asked.

'When do you think? When that growth-hormone-overdosed mouth feeder was beating on Merrill.'

'Taking a piss.'

'You were supposed to be watching our backs and keeping an eye on him,' Miska said, nodding towards the snivelling Merrill.

'Is he anybody's bitch?' Nyukuti asked, pointing at Merrill. The hacker burst into tears again. Both Torricone and Miska turned on Nyukuti.

'Nobody's anybody's bitch now, remember?' she asked dangerously.

Torricone looked ready to go toe-to-toe with Nyukuti. Miska was pretty impressed with this, because even she was starting to suspect that they'd seriously underestimated what a psycho he was. Nyukuti shrugged as if it was no big deal. Torricone turned back to Miska.

'You're angry with me? I got the guy off of him!'

'It wouldn't have happened at all if you'd been doing your job!'

Torricone was staring at her. He looked pretty angry.

'It's not my fucking job. My fucking job is to be frozen until such a time as society deems me to have been rehabilitated.' Miska opened her mouth to retort. 'What? You going to threaten to blow my head off?' Miska was pretty sure she could take him if push came to shove, but there was something dangerous in his eyes. She resisted the urge to look him up and down.

'Where'd you learn to fight?' she asked trying to defuse the tension a little.

'My mum taught me,' he told her.

'For fuck's sake,' Miska muttered. She'd thought it was a reasonable question. 'I'm going out, you guys stay here. Try not to fuck up and I don't want anybody crying by the time I get back.'

'Where are you going?' Torricone demanded. Miska's head whipped around to face him.

'I know you don't like it but you're a soldier now, just fucking deal with it.'

'And remember my place?'

Miska stormed out of the room.

Great leadership skills, Corbin! Miska excoriated herself as she walked out of the stack of cargo containers into one of the narrow streets in the central hub. May '68 was in its night cycle at the moment. The whole place was illuminated by ultraviolet light to provide energy for all the plants, many of them fruits and vegetables that seemed to take up every spare bit of space. Miska knew that there were vast hydroponics farms within the free port as well.

She spent some time wandering around, enjoying the UV on her skin, looking at the stalls, the smell of street food making her hungry. Every so often she would glance up at the streets above her head on the bulkheads of the repurposed ore carrier. From the core the houses were inverted, and she could see people wandering around

Her mind wandered and she found herself thinking about the

Ultra. She wasn't sure why. There had to be more to it than his technologically sculpted beauty. She hoped she wasn't that shallow, though she had to admit he had a presence, even while frozen. There was a momentary rush of paranoia, the near-superstitious dread surrounding the technology of the Small Gods. She found herself wondering if her preoccupation with the Ultra was some kind of subtle hack. There were sequestration programs out there, the meat/electronic border ran both ways and every hacker had heard stories about possession. She almost ran an extensive diagnostics on her neuralware.

Get a grip, she told herself, *it's just a crush*. She had been told on more than one occasion that she had questionable taste in men.

She wasn't really trying to find the guy she'd seen in the Revolution Will Be Televised. She knew that he would reveal himself to her as and when. But eventually she found him sitting at a table in the open front of a bar made from two cargo containers, one on top of the other. He was sipping from a complicated-looking double cocktail bulb with a pointless umbrella sticking out of it.

She went into the bar, ordered a beer and then pulled herself up to the first floor. The place seemed much friendlier than the previous bar. She sat at a table close enough to the open front to see the street but not so close that she was completely exposed. A few minutes later he sat opposite her with his ridiculous cocktail.

'What happened to discretion?' she asked.

'Huh?' he asked.

She nodded at his cocktail. 'You on holiday?' He just smiled.

'So how's General Corbin?' he asked and Miska gave him the finger. 'Quite a display you guys put on.'

She shook her head and sagged in her chair. 'What do you expect, Raff? You know what I'm working with, and I'm not an officer. I wasn't even a very good soldier. I liked working on my own ...'

'Which made you good for us,' he said. Miska just nodded. 'So?' he asked.

She shrugged. 'I feel a bit sorry for the miners and the TCC are assholes.' Miska toyed with her beer. Rafael nodded.

'We've—' he started. Miska looked up.

'We?'

'I'm in this with you.'

'Really? I thought I ... all of us were deniable?' It wasn't really a question. She knew what the score was. She was just lashing out. Raff was a good handler, but the argument with Torricone had left her feeling unusually tense.

'Look, we can collapse this right now, you walk away with me. We let those idiots in Group 13 know where they can find their prison barge, and we set you up with a new identity, a new life somewhere else.'

'You know I can't do that.' The sad thing was it didn't even sound all that appealing. It would mean an end to her operational life. Raff nodded. He knew her reasons.

'You need anything?' he asked.

'Yeah, a shitload of hardware, food, and medical supplies, maybe access to one of the slush funds. The FBI and the Marshals off my back would be nice as well.'

'You know we can't do that. People are watching, asking questions about you. It's got to appear real. Maybe later, when you've got some funds behind you, we can arrange slush access for you, put some surplus hardware your way at a knockdown price through one of our intermediaries.'

'Who's asking questions? The NSA?' she asked. Raff didn't need to answer. It was to be expected when you stole one of their experimental spaceships. 'They send Angela?'

'It was her ship.'

Miska grimaced. 'Yeah, she's gonna be pretty pissed.' More than anything this was why she suspected her operation was deniable. Never mind six thousand civil rights violations, the NSA could never find out that she had been on active duty when she stole their ship. It would cause a war between the NSA and the CIA. 'What's the Company line on Faigroe Station?'

'Capitalism is king, everything else is weakness and possibly communism. The miners can't succeed. Various forms of co-ops, socialism etcetera have been tried throughout history. They've only ever acted as a destabilising force.' He seemed so earnest, Miska had to laugh.

'Seems to be working okay here,' she pointed out and took another sip of her beer.

'This is a black market, little more than a tax loophole. How much more capitalist do you want? Every society has criminals.'

'Surely Communism hasn't been a threat for hundreds of years?' Part of her was wondering if the CIA needed another straw-bugbear to justify budget increases.

'Yes, because of our constant vigilance,' he told her. Miska wondered if he really believed that. It was always difficult to tell with intelligence agents. 'Capitalism, particularly the profit motive, is synonymous with freedom. You know this.'

She really wasn't sure she did. She could never quite make the connection.

'So fuck the miners?' she asked. He shrugged.

'It's not quite that simple,' he told her. *Here we go,* she thought. 'The miners can't be allowed to succeed, but nobody's

129

going to cry if the TCC get humiliated. It looks like they're moving towards declaring the system independent ...'

'From where I'm sitting it looks like they already have.' Still, it was a ballsy move. The US government couldn't not respond.

'They've been in contact with Mars. It gives the Small Gods another foothold in the colonies. If they go independent with Martian backing then they'll legalise the tech.'

Miska knew enough about politics to know that wasn't good. The sophisticated nanotech that the Small Gods utilised was severely restricted in most human-controlled territories, in part because it was so powerful. She suspected that if the Small Gods were more reasonable then they'd already have many more allies among the hypercorps.

'Turn us loose on the TCC, then,' Miska suggested but Raff was shaking his head.

'We can't, because—'

'Capitalism is king.' Miska finished.

'It's our way of life.'

In many ways it was a typical briefing in that it contained conflicting instructions or, as she liked to think of it, just enough rope to hang yourself. She felt a hand on her own. She looked down to see Raff holding hers.

'Look, I've got some time—' he started.

'Well how fucking professional,' Miska said, genuinely irritated now.

'It never stopped us before ...'

'It's always stopped us before, except for that one time we were both really, really drunk.' Raff opened his mouth to say something else. 'Actually, maybe you can help me with something. How come when you've slept with a guy once they think they've got some kind of claim on you?'

He pulled his hand back into his lap. Idly she wondered how many cocktails he'd had.

'I don't think I have ... I just thought ... it'd be nice ...'

'We're working, grow the fuck up. I need your mind on the job.' She stood up.

'Have you got a name yet, for your penal legion?' he asked.

'For fuck's sake, I'm working on it, all right?' She realised that she was being a little defensive but her inability to come up with a name was starting to bother her. It should have been a simple thing after all.

'Who was that?' Torricone was waiting for her just outside the bar. Miska hadn't expected to see him in the street. She was pretty sure that he hadn't expected to be grabbed by the bridge of the nose, torn off the stikpad carpet, pushed into what passed for an alleyway in the free port, and rammed up against the side of a colourfully painted cargo container.

'Seriously?' she hissed. *Is he one of them?* she wondered. *Did he help kill my father?* She moved in close enough to smell the soap he used, the spearmint on his breath. 'I don't think you realise how this works. I tell you what to do and you do it.'

'Yeah, the amount of times you have to tell us that—' he started. She pulled him away from the container – he weighed very little in the microgravity – and then slammed him back against it, hard.

'Get back to the hotel, now,' she barked.

He just looked at her with his soulful brown eyes. It was the judgement she read in his eyes that made her snap. He let out a yelp as she threw him up into the air. He scrabbled for purchase against the container but the move had taken him by surprise. She watched him spin out into the air away from the central hub and towards the residential streets on the bulkhead walls. She'd had to, Miska told herself, it was either that or she would have kissed him.

CHAPTER 9

They were in the passenger compartment of an ore transporter shuttle on their way to Faigroe Station. The air was full of rock dust and smelled of old sweat. She had actually been surprised that the shuttle was more run-down than her own, ancient prison shuttles. She had been sitting on her own, brooding, occasionally glancing over at the 'other' data warfare specialist Chanar had hired, the nondescript mercenary from the bar. Miska had discovered that his name was Joshua, and although there was no doubt that he was ex-military he stuck out like a sore thumb for reasons that she couldn't quite put her finger on.

Chanar was on the shuttle but not in the passenger compartment with them. The last time Miska had seen the big miner he had looked awful. Pale, feverish, covered in sweat, more than ever it was clear he was going cold turkey off something. Stainless and his crew were there too, occasionally casting glares in the direction of Miska and her people. There were a few other crews with them as well. All of them looked like the kind of desperate, bottom-feeding mercenaries that she and her people didn't have to try too hard to mimic. The odd one out was Joshua.

'That was a pretty childish thing to do,' Torricone told her as he slid into the seat next to her. Miska sighed. She was beginning to think she should have listened to her dad; the car thief was starting to become a pain in the ass.

'I thought it was funny.'

'You going to tell me who that guy was, now? Or just throw me out an airlock?'

'No,' she snapped.

'It's our lives as well ...'

'Shut up now, okay?' It wasn't an order this time. She had phrased it as a request.

He followed her eyes as she glanced around the passenger compartment at the hard, desperate faces. He understood the message. It wasn't a safe environment to discuss this.

'So are you going tell me who did teach you to fight? You've got more skills than just what you've learned in training.'

'I told you, my mum taught me.' She glanced at him irritably. 'I'm telling the truth.'

'What is she, a pro pit fighter?'

Now Torricone was laughing.

'She's a priest,' he told her. Miska raised an eyebrow, not sure if he was serious or not.

'So where'd she learn to fight?'

He shrugged. 'She grew up in a rough neighbourhood, I guess.'

Miska couldn't be bothered to dig further. It wasn't such a ridiculous idea. Her mom, a member of the UK's SBS special forces, doubtless would have taught her daughters to fight if she'd lived. Thinking of her mom caused a spike of maudlin.

She pushed it to the back of her mind. She was worried that she was losing her focus. She went back to watching Joshua.

'What's wrong with this picture?' she muttered to herself. Torricone followed her gaze.

'He looks like he's wearing his old clothes,' Torricone said after a moment or two.

'Imagine you walk into a shady deal and that guy's sitting there?'

Torricone glanced over at her. 'Shady deal?' He smiled, then turned back to Joshua and studied him for a bit longer. 'UC,' he said finally. The initials stood for undercover.

'And if he's got any training it's rudimentary, he's running a skillsoft telling him how to do it.' She was pretty much thinking out loud now but Torricone was nodding along with her. Suddenly it seemed obvious.

'TCC?' Torricone asked. It would have been her guess. She wasn't sure what irritated her most: that they'd sent other contractors, or that they'd sent someone so bad at their job. They certainly didn't seem to have much faith in Miska and her people.

'So? Leave him in play, what difference does it make?' Torricone asked.

Miska glanced back to the rows of worn seats where Gleave, Merrill and Nyukuti were sat. Gleave was staring out of the window at the dim light of the distant star. Merrill was tranced in. Miska had, somewhat reluctantly, activated his integral computer and the hacker had been writing the software he was going to need for the job. With a thought Miska sent him a text telling him to drop out of the trance. Nyukuti had stripped down the only M-19 they had brought with them and was cleaning it. Miska glanced at the stand-over man. She couldn't

135

shake the feeling that there was something sexual about the way he handled the assault rifle. She caught his eye and he started to rapidly reassemble the M-19.

'Wait—' Torricone started as she stood up and headed up the aisle towards where Joshua was sitting. She passed Stainless and his crew on the way. She reached the two seats that Joshua was sitting across. He looked up.

'Hi!' she said cheerfully, drawing the Glock and aiming it at him.

'Hey!' he said. 'What are you doing?' English accent, cultured, posh even; he sounded like officer class to Miska.

'I'm going to search and disarm you, okay? I know you're wired. I'm wired faster. You move in a way that I don't like and I'll put two in your face, see if your dermal armour will hold up. Do you understand me?'

'What do you think—' His voice was a borderline arrogant snarl.

'I said do you understand me? Any response other than "yes" and I shoot you in the face.' She suspected that her continued cheerfulness was irritating him.

'Yes,' he said. She noticed that an occulted text had appeared in her business inbox. She opened it and read it in her IVD. It simply said: *We're on the same side*. She composed a reply in her head and sent it: *Change of plan, thought you'd been updated, you're blown but I can keep you alive if you go along with it.*

'Put your hands behind your head and lace your fingers together.' He did as he was told, glaring at her.

'Hey, what's going on?' Stainless demanded. He and a few of his crew were on their feet.

Nyukuti stood up. He wasn't exactly aiming the M-19 at

them but the message was clear. Merrill had stood up as well.

'Yeah! Ease back, motherfucker, or get beat down!' the hacker cried. The embarrassment everybody felt for Merrill was palpable. Miska blinked and wished she'd left him tranced in. Joshua smirked and she had to resist the urge to pistol whip him. With a thought she sent a text to Gleave.

'Merrill, go and find Chanar,' Gleave told the hacker.

'But—' Merrill started.

'Now!' Gleave roared. Merrill practically ran from the passenger compartment, despite having seen Gleave's crying jags. Miska couldn't shake the feeling that Gleave had more authority over the boy than she did.

Miska held the Glock against her body, as far from Joshua as possible, using her left hand to search him. Ideally you wanted someone to cover while you searched but frankly she was just finding it easier to do things herself. She took a SIG-692 gauss pistol off him. An older model of the pistol she normally carried, and one favoured by British special forces, it was a dead giveaway. He also had a folding fighting knife and a compact backup pistol in an ankle holster. She removed them all and tossed them on a free seat behind her.

'You again,' Chanar said as he walked, somewhat unsteadily, down the aisle of the passenger compartment.

'He's a contractor,' she told him. 'TCC plant.'

'This woman's deluded,' Joshua said glaring at her. 'She's trying to eliminate her competition for a bigger share.'

'Where's your proof?' Chanar asked, looking between the two of them. Miska sent another text to Gleave and Nyukuti.

'Boss, can I borrow Nyukuti?' she asked.

Gleave almost managed to look like a professional as he took the M-19 from Nyukuti. He remained in character despite the text Miska had received begging her not to get him involved. Nyukuti strode down the aisle to join Miska and Chanar.

'This is Nyukuti,' Miska told the contractor. 'Do you know what a stand-over man is?' She could tell by the expression on his face that he did. 'Well, I know how you've been trained. You can withstand interrogation but you know that everyone breaks. Nyukuti's thing is to drop people into a custom VR construct and torture them until he's got what he wants. Now, you'd hold out much longer than some pissant but you'd break eventually because we all do. In VR, with time contraction, every minute is a day. Maybe you'd last five minutes.'

'A lot of effort to go to,' Joshua said.

'It's not effort when it's a vocation,' Nyukuti pointed out and grinned at Joshua.

Miska sent Joshua another text: *Play along*. She received one back: *You'd better keep me safe*.

'Just one question,' she said. 'You're a contractor working for the TCC, aren't you?' He sagged in his seat and nodded.

'Son of a bitch,' Chanar snapped. She could tell he felt as though he'd been personally betrayed. She was starting to suspect the miner was far too soft-hearted for this business.

'Ex-SAS?' Nyukuti asked.

'Eighteen Signals, at a guess,' Miska said. 'They handle communications and electronic warfare for UKSF. I don't think he's full special forces, probably two-six-eight Squadron, attached to their special forces support group.' Joshua was giving nothing away.

'Look, no pay packet is worth this, just let me go and ...'

'You'll go back and tell your bosses everything you've learned,' Chanar said. 'I don't think so. You'll be humanely treated.' He glanced over at Nyukuti, who was still grinning at Joshua. 'We're not savages.'

Oh, I'm afraid we are, Miska thought.

'What company are you with?' she asked.

Joshua smiled. 'Sorry, but your employer has just said that you won't be torturing me.' Miska noticed that she had received another text: *Go fuck yourself, bitch*.

It didn't matter, in one fell swoop she'd removed the competition and proven herself to Chanar and …

'We need to talk about your electronic security; there's a reason they sent a hacker,' she told Chanar, sounding just the right amount of angry. He nodded, looking pale.

… hopefully bought herself access to Faigroe Station's systems.

The ore shuttle manoeuvred carefully around two independent small, fast-looking freighters and a large transport shuttle, all docked at the station's main dock area. Miska guessed the indy ships were smuggling supplies to the miners.

Her mind was drifting. She caught herself thinking about her dad again. Not her real dad, though. Not the proud, lonely man at home on his own except for those few times a month he met up with his dwindling group of buddies to relive old glories. Not the man living vicariously through both his daughters. He never hid how pleased he was to see them, though he had tried to hide the relief. She had known that after a life of service he had struggled to enjoy his retirement. Clutching at consultancy work in a bid to be, in his eyes at least, useful. She should have spent more time with him. As should Angela, her bitch sister, but they were always too busy living their lives.

The problem was, that wasn't the dad she was thinking about.

She was thinking about the hard-charging, no bullshit, spit bullets, larger than life gunnery sergeant running Camp Reisman as though it were a real place. Worse still, she had started to think of him as a real person. She wanted this ghost, this fantasy, to be real and then she wouldn't really have to mourn her father. She squeezed her eyes shut. She knew she needed to focus or she was going to get everyone killed all over again.

She opened her eyes and looked out the closest porthole as the shuttle made its way towards a secondary industrial dock growing out of the huge potato-shaped asteroid. Presumably this was for delivering the refined ore to shuttles and freighters. The shuttle's cargo bay plugged into an airlock with the extending conveyor. Miska, her crew and the other mercenaries all left by the ancillary passenger airlock. Nyukuti escorted Joshua, who they'd secured with industrial memory cable and searched more thoroughly. Miska had also disabled his neural computer. At gunpoint, the contractor had allowed her access to his systems.

They had exited the ore shuttle into a cramped dock over the conveyor. Miska found herself surrounded by piles of rubble and the hulking forms of some of the heavier mine machinery. The asteroid was like a hundred other mining stations that she had visited. Corridors cut out of rock, lights bolted to the wall, metal catwalks for a floor. Cramped, minimalist, cheap, no unnecessary expense whatsoever. That included the life support system, it seemed. The air was somewhat fetid and soupy. Miska reckoned it provided the bare minimum for human life to function. It smelled of too many people. It would make the miners happy to put on suits and go to work for the fresher bottled air. She suspected that was the point. She wondered what life support had been like in the executive offices.

There were armed miners in the industrial docking area,

wearing the printed armour and carrying the replica AK-47s she'd seen during her initial attack.

As they were led through the rock and metal she saw more of the miners-turned-revolutionaries patrolling the facility, suspicious eyes cast their way. They almost looked like soldiers, it was clear that they'd been practising. Miska felt Torricone looking at her.

Chanar spoke with some of the miner-soldiers and Joshua was taken away. It was clear from the body language that the big shift boss was well respected.

Something else was also becoming apparent.

'They're all going cold turkey from something,' Torricone said, giving voice to her thoughts. Corporate-enforced addiction. It wouldn't be the first time, and sadly not the last. 'At least we're on the right side now.' Miska was getting a little tired of his moralistic bullshit but didn't say anything. The mercenaries were led off towards the mine workings, while Chanar went towards the ops centre.

It took a moment for Miska to work out the function of the room they had been shown into. It was in a corridor that branched off from the main passage to one of the mine works. Like the rest of the mine it had been carved out of solid rock with mining lasers but this area had a once-thick but now-threadbare carpet on the floor. Fading but child-friendly, educational, once-interactive holograms covered the rock walls. There were a few sad, mostly broken toys on the floor and there was a badly damaged droid with bits peeling off its metal carapace. Slowly Miska came to the conclusion that this was the mine crèche, and it looked like it had been run by a droid that had been old when her dad was young. Much of its body had been damaged and torn in such a way that it might as well have been covered in spikes. It would have been lethal for the thing to pick up a child.

'They were breeding the next generation,' Nyukuti muttered. Miska took a closer look at the 'educational' holograms. They were all about how much 'fun' it was to be a miner. 'See, this is why I tortured people for money.'

A couple of the other mercs turned to look at him but Nyukuti was oblivious.

'What!' one of the other mercs spat. 'We supposed to feel sorry for them? Life's hard all over.' The mercenary was right. This was a bit manipulative, which, to Miska, suggested that it was unprofessional.

'Fucking A!' Merrill agreed, trying too hard.

'Shut up,' Miska snapped, and then ignored the wounded expression on his face. The door to the crèche slid open and Chanar came back into the room. A short, stocky, black woman with an endomorphic build followed him. She wore worn working clothes similar to Chanar's. Miska knew that this was Walentyna Uboka, one of the miners mentioned in the TCC's personnel files. She was, according to corporate intelligence, 87.435% likely to be the miners' ringleader. Her hair was cropped short, like Chanar's, and judging by the blocky features and bulges under her clothes she had similar cybernetic modifications. If she was going cold turkey then Miska couldn't see it.

'Thank you for coming,' she said. She had an African accent. Miska couldn't quite place it. It always surprised her that the incredibly wealthy equatorial states of Earth somehow still had people so poor that they'd risk coming out here. 'My name is Walentyna Uboka. I speak for the council, who in turn represent the Faigroe Station Collective.' There were a couple of sniggers and more than one mercenary had a sneer on his face. Miska kept her expression impassive.

'Why are we in a fucking nursery?' one of the other mercenaries asked. He wore a bandanna and had what looked like gang tattoos on his visible skin. She suspected the only soldiering he'd ever done had been for a street gang. Miska could tell that he considered it beneath him to be here. 'Couldn't we at least have done this in a bar?' There was more than a little grumbled agreement. Miska saw Merrill nodding. She resisted the urge to slap him around the back of the head.

'We don't want your pity, we don't expect sympathy. We'll fight for what we need right alongside you, and you'll be rewarded for your work. The reason you're here is to make one thing clear:

'This was where our children were expected to be deposited every day. A child got hurt on a weekly basis, there'd be a serious accident every couple of months and maybe a fatality every year.' Her face hardened but it was clear there was a great deal of powerful emotion being held in check behind the mask. 'This is not ideological. We are not trying to "stick it to the man". This is survival, plain and simple. We were left with no choice.' And Miska believed her. Even the more outwardly cynical mercenaries had gone quiet and were listening now.

'What's the tactical situation?' Gleave asked, all business. Uboka turned to him.

'We've been assaulted once, we think it was a probing attack, or they severely underestimated our resolve. Either way, I don't think it went as well as they had hoped. When they come back we suspect they'll come in force. Obviously they want the facility intact, which means they'll have to do it the hard way.'

It was the perennial problem of space combat. If you didn't

143

want to completely destroy your objective then that meant an assault, which in turn meant taking the ship, station, whatever, corridor by corridor, the hard way. There were no shortcuts. Even fuel-air-explosives and gas didn't work because it was so easy to isolate areas in spacecraft or facilities designed to withstand the rigours of vacuum. Miska had no doubt that if the TCC came in mob-handed they could take the station, but they were going to have one hell of a fight on their hands.

'Your people look like they've had rudimentary training,' Stainless said.

'Some,' Uboka admitted.

'I thought you said this wasn't ideological?' Gleave asked.

'It's not.'

'So where did the training come from?' Gleave pushed, his grasp of the situation impressing Miska.

'Obviously we don't know you, and as I understand it there have already been problems. Some things are just going to have to be "need to know".'

'There's an argument we need to know who we're getting into bed with,' Stainless pointed out.

'Does that matter?' another merc, not part of Stainless's crew, demanded. His face had been crudely, cybernetically reconstructed and looked like the face of an armoured robot. At least one of his arms was artificial as well.

'It does if we end up on a terrorist watch list or in bed with Mars,' Miska pointed out. Uboka was shaking her head.

'We're using virtual training,' Uboka said.

'It's not the same as real skills,' Stainless told her. Miska could see that he wasn't trying to give Uboka a hard time, he was just asking sensible questions that all of them needed answers to.

144

'I understand that,' Uboka said. 'We bow to your superior knowledge in these matters.'

'Which brings me to my next question,' Stainless said. 'Who's in charge?'

'I speak for the—' Uboka started.

'I get that,' Stainless said. He waved his thumb around, gesturing at the mercenaries. 'Of us. We've got a number of disparate crews here.' Miska sent a text to Gleave with a thought. 'And do we work on our own, or do you want us integrated with your people? Because, no offence, but I'm not entirely comfortable with that.' There was muttered agreement from some of the other mercenaries. 'If, on the other hand, you want us to start training your people up, then we can do that.'

'I'm happy for ...' Gleave gestured at Stainless.

'Reg,' Stainless, now Reg, told him.

'Reg, here to have the headache of being in charge,' Gleave said. There was some grumbling from the other mercenaries.

'Really, guys?' Miska asked. The grumbling subsided, mostly.

'Thanks,' Stainless said. His metallic smile looked somewhat rueful. 'We weren't introduced when we exchanged threats.'

'Gleave.'

'I'm happy that Gleave shares my headaches as my second. Anyone got any problems with that, step up now.'

Gleave nodded. Miska saw the sweat on his brow because she knew to look for it.

'Can we discuss this again once we've seen your work?' one of the mercs asked. He'd been quiet so far, a tall, thin guy in an armoured duster that gave him the look of a professional gunfighter.

'That seems reasonable,' Reg said. Gleave just nodded again. 'Decide among yourselves when you want to review it.'

'We need to know what you guys are coming down off of,' Torricone said. A couple of the assembled mercenaries nodded, a few looked surprised and then unhappy. Miska could understand that. Combat drug use was pretty standard among the military, some of it encouraged, some of it not, and recreational drug use wasn't unheard of, but mercs trusted themselves and their friends on drugs. They didn't want to fight alongside a virtually trained, civilian militia of junkies. 'Some kind of new drug TCC were pushing on you?'

'Old drug,' Uboka told them. 'Ever heard of Slaughter?' Torricone was shaking his head.

'It's a combat drug,' Miska said. 'Or it was, developed during the War with Them.' Uboka was nodding. 'It's sometimes called Red.' Some of the older mercenaries were nodding now as well.

'The TCC were using a derivative of it. They gave us ridiculous quotas that we had to make if we wanted to make a living wage, then they sold us the drugs to help make the quotas ...'

'Not all of us took the Slaughter,' Chanar said, looking at Uboka. Miska was starting to understand why the African woman was in charge.

'Many of us ended up hooked on the drug, more of our wages going on the Red, families going hungry, and between the drugs and the cheap 'ware we needed for the job there was more than one psychotic breakdown.'

Miska had started with a pretty low opinion of the TCC. It wasn't improving. She could feel Torricone, and his bleeding heart, staring at her again. She knew that sooner or later she was going to have to square that boy away.

'What about your electronic security?' Miska asked. 'We've got two electronic warfare specialists on our team and you've already had one close call.' She glanced at Chanar, who was

146

looking down at the floor. She noticed that one of the crèche's security lenses had turned towards her. Uboka was looking at her but saying nothing. Miska wondered if she was in communication with someone else, like the Che virus.

'Like I said, we're going to have to get to know you first,' Uboka told her. Miska couldn't be sure but she thought she heard suspicion in the council leader's voice. *Too soon?* she wondered.

'I understand that, but they're going to come at you hard through your systems,' Stainless surprised her by pointing out. Electronic warfare was the only shortcut when dealing with space-borne assaults. Take control of a ship or facility's systems and they were wide open. It was why they were so heavily protected.

'We're confident that our systems are pretty secure—' Uboka started.

'And given that our lives are on the line you can understand why we'd want to review that, and given our experience you can maybe understand why we'd be better suited to advise you on said security.' Miska was starting to like Stainless, or Reg, despite his display in the Revolution Will Be Televised.

'And you can understand with what happened on the shuttle why we would be reluctant to allow strangers into our systems. They have already withstood one assault, it was the only competent part of the probing attack.'

'The botched attack was probably a diversion for the net assault,' Reg pointed out. 'Mind me asking how you fought off this net attack?' Uboka didn't answer.

The lens Miska had noticed earlier seemed to have been following the discussion. Nyukuti was watching it, transfixed. The silence stretched out. Reg shook his head, his crew looked less than happy. Miska sent another text to Gleave.

'We need more weapons,' Gleave said. 'Arm us with what your people are carrying so the parts and ammunition are ubiquitous.'

'Give us a list of our duties and we'll work out a roster,' Reg added, seemingly less than pleased that his questions weren't being answered. 'Where we bedding down?'

'Here,' Uboka told them. It was clear that the miners didn't want their mercenaries forgetting why they were fighting any time soon.

CHAPTER 10

The miners were keeping the mercenaries on a short leash. It made sense – leaving aside the fact that they'd already discovered one TCC plant, the collective had to be worried about the possibility of the mercenaries trying to take over. Miska shifted the printed AK-47 a little. The slugthrower was somewhat hefty compared to the laser carbine she normally carried, but she kind of liked that. She was patrolling the mine's recreation area with Torricone. He seemed less pleased to be toting the slugthrower. The rec area looked like it had been a natural passage in the asteroid that had been widened into a street, with two- and three-storey buildings also carved out of the rock. There were a number of bars, no restaurants but a few automated fast food joints and vending machines, a nightclub, a sad-looking strip club/thinly veiled brothel, and more tellingly, two archaic-looking sense arcades. The whole street practically stank of desperation, of needing to escape by any means necessary. For some reason the faux-neon and holographic signs had been left running and they bathed the street in hellish reds, cold blues, garish greens, and, to Miska's mind anyway, nauseating pinks.

She wondered where they had sold the Red. Did they deal it properly like seedy drug dealers in seedy bars? Did they have some kind of on-station crack-house equivalent? Or had it just been out of the corporate offices, or even the mine shop? Boots, spacesuits, laser torches, performance enhancing drugs etcetera.

Everywhere they went Miska could feel the security lenses following them. The miners seemed reasonably optimistic, despite the fact that many of them were suffering withdrawal symptoms. She reckoned they were buoyed with false optimism as a result of her own people's disastrous first assault. Due to the current situation the mine had been shut down except for the automated processes. Everyone over sixteen years of age was under arms. There were no old people on the station. Mining was a harsh job even without abusive employers. The miners seemed to view themselves as citizen soldiers. Miska might have to return the station to the TCC, but she was going to do her best to keep them alive.

She saw a small group of grubby children playing in one of the bars' malfunctioning holographic signs and then felt Torricone's eyes on her. She sighed internally.

'What now?' it was out of her mouth before she had time to think.

'You know what,' he said and nodded towards the children.

'That's life during wartime. Nobody made their parents rebel against their employers or steal an extremely expensive mine. We've all got to live with our decisions.' *Why am I engaging?* she wondered. It just provided an opening for him.

'Doesn't look to me like they had much of a choice.'

'Yeah, well, that's capitalism for you,' Miska said as they passed one of the sense arcades. The place was empty but she

158

could see the spider webs of the trode sets designed to plug customers into a full-on sensory fantasy. She was pretty sure the arcades must have done a roaring trade under the TCC.

'I thought capitalism was supposed to reward you for working hard. Where's the reward for these guys?'

They had reached the end of the street and started up a flight of steps that had been cut into the rock. They were going to make their way through the retail area, such as it was, and into the ops and admin offices. They still weren't allowed into the ops centre itself, which made sense, but Reg had let Gleave handle the rotas. The patrols were basically busy work for the mercenaries as, other than themselves, the threat to the station was external. The fighting would be around the airlocks, but it did allow the mercenaries a chance to get to know the station. Gleave had made sure that Miska and her crew were assigned to patrols that took them as close to the ops centre as possible. The centre could provide them with direct access to the station's systems. The systems would still be protected but it would be one less hurdle to overcome. The ops centre would also provide them with a reasonably secure area to hole up in until the assault team took the station.

'You realise that we're fighting for the wrong—' Torricone started as they were walking past a mining goods store. Miska turned on him.

'Oh, you have to lighten up! I mean seriously, does your menstruating heart bleed enough for everyone here?' Their relationship should be so much simpler, she decided. *He does what I tell him, I don't explosively decapitate him.* She read the anger in his expression as he opened his mouth to retort. She pointed at him with her left hand, the right still holding the slung AK-47. 'No! I get it, you don't like the hand you've been

151

dealt, well tough shit, you shouldn't have robbed cars. You need to un-fuck your head because all this bullshit is going to get us blown, and if you go to work second-guessing everything then you'll get yourself and the rest of us killed.'

They were starting to attract attention. Miska was worried about how many lenses were pointed at them. She leaned in close, her voice a hissed whisper. 'Boohoo for the miners, they're one of any number of people all over the colonies and probably back on Earth who get fucked on a regular basis by those with more power than them. That's life. If we don't do this then another outfit will and they won't give a shit about trying to keep the casualties down. Understand me? So either stop whining, or go and curl up and die somewhere.' Torricone was staring at her. At this moment it wasn't difficult to see the rage just below the surface that had resulted in another prisoner getting beaten to death.

'It's not whining,' he whispered through gritted teeth. 'I just keep hoping that you'll stop pretending to be the monster that you want us to believe you are.'

She moved in closer to him, close enough to smell him again, intimate, close enough to really hurt him. 'Want to see my résumé? All I need from you is to get us into the ops centre, understand?'

'Yes sir,' he whispered.

She wasn't sure she would put up with this from many of the other prisoners, she thought as they stared at each other. *Now it's just a case of who turns away first.* She did.

Their earlier recon had told Miska pretty much what she had expected from the information provided by the TCC. The ops centre was guarded by a blast door. Two miners with printed armour and AK-47s stood guard outside the closed door, and there were a number of security lenses watching over the area.

Torricone was carrying Merrill, who was tranced in and, judging by the twitching and drooling, already going toe-to-toe with the Che virus. Miska hadn't dared so much as glance sideways into the net before they were ready to attack in case they tipped their hat. Now they had dropped Merrill into Faigroe Station's information reflection practically blind. The hacker had gone after the virus with some very powerful but not terribly subtle attack programs and anti-virals. Merrill had developed the programs himself and Miska had helped augment them. The young hacker was also bolstered by some of the best protection programs that she had. Miska assumed that everyone in the ops centre was going nuts at the moment but you wouldn't know it from strolling down the corridor towards the centre's blast door.

Net feed appeared in a window in Miska's IVD as she walked towards the two guards. Everything was fire and lightning. Merrill's armoured demon icon looked exactly as Miska expected a sense-game-obsessed and deeply insecure kid's net representation would. The black lightning was coming from Che's gun as the virus fought back. The virus and the hacker were tearing up the seventeenth-century Caribbean pirate port that the station's site had been transformed into. There was nothing subtle about the attack. It looked like two wizards battling in some old-fashioned fantasy. Over Torricone's shoulder Merrill's body spasmed and shook from the biofeedback. The subtlest program that Merrill had used was an infiltration-spoof routine designed by Miska's ex-employers and further adapted by her. The program had one job and one job only: to infiltrate the station's security systems while the Che virus was distracted, and spoof the security lenses in the corridor outside the ops centre. Miska assumed it was working because the two guards outside the blast door weren't shooting at them.

'What happened to him?' One of the guards asked as they approached the door.

'Oh, he's—' Miska started and then brought the shotgun up on its sling and fired twice at point-blank range. The taser rounds, basically flying spiked batteries, hit both guards in their lightly armoured faces. The barbed spikes hooked into dermal armour and flesh and delivered fifty-thousand volts each. Miska heard the crackle of electricity as the guards' muscles contracted, contorting their facial features. The miners' various cybernetic augmentations protected them from a number of environmental threats inherent in mining. Fortunately for Miska, electrocution wasn't one of them. One of the guards went down like he was poleaxed. The other staggered back. There was a popping noise as Nyukuti fired the M-19's grenade launcher. The 30mm gel shot hit the staggering guard in the chest, picked her up off her feet and slammed her into the rock wall.

'Jesus Christ, Nyukuti,' Miska started.

'They didn't go down quickly enough,' the stand-over man told her.

'Here,' Torricone handed Nyukuti Merrill and then knelt down by the blast door.

The car thief had only been able to glance at the mechanism when they had passed it earlier in the day. Begrudgingly he had admitted that he could probably get it open. It seemed that the TCC had skimped on everything at Faigroe Station, including the door mechanisms.

'Gleave, cover down the corridor,' Miska said as she re-loaded the shotgun's tubular magazine with more taser rounds.

It seemed that playing a character only went so far. Now, with a gun in his hand, the conman was shaking like a leaf. Miska was worried that he might accidentally pull the trigger. She would have left him behind but there was a chance that the miners could have captured him and tried to use him against her. Miska didn't want to kill him unless she had to. He'd been very helpful so far but she suspected that his usefulness was at an end. She just hoped he didn't become too much of a hindrance. She finished reloading the shotgun and let it drop on its sling, bringing the AK-47 up and covering the corridor in the opposite direction.

Nyukuti loaded another gel round into the M-19's grenade launcher as Torricone used a handheld laser torch to cut around the lock mechanism. He prised it out with a knife, careful not to burn himself on the red-hot metal surrounding it. He inspected the innards of the mechanism.

'Well?' Miska asked. Torricone ignored her. Instead he hooked up a lock burner to the mechanism's guts. Nothing happened. Miska resisted the urge to glance up at the security lens. If the spoof had worked they would be none the wiser. If it hadn't then they would walk into a wall of exploding bullets.

'Torricone?' Miska asked again.

'Patience,' he told her.

'The longer we're out here the more chance that someone discovers us and we have to kill them,' Miska pointed out. The car thief hadn't quite refused to come with them. If he had she would have had no choice but to kill him. He had, however, made it clear that he wanted nothing to do with killing the miners.

'It has to cycle through every possible combination—' Torricone started to tell her and then the door opened. Miska removed a multi-spectrum stun grenade from a pouch on her webbing, popped the cap and pressed the button. Nyukuti was doing the same. She threw to the right, Nyukuti to the left. She could hear shouting from inside the ops centre as she took cover behind a rock wall, looking away from the door and squeezing her eyes shut. Despite looking the other way, despite the flash compensators built into her artificial eyes and the dampeners built into her ears, the flash still seeped through the membrane of her eyelids, and she still heard the explosion.

She spun round and stalked into the ops centre. Another artificial cave, with workstations on a raised catwalk running all around the wall, flickering holographic displays delivering information on everything from life support systems to mine automation, security to maintenance, supplies to telemetry on their orbit, and all the various sundry information required to keep an asteroid mine running. Several screens also showed the war in Faigroe Station's net between Merrill and the Che virus.

The chamber was in chaos. Like electricity, stun grenades weren't something that mining cybernetics were set up to deal with. The two guards, four technicians and Uboka were all momentarily blinded, several of them making strange keening noises because they couldn't hear the sound of their own voices. There was no point in talking to them. They wouldn't hear the order to surrender. Miska shot the guards on her side of the room first. Flying barbed darts hooked into facial dermal armour and then delivered their voltage.

Out of the corner of her eye she saw Nyukuti throw the tranced Merrill at one of the guards, catching him high on his torso and sending both of them tumbling to the ground. She had no time to deal with that now. Another taser round hit an unarmoured technician in the back and Miska watched as she hit the ground, gyrating as electricity coursed through her body. She heard the pop of the grenade launcher on Nyukuti's M-19 firing, followed by a cry of pain. Miska fired the shotgun again. The taser round caught another technician in the throat and he went down as well. She quickly checked her side of the room, no more targets. She swung round, taking in the situation very quickly. Gleave was still outside, covering the corridor. Torricone was in the doorway, AK-47 at the ready, in theory covering their backs. There was another pop and it looked like a technician attempting to surrender was knocked off his feet by a gel round fired from Nyukuti's grenade launcher. The guard that Nyukuti had thrown Merrill at had managed to wriggle out from under him. Miska took a moment to ensure that there was no flesh-to-flesh contact with the hacker and shot the guard with a taser round, leaving him writhing on the rock floor.

Uboka, however, was on the move. Nyukuti had the M-19 at his shoulder as he triggered another round from the underslung grenade launcher. The 40mm gel shot hit the mine leader in the side, partially spinning her around, but it didn't take her down and she was dragging a sidearm out of a holster on her hip. Miska fired her shotgun. The taser round hit Uboka in the torso, hooking itself into the printed armour she wore. Uboka's face contorted as the electricity made her muscles contract, causing her to squeeze the sidearm's trigger. Bullets sprayed out across the ops centre. Miska heard a cry of pain from behind her. She felt a round hit her, its force dispersed by her armoured jacket, the impact little worse than a punch. Nyukuti grunted and staggered slightly as he was hit as well. Miska let the shotgun drop on its sling and grabbed the AK-47, bringing it up. Someone charged past her. Torricone. Uboka's pistol ran dry. Torricone leaped into the air curling his legs up underneath him, both knees catching the mine leader in the face, sending her crashing to the floor. Torricone landed just behind her. Somehow Uboka still had the presence of mind to eject her pistol's magazine and reach for another. She cried out as the final gel round from Nyukuti's grenade launcher hit her in the stomach, driving the air from her lungs. Miska's finger was curled round the trigger. She wasn't sure why she didn't fire. Uboka slid the replacement magazine home just as Torricone's knee landed on her throat and he tore the pistol out of her grip. It was bullshit martial arts of the kind that had more chance of getting you shot than actually succeeding but he'd been lucky enough to get away with it.

Miska advanced as Torricone rolled a struggling Uboka on to her front. Miska leaned in just close enough to let the mine leader feel the barrel of the AK-47 against the back of her head. Just enough so she knew it was there, then she backed quickly away, still covering the mine leader. Torricone managed to get industrial memory cables around Uboka's wrists and ankles, and then he connected the two.

'Gleave, get in here!' Miska shouted, and then to Torricone: 'Get that door closed!' She left out: *And stop fucking around.*

Torricone ran over to the door mechanism and knelt down next to it as Gleave backed nervously into the room. With some irritation she noticed that he had his finger curled round the trigger of the AK-47.

'Trigger discipline,' she snapped. Gleave looked down at his shaking hands and moved his finger so it was curled around the trigger guard. She looked over at Nyukuti, who at least was doing his job, looking around the room at the stunned, bludgeoned, and recently electrified miners. There was some moaning, a bit of movement but none of them were showing much in the way of resistance. One of the technicians had taken a stray round from Uboka's pistol in the foot. There wasn't much of it left. With a thought she texted Gleave: *You running a skillsoft for trauma medicine?* He nodded and she sent another text: *Find a first aid kit and see to that foot.* She had enough field medicine training to help but the plan called for her to be doing other things.

With Nyukuti covering her, Miska went from prisoner to prisoner, tying them with memory cables. They brought in the two guards from the corridor and did the same with them just before the blast door slid shut. Miska searched every one of them, removing any weapons and ammunition, piling it at the opposite side of the ops centre to where they'd dragged the prisoners. She glanced at the hologram displays. Merrill's armoured demonic icon seemed to be holding its own against the Che virus in the net. Though, glancing down at the hacker, she didn't like the way he was spasming, or the blood seeping out of his nose, assuming that wasn't the result of being used as a thrown weapon by Nyukuti.

Miska checked one of the hologram displays. It showed lens feed from the fat, stingray-shaped drone craft harvesting combustibles within the gas giant's atmosphere. Turning away from the screen, she nodded to Nyukuti to follow her as she crossed the ops centre to kneel next to Uboka.

'You changed the access codes. Give me the new ones.'

'Go and fuck yourself, you corporate whore!' the mine leader spat.

'Don't waste my time. He used to be a stand-over man. Either you give us the codes, or he tortures it out of you. Drop you in a time-dilated program it won't even take that much longer, though it'll seem a lot longer to you.'

Uboka managed to twist her head around to glare up at Miska.

'You people really are bastards, aren't you,' she spat. Miska could read the hatred in the mine leader's eyes. She couldn't really blame her. One thing was for certain, she had more backbone than Joshua. Miska stood up. It was a bluff anyway. She had no intention of letting Nyukuti torture Uboka. With some trepidation she left the stand-over man to guard the prisoners.

'We're going to do this the hard way, then,' she muttered to herself as she crossed to Merrill, lifted him up and carried him to a couch near to where Torricone was standing looking at a hologram from the security lens feed. The miners knew something was wrong now. There were four of them outside the ops centre's blast door examining the mechanism.

'So I made a mess of the door mechanism on that side,' Torricone told her. 'In theory it can now only be opened from this side. If they're smart they could drill through the rock to get to the mechanism on this side of the wall. More likely they'll try and cut through the blast door.'

'Try?' Miska asked. The car thief shrugged.

'Succeed. It's a mine, they've got the tools.'

Miska leaned in close and nodded towards where Uboka lay face-down and bound.

'What was that about?' she whispered.

'She didn't deserve to die,' Torricone said quietly, looking away from her.

'You're going to get somebody killed.' He said nothing. 'I'm trancing in now, we need you watching our backs, understand me?' She didn't need to add that if she died then the rest of them did as well.

*

Miska was using every net-stealth trick she knew, hopefully rendering her cartoon icon invisible. She did wonder for a moment if she should have bothered when she appeared in the middle of a sandstorm. Either Che, or more likely Merrill, had weaponised the sand on the pirate port's beach. It flayed her skin as she dropped a number of heavily occulted hacks, invisible worms that buried into the remaining sand. One an order, the other a signal. Then she started to heal her wounded, partially flayed icon. She knew that back in the real world her body would be shaking from the biofeedback.

She could just about make out Merrill's icon as a monstrous shadow amid the sharp swirling sand up on one of the towers on the fort. Black lightning and flame still flashed within the storm. It looked positively mythological, Miska thought. Everything she'd found out about the virus, however, suggested that a frontal assault against it was a complete waste of time. Merrill was bringing some big guns to bear in terms of his augmented anti-virals and attack programs. His augmented net defences meant his icon and systems could take more damage, and to give the kid his credit he was standing his ground, but the attack was never meant as anything other than a diversion.

She knew that she couldn't destroy the virus without stripping out the station's systems. So that left isolating it. Merrill had fought the virus through various systems. They were now standing on part of the fort that symbolised the station's automated ore refinery control systems. Miska dropped more invisible worms into the sand, the force of the storm forcing her to kneel, the whirling sand outlining her supposedly invisible icon. While the Che virus was distracted, or rather while its resources were concentrated elsewhere, the worms slowly went about isolating the refinery systems from the rest of the station.

'This is Hangman-One-Actual to Hangman-One-Four, do you copy?' Miska subvocalised.

'In here, you call me the God of Fuck,' came Merrill's heavily modulated supposed-to-be-scary reply. She made a mental note to add correct radio procedure to the list of topics of conversations the infiltration team would be having with her dad when they got back to the *Hangman's Daughter*.

'Hangman-One-Four, stop screwing around and get ready to burn that virus, understand?'

'Solid copy, Hangman-One-Actual.' The sandstorm became a firestorm. Virtual silicon was burned to virtual glass as Merrill's demonic icon burst into flames and then flew from the tower, ejecting himself from the refinery systems just before his program isolated them. Flame dispersed and the remaining sand showered back down onto the beach and the deserted pirate town.

With a thought Miska made her icon visible as she made her way up the hill towards the colonial fort. Merrill's armoured demon was now perched on one of the other towers. She could see tall sailing ships setting sail from the dockside out on to the smooth, black, glass-like ocean. She assumed that they were the indy ships' net representations. In the real world the crews of the ships would be aware that something bad was happening on the station and would be making a run for it. On the tower that contained the ore refinery the Che virus was imprisoned in a complex glass cage. As Miska trudged up the beach she watched the revolutionary icon explode into a mass of pseudopodia as it tried to seep through the cage and back into the station's systems. The demon flexed huge, bat-like wings and took to the air, circling Miska as she used military grade intrusion and suborning programs to take control of the

162

station system-by-system. There was a minor explosion of sand as Merrill landed next to her.

'Status?' she asked the demon as window after window appeared in the air around her, providing information on the newly suborned systems.

'I am ready to crush the skulls of my enemies and sup the marrow from their ...'

'Merrill, stop fucking around!'

'Yeah, I couldn't have taken much more of that,' the demon admitted. Even through the modulation she could hear the frightened child in his voice.

'Okay, I'll take over in the net. Get out, get some rest, start running repairs on your systems.' She pointed at the mass of pseudopodia trying to break through the glass cage. 'That won't hold it forever, and there will be traces left in the rest of the system, it'll be trying to rebuild itself. While we're here we need to be constantly looking for it, burning it out where it's weakest, isolating it where it's too strong until we can make this the TCC's problem.'

'Understood,' the demon said and turned to smoke as Merrill tranced out of the net. With a thought Miska accessed the comms system.

'Hangman-One-Actual to all Hangman call signs, we are now in control of the target's net, over.'

CHAPTER 11

FIVE MONTHS AGO

The net representation of the USSS Jimmy Carter *was a metallic skeletal raven. Miska's cartoon icon was sitting in the skull of the raven, the enlarged eye sockets of which showed lens feed from the real world. She was in orbit high above the white surface of Proxima E. Proxima Centauri was huge on the planetary horizon, its reflected light making the ice that covered the planet's deep oceans look blood-red. From where Little Jimmy orbited, drifting around the cold planet, she could make out the 'spoke', the equatorial space elevator designed to pull the bounties of Proxima's rich sub-ice ocean into orbit for export. The spoke had been grown, rather than built, by Small Gods who had named it Yggdrasil, after the world tree from Norse mythology. It looked different to other space elevators that Miska had seen. It was clear that the mega structure was all tech, but there was still an organic look to it, an aesthetic presumably inherited from its name. Through the lens feed she could see*

164

the light of High Yggdrasil, the spoke's entrepôt. Freighters of various sizes docked with the station, and high above that was the asteroid tether that helped hold it all in place. Miska had worked on Proxima E, so she knew that if she magnified the lenses providing the feed she would be able to make out the ice-formed settlements surrounding the arcology-sized base of the huge spoke's structure. Most of the inhabitants of the planet lived and worked in the oceans far beneath the ice, however.

Since she'd tranced into Little Jimmy's systems, the ship was basically her body now. She wasn't as close to Little Jimmy as the Chimera, who hard-wired themselves into their vehicles for optimum speed-of-thought performance, but it wasn't far off. The ship was in full stealth mode. Miska didn't dare use any of the active scanners, but the passive scanners were her eyes and ears as she searched the lower orbits until she found what she was looking for: the Mjölnir. The intimidating, hammer-shaped orbital defence platform that controlled the protective network of satellites encircling the ice planet. With a thought she magnified the image. Almost the same size as the Mjölnir was the ship docked with it for a high security prisoner transfer, the Hangman's Daughter. The prison barge was long and rectangular, the tower towards the rear of the ship looking as much like a prison gun tower, to Miska's mind, as it did a conning tower. Miska smiled, and with a thought an old rock ballad started to play within the Little Jimmy's net representation.

A countdown appeared in the air before her. The numbers were rapidly approaching zero. Miska used the compressed gas jets to shift the position of the ship, hoping that the information on the Hangman's Daughter's flight path that Rafael had provided was correct. She got the ship in position and just as the counter reached zero she triggered the long burn. In the real world she knew that the acceleration, fighting with the ship's artificial gravity, would be tugging at her tranced-in body, but in the net she felt nothing. The burn was the trickiest part of the operation, where she risked the greatest chance of discovery. Stealth or no stealth, it was difficult to hide exhaust plumes of any significant magnitude, which was why she had done it so far away. She retracted the thrusters to mask their heat, using extruded fins to bleed off any excess into the coldness of space as quickly as possible. The manoeuvre was made more difficult due to having to change orbits. Even with the ship's nav systems doing most of the work, the maths had made her head hurt. She'd always hated maths.

Miska held up her hands and, with a gesture, conjoined the two eye socket lens feeds from the real world, turning it into one large window and then moving it to one side, leaving it hanging in the air. Through the hollowed eye sockets of the raven's skull she was looking down at Proxima E's planetary and orbital net. Down on the planet solid lines of neon light criss-crossed, making a sparse network in the shape of a sphere. Here and there the lines joined up to form nexus points at towns, villages or other settlements. Beneath that sphere was a much more extensive and fuller one, with many more and much larger nexus points: the communications net of Proxima E's submarine world. Both the inner and outer spheres fed into Yggdrasil. The spoke's net representation was of a giant tree that towered over the planetary net. Mjölnir also looked like its namesake, a giant stone hammer decorated with glowing neon runes, lightning wreathing its haft, which was pointing down towards the planet. Gossamer neon threads of varying permanence connected it to the spoke, to the planet, and to the various ships in local space. It looked as though it had just drifted through a spider web made of light.

'Pretty!' Miska announced to herself as the ballad ended and something faster and more aggressive took over. She was running stealth programs designed to occult the Little Jimmy in the net as well, the skeletal raven invisible to all intents and purposes. She glanced over at the lens feed from the real world and, with a thought, triggered the compressed gas manoeuvring jets, which were not nearly as efficient as the normal manoeuvring jets but were almost impossible to detect. The Little Jimmy rolled and the planet, both in the real world and the net, seemed to spin around the ship. Miska was grinning. The maths was over and done with. This was what she lived for.

She turned back to the eye sockets and the view of the orbital net and took a closer look at the prison barge. In the net the Hangman's Daughter looked like a cross between some vast and rotting wooden prison hulk and Charon's ferry.

'Maybe just a little too oppressive,' she muttered. She pushed aside thoughts of redesigning the prison barge's net representation to focus on the job at hand. She checked the countdown, which had reset, then glanced at the window into the real world, cartoon brow furrowing with comical worry. The frown disappeared and she smiled as she watched the umbilicals connecting the Hangman's Daughter and Mjölnir separate in clouds of venting gases. Manoeuvring thrusters glowed, pushing the prison barge away from the orbital defence platform. It had been the weakest part of the plan as it had relied on two bureaucracies, the ship's and Proxima E's authorities, to do something at the time they said they would, but it looked as though it had paid off.

As she dropped into a lower orbit, the Little Jimmy glided into a wall of low-powered lasers and radio waves from the

Mjölnir's *lidar and radar systems. Miska was interfaced so closely with the ship that the active scans felt like the caress of a particularly inept lover. In theory, the ship's design and various stealth systems would either make them invisible, or the signature would be so small that operators and expert systems alike would read it as an anomaly. If, however,* Mjölnir *detected the ship then her best chance would be to run – but even then she didn't like her odds against the formidable weapons platform.*

She checked her window into the real world again and saw the glow from the prison barge's huge main engines at its stern. The Hangman's Daughter *was rising as Miska was falling. She got a much closer view of the industrial-looking superstructure, a mass of spars and girders that surrounded the ugly ship. She could see the lights from the bridge, the holographic displays over the work stations, even the crew tranced in, interfacing with the ship in their reclined bucket seats. The only reason they couldn't see the* Little Jimmy *was because of the photoreactive camouflage that coated the stealth ship's exterior.*

'Ninja!' Miska announced. This was cool, and sneaky. She liked her new ship. It felt like she had cleared the front of the still-accelerating prison barge by a hair's breadth, and in spatial terms this was true even though there had been hundreds of feet between Little Jimmy *and the* Hangman's Daughter. *It didn't stop her feeling like a tiny dinghy about to be run over by a super tanker, however. The prison barge threw her into shadow as it passed over her stealth craft. She triggered the compressed gas jets, a long, hard burn heavily depleting the reserves as she tried to match the prison barge's speed. A little downward squirt had the* Little Jimmy *rising towards the* Hangman's Daughter's *superstructure. She got a closer look at its weapons systems. Ball-mounted lasers and rapid-firing multi-barrelled railguns*

168

for point defence, missile batteries and heavier laser cannons for offence. The whole ship was covered in thick armour pitted from micrometeorite impacts. Miska let a little whistle escape through her lips. It wasn't lost on her that the Hangman's Daughter could swat the Little Jimmy like a bug if she was discovered.

She used most of the rest of the compressed gas reserves to weave her way through the superstructure to the ship's hull. She flew as close as she could, then extended the landing gear and let the electromagnetic anchors suck the ship onto the prison barge's hull over an airlock, but she didn't try and connect to it as that would alert the crew to her presence. Miska then partially retracted the landing gear so the Little Jimmy sank closer still to the prison barge, further reducing its signature.

Suddenly Miska went very still. Through the window into the real world she could see an insectile maintenance droid crawling across the skin of the prison barge little more than twenty feet away. It paid no attention to her and continued on its way.

'Phew,' she muttered, then, with a thought, extended the ship's tendrils. The flexible tentacle-like appendages crawled across the hull of the Hangman's Daughter in a way that Miska found a little creepy. They looked even more unpleasant in the net. The appendages were guided by the prison barge's blueprints that Rafael had provided. They were scanning for hardwired systems that were close to the hull. One of the appendages found something. A cowl covered the laser torch on the end of the tentacle as it drilled through the armour plate. Soon all the appendages were doing likewise.

The laser torches were retracted and tendrils of carbon nanotube wriggled through the still-hot holes in the hull. They *wrapped themselves around hardwired systems, piercing them. Miska launched the ship's intrusion and suborning software programs like a wizard in an old viz casting spells. The prison barge's systems had excellent intrusion counter measures. It needed them to stop external parties from trying to break prisoners out. But between the NSA intrusion software and the library of system backdoors that the agency kept on file, she might as well have been hacking a coffee machine. The prison hulk lit up with lines of neon light, a bright nexus point appearing far above her. Miska found herself smiling as she bathed in the light and the* Hangman's Daughter *opened itself to her.*

The first thing she did was spoof the security systems on the airlock she'd landed the Little Jimmy *on top of. Airlocks were among some of the most secure systems on ships and stations, but none of that mattered if you effectively opened them from the inside. In the real world the* Little Jimmy *connected itself to the airlock with a concertinaed umbilical of smart material and started to pump air, equalising the pressure. She was in.*

Miska had made her way through the guts of the ship, spoofing the security lenses to replay footage of empty corridors. Doors lied to the monitoring crew members about opening and closing, other security systems just ignored her. She made her life easier by eschewing the lifts and, instead, climbing a maintenance ladder that took her up the conning tower. Even with her enhancements and her high level of physical fitness it left her a little out of breath. A panel popped open for her and she crawled out, moving into a crouch, her M-187 laser carbine at the ready. She was in another corridor, like many others she had been in on various ships. It was dull, institutional and looked like it had seen better days.

She had windows open in her IVD showing the feed from the local security lenses. A squad of guard droids were about to turn into her corridor but that was fine, they were under her control. They marched past. Miska knew that the automatic shotguns they carried were all loaded with non-lethal gel rounds.

She followed them quietly. They marched around the corner into another longer corridor that ended in the blast door that led to the bridge. There were two people in the corridor. Guards. She guessed they had just left the bridge. They watched the squad of eight droids march past, confused looks on their faces. This was where things could go wrong: people, it was always people. Through the lens feed she could already see one of the guards subvocalising. She found his comms link and shut it off.

Miska moved round the corridor quietly, slinging her carbine behind her back and wishing she'd brought non-lethal weapons with her, though she'd never really needed any before. These guys didn't deserve to die. They weren't soldiers, terrorists or criminals. They were just trying to do their job. She couldn't afford to use the droids. Their shotguns were too loud. At the same time, she couldn't afford to be too gentle either. They needed to be removed from the equation for the time being.

She moved up behind the first guard and grabbed either side of his head. She pulled at the same time as she kicked the back of his knee, hard, sending him to the ground before stamping on his face. The other guard was turning, subvocalising at the same time, but Miska had already taken care of that. The guard was pulling out her shock stick. That was fine, Miska let her, her armoured leather jacket was insulated and her dermal armour was resistant to electricity as well.

She grabbed the woman's hand and wrist and changed the direction of her strike. It was movie kung-fu bullshit but worth the risk because Miska was effectively immune to the shock stick. Miska held the electrified baton against the side of guard's face until she collapsed. Only then did Miska wrench the baton out of the woman's death grip. The guard with the broken face was trying to get up, dripping blood down himself, reaching for his holstered Glock, when she hit him with the shock stick and left him drooling blood onto the corridor floor.

Miska followed the squad of droids into the bridge. It was open plan, on three different levels. The bottom level looked like some kind of command & control centre, holographic displays showing the telemetry and lens feeds from the cellblocks and the virtual construct used for retraining and, in theory, rehabilitating the prisoners. The second level, the one she'd come in on, was the flying bridge that surrounded the C&C level on a wide mezzanine catwalk. The displays were also showing telemetry, feeds from engineering, various external feeds – including targeting information from the weapon systems – and holographic displays of local space, which showed nearby ships, as well as Mjölnir and Yggdrasil. Above the bridge was the executive level, presided over by the Hangman's Daughter's captain. He looked like her ideal of an old-time sea captain: chiselled features, short salt and pepper hair, a beard to match.

Four of the droids were marching down into the C&C area, the other four were spreading out around the flying bridge. All of them were levelling automatic shotguns at any armed personnel.

She'd kept the carbine slung and had the SIG Sauer GP-992 levelled at the captain. The pistol was better in close quarters like this.

'Hands in the air!' she shouted. 'Do as you're told and

everyone gets to go home and see their loved ones.' The captain nodded and raised his hands. He looked confident, calm, and somehow in control of the situation. He wasn't. Miska made her way around the mezzanine towards the steps up to the executive level.

'Please, just remain calm,' the captain said as she passed one of the guard droids covering an armed crew member. There wasn't quite enough room and she made a mistake. She passed in front of the guard droid. The droid raised its shotgun as she did so. The crewmember went for his Glock. Miska's eyes widened as she realised what was happening, what she had done. Instinctively she grabbed his gun hand with her free left. Then training kicked in. She brought the butt of the gauss pistol down on the crewmember's wrist with enough boosted muscle to break it. He screamed. The Glock fell onto the catwalk. She drove the edge of the gun up and into his nose, breaking that as well, spreading it across his face. She cleared the guard droid even as it was extending a shock stick from the palm of its left hand, its right still holding the automatic shotgun now, once again, covering the crewmember. The guard droid electrocuted the man until he hit the ground a drooling, spasming mess. One of the droids fired a three-round burst from its shotgun as another member of the bridge crew tried to go for their sidearm.

'I am calm,' Miska told the captain as she climbed the steps to the executive level and his chair. 'You're in my seat,' she told him. He had a bemused expression on his face. 'Arr!' she added, pirate-fashion, and grinned at him.

The same scene, sans Miska's involvement, had been repeated all over the ship. The guard droids had turned on the human personnel, disarming and then securing them with little

173

resistance. There had been a brief firefight in one of the guard-rooms. Fortunately no one had been killed, though a few guards were the worse for wear, but none of the droids had been too badly damaged.

The droids had then escorted all of the ship's personnel to one of the larger lifeboats. Miska had noticed that there weren't enough lifeboats for the prisoners. The captain had remained calm, the bemused expression never really leaving his face. The warden – Miska vaguely seemed to remember his name was Oates, bald, bullet-headed, a slug of a man – had not gone so quietly. He'd been dragged to the lifeboat screaming threats to the point that, even though she was watching through lens feed, she was considering having him tasered. Then she acted on the thought. One of the droids touched him with a shock stick and then it was quiet again.

She started uploading the upgraded, nearly sentient, dumb-AI autopilot into the Hangman's Daughter's systems. The improved software had been another gift from Rafael, as had the copy of the sophisticated virtual training construct that the USMC Special Operations Raider Regiment used. The size of the two programs meant that they would take a while to upload. The ship was holding its course, making its way out of Proxima E's gravity well to set sail. She was sending standard comms replies to High Yggdrasil's traffic control taken from recordings she'd found in the bridge-systems' memory. She would launch the lifeboat at the last minute.

An icon appeared in her IVD telling her that the upgraded autopilot was finally uploaded, integrated, tested and diagnostics had come back to tell her that it was running close to peak. With a thought she sent the autopilot the new coordinates. Dead-space between systems, the coordinates had once been used as a rendezvous point for the Company. Rafael had assured it her that it was as good a place as any for several months of uninterrupted training time.

For a moment she enjoyed the peace and quiet, all alone in the bridge, looking down at the ship stretching out in front of her, master of her domain. The ship's sails unfurled, looking incongruous in comparison with its blocky, industrial mass, like butterfly wings on an oil tanker. With a thought the Hangman's Daughter *launched the lifeboat, which started broadcasting its automated mayday immediately. The ship accelerated, the light from the stars blurred. Another thought and she started to upload her most precious program. Her father.*

A lot of the prisoners had to be tasered by the guard droids' shock sticks when they were removed from their pods to get them into the explosive collars. It was a four-droid job. Two to hold the prisoner and administer the occasional tasering, one to cover, and the fourth to put the lowjack on. It was time- and resource-intensive. The exercise yard wasn't big enough to hold all six-thousand-plus convicts so they were doing it cellblock by cellblock.

The Hangman's Daughter *was an all male prison barge. This was probably due to tradition, in part, though gender was much less rigidly defined these days. Miska suspected, however, that having the population all male was simply easier in terms of administration and resources. It was also a hold over from the ultramax prisons that most of the convict population came from. The ultramaxes didn't put their prisoners into suspended animation and therefore were segregated. She knew there were all female prison barges out there as well.*

Miska was leaning on the wall just outside the security doors to CB1. She could see the thousand assembled hard-faced convicts milling around in the exercise yard through the security lens feed in her IVD. A number of them had toyed with their lowjack collars only to be warned to leave them alone by the guard droids. The automated gun turrets had been set to track anyone exhibiting aggressive behaviour as well, but it had taken a while to thaw, collar and assemble a thousand ultramax convicts. More than one fight had broken out. The majority of them had been broken up by the guard droids firing gel shots down into the belligerents. The worst fight had resulted in three prisoners splattered all over the exercise yard, however, after she'd been forced to order one of the turrets to open fire.

Today was all about stick. Carrot would come later.

'All right, maggots!' Every hard face in the yard turned to look at her father's giant face, six storeys tall. A few of them jeered, more of them joined in, soon most of them were shouting. 'Quiet!' He very nearly got it as well, such was the degree of command in his voice. 'You need to listen, what I say next could very well save your life!' They were quieter still. 'The Hangman's Daughter *is under new management. We don't give a flying fuck for your wellbeing, your safety, or your rights. You are now a penal legion. We will train you. You apply yourself and you will do well. Don't do as we say, we will kill you.'*

The convicts were screaming at the screen now. Some of them were hitting the doors, or tearing at the walls of the sunken exercise yard. Miska had made the guard droids remove all the equipment so they had nothing to throw. A few of them tried to scale the walls and reach the catwalk running around CB1. A few bursts of gel shot discouraged them. Miska wasn't sure she'd ever seen such naked aggression before, even in the marines, and that was saying something. 'Caged animals' didn't really do them justice. It was the prisoners that weren't ranting and raving in ultimately futile displays of rage that interested her, though. The thinkers. She had programmed the security lenses to make note of them, cross-reference them with their files, and flag those files.

'Let me introduce you to your new commander!' It was her cue. She realised she was nervous. She had no fear doing an Orbital Insertion Low Opening parachute jump into a hot landing zone, but public speaking freaked her out. It was something that she would just have to get used to. Also she wasn't happy about what she had to do next.

The security doors clicked open at a silent coded command texted from her integral computer. She went through the second set of doors and stepped out onto the catwalk. It suddenly went very quiet in the exercise yard below as they looked up at her. She made it about a quarter of the way down the length of the cellblock before it began. Many of the screamed threats were what she had expected. Some of them, however, were so graphic and imaginative that they would make a marine blush. She knew her dad would be in a fury but she couldn't help but smile. They were really, really afraid.

Miska walked out onto the catwalk at the end of the cellblock underneath the massive Orwellian presence of her father.

'Quiet down,' she told them. Her voice was amplified but she hadn't raised it. If anything the screamed promises of pain and violation redoubled. She just nodded. 'Quiet down,' she said again. 'Second and last chance.' She was met by a wall of sound torn from the throat of nearly a thousand very dangerous criminals. She pulled a conductor's baton from inside her leather jacket as music started to play softly through the ship's

PA. She pointed the baton at one of the screaming prisoners. The information on him scrolled down her IVD. Muldoon, Jacobi, convicted paedophile. His collar blew and his head tumbled into the air. Nearby convicts backed quickly away from the headless corpse before it toppled to the deck. Now she had their attention.

'There are no third chances. Now, there's no need to panic, but you need to understand how serious we are.' The music was louder now. Tchaikovsky's 1812 Overture. 'I say there's no need to panic, but what I mean is there's no need to panic unless you're a convicted sex criminal, or you've ever hurt a child.' Suddenly the music was very loud and the cannons started. With each cannon blast she pointed the baton, a collar exploded and a decapitated head went spinning into the air. Her words didn't seem to matter. There was still quite a lot of panic.

She didn't want to do it. There were no tears for those she killed and in the course of her duty Miska had killed many people far less deserving than them. But an enemy soldier was just doing their job. This was in cold blood, an act of barbarity. It made her point, however. She would kill anyone who wouldn't cooperate. It also got rid of prisoners who none of the others would work with, who would cause dissension among the ranks, and who, frankly, she wanted nothing to do with. She could be pretty sure that none of them were her father's killers. Nobody would build a cover as sex criminal. It would dramatically lower their life expectancy. They were the lowest of the low in the penal system, hated by guard and fellow inmate alike. Still, as she painted the world red with her baton to the bombastic strains of Tchaikovsky's Overture, she did not relish the other five mass murders she would have to perform for her convict audience. They had to think she was insane. It was a *message that wouldn't be completely at odds with some of her final psych evaluations in the marines. She'd have the droids clear the bodies away between the performances but she'd leave the bloodstains. She suspected the smell of evacuated bowels would take some time to dissipate.*

CHAPTER 12

Cartoon Miska was sat on the beach in the net, leaning on her club. She'd caught glimpses of forms growing out of the sand and forming from the black liquid of the sea a few times, but probing attacks from her offensive software had seen off whatever they had been. She suspected they were either residual intrusion countermeasures, or remaining tendrils of the virus trying to grow.

She had multiple windows open in the air around her. A number of them showed security lens feed from various areas around the station. A new window opened, her father's craggy face appearing in it, a private link to the *Hangman's Daughter*.

'Bit busy, Dad,' she told him. Many of the miners and mercenaries were locked down in rooms designed to be secure in the face of fires or decompression and, as a result, were reasonably secure. Their small arms were of little use against solid rock and blast doors. More worrying were those who had access to the mining gear, but they were few and far between. They would, however, have to be prioritised when the assault team arrived.

Through the security lens feed Miska could see a small group of miners in one of the stores assembling a portable mining laser. There were also a number of miners and mercenaries loose in much more open spaces like the rec and shopping areas. It didn't make that much difference – those areas were still locked down. It just meant they had more room to roam until her Wraiths got there. Realising that they would be watched, a number of the locked-down rebels had tried to destroy the security lenses, but they were well armoured as they had been the butt of miner anger many times before.

'Just wanted to see how you're doing,' he said. He was worried. She could hear it in his voice. This was her dad of nine years ago, when she had been a teenaged trouble magnet. He hadn't been there when she'd passed basic training, qualified as a Recon Marine and then a Raider. Annoyingly, she was still his little girl, however troubling.

'Just fine, Dad,' she told him, not really looking at him, checking a blank window. Unlike the miners, the mercenaries had succeeded in knocking out the lenses in the crèche where they'd been bunking. This was a worry. They would have to be prioritised and would probably be the stiffest fight. On the other hand, they also had enough tactical acumen (and/or common sense) to realise they didn't have the gear to win a fight against power armour, even a hundred-year-old design like the Wraiths.

Making sure none of them got near the two remaining mining mechs was crucial. Fortunately nobody had been locked in the shed with the machines, otherwise she would have had to risk a sortie to go and deal with them. That could have been all kinds of complicated. It was another reason why the miners with the cutting laser needed to be dealt with, however.

'Torricone?' he asked. Even in her cartoon net icon she felt herself tense. She tried to concentrate on what she was doing. The biggest problem would be the docks. The indy ships had left, and if they were still nearby then they were either hiding from the station's rudimentary radar and lidar, or she wasn't reading it right. The docks, not surprisingly, were the most heavily protected part of the station. Twenty of the miners had been stationed there, supported by four of the mercenaries. Again the majority of them were armed with slugthrowers that would do little or no damage to the Wraiths, even with the airbursting explosive bullets. The industrial printers on the station lacked the sophistication to make complex weapons like railguns, heavy lasers, plasma weapons or missiles, but it looked like they had managed to print two archaic-looking, almost portable, 20mm cannons. Some bright spark had then added homemade gauss-kisses to the ends of the cannons' barrels, turning them into rudimentary railguns. They'd be no use against the port's thick blast doors but they might give her Wraiths pause.

'He worked out just fine,' she tried not to say through gritted teeth.

'You know you were always a terrible liar,' he told her. Miska sighed. 'This Torricone, tattoos, criminal tendencies. He sounds just your type.' She couldn't quite believe what she'd just heard.

'Really Dad? You want to discuss this now?' She was staring at the floating window, with his disembodied head in the centre of it, now.

'Who was that knucklehead you took to the prom?'

'Chet,' she muttered, silently cursing herself for getting drawn into this.

'That's it Chet, the biker.'

'Brad was the biker, Chet was one of Uncle Jakob's ranch hands ...'

'Not a one of them with a two-syllable name!'

'I went with Chet because you let it be known on base that you'd personally castrate any marine that dare date your youngest daughter, though I noticed that you let Angela go to her prom with a second lieutenant ...' She was getting angry now. Thinking about her older sister had that effect.

'That was different, he was an officer, and a gentleman.'

'Is there a point to this? Or have you just opened a comms link to piss me off when I'm working!'

'Torricone, he didn't work out, did he?'

'He's an insubordinate asshole but he's done his job, you can tell me "I told you so" later!' Her father opened his mouth to retort and she severed the comms link. She stared at the empty space above the sand where the window had hovered moments before, still not quite able to believe the conversation she'd just had. 'Now he wants to play the protective dad?' she muttered.

She tried to suppress her anger and focus again. She knew the docks would be where any remaining traces of the Che virus would try and consolidate, take control of the defences and blast any shuttle that tried to dock carrying an assault team. So Miska had decided that she wouldn't do that.

'Hangman-One-Actual to Hangman-Two-Actual, what's your status?' Miska subvocalised over the secure and heavily occulted comms link.

'Hangman-Two-Actual, really ... busy,' Mass replied over the interference-heavy link. Miska smiled. She looked at the window she'd just opened showing the lens feed from the prison shuttle. It was being kicked around in Proxima G's upper atmosphere as it linked with the now-stationary fuel scoop drone craft. The armoured, deceptively spindly-looking, humanoid shapes of the Wraith combat exoskeletons worn by the prisoners were stepping out of the shuttle cargo bay and onto the drones. Even using the electromagnets on their boots to steady themselves, it looked pretty hairy. Miska was more than impressed with the pilots trying to keep the shuttle steady high above the vast swirling storm fronts of the gas giant. Miska, for her part, was concentrating on hiding any trace of what was happening to the drones from the station's systems just in case the virus's inevitable residual presence detected it.

Four of the Wraiths made it onto the first drone craft and knelt down, each prisoner using one hand to provide a third electromagnet to help steady their power armoured suits. In their other hand they all held the 20mm Retributors converted to fire rubber bullets. The shuttle, its cargo bay still wide open, moved away from the drone as it rose. The next drone came up to take its place and the shuttle's manoeuvring engines burned brightly as it attempted to negotiate the upper atmospheric winds to get close enough. She couldn't hear the squad-level comms but a couple of the Wraiths looked reluctant to step out of the rear of the shuttle. She couldn't really blame them. A misstep here meant death in the crushing atmosphere far below the gas giant's clouds. She would have been interested to hear the persuasion methods utilised by Mass to get the assault team out of a perfectly serviceable shuttle and onto the automated fuel scoops.

When the third and final drone was on its way Miska diverted the lens footage from the fuel storage landing area to her integral computer, and then spoofed it with older footage to hopefully fool any of the virus's residual presence.

'May I speak with you?'

Surprised, Miska looked around, readying her various attack and defence programs with the simple symbolic gesture of hefting her club. It took her a moment to realise that the voice came from within the complex glass geometry of the cage on top of the tower. The virus looked like Che Guevara again. She frowned and moved a little further up the beach towards the cliff-top colonial fort.

'You shouldn't be able to do that,' she said.

'I'm sending a request via an emergency monitoring system for the refinery. Your systems are checking the messages for any vectored threat. I could only use it to escape if you allowed me to, and even then it would take a while.' Shielding her eyes with her hand from the virtual sun, she could just about make out his lips moving within the cage. With a thought Miska double-checked her systems. As far as she could tell he was telling the truth. She still didn't like it.

'Yeah, I'm going to shut it down anyway, just to be on the safe side.' She had no idea why she was telling him – no, it – this, as opposed to just doing it.

'Can I show you something first?' Che asked. He spoke with what she was sure was a South American accent, from Earth.

'I see you're not a mass of tentacles any more. That look not working for you?' she asked.

He shrugged. 'Right tools for the job.'

'True that,' Miska nodded.

'So, may I show you something?'

She sighed. 'You know what, whenever anyone's on the back foot, that's when the sob stories come out. Somebody wants something another person has, we fight. Sure, we'll dress it up in all sorts of words: belief, ideology, security. It's all bullshit. Two people fight, one wins. I really don't care about all the bad things that happened here. If I did I'd be a fucking social worker instead of a mercenary.'

Even to her ears she sounded a little defensive. Out of curiosity she magnified the view of Che ... the virus in its cage. It had an eyebrow raised over one of its dark eyes. The icon was well animated.

'So then there's no harm in looking at what I have to show you,' he suggested.

'Well it might make me feel bad about what I'm doing,' she said. *Shut this down, now*!

'So you're not a psychopath then?'

The jury's out, she thought. 'Bye,' Miska said, turning to walk back down the beach.

'We know who you are, what you've done,' he said.

We? She looked back. 'Threats?'

'I suspect you wouldn't want me in your systems. What if all those collars suddenly stopped functioning?' He seemed to be studying her. Miska turned around, hands on her hips, the end of the club resting on the sand.

'Well, there's your answer then. I mean, if you feel like protecting some of the worst scum the colonies have to offer.'

'Protecting them? I could lock you in there with them. Hand you over to the authorities.'

'Doing the man's job for him?' She couldn't help but smile at how absurd she sounded.

'Are all of them irredeemable scum?' he asked, ignoring her question. Suddenly she was thinking of Torricone despite herself. 'No victims of circumstances, nobody using their time to try and better themselves, nobody falsely imprisoned?'

'Bring it, then,' Miska said, shrugging. Sounding absurd even to herself.

'We don't approve of what you've done, but there's worse than the likes of an amoral little sociopath like yourself.'

She raised an eyebrow. 'Good negotiation technique for a guy in a cage,' she muttered.

'What you do with your convict army is another matter. Too many actions like this and we'll have to do something about you.'

'I'll bite, who's we?' He just smiled. 'What do you want me to look at?'

'I want you to see what it was like . . .'

'Before the miners took the station?' Miska asked. 'Sorry, pal, things are tough all over.' She cut the link to the virus and wondered what she had been thinking engaging it in conversation for so long. She blocked the connection as well, just to be on the safe side.

She looked around at her windows again. It looked like the miners trapped in the stores had almost finished assembling the mining laser. The fuel scoop drones had left the atmosphere and were making their way towards the station, their engines flaring as they made small course adjustments. There was still a group of miners outside the ops centre but they were effectively locked in that corridor. Though Chanar was one of them, which she hadn't noticed before. The big shift leader was staring at the lens, as though he could reach through it and crush her head with one of his big fists.

She checked the feed from ops centre itself. Gleave was sat in one of the chairs, his AK-47 on the workstation, his head in his hands. Merrill was reclining on another chair, his feet up on the workstation. Miska wasn't sure she liked that he had got hold of one of the archaic-looking slugthrowers. Nyukuti was guarding the prisoners and it didn't look like he'd hurt any of them, which was a good thing. Torricone was kneeling down next to Uboka. It looked as though the pair of them were talking. Miska didn't like that either, not at all. She checked the ETA on the drones. She had another five minutes or so.

'Hangman-One-Actual to Hangman-One-Four,' she subvocalised. There was no answer. 'That's you, Merrill.'

'Oh shit, yeah, sorry, Miska, I mean Hangman-One-Actual,' came the reply. Miska sighed, rolled her eyes, added it to the list, and tried to remember a time when she'd actually enjoyed her job. This all felt far too much like being an adult.

'Can you take over in the net for me for a while?' she asked.

'Sure, boss.'

Miska glanced up at the fort where the artificial sun caught Che's glass cage and made it glow like a prism. Somehow she still knew that he was watching her. Out of the corner of her eye she caught little eddies of wind kicking the sand about.

'Gleave, pay the fuck attention,' Miska said when she opened her eyes back in the real world. 'At least watch the feed from the lenses, keep an eye on that lot just outside the door.' She didn't like the irritable tone she heard in her voice, it made her sound whiny, which she equated with weakness. That wasn't good with eight enemy potential-combatants in the room, no matter how secure they were. 'Torricone, what are you doing?'

Torricone looked up at her from where he was knelt next to Uboka. He didn't look even remotely guilty. He didn't look like someone who'd been caught doing something they shouldn't. If anything he looked angry.

'You need to listen to her,' he told Miska. Miska rolled her eyes and pushed herself out of the bucket seat. She grabbed her AK-47 and made her way across the ops centre towards Torricone.

'Everybody has a hard luck story, everybody. Everyone's got an excuse. You listen to them all and you're frozen, you'd never do anything, understand me? Now get away from her, do your fucking job, and I'll gag her.' He didn't move. 'How far do you want to take this?' she asked him. She didn't want to blow his head off but she would if he forced her to. She could tell by the set of his jaw that he was going to push this.

'Please, just listen to her. That's all I ask,' he said quietly. He wasn't quite pleading with her.

'You don't understand. I heard her sob story on the way in. That's not the point, this has got nothing to do with wrong-or-right, it's to do with chain-of-command. You don't respect it,' she made a circular gesture with her finger, 'you maybe get all of us killed, including your precious rebel leader here.' She leaned in towards Torricone. 'Please don't make me ask again.'

Torricone opened his mouth to reply but it was Uboka who spoke: 'What's your sob story?'

Miska looked down at her. 'My own business,' she finally said.

'Your dad, your real dad, is dead, isn't he?' Torricone asked. Miska's hand darted out. Steely fingers grabbed his jaw. She knew that between real and boosted muscle all she had to do was squeeze and she could powder the bone. That would shut him up.

'Not now,' she told him, desperately trying to control the boiling rage she felt. 'Not ever, do you understand me?'

'Funnily enough, the thing that broke me wasn't when we discovered that all our medicals had been faked, and the Red was destroying our nervous systems,' Uboka started. 'It wasn't

189

when Jarrod, an old and trusted friend of mine, went berserk and stabbed a hooker to death, an action so uncharacteristic of him before the Red it would have been impossible to predict.' She was struggling to look at Miska from her uncomfortable position face-down on the metal grill of the floor, her wrists and ankles cabled together. 'It wasn't even when Baby Jemima died. No, it was when they tried to hook my fifteen-year-old son on Red, and get him to sign an indentured drugs-for-work contract.'

Torricone slapped her hand away. Or rather, she let him slap her hand away.

'In my experience, people will say anything when they're up against the wall,' Miska told him.

'Easy enough to check,' Torricone replied.

'Get back to work.'

He just crossed his arms.

'You going to blow his head off?' Merrill asked over comms, presumably having been watching the whole thing from the net. And she knew she really should. She'd undermine her own authority if she didn't. Except that he was right and the TCC, even for an amoral corporate entity, was wrong. Over the years she'd had a lot of problems telling the difference. It was one of the reasons that she'd made such a good covert operator – she was morally flexible. But this seemed reasonably clear-cut.

'Nyukuti, relieve Torricone of his sidearm,' she said.

'Huh?' Nyukuti said. It was the only time he'd questioned an order. She just turned to look at him, and then, stand-over man or not, he moved to obey.

'I think you'd better put me with them,' Torricone said and nodded towards the miners all face-down on the floor.

'I don't give a fuck what you think,' Miska told him. She

gestured to a chair on the other side of the room. 'Go and sit there, and be quiet.' If he didn't do what she told him to this time then she was just going to trigger the collar. Her dad had been right, it had been a mistake to bring him on this mission. She should have brought more like Nyukuti. Torricone must have read something in her face because he held his peace, crossed the room and sat down. Miska felt eyes on her. She looked down to see Uboka craning her neck to look up. 'Do you want to live?' she asked the rebel leader.

'Why do you fear words so much?' she asked. Miska almost drew her pistol and shot her there and then. She was aware of how quiet and still it had suddenly become in the ops centre. 'I want to live but I don't want to be a slave.'

'You can only have hope when you're alive. Do you have any doubt whatsoever that I will put two bullets in your head if you try messing with my people again?' Uboka didn't say anything. It seemed that she believed Miska. 'Then lie there quietly.' She walked away from the rebel leader before someone had to die.

She could see the diverted feed from the station's external lenses in her IVD. The drones were about to dock. She checked the other feeds. The miners with the cutting laser were almost through the blast door.

Miska kept the squad of twelve Wraiths in fire teams of four to begin with. The four from the first drone, call signs Hangman-Two-Five to Hangman-Two-Eight, she sent to the stores at a run. Doors opened in front of the sprinting power-armoured figures and closed behind them. They took fire as they raced down corridors, rounds sparking off their armour or exploding in the air close to them. Miska ordered them to ignore the re-sistance. They could mop up later but she needed to stop that laser getting into play. Another group of armed miners, who'd been in the corridor outside the stores, had joined those with the laser. They were trying to manhandle the cumbersome cutting tool through the still-red hole in the blast door without burning themselves on the molten metal when the Wraiths came round the corner.

The convicts didn't waste any time. They just opened fire with the Retributors. Long, wasteful bursts, nearly silent because velocity on the weapons had been dialled down to subsonic so the rubber bullets didn't kill anyone, cut the miners down. It must have been like being hit by a sack full of hammers.

'Fire control, fire control!' Miska subvocalised over the comms link but her convict soldiers seemed to be having too much fun. All the miners on one side of the door were down. The Wraiths stopped firing. Two of them moved to cover up and down the corridor. The third covered the fourth Wraith as it knelt to check the still-glowing hole in the blast door. For a moment they almost looked like competent soldiers. Miska checked the lens feed from inside the stores. 'You've got two more inside, one immediately to the left of you ... no, your other left.' Then Miska was watching chain-fed, electromagnetically driven rubber bullets bounce around the inside of the stores. The Wraith by the hole shifted his position to the right and fired, just as a miner tried to make a run for it. Miska watched as the rubber bullets caught him in the back and side, spinning him around in mid-air and slamming him into the ground. The Wraith was suddenly wreathed in sparks and enough small explosions to stagger the power armour.

'Christos!' Hangman-Two-Five's operator spat. Miska sent an order to the blast door to open. It opened a few more inches and then jammed.

'Okay, your shooter is towards the back of the stores, he's behind a stack of what looks like regolith cement,' she told Hangman-Two-Five. The Wraith started firing from one knee. Hangman-Two-Six, who was supposed to be covering, leaned down and joined in. Inside the stores everything seemed to be airborne as they fired rubber bullet after rubber bullet into the space. Miska had no idea what hit the last miner, a direct shot, a ricochet, flying debris or all of the above, but he was down. 'Cease fire. Cease fire Goddammit!' She checked her IVD for the telemetry feed from their Wraiths. They'd used almost half of the rounds from their back-mounted ammunition pods. 'Hangman-Two-Five, secure that laser. Hangman-Two-Six, can you get in there?' She watched as Hangman-Two-Six tried to prise the door open. It budged a little under the Wraith's mechanical strength but not enough.

'That's a negative, Hangman-One-Actual,' Two-Six told her. Two-Five had slung the laser and was in the process of securing the miners with memory cable cuffs. She told them which area she wanted them to pacify next and turned her attention to the lens feed from the docks.

The docks were a wide-open area where cargo could be stacked, interspersed with three airlocks, each about a hundred metres apart – just enough room to allow access for a medium-sized freighter or some of the larger cargo shuttles. The dock was mainly for goods in. Goods out were fed directly from the automated refinery, where the shuttle carrying Miska and the other mercenaries had docked. The miners had two fortified positions between airlocks A and B, and B and C. The idea presumably being that the two strongpoints would enable them to cover all three airlocks. It wasn't how Miska would have done it, but it did mean that both of the cannons were pointed towards the airlocks. Most of the miners were behind the powdered-regolith-filled bags they were using as cover, but three of them were examining the two blast doors, trying to get them open. There were two miners at the left-hand door and one on the right. They were more than a little surprised when the blast doors slid open and Hangman-Two-Nine and Two-Ten strode in through the left blast door, while Two-Eleven and Two-Twelve strode in through the right.

Two-Nine picked up one of the miners as he tried to run and slammed him into the wall.

'Easy, Two-Nine,' Miska subvocalised over comms. Two-Ten and Two-Eleven cut the other two down as they attempted to flee back to the strongpoints. The rubber bullets sent the miners rolling across the floor from the multiple impacts. 'Concentrate your fire on the cannons.' *You idiots*, she decided not to add. The miners were struggling to bring the cannons around to bear on the new threat as rubber bullets impacted the multi-layered protective wall of regolith-filled bags. Miska couldn't believe what she was seeing. The four Wraiths were trying to walk the rounds in on their targets. Rubber bullets were flying everywhere. They were even shooting each other's power armour. Miska was relieved they weren't using real rounds. 'Get out of each other's fields of fire!' Miska wasn't subvocalising now. 'Use your smartlink, aim your shots, close in on the strong points.'

The four Wraiths moved closer to the wall so they weren't catching each other in their crossfire. Then they started taking short, controlled bursts. One of the cannons fired, then the other, but both shots were wide. The miners didn't dare raise their heads high enough to aim.

'Suppressing fire, close with them,' Miska told them. She was pleased that at least they had the presence of mind to do as they were told.

They marched towards the strongpoints firing short bursts. One miner who did raise her head took a nasty hit. The rubber bullet whipped her head around and she slithered back down out of sight. AK-47s were fired blindly over the top but the fire was wild and wouldn't have penetrated the Wraiths' armour anyway. Miska saw fingers, hands and wrists broken from the incoming rubber bullets, the archaic slugthrowers bent from impact. The Wraiths soon had the angle to fire into the strong-points. It was a shooting gallery as rubber bullet after rubber bullet hit the defenders.

'Okay, cease fire,' Miska told them.

'Uh, boss-lady, er ... I mean, Hangman-One-Actual,' Hangman-Two-Nine asked. 'Do you want us to junk these cannons?'

Miska took a moment to think about it. 'Negative, Two-Nine, secure them both and any ammo; bring them to me once you're finished.' She wanted to see them up-close. They might be useful.

She split the fire team into twos and sent them onto the next area she wanted pacified. Then she turned her attention to the third group, commanded by Mass, who had just reached the mercenary-filled crèche.

'Hangman-One-Actual to Hangman-Two-Actual, you want those doors opened?' she asked over comms. Out of all three patrols this one looked the most professional. Hangman-Two-Three and Two-Four covered the surrounding area while Two-Actual – Mass – and Two-Two covered the door to the crèche. Of course the problem was that Miska didn't have eyes on what was happening inside because the mercs had taken out the lens.

She was pretty sure they didn't have anything that could beat the Wraiths' armour, though. Pretty sure. They were certainly about to find out.

'Hangman-Two-Actual to One-Actual, sure, that'd be nice,' Mass replied. With a thought Miska sent an instruction to the station's systems to open the blast door. It slid open on a darkened crèche. Nothing happened.

'Well, that was something of an anti-climax,' Miska mused.

'Surrender or get hurt and then you'll have to surrender anyway, your choice.' Mass said, the Wraith's loudspeaker amplifying his voice. He sounded pretty relaxed. It was a compelling argument, she decided. Nothing happened. Mass's Wraith's head turned to look at Two-Two and nodded. Both of them fired a burst into the crèche. Miska thought she heard someone shout from inside and boosted the audio.

'... mind if I come out and speak to you?' Miska couldn't be sure but she thought it sounded like Reg. Mass didn't answer immediately.

'Sure,' he finally said. 'But no weapons, hands where I can see them.'

Reg emerged from the darkness, his hands held away from his side, no weapons on display. The mercenary commander took his time looking at the four Wraiths and then shook his head.

'Guys!' he shouted back into the crèche. 'We've got nothing that can touch them.' He turned back to Mass's Wraith, looking up at the power armour towering over him. 'Will you accept my parole if we surrender?' he asked.

'Your what?' Mass asked.

'Give my apologies to Reg, but no,' Miska told Mass. 'I'm afraid it's unconditional. They'll be disarmed and cuffed but 'not mistreated, they have my word on that.' Mass repeated what Miska had told him. Reg looked rueful but nodded.

'That's what I figured, nobody trusts anybody any more,' the mercenary commander said as his people emerged, unarmed, hands in the air. Mass somehow managed to get his Wraith to shrug.

'Good work, Mass. Now tell me that wasn't a rush?' Miska said.

'It didn't suck, bella,' he replied. She could hear in his voice that he was smiling.

They hunted down the rest of the miners. Some ran. Rubber bullets caught them in their backs, lifting them off their feet and sending them sprawling. Some surrendered, and Miska couldn't blame them. They didn't really stand a chance. They would have to explain their lack of bruises to their compatriots. The majority, however, fought. It was futile. The Wraiths strode among them like demigods, shrugging off gunfire and cutting the miners down, battering the fight out of them with rubber bullets until they could be disarmed and cuffed. A few hid. Most were found, some weren't. Miska knew that they would have to be rooted out the hard way. She was hoping to make that the TCC's problem.

'The station's ours,' she announced. It was time for them to get paid.

She didn't look at Torricone but she could feel his eyes on her.

CHAPTER 13

Chanar had gone by the time the two Wraiths arrived outside the ops centre's blast door. This was something of a worry as the corridor should have been locked down. There was a degree of inevitability in it, Miska decided – after all, the miners knew the station a lot better than she did. Ideally she wanted the relief forces that the TCC would be sending to handle Chanar and the other unaccounted-for miners. She had, however, posted two Wraiths – Hangman-Two-Three and Hangman-Two-Four – in the stores area where the industrial printers were. The printers were Chanar's best chance at securing more arms, though there were explosives in the stores as well. Hangman-Two-Five to Two-Eight were guarding the prisoners. A lot of them were pretty banged up but nobody was critical. Finding where the children had been hidden in a pressurised section of the mine had given her pause but she had assigned Hangman-Two-Nine to watch them. It had been made clear what would happen to him if anything happened to them. The thought of firing rubber bullets into a room full of children made even Miska's stomach turn. That left Two-Ten, Two-Eleven and Two-Twelve patrolling the vast station. It wasn't ideal but it would have to do. Hangman-Two-Actual and Two-Two were the Wraiths waiting for her when the blast door hissed open and Miska walked out into the corridor.

'Boss,' Mass's amplified voice said, the Wraith's head nodding in greeting.

'Good work, Mass, pass it onto your squad. I'm very pleased,' she said. Mass nodded again. Mass and Two-Two were carrying the cannon weapons taken from the strongpoints at the dock. Mass held his out and Miska examined it. Her integral computer ran through the data it held on historical weapons. It appeared that it was printed replica of something called a Lahti L-39 anti-tank rifle, which was more than four centuries old. Each weapon fired a 20mm bullet. The series of electromagnetic coils on the end of the ungainly and cumbersome weapon's barrel, the gauss-kiss, was designed to turn it into a rudimentary railgun. The gauss-kisses hadn't come from a printer, either, which meant they couldn't be easily replicated. It even looked as though they had primitive smartlinked targeting systems. The rounds were tungsten-cored penetrators.

'Would they have done any damage to us?' Mass asked.

Miska looked up at the armoured figure towering over her. 'I think they could have,' she told him. Of course the fast-moving Wraiths were always going to have the advantage in terms of manoeuvrability, but she was pretty sure the two anti-tank rifles were gun enough to penetrate the old suits of power armour.

'Uh, boss,' Two-Two said. His bio rolled down her IVD. Halliwell, James G, possession of illegal weapons, assault with a deadly weapon and three counts of second-degree murder stemming from a gang fight. He had been a member of an ice-forming construction gang on Proxima E. 'You're pleased with us right?'

'I just said so,' Miska said, not liking where this was going. She knew she had to incentivise the prisoners for active duty, but this really wasn't the time to sort that out.

'Well, I was wondering if we could round up some of the prisoners, y'know, for fun?' Miska stared up at Halliwell's Wraith. Mass's Wraith was shaking its armoured head. It was a weirdly human gesture.

'He's speaking for himself,' Mass said.

Halliwell's suit's head turned to look at his squad leader's and then back down at Miska, her face a mask of consternation.

'For non-consensual fun?' Miska asked.

Halliwell tried to make his Wraith shrug, but it didn't look right when he did it.

'Sure,' he said.

'You remember when I executed all the sex criminals, right?' she asked.

Halliwell shook the Wraith's finger at her. 'Ah! Ah! But you didn't, though,' Halliwell said. Miska's eyes went wide. 'You executed all the *convicted* sex criminals. I've never been convicted of any of that shit.'

'Jesus Christ,' Mass muttered holding his free hand to his Wraith's nearly featureless armoured face in another incongruously human gesture.

'Morally, what do you think the difference is?' Miska asked, genuinely interested in the answer.

'Well it's legal, innit?' he said.

Miska considered Halliwell's answer.

'Well, can we?' he asked again.

The Wraith rocked slightly but didn't fall over. The armour

contained the lowjack's explosion so well that she didn't even hear it.

'Shit,' Mass said. 'I ain't cleaning that up.'

Miska looked up at the Mafia button man. 'Did that sound like suicide to you?' she asked and then noticed that a blinking icon had appeared in her IVD. It was letting her know that she'd had an answer to the communication she'd sent some ninety minutes ago to Laura Gobbin on Proxima E. 'I want you on roving patrol with Ten, Eleven and Twelve, okay?'

'Sure,' Mass said and turned to head back down the corridor as Miska accessed the communication.

No visual, no audio, just text: *Execute all remaining miners on the station*. Miska froze and then read the message again. She had made a point of telling Gobbin in her original communiqué that she'd taken the station without killing anyone. She turned and headed back into the ops centre. It must have been written all over her face.

'Problems?' Torricone asked from where he was sat at one of the workstations.

She ignored him and composed a reply: *We don't do that. We've done what you hired us for. If you want the station then pay us and you can do what you want when you take possession*. It would take at least another ninety minutes before she heard a reply.

'They've told you to execute us all, haven't they?' Uboka asked.

'Quiet, please,' Miska said with a cheeriness she wasn't quite feeling.

'Have we got enough ammunition for that?' Nyukuti asked, causing a ripple of unease among the prisoners still in the ops centre. It had been a mistake not to have Mass move them to the nightclub where they were holding the rest of the miners. Though she still would have had to keep Uboka separate.

'We're not executing them,' Torricone said.

'Who do you think'll take the fall for it? They'll hang us out to dry,' Gleave said quietly.

'Okay, that's enough,' Miska said. She was starting to understand why Gobbin had hired them.

Ninety-two minutes later the shape of the HR executive's plan became even more apparent. Gobbin's reply had been very simple: *Understood. Relief forces en route.* Moments later a sleek, violent and very modern-looking frigate hove into view suspiciously close to the station.

'Transponder says it's the *Excelsior*,' Gleave told her. It seemed he'd uploaded a sensor operations skillsoft from somewhere. He might have been a blatant coward but he continued to make himself useful. 'It belongs to a military contractor outfit. Stirling Security Solutions.'

'Where the fuck'd that come from?' Merrill asked from the net where he was monitoring the situation.

'Probably hiding in one of the cored asteroids,' Miska muttered. She'd heard of Triple-S. They were run by and recruited from ex-members of UKSF and their support units. If they were close by then they would have been more than capable of taking the station themselves. Which meant that Miska and her people were there for another reason.

Torricone had come to the same conclusion. 'Wow, have we been betrayed by the greedy and abusive hypercorp with a secret to hide? Who would have thought it?'

Miska ignored the car thief and sent a text message to her dad on board the *Hangman's Daughter*: *Dad, can you bring the ship out to play? We've got a frigate in our space. I want you to put yourself in a position to fire on it if need be.* She was still too angry to speak to him.

She received a text reply a moment later: *Will do, Pumpkin.* It was about as close to contrition as her father ever got, with his youngest daughter anyway. *But we've only got the autopilot. If it turns into a shooting war then they'll fly rings around us.* It was something that she already knew. She sent a terse acknowledgement and let him know that the contractors were about to come on board. Standing in the middle of the ops centre she felt as though all eyes were on her.

'You know that they're going to massacre all the prisoners and blame us – well, you – for it, right?' Torricone asked.

Miska opened her mouth to answer but another icon appeared in her IVD, an incoming message from the *Excelsior*. This one had sound and vision. Salon-styled black hair, parted in the middle like a wave, a weak chin, and slightly podgy face, though from what she could see of his shoulders she suspected he was in good shape. He undoubtedly had 'ware but she couldn't see any, which suggested subtle, which in turn suggested sophisticated and expensive.

'Good day, Corporal Corbin.' He had a posh English accent, upper middle class at least, Miska reckoned. 'It is Corporal Corbin, isn't it?' His tone was just patronising enough so you knew your place. It was clear he felt he was dealing with an NCO who was in way over her head. She wasn't entirely sure he was wrong but that didn't mean he had to be a jerk about it.

'Miska's fine,' she told him.

'I am Major Sheldon Cartwright ...' he told her. Miska burst out laughing.

'Oh, I'm so sorry,' she subvocalised, trying to control herself. Gleave, Torricone and even Nyukuti were all looking at her now. 'But what a name. I thought you were going to say "the third", or something, at the end there.'

He frowned. 'The fourth, actually.'

Miska burst out laughing again. It was obvious he couldn't see the reason for the laughter. As she tried to control herself it became clear from the expression on Cartwright's face that there was going to be something of a gulf in their worldviews.

'I am so sorry,' Miska said, managing to pull herself together.

'That's quite all right,' he told her in a way that made her suspect that it wasn't. 'I understand there's some issue with your orders?'

'None whatsoever,' Miska answered.

'Then the prisoners …?'

'Are all fine and well.' She gave it some thought. 'Well, maybe a little the worse for wear.'

Cartwright sighed. 'Corporal—' he started.

'Miska,' she told him.

'I can't really think of a way to put this delicately. You're in charge of a small army of murderous scum …'

'Quite a large army, actually, practically a Roman legion's worth.' She could tell that he neither liked nor was used to being interrupted by the rank and file. Though she was pretty sure he'd never commanded six thousand 'soldiers'. It also told her that he wasn't a good special forces officer. They had no problems dealing with enlisted personnel on an equal basis.

'Nevertheless, your men are clearly the right people for this particular job, distasteful though it may be.'

'We were hired to take the station and, despite the bad intel, we did it. You want to commit a war crime? You go right ahead and do that, but only after we've been paid for the job we've done, understand me?'

'Miss Corbin, I'm not sure that you're entirely cut out for this line of work—' he started.

'Is it my army of "murderous scum" that gives it away?' she asked, more bemused than angry.

'Big boys' games, big boys' rules. We shouldn't even have to be having this conversation; what you were expected to do was implicit in your briefing.'

'I'm a very literal person,' she told him, crossing her arms. Now she was tiring of him being a patronising cockbag.

'Okay, enough of this. One of my men is on board, you should consider him in charge and follow his orders. I'll have him make himself known to you,' Cartwright told her.

The comms screen went blank. She waited. A few moments later he appeared in the window again.

'Having problems getting through to him?' she asked. Joshua would have been comms-silent during his infiltration. Without a powerful transmitter of his own, which in itself would have been something of a giveaway, he would have had to sneak any comms through via the station's systems. It would have been too much of a risk while the Che virus was in control.

'Miss Corbin, I hope you haven't done anything too foolish.'

'I once ate some chilli chocolate that was six-point-four million on the Scolville scale,' she told him. Judging by the look in his face they didn't share much of a sense of humour either. 'He's safe, but I can't think of a terribly compelling reason to hand over my command to him.'

'Miss Corbin, you're being neither terribly reasonable nor professional ...'

'Reasonable and professional would be for the TCC to pay me what's owed ...'

'Has it escaped your notice that we have a frigate loaded with seasoned operators—?' he started.

Miska muted the conversation with a thought,

'Gleave,' she said out loud. 'Any sign of the *Daughter*?'

'Just hove in view over the planetary horizon,' Gleave told her.

She unmuted the conversation.

'—please don't let us go down the path of exchanging ...' Cartwright stopped and concentrated. Miska guessed he was receiving information, probably about the appearance of the *Hangman's Daughter*.

'Big boys' rules?' she asked. 'Mine's bigger than yours. Tell Gobbin to deposit the money and the station's all yours.'

In the end Miska agreed that Cartwright and three of his people could come on board to get eyes on the situation. If it was as Miska claimed, then he would advise Gobbin to release the funds. In the meantime Miska had contacted her dad and told him to assemble a QRF, or Quick Reaction Force, made up of the most promising of the remaining prisoners that they had the resources to equip. That would amount to something like one hundred men, two platoons worth, plus the other twelve Wraiths. They could well be massacred if Triple-S fielded even a tenth of that number. Then she contacted Mass and warned him that they were about to have company. She told him to take Hangman-Two-Ten, Eleven and Twelve and the two anti-tank rifles and lay low. To Mass's credit he didn't ask her what was going on, he just did it.

'What's going on?' Torricone – clearly Mass's diametric

opposite in terms of discipline – asked. She didn't answer. She was too busy doing a surface search of Faigroe Station's systems looking for where Chanar had stowed Joshua.

'I've got an assault shuttle leaving the *Excelsior*,' Gleave told them. There was a lot of nervous shuffling and muttered conversation in the room. 'It's heading this way.'

Miska checked the status of the station's weapon systems. Those that the *Hangman's Daughter* hadn't destroyed during the initial assault seemed in reasonable working order, though she would have to rely on their automated targeting systems. They might, *might*, get the assault shuttle but a frigate that size carried more than one shuttle and it was capable of standing off and destroying the station's weapons from afar. The weapons were there to dissuade opportunistic pirates, not go toe-to-toe with military-grade craft.

'Are we under attack?' Gleave asked, unable to stop his voice from shaking.

'No, they're sending people on board to check we've done what we said we've done,' Miska said.

'Then why the precautions?' Torricone asked.

'Because we're all cautious people,' Miska said, and then smiled brightly.

'You're not,' Torricone pointed out. 'And you know that they're going to come in here, kill the prisoners.'

'What's that got to do with us?' Miska asked. It sounded harsh even to her ears but they were mercenaries now. Torricone looked as though she'd slapped him. He was off his chair and striding across the ops centre towards her.

'There are children here!' he said pointing through the rock.

'What do you want me to do?' Miska asked, once again

wondering why she didn't just blow his collar. On the other hand, she had the feeling that she might need his services soon.

'Release the prisoners, join forces with them,' Torricone said. He was almost pleading. It had gone very quiet in the ops centre.

'To what end?' Miska asked.

'What do you mean to what—' Torricone started.

'We work with the miners, perhaps the QRF get here in time to help, maybe the *Hangman's Daughter* even frightens off the *Excelsior*. Fine. Then what? You think the TCC is going to give up just like that?'

'She's right,' Nyukuti said quietly. 'They'd just come back here and do what they were going to do anyway.'

'Except we'd be dead as well,' Miska added.

'We do what they were going to do,' Torricone said pointing at Uboka. 'Hold out long enough for it to become unprofitable for them to take it back.'

'How'd that work for them?' Miska asked nodding towards Uboka, trussed up face-down on the floor. She could see the desperation writ all over Torricone's face. She glanced up at the crown of thorns tattoo circling his head. 'They can't afford to fail here and they are effectively a nation state in this system, with a nation state's power to bring to bear.'

'Makes you wonder why they bothered with you, doesn't it?' Uboka said from the ground.

'Then we evacuate the station,' Torricone said. 'Take them somewhere else.' Miska just laughed.

'Then how do we profit from it?' Miska asked.

Now Uboka was laughing. 'You do not know the TCC,' she said. 'There is no profit here for you. They will blame our massacre on your undisciplined penal legion. They will make themselves the heroes but too late for us. Witness the price of betrayal.'

Torricone was nodding as Uboka spoke.

'They're requesting permission to dock,' Gleave said.

'She's right, you know she is,' the car thief said and Miska did know, or at least strongly suspected. *But we have to play this through. We can't be the guys who broke contract, or nobody will ever touch us again*, she thought.

'Gleave, give them permission to dock. Nyukuti, Torricone, I want you there to meet them. Only four come on board. They can keep their weapons but no power armour,' she said. Torricone opened his mouth to protest. 'Look at it this way,' she told him. 'If it kicks off, *these* guys you can fight.'

Torricone turned away from her and stormed across the ops centre to grab his Glock and an AK-47. 'Oh, that won't be a problem,' he muttered as he made for the blast door, followed by Nyukuti. 'That won't be a problem at all.'

With a thought she dipped into the net, not a full immersion. She watched her cartoon icon, little more than a ghost, skip across the virtual distance between the station's pirate port net representation and the *Hangman's Daughter*'s prison hulk in a window in her IVD. Her access allowed her to view the cellblocks on the prison barge through the security lenses. She skipped through them until she found the one she was looking for. Then she made the arm rotate until she was looking at the alabaster sculpture that was the Ultra.

'What are you doing?' Her dad was standing next to the ghost of her cartoon icon in the *Hangman's Daughter*'s net architecture, looking at the window showing the feed from solitary. It would have taken her longer to go in unnoticed, and she probably would have had to do it tranced-in. He would have known she was in the systems as soon as she had used her access.

'I don't like how this is going down,' she admitted.

'You think these people are the answer?' he asked. She could tell from his voice that he was starting to have some very serious doubts about his daughter. For her part she was still pretty pissed off with him. The marines had trusted her with multi-million-dollar weapons systems like power armour. The CIA hadn't thought twice about sending her to assassinate terrorist leaders. Her dad, on the other hand, didn't trust her judgement.

'That's the thing, Dad. I don't think they are people, they're weapons.'

'Some weapons you just shouldn't use,' he said, after a long pause.

'And yet somehow the trigger always gets pulled,' she mused, but she knew the Ultra wasn't the answer, not yet. She suspected the three in solitary were weapons of spite, a human scorched-earth policy. They weren't there yet.

Miska closed the window, her full attention now refocused on the ops centre. She turned towards one of the holographic displays showing lens feed from the dock's exterior. The assault shuttle, a sleek, angular, predatory craft, heavily armoured and bristling with comms antennae, sensor pods and weapons, was backing towards one of the airlocks, its manoeuvring jets burning as it made incremental positional changes. She glanced down at the prisoners and wished again that she'd moved them.

CHAPTER 14

Miska watched the docking bay's lens feed as Cartwright came on board. She saw Torricone hold up his hand. He wasn't broadcasting but she guessed he was telling the major that he could only bring three more men with him. Something about the body language suggested to Miska that Cartwright had a lot more people in the ship. That was confirmed when Torricone subvocalised over the comms link that he'd seen at least three more contractors, one of whom was wearing power armour that looked a lot more up-to-date than their Wraiths.

Cartwright had a good look around at the docking bay as he walked through, seeing the results of the brief battle. It looked as though he was trying to engage Torricone and Nyukuti in conversation, but neither of them were having any of it. Even through the grainy lens feed Torricone's disgust was obvious.

Miska tracked him through the station as the contractors made their way towards the ops centre. She had made sure that they weren't going near where the prisoners or the children were being held, nor where the Wraiths were on guard, for the time being. She had a chance to have a better look at the contractors. They wore their night black fatigues and body armour like sports casual. It made them look like designer corporate storm troopers. The way they moved suggested that they had been extensively augmented but nothing was on show, any 'ware was subtle. Their gear was the best that money could buy. They carried Martian Military Industries gauss personnel defence weapons. The compact, ergonomically designed weapons were perfect for close quarter battle in confined spaces like ships and stations. Each had a single shot 25mm grenade launcher mounted on a rail just under the main weapon's stubby barrel. Miska remembered what Rafael had told her about the TCC having a possible Martian connection. It made her wonder if Cartwright and his people had been augmented with Small Gods' tech.

'Hangman-One-Four to Hangman-One-Actual,' Merrill said over the comms link from the net. The modulated demonic growl of the icon was still not quite enough to disguise the boy doing the talking. 'One of them's a hacker, the woman I think. She's having a surface look around.' Miska looked back at the lens feed. They were making their way through the dorm area, a diversion designed to bypass the rec area to avoid the nightclub where the prisoners were being kept. Cartwright and his people were walking in a rough diamond formation. The only woman with them was tall, muscular, with dark hair, shaved at the sides, longer on top.

'How long do these people spend on their hair?' she muttered to herself.

'Boss?' Merrill asked.

'Has she seen you?' Miska asked.

'No, I'm stealthed.'

'Stay that way, let her have a look around. She seen the virus?'

'The crystal cage kind of acts like a prism in the sunlight.'

Miska just nodded to herself. 'Seen any indication of the virus resurgent?'

'Pirates made of sand keep trying to grow out of the beach, and drowned pirates made of the black water keep on trying to walk out of the sea. I'm squashing them when I see them.'

Miska gave this some thought. 'Don't,' she finally said.

'You sure? If it gets strong enough they can try and bridge into the ore refinery systems and release the main virus.'

'If it goes according to plan then the station will soon be changing hands. They look capable, we'll SEP it.'

'SEP it?'

'Someone else's problem,' Miska explained.

Nyukuti, Torricone and the four contractors were in the corridor outside the ops centre now. Miska wandered over to meet them as they reached the open blast door. Cartwright was looking up at the stationary Wraith that Halliwell had been piloting before he'd committed suicide with his mouth. His body was still inside. Cartwright pointed at it.

'Discipline problems?' he asked. Miska didn't like how astute a guess that was but she did her best not to show it. Instead she just smiled as he went on, 'I do apologise for my manner over comms. Major Sheldon Cartwright, Strategic Security Solutions, pleasure to finally meet you face-to-face.'

Miska managed not to laugh at his name again as she shook his proffered hand. 'Miska,' she told him, noticing that an intro-duction to the three contractors with him wasn't forthcoming. 'Strategic Security Solutions. See, that's a good name for a mercenary crew.' His lips twitched a little at the description. 'I'm really struggling to come up with a name, well, not really a name, a brand. Do you know what I mean?'

'I had nothing to do with it, I'm afraid. It was our marketing and PR department that came up with it.'

'Marketing and PR department? We'll have to get one of those.' Miska decided that she would rather choke to death on her own vomit than get a marketing and PR department.

'Indeed.' Cartwright's smile suggested that he was patiently, if somewhat patronisingly, humouring her. 'Perhaps something visceral that suggests your origins as a penal legion.'

Miska wasn't really sure if she was being made fun of or not. She'd had this feeling in the past when dealing with the British officer class. One time it had resulted in a broken nose – not hers – and a demotion. Hers. She did notice that one of the men with Cartwright was trying not to smirk.

'I'll give it some thought. So I checked our account, it doesn't look like there's anything there.' She hadn't changed her expression. She was still smiling. Cartwright, however, looked somewhat sheepish.

'Ah, there we must apologise. It seems there's been a degree of confusion. One hand not knowing what the other hand was doing, I'm afraid.'

'And our money?'

'Our?' one of the contractors asked. He wore his blond hair short and spiked up, and had a compact, powerful build and broken nose that made Miska wonder if he'd played rugby. 'I thought your men were slaves.' Miska turned to look at him, not letting her smile falter. Contempt was written all over his face.

'Aren't we all?' she asked. He opened his mouth to retort but Cartwright held up his hand.

'That's enough,' he said quietly. The blond contractor went back to looking around at the ops centre. The other two were

214

doing the same. The woman was also, presumably, simultaneously surface-checking the net. They never let their situational awareness drop. Even Cartwright was looking around, his right hand always on his PDW's ergonomic grip.

'Does this confusion explain the goalposts moving when you tried to give me orders?' Miska asked cheerfully.

'Yes. We were told one thing, clearly you were told another.'

'So, you going to kill all the prisoners?' Torricone demanded. Cartwright didn't look at the car thief, just raised an eyebrow.

'Okay, that's enough,' Miska said. Then she sent Torricone a text strongly recommending that he shut the fuck up. He lapsed into a fuming silence. Cartwright held up a small cred stick.

'Your money,' he said. Miska stared at the black cred stick. She could upload the electronic funds into her account through social media, but until such a time as the information had been ratified with her bank, i.e. she had sent the signal and had it confirmed, the information would remain in her head. Her bank's closest branch was on Proxima E, more than forty light minutes away, and she would need to broadcast it via the stations transmitter, which she still didn't fully trust. The last thing she wanted was the Che virus tracking her money.

A blinking icon in her IVD told her that she had received a text from Nyukuti. It read: *Boss, part of what I used to do was torture codes for internal fund storage from people. If they've got a cracker good enough they'll be able to recover the funds from your corpse's neuralware.* She'd worked that out herself but it was nice that he cared.

'Is there a problem?' Cartwright asked. She could feel both Torricone and Nyukuti tense up but she took the black cred stick from Cartwright. Her integral computer made contact with the stick and started running diagnostics on it, looking for

215

any viral infections. If it was clean she would risk uploading it to her internal systems.

'Just out of interest, why didn't they just give you guys the job in the first place?' Miska asked. She was pretty sure she knew the answer but she wanted to see what Cartwright would say.

'Honestly?' Cartwright asked. *No, I want you to lie to me*, she decided not to say and just nodded instead. 'The TCC modelled it and the most likely outcome was that your people would massacre the miners.' Miska was both impressed and somewhat suspicious of his forthrightness. She was aware of Torricone shaking with rage.

'Murderers!' Uboka spat from the ground.

'Seems my people were a little more disciplined than you thought. They're good boys,' Miska said, ignoring the mine leader. There was a snort of derision from the blond contractor.

'It must come easier when your men all have explosive collars on,' he said.

'You'd be surprised,' Miska told him. 'But I'm afraid it does mean you'll have to do your own dirty work.'

'Fucking scum,' the blond contractor muttered.

'We're scum?' Torricone spat. Miska caught his eye and shook her head. She was pretty sure that Cartwright noticed.

'You're no better than them,' Uboka cried. 'You're just going to let them kill us!'

Torricone looked stricken.

'Well, let's start,' Cartwright said. He drew his sidearm and put two rounds in the back of Uboka's head, hollowing it out, spreading her face across the metal grill of the floor, blood dripping through onto the rock. The prisoners screamed.

'No!' Torricone was bringing his AK-47 up. He might as well have been moving in molasses in comparison with Cartwright.

216

Miska moved herself between Torricone and the major, arms upraised. Nyukuti was reacting as well but the female contractor, their hacker, had him covered with her PDW. The blond contractor was covering a pale, shaking Gleave, and the fourth, a small, quiet, nondescript man, was covering the open blast door.

'Can't let the prisoners mouth off like that, particularly not in your situation,' Cartwright said, his pistol now still hanging loose at his side. 'Bad for morale, you see?' He smiled at her.

Miska would have quite liked to have shot him there and then. She could feel the anger pouring off Torricone behind her. She hoped he realised that she was just trying to keep him alive. A glance to her side at Nyukuti told her that the stand-over man wasn't terribly happy either, though she suspected for different reasons. Miska lowered her hands and went to put her right hand back on the grip of her AK-47.

'Maybe just keep your hand off the weapons?' Cartwright suggested.

'Okay, look, you seem really polite and everything but it's obvious that you're an asshole—' Miska started.

'It's pronounced arsehole, you ignorant bitch,' the blond contractor told her. Miska decided that if the opportunity presented itself she was going to kill him.

'So why don't I just take my people and our money and leave you to your war crime?' Miska asked over the prisoners' sobs. She felt Torricone flinch behind her.

'Where is my man Joshua?' Cartwright asked.

'He's around here somewhere,' Miska said. 'I'll probably remember, once me and my people are off the station.'

'My people and I,' Cartwright corrected. He was starting to affect her normally-cheery demeanour.

'Whatever. Maybe you guys should lower your weapons in case we start to get the wrong idea.'

'Maybe you should just answer the fucking question,' the blond contractor snapped.

'Yeah, that should work,' Torricone muttered. Miska glanced at the blond and then back to Cartwright.

'Starting to feel a bit hostile in here, isn't it? Just because we kill people for a living doesn't mean we have to be all aggressive,' she said sounding more reasonable than she felt.

Cartwright motioned for his people to lower their weapons, which they did, the blond one reluctantly. Miska's diagnostic check on the black cred stick was done. She started uploading the funds into her own systems to hold. If it was a burn, and it was certainly starting to look that way, then she was damn well going to make them work to get the money back.

'Kill them now, later, what difference does it make?' Cartwright asked, to the sound of renewed tears and begging from the prisoners on the floor.

'Shut the fuck up!' the blond shouted, cowing them into near-silence except for the snivelling. Miska prayed that Torricone didn't do anything stupid. She could still feel him seething just behind her.

'The virus?' Cartwright enquired.

'Contained,' she told him. The major looked at the female contractor, who just nodded.

'Then you just need to bring me my man ...' he paused for a second. Miska was pretty sure that he was receiving a message. 'And we can arrange the changeover.'

'I've told you, when we're clear we'll let you know—' Miska started. Cartwright pointed his gauss pistol at her head.

'Oh, don't do that,' Gleave moaned just loud enough for everyone to hear.

The blond contractor took a couple of steps to his side so that he could cover both Torricone and Nyukuti, and the woman turned to cover Gleave, who looked just about ready to expire from sheer terror right there and then on the spot.

'Are you out of your mind?' Miska asked as she composed a text. 'Army of six thousand psychos?'

'Best estimate, you can maybe field a hundred,' Cartwright said. *Well shit*, Miska thought.

'And the heavily armed ship with a metric fuck-tonne of ordnance pointing at your little frigate?'

'I've got two ships slowing down from sunward,' Gleave said. Miska was impressed that he'd managed to keep an eye open through his fear. *The message Cartwright received*, she thought.

'Class?' Miska asked.

'I'm no expert,' Gleave told her, sounding shaky. 'But light cruisers, I think.' Miska guessed that they were TCC's own private navy. Either cruiser was probably a match for the *Hangman's Daughter*. Miska sent the text.

'Now, I think you should perhaps put your weapons on the floor,' Cartwright suggested.

'If you're about to try and shoot us it would seem like a good idea to hold onto them,' Nyukuti pointed out with, to Miska's mind, faultless logic.

'There is always hope,' Cartwright told him. 'Not laying your weapons down is the absence of hope.'

'Please! Just do what they're asking!' Gleave cried as he put his Glock on the floor and slid it away from him.

219

'You must know I won't hesitate to shoot you in the head,' Cartwright said, and Miska believed him.

'Please don't,' Gleave begged him. Miska could see the curiosity on the major's face. She was trying to will Gleave into silence. 'Because if you kill her it triggers the collars and we all die.' Miska's heart sank.

'Really?' Cartwright said.

'Why the fuck would you tell him that?' Torricone demanded.

'I am very angry with you,' Nyukuti told Gleave. Miska saw the conman blanch further.

'Do it,' Miska told them. She put her AK-47 down on floor and then reached for her sidearm.

'Slowly, and carefully, two fingers only. It sounds like we can't afford any accidents here,' Cartwright said, smiling. Neither Nyukuti or Torricone had put their weapons down. 'I will have them shot,' Cartwright promised.

'Do it,' Miska ordered. Torricone put his AK-47 on the floor and then the Glock that he wore at his hip. Much more slowly Nyukuti laid his M-19 down. Miska drew the SIG Sauer GP-692 that she'd taken off Joshua, and dropped it on the floor.

'You sure?' Merrill asked over their comms link from the net, answering the text she'd sent him. Only Miska could hear it. Cartwright glanced down at the SIG.

'He'd better still be alive,' he said.

'Uh huh,' Miska said as she hooked her finger through the ring at the end of her knife's hilt and slowly drew it from the sheath on the front of her jacket. She appeared to be answering Cartwright but she hoped that Merrill understood.

Nyukuti had put his Glock down on the floor. He was staring at the blond contractor as he slowly drew the folded boomer-sword. Suddenly all the lights in the ops centre went

220

off, the blast door started to close, and every holographic display showed the red-coloured, manically laughing head of Che Guevara as Merrill released the virus from the refinery's systems. A muffled explosion, little more than a dull *crump*, and Gleave's head went tumbling up into the air.

CHAPTER 15

6 MONTHS AGO

Miska was so tired that she barely felt atmospheric entry. She was aware of fire licking around the view ports of the military transport shuttle. She was sat in the barely padded metal frame of one of the bench seats, her head lolling back, eyes rolling up, as she started to nod off before the shuttle jostled her back into something approaching wakefulness. The cavernous shuttle bay was practically empty. It had the same uncomfortable and utilitarian interior that seemed common to all military vehicles. Inanely she wondered if the military vehicles owned by the rich equatorial states of Earth were more luxurious.

You're hysterical, *she told herself. She needed some sleep but she was heading back to the closest place that she had to a home. Sirius 4. Or Dog 4 as most military personnel still referred to it, a holdover from the War with Them. She wouldn't quite describe herself as excited. She was, however, looking forward to going home. It had been a rough mission. Extended stealth* recon, nightside on a cold, tidally locked, moon, the sort of place that humans only went if they wanted to hide something. In this case an illegal nanotech manufactory. Seven weeks of living in a pressurised tent buried in the methane ice with two Special Forces guys. Eating crappy rations and shitting into a flask, only for the manufactory to be destroyed by a missile strike that caused a cryo-volcano eruption that destroyed any evidence. The missile strike had caused so much interest in the moon from some of the other governments in-system that the three of them had to hump it deeper into the hot dayside for a somewhat perilous shuttle pickup.

Her eyes flickered open again as they hit turbulence in a cloudbank. She had no idea what the local time was, she had shut down the majority of the displays in her IVD, but as the shuttle dropped out of the cloud, somewhere in her exhausted brain, Miska realised it was night over Camp Basilone. The camp stretched out below her lit up like a very orderly city, the low, prefab and printed buildings all set out in precise military fashion. Beyond the command centres, administration offices, real and virtual training facilities, armouries and munitions storage, garages, workshops, vehicle, power armour and mech parks, were acres of wilderness that the marines used for running exercises, and beyond the marine base, the terraformed prairies. It was cattle country, mostly British and American territory. Her mom's family had lived here for two generations, which seemed like a long time in the colonies.

Sirius B had set, Sirius A was dropping towards the horizon, its pale light bathing the landscape in a deep blue twilight that Miska had always loved when she was growing up. She'd called Basilone City, the large town that bordered the marine base, home. The town simultaneously provided civilian services to the base as well as acting as a railhead for the local cattle industry, to transport stock two thousand miles south to the imaginatively named equatorial Capital City, and the planet's only orbital elevator.

She had drifted off again, and it was the thump of the landing that woke her. She forced herself to stand up, swaying a little, then she grabbed her pack, slinging it over one shoulder, and picked up her laser carbine. The Special Forces guys were doing likewise. If they felt anything like her then they were probably too tired to feel uncomfortable about being the only two army dogs on a marine base.

The rear ramp on the transport started to come down as she made her way towards it. The widening gap in the rear of the transport shuttle letting in the cold, prairie night air, that and the blue light, made it feel like home and promised sleep. Instead, the lowering ramp revealed Rafael, her CIA handler, along with a number of military police SWAT team members, including two in M-984 Honey Badger power armour suits.

'Huh,' Miska said as she saw them. 'They here for you guys?' she asked the two Special Forces guys. One of them grunted in reply, signalling a negative. Miska racked her brain trying to remember just how drunk she'd got the last time she'd visited Camp Basilone.

Rafael was approaching them. He was gesturing for the two Special Forces guys to move away from her. They both stopped and looked at Miska. They may have got on each other's nerves stuck in the pressure tent for so long but they were good guys.

'It's all right,' she told them both. They nodded and moved away. Miska glanced at Rafael and the MP SWAT guys.

'What's going on, Raff?' she asked.

'Do you trust me?' he asked her. There was something very

wrong here. He sounded either really worried, or really scared.
She couldn't work out which. She just shrugged. She was too
tired to really think about any of it right now.

'We need you to put your weapons down,' he told her. That
got her attention. She took a step back, ready to drop the pack
if need be. She was aware of the SWAT guys tensing. A quick
glance told her that most of them had non-lethal weapons in
their hands but they were carrying lethal weapons as well.

'Why do you need me to trust you while I'm unarmed?'
She had family members she didn't like to be around without
her knife at least. 'What are they doing here? Are they here to
arrest me?' She'd done a lot of naughty things for the CIA. She
wouldn't be the first operative burned out of political necessity
when the winds of change blew through the Company.

'No, nothing like that,' Rafael told her. Now she was proper-
ly awake, and worried. He had something to tell her and he was
so worried he'd brought along a SWAT team.

'What?' she said, stepping forward. The MPs stepped for-
ward as well. 'Is it Angela?' She wasn't quite sure what her sister
did for the NSA but she'd heard rumours that she was Black
Chamber, their blacker-than-black ops team. It meant that she
was on the sharp edge.

'Your weapons,' Rafael said.

'Fuck's sake, Raff!' Miska snapped. She dropped her pack.
Leaned her laser carbine on it, and put the gauss pistol on top
of it.

'And the knife and grenades,' Rafael told her.

'Raff, I can kill you with my bare hands. Stop fucking
around!' She was walking towards him now and he was backing
away as the SWAT team members came forward. 'Tell me what
the fuck's going on!'

'It's your dad. He was killed ...' he told her.

Everything seemed to stop. It didn't make sense. Killed, not dead. Dad hadn't been on active duty in years, and that was before he retired. She heard screaming. It was in her head. Then it wasn't. It was her. It took her a while to work out what had happened. She hadn't lost control like that since high school, maybe basic training. She hadn't been trying to kill Raff, she knew that, because she hadn't used her knife. She was pretty sure that she hadn't meant to throw a grenade at one of the Honey Badgers. They'd hit her with a lot of gel shots and taser rounds. In the end it had been the other Honey Badger that had yanked her off Raff and stood on her, pinning her as she fought and screamed, bloodying herself on the ground.

They'd restrained her, as much to stop her from hurting herself as anything else, and then put her in lockup until she'd managed to calm down. Eventually she'd worn out from sheer exhaustion. She'd woken up, remembered and filled several hours with crying jags. No tears from her artificial eyes. In some ways it had been a blessing that she was locked in a cell for that time. Raff and the MPs had been good enough to just let her get it out of her system. Eventually they let her out. She showered, changed. Stowed her gear on automatic and found Raff waiting for her outside the dorm block where she'd been assigned a room. He was leaning on a rental four-wheel-drive.

'Take me home,' she told him. She'd beaten the shit out of him, his neck was covered in multiple bruises the size and shape of her fingers. He was lucky she hadn't killed him, so was she, but yet here he was. He opened his mouth to say something but one look from her and he shut it again.

They made one stop on the way there, a liquor store. Because that'll help, *she thought.*

They'd broken the sealed crime scene tape on her father's bungalow. This had alerted the police but it seemed that Raff had some pull locally, and with one call he'd persuaded the authorities to leave them alone.

Miska had walked into the house that she'd spent most of her teenaged years in, the place that, after years of moving from system-to-system, base-to-base before her mom died, still seemed most like home. Now, however, with wall screens inert, with pieces cut out of the carpet where it had been taken for forensic analysis, with boards over smashed windows, with holes punched and shot through the wall, with the blood splatter, now it was an alien environment. It was clear that her father had put up a fight. What she didn't understand was why he hadn't won it.

She broke the seal on the bottle of Scotch and took a long swallow from it. Let it burn all the way down her gullet.

'Where's the furniture?' she asked. She was sitting on the floor next to the French windows looking out at the overgrown garden and the roofs of the neighbours' houses. The bungalow was in a faceless suburb not far from the base. Her dad had never managed to make it too far from the marines. Even after he'd left the Corps he'd worked as a consultant and civilian trainer, never quite able to fully retire and live the life of leisure both his daughters felt he deserved. A life he'd never really wanted.

She'd been happy here, Miska decided. She hadn't known it then; she'd been too young, still too angry at the death of the mom she'd barely known. A lot of the trouble she'd found when she was younger had been her own doing, she reflected.

'Angela had the place cleared out once the investigation was finished. She put it all in storage.'

'Well she's nothing if not efficient,' Miska muttered. 'Still, I'm surprised she turned up.'

Raff came over to lean against the window frame. He didn't say anything. He just reached for the bottle of Scotch.

'Bad time to be a bitch?'

Raff shrugged. 'Families,' he said as though that explained it.

She looked up at the cuts and bruises he had on display. 'Shit, I'm really sorry, Raff, you didn't deserve that.'

He tried to laugh. 'Ow! I went into it with my eyes open. I knew what was going to happen.' He considered something for a moment or two. 'Though I had hoped the SWAT team would be more use.'

Miska laughed. There wasn't much humour in it but it was the first time she had done so since he'd told her.

'They're just MPs,' Miska told him. 'You shouldn't have come forward.'

'Yep,' he said smiling ruefully. 'I should have stayed behind them, broken the news with a loudhailer.' She laughed again.

'Transfer the file over,' she told him. He opened his mouth to say something. 'Let's assume we've had the conversation where you tell me this is a bad idea.' He slid down the window frame to sit on the floor opposite her and passed the Scotch back. Miska saw the icon of the texted file blinking in her IVD. She steeled herself and opened it.

Half a bottle of Scotch later she leaned back against the frame and crossed her arms.

'This seem legit to you?' she asked. She watched Raff sigh.

'Miska ...'

'Just answer the fucking question,' she told him.

'They got the—' he started.

'Oh bullshit!' She was angry again but this was a cold anger. This was something that she could hold onto.

'Dad wasn't paranoid but we had strong doors, good locks and a half-decent alarm. They bypass all of them ...'

'So they were competent—' Raff started.

Miska pointed at the holes in the wall.

'Dad comes out shooting with his old SIG, because he's too fucking stubborn to update to the 992. He's carrying his antique .45 as backup. He shoots through the wall, EM-driven penetrator round. Tags them, and they don't go down.'

'They were armoured ...'

'That's pretty high-spec armour. They tag him, through the wall. They either know what they're doing, or they're wearing thermographics, possibly both ...'

'Thermographics are available to civilians ...'

'And the weapons they're carrying—'

'Are civilian,' Raff protested.

'Yeah!' Miska cried. 'A Void Eagle, big bore alien hunter firing AP rounds, and a Remington Compact 12-gauge firing discarded sabot-fin-stabilised armour-piercing rounds. Are you fucking kidding me?'

'You get a decent printer and—' Raff started.

'Both weapons with gauss-kisses,' Miska pointed out. Raff was quiet. 'It sounds like they knew who they were dealing with – a veteran with military grade dermal armour – and they brought the tools they needed to do the job.' Raff opened his mouth again but Miska held up her hand, silencing him. 'Now, even if we assume that they just happened to be competent and well-armed criminals, it kind of comes apart for the next bit.

229

He gets close enough to engage them in hand-to-hand. Two criminals against my dad.' She just shook her head.

The look of sympathy in Raff's eyes would have made her want to hit him if she wasn't already feeling so guilty for the beating she'd given him the day before.

'We all think our dads are immortal—' he started.

'He was a Devil Dog, Raff, a fucking ... Raider. He's a legend in the Corps and that's with most of his missions still being sealed. There're some hard men and women in special operations who still have awe in their voice when they tell stories about him. He won the fucking Colonial Medal of Honour during the Ahriman invasion. I mean, c'mon!'

'He was in his sixties ...'

She leaned in close to him. 'Listen to me. He would have eaten them. Unless ...'

'They knew what they were doing,' Raff finished. Miska wasn't sure if he was humouring her or not. On the other hand he couldn't have read the report and not seen the same things that she was seeing. She leaned back against the frame of the French windows. The only light in the room was coming from the street lights outside. It was as dark as it got on Dog 4. Both suns had set to give the planet its short night-proper.

'And why do it?' Miska asked. 'A home invasion, you hit a family. You threaten the kids so the parents provide access to their accounts, which they do because it's all insured. Nobody steals things any more because the only thing that's worth shit these days is information. So why come to an old man's house?'

'They wouldn't have known ...'

'You're the one telling me that these guys were super-competent. A search on social media and you find out that he's an ex-scout sniper and winner of the CMH. What, they plan *everything but that?' Raff didn't answer. 'The most valuable things my dad's got are his CMH, that antique four-five, and great-great-grandfather's Mastodon. They didn't take any of it.'* Thank fuck, *she thought. Angela could have the .45 and the CMH but Miska was taking the big Mastodon.*

'Because they didn't have time, because of the gunshots.'

'And yet the place was trashed. Why?'

Raff considered the question. 'Because they were looking for something.'

'Some-thing,' she repeated. 'Know what I didn't find in the report?' He shook his head, looking down. 'Information on the house net. I checked. It's been trashed, extensively, as though someone was covering their tracks.'

'Your sister just being careful?' Raff asked.

'Maybe. Know what else is missing? Any evidence from his own neuralware.'

'They had the guys cold, it wasn't needed. Besides he's ex-SF, MARSOC would have redacted it,' he told her. In this he was probably right. The Marine Corps Special Operations Command wouldn't want Basilone City PD poking around in the head of one of their operators, even an ex-operator.

'Okay fine, but I've got clearance. I want to see his body, check his neuralware, see if it's been tampered with.' As she said it Raff looked stricken. He took another mouthful from the bottle. 'What?' she demanded.

'I'm afraid he was cremated,' he told her. Miska stared at Raff, unable to believe what she was hearing.

'He's been what?' she managed. She was starting to shake again. Raff pushed himself away from her. 'The funeral's not for another three days!' she screamed. 'He wanted to be buried out at the ranch, not fucking set fire to!'

'Apparently it was a screw up ...'

'A screw up! A fucking screw up!' Miska had to force herself to calm down. She grabbed the bottle from Raff – he flinched away from her – and knocked back about a quarter of it, then threw it against the wall and screamed.

Raff was on his feet, making calming motions with his hands.

'Fine, I want to speak to whoever did the autopsy,' she managed. If they'd not had much time she could at least find out if his neuralware had been cut out of his head.

'She's dead,' Raff told her. 'Car accident.' Miska stared at him.

'Come on, Raff!'

'It was an op,' he admitted. She knew he hadn't been trying to cover it up. It was their method for debriefings. He'd been playing devil's advocate, making her examine the conclusions she was reaching. 'They covered their tracks well.'

'You said they got the shooters?' Miska asked. Though she was pretty sure she knew what was coming. 'If they're in county, I can sneak in there and torture the truth out of them.'

'Caught, arraigned, tried, pled guilty and incarcerated all in six weeks,' he told her.

So it all happened while I was away, Miska thought. How convenient.

'What is that, a fucking world record?' she demanded. 'Who were they?'

'All their records were destroyed by a virus after they were incarcerated.'

'Oh wow,' she said. 'Subtle. You said incarcerated. Where? New Fintry? High Rock?'

'Hangman's Daughter,' Raff told her. Miska shook her head. 'One of Group 13's prison barges.'

'Which I'm guessing has left the system?' she asked. He nodded. 'So that's that, then?'

'Maybe not. Whoever did it had people on the ground. The virus, however they managed to influence the courts and the DA's office, everything leaves tracks. We're looking into it.'

'But the shooters will be taken off at the next stop,' Miska said.

'It's not that easy. We don't think that Group 13 are compromised. Your father made life difficult enough for them that they walked out of the house and into the police, at which point they were improvising wildly. Their best way out was the prison barge. The earliest they can get off is in a month's time at Proxima, but they won't.'

'Why not?'

'Because we'll have a team there waiting and we'll make that obvious. Besides which, it's Small Gods' territory and the folks at Mjölnir owe us a favour. They need to get into friendly skies and they need time to set up an out.'

Miska nodded, giving this some more thought. Now it was starting to look like there was a glimmer of hope.

'Wait a second. It doesn't take a month to get to Proxima,' Miska said.

'No, but those barges only come into system when they have to because they're supposed to be impregnable.'

Miska smiled. 'And when they do I'll be waiting.'

'It's not that simple. Their net coverage has been incredible. They must have had an extremely talented hacker supporting them.'

Miska felt her heart sink again.

'They'll have changed the files?' she said. Raff nodded.

'And their prisoner processing is automated,' he told her.

'Which means we can't even interrogate the guards?'

'The prisoners are held in cold storage. They're only allowed out for their UN-mandated exercises. They're watched over by guard droids and automated gun turrets. Rehabilitation happens in a VR construct. The human guards barely see them.'

'How the fuck does this happen in a surveillance society?' Miska demanded.

Raff shrugged. 'Bureaucracy.'

'How many suspects?' she asked.

'Six-thousand-plus.'

For some reason she remembered a conversation with her dad, who was something of a military history buff. A Roman legion was roughly six thousand strong.

'So that's it then?' she asked. She felt like crying. The rage was better, she decided. She noticed another file icon blinking in her IVD.

'What's Operation Lee Marvin?' she asked.

Operation Lee Marvin was an old plan that the CIA had developed some years ago after a spate of particularly violent colonial independence movements. In the face of the spokes-controlling equatorial states, the hypercorps, the Small Gods and Mars, America was pretty much a spent force in the Sol System. They had a few habitats, some asteroids in the belt and a spattering of colonies on a few moons not claimed by their Small Gods namesakes. The only thing that still allowed them a seat at the table was their colonial holdings. After the War in Heaven and the havoc of the creation of the Small Gods, manifest destiny had taken hold again and the crowded, overpopulated US had aggressively sought new worlds to terraform and colonise. This meant that holding onto those colonies suddenly became very important, and a deniable army of criminals in the nominal service of the CIA seemed like a good idea. To many in the Company it was also a good use for the violent criminals that still plagued humanity. It was also appealing to the powers that be because, in theory, it should be self-funding. The only problem being that it was a monstrous violation of human rights that would cause a huge scandal, loss of funding, and probably jail time if a link to the Company was ever discovered. That was until the opportunity to kill two birds with one stone presented itself in the shape of a vengeful Miska Corbin. It might have been convenient, and it was definitely empire-building on Raff's part. He wanted to be seen as an aggressive young case officer, capable of thinking outside of the box. She didn't begrudge him taking advantage of her father's death, mostly because it suited her as well.

All of this was running through her head, as well as a killer whisky headache, as a way of not dealing with the fact that she was lying face-down in a hotel room bed, with Raff next to her, on the morning of her father's memorial service (recently demoted from a full funeral).

You just don't stop fucking up, do you? It wasn't lost on her that she'd tried to kill him a little over sixty hours before. She tried to suppress a smile thinking about how gentle she'd had to be with him last night.

She tried to sneak out of bed but Raff's arm had been stretched out across her back.

'Hey,' he said. So much for being sneaky, she thought as she gathered her clothes. 'You want me there today?'

She didn't look at him, instead she looked out of the hotel window across the cattle pens, the railhead and out over the prairies. 'This was a mistake.' She knew she should report the

235

liaison, assuming the Company didn't already know, and ask to be reassigned to a different case officer, but she'd never been very good with the rules. 'It can't happen again, understood?'

Now she did look at him. He nodded. She couldn't read the expression in his face, but then he was a spy. 'I need to borrow your Jeep.'

'Why don't you let me drive?' he asked. Because I don't want you there, because it makes me feel weak, she thought. 'I'd like to pay my respects.'

She wanted to say no, she really did. Instead she just nodded.

Working on getting mean drunk wasn't doing last night's whisky headache much good. She was sat in a corner of the sprawling, open plan lounge, close to one of the panoramic windows, in Uncle Jakob's log-built ranch house. She was looking out over the small lake and beyond to the violet grasses of the prairie, spotted with genetically modified highland cows. She was in her dress blues, the ceremonial uniform of the USMC, that Raff, resourceful Raff, had found from somewhere. She was uncomfortable, struggling to deal with platitudes from her father's friends, Corps buddies and even family.

The ranch had belonged to her mom's family but after her death there was only her uncle Jakob and his kids left on that side. She didn't think that her dad had known all that much about his family.

She'd loved it here as a kid. It had seemed peaceful, just the sound of the wind in the long grass powering the whirring field of windmills, the dogs barking occasionally, and the horses in the stables. The last two summers before she'd joined the Corps she'd come up here to work as a cowhand during her vacation. It had been a refuge for her, her dad and even her sister. She'd even run away here once during one of the more tumultuous periods of her teenaged years.

Sirius A was behind the house now and starting to dip, but Sirius B was still high in the sky, casting its strange pale light over the landscape. Then someone cast a familiar shadow over her. Miska sighed and drained her whisky. She looked up at her sister.

The elder Corbin had got their mom's looks and their dad's height. She was classically, and annoyingly effortlessly, beautiful, seeming to inherit the best parts of their family's complicated Slavic, Celtic, Germanic and Thai background. She wasn't wearing a uniform, unless you considered the black skirt suit an NSA uniform. Her long, ash-blonde hair was tied back in a complicated looking and severe bun. Her height and athleticism gave her a statuesque build, which, along with her piercing blue eyes and high cheekbones, meant that she had been mistaken for a Small Demigod before.

'I thought I might hear from you before today,' Angela said by way of a hello.

Miska sighed. 'What? You want me to lie? I was avoiding you. This is hard enough without having to put up with your sanctimonious hypocritical bullshit.' She could see Raff glancing her way. He was talking to a retired full-bird colonel that Miska vaguely recognised. 'At least you didn't come in dress uniform.'

As the eldest, Angela could remember their mom better, and she'd honoured her memory by being the good daughter, the dutiful daughter. Miska had been the trouble magnet, but in some ways Miska suspected that her sister's rebellion – joining the army instead of the Corps – had been more painful for her dad. Though he'd never said anything.

'Really? Here? Even now?' her sister asked. Out of the corner of her eye she could make out Raff trying to edge closer. She noticed a text icon in her IVD from him. She assumed it was asking if she was okay, if she needed rescuing. She ignored it. She was angry.

'What do you mean here? Now? Your opening salvo was passive aggression one-oh-one.'

Angela leaned down to get right in her face. 'Because I'm upset, because I'm angry, because even now it seems you're still the same spoilt, selfish little girl that broke his heart when you were a teenager.'

'How the fuck would you know?' Miska demanded. 'You were gone by then.'

'Ladies ...?' Raff asked. Both of them turned to look at him. He spent a moment looking between them and then wisely backed off.

'Did you do this?' Miska blurted out. Angela turned back to stare at her, eyes wide, anger written all over her face.

'What?' she demanded, her voice cold and brittle. Miska stood up. Her sister had a good six inches on her. She was aware of various members of Uncle Jakob's extended family casting glances their way. Everyone in the family knew there was no love lost between the Corbin girls.

'You heard,' Miska said trying to keep her voice down. 'You've seen the report, you must have worked out it was an operation. You don't give a fuck about family ...'

Miska crashed through the window. She tried to roll to her feet but got tangled up in her dress uniform skirt.

'Fucking skirt!' she muttered, shrugging off her dress jacket. She had her knife in an upside down scabbard underneath it. The knife her dad had given her. She reached for the hilt. The smartlink sensors impregnated in her hand connected with the knife, sending a signal to the smartgrip sheath to release it. She drew the blade just as Angela stepped through the hole in the glass she'd made by kicking Miska through it.

'You're going to use a knife on me?' Angela demanded.

'It's not for you,' Miska muttered, cutting a slit in her skirt and then throwing the knife close enough to where Angela was standing to make her duck out of the way. The knife embedded itself in the wooden window frame but it had done its job, distracting her sister. It was a dirty trick but Angela was the better fighter. Miska had already been moving the moment the knife had left her hand. She hooked a kick round Angela's knee, staggering her, almost knocking her over. Her sister took the elbow Miska had thrown on a raised arm. She took advantage of her height and hooked a punch down onto Miska's temple, staggering her. An uppercut from Angela's left rattled all the teeth in Miska's head. Miska swung her own hook. Angela broke the punch's momentum by punching her in the arm. Then she grabbed the halted arm, jumped and brought her elbow down on Miska's nose, breaking it. With bewildering speed, she side-kicked Miska in the upper thigh, kneed her in the chin and then delivered a stepping kick to the centre of her chest, driving Miska to the ground. From the ground Miska kicked out, hitting Angela in the ankle, then the knee, staggering her and then, balancing on one foot and both her hands, she kicked straight up and caught Angela under the chin, picking her up off her feet and sending her crashing to the ground. Miska was back on her feet now and making her way towards her sister to stamp on her head.

'Enough of this shit!' She didn't think she'd ever heard her uncle Jakob raise his voice. 'This is your dad's funeral, and your mum's house! Show some damned respect!' Her mom's side of the family had a long history of military service – also criminality, and arguably terrorism, depending on your perspective – but her uncle hadn't served. He had, however, fought with the resistance during the Cult of Ahriman's occupation of Sirius 4. The sound of command in his voice was unmistakable. A number of his sons – her cousins – as well as his cowhands, not to mention some of the marines present, all looked ready to intervene. Miska looked over at the marines. People who lived lives of violence but for them, somehow, this was too far.

'I'm sorry, Uncle,' Angela said from the ground. The contrition in her voice was just too much to bear. Miska wanted to scream at them: She kills people! So do I!

'Fucking buncha hypocrites,' she managed through the blood and mucus dripping out of her broken nose. They all looked like strangers to her. She glared at Angela once more, and then turned and stormed towards the Jeep. Stopped. Turned round and they all watched her as she marched back and retrieved her knife from the window frame and then stormed back to the Jeep again. She was vaguely aware of Raff making his apologies and then rushing after her.

'So that was fun,' Raff said as he drove them down the long winding gravel road that led back to the highway. She was dabbing at her nose having just reset it and in doing so covered her dress blouse with nasal blood.

'Fucking bitch,' Miska managed. Somehow she was still surprised at the level of violence that had been involved. She could feel Raff looking at her. She turned away from him and looked out over the prairies. It was getting dark again. She could see one of the low energy rotor drones that her uncle used to keep an eye on his herds, high above the prairie. She could make out *the running lights of a few more of the drones in the distance.*

'Want to get your own back on her?' Raff asked. Only now that Miska's anger was subsiding to manageable levels was she starting to feel the pain from the kicking her sister had administered. She still had broken glass in her hair. She hoped Angela was in a similar amount of discomfort.

'Doesn't sound terribly professional,' she muttered. Though the truthful answer was an unequivocal yes.

'Your sister has access to a ship that might help. I happen to know where it's berthed.'

Miska nodded. The synchronicities in her life just seemed to keep mounting up.

'There's one other thing,' she said, as they turned onto the highway. The blacktop was empty in either direction. In the distance lightning arced out of the dark blue sky, bathing the prairie in violent neon light. Raff glanced over at her. 'My dad's upload from back when he was on active duty.'

'Oh … now … I don't think that's a very good idea.'

'It's non-negotiable.'

CHAPTER 16

Cartwright made the wrong decision on a number of different levels. He shot Merrill, who was still tranced in, assuming that he was responsible for the current net attack, which was partially correct but it didn't solve the contractor's problems.

'No!' Miska was surprised to find herself shouting. It didn't stop her from moving. She used the ring at the end of her knife's hilt to spin the weapon up into her hand. She hammered the blade into Cartwright between a gap in the hard plates of his body armour. She felt his inertial armour undersuit harden as the point of her blade hit it but despite the awkwardness of the blow, her boosted muscle and the titanium blade's diamond edge drove it through, where it lodged in Cartwright's dermal armour. Wired reactions made the world slow down, though Cartwright himself sped up. His reflexes were wired at least as high spec as hers, possibly higher if he'd been augmented with Martian nanotech. She pulled the blade out and stabbed him higher on his side, trying to push it into his chest cavity, but again truly excellent dermal armour stopped her. She tried to stab him in the face but he managed to get both forearms in the way, blocking the blow, but at least it meant he couldn't shoot her and he was momentarily blind. She spun and swept his legs out from underneath him. The blast door was closing. It was time to leave.

The blond contractor was raising his PDW. He had her dead to rights until Nyukuti's boomer-sword came down on the contractor's head and split it in two down to the neck. The man sank to his knees. The small, unassuming contractor was turning towards Miska, bringing his weapon up. Torricone kicked him in the arm, knocking him around.

'Run!' the car thief screamed. The female contractor was bringing her PDW to bear on Torricone. Miska threw her knife. The blade spun through the air and embedded itself in the contractor's face. It was stuck in her dermal armour and hadn't gone deep enough to do any significant damage but it didn't matter who you were, you got a knife stuck in your face, it was distracting. Miska dropped a multi-spectrum stun grenade and ran after Torricone, Nyukuti following her. She heard the hypersonic scream of electromagnetically driven rounds. Felt something just touch her leg and almost tear her off her feet. Something ripped open a line of flesh through the dermal armour on her cheek. Torricone dived through the hole in the blast door. She followed, rolling to one side and up onto her feet. She turned her head to one side and closed her eyes as the stun grenade went off in the ops centre. The contractors would be augmented with flash compensation and audio filters, they'd recover quickly from the grenade but it was another distraction, another extra moment to widen the distance.

Nyukuti seemed somewhat disoriented by the stun grenade as he staggered to his feet in front of the narrowing hole in the blast door.

Miska reached for him. Some of what was Nyukuti spattered against the wall of the corridor as spinning, dart-like hypersonic rounds made tunnels through his flesh. Nyukuti staggered forward, dancing a little with each round before collapsing to the ground. Miska turned and ran past an appalled Torricone.

'Move!' she shouted in her best parade ground NCO's voice. She heard him running after her. She glanced behind her and saw the small contractor tumble through the narrowing gap in the blast door that she would have sworn was too narrow for someone in all that gear. He rolled over Nyukuti's body and to his feet as they reached the corner of the corridor. She heard the familiar pop of a grenade launcher. She was running so fast as she cornered that she ran up the wall, Torricone following suit. She sprinted down the corridor as the grenade hit the rock wall behind them and exploded. Later she would work out that it was a high-explosive armour-piercing grenade, presumably loaded to use against the Wraiths, and that probably saved their lives. The armour-piercing tip penetrated deeper into the rock than other grenades would have, and that contained the explosion to a degree. It didn't feel that way as the blast knocked them both off their feet and fragments of rock tore open exposed skin and hit her dermal armour, knocking the air out of them. Had it been a fragmentation grenade they'd both have been dead.

Miska pushed herself to her feet, her ears ringing. The corridor was full of rock dust and the open blast door at the end of it looked very far away. Torricone was making the kind of keening noise that Miska associated with ordnance-induced temporary deafness. She grabbed him and pulled him to his feet, dragging him into a run. There was no way that they'd make the end of the corridor before the contractor turned the corner and blew them away but they had to try. She pushed Torricone in front of her, putting herself between the shooter and him. It wasn't heroic, just simple expedience. Torricone didn't have any dermal armour, she did and it was military spec, therefore she had a better chance of surviving a hit. Not that it would make that much difference with the penetrators the contractors were using, and if she died, he died anyway. She kind of wished Gleave hadn't told the contractors that.

Ahead of her an air vent high up on the rock wall swung open on servo-driven hinges.

'Torricone, on your right!' Miska cried out loud and over the comms link. Then came the hypersonic scream of a PDW being fired.

Torricone was leaping for the vent as three electromagnetically driven rounds hit her, centre mass in the back. Her armour hardened but not enough. Air exploded out of her diaphragm as she stumbled and Torricone grabbed her and dragged her up into the vent as bullets impacted all around her, powdering the rock.

Miska scrambled into the air vent. It was just about big enough to crouch in. She pushed Torricone ahead of her, moving as fast as she could. Her back was agony. She could feel blood running down it. Red icons appeared in her IVD from her medical systems but it looked as though her armoured jacket and dermal armour had slowed the rounds enough that they hadn't caused too much damage.

More hypersonic screaming and EM-driven bullets tore through the grill in the air vent hatch. Miska brought up the schematics for the air vents from the files that the TCC had given her as they came to a junction.

'That way,' she pointed to the right. She heard the sound of an explosion behind them. She had a moment to recognise it

245

as micro breaching charges and then the pressure wave, forced through the vents by the blast, battered into them, knocking them off their feet.

'What's that?' Torricone demanded from underneath her.

'The air vent being blown off, he's in the vents now,' Miska told him. She didn't need to add that he was armed and they only had the knife and the compact pistol she'd taken off Joshua. Neither of which would be any use against the contractor's armour. She was trying not to grin fiercely. She knew that she wasn't supposed to be enjoying this, particularly as the rest of the infiltration team were dead, but she kind of was. They reached another junction. Miska heard something in a vertical vent directly above them. She looked up to see a vaguely insectile maintenance droid crawling down the vent towards them. There was a blinking comms icon in her IVD, an incoming message that she was loath to open in case it was being used as an incoming attack vector.

'This way.' Miska all but pushed Torricone into the left-hand, downward-sloping air vents. The maintenance droid crawled into the vent they'd just come from, filling it. Moments later came the hypersonic scream as a short, controlled burst from the contractor's PDW killed the maintenance droid.

'Shit!' Torricone cried out as bullets ricocheted around them. Behind them Miska could hear what she suspected was an inert maintenance droid being kicked out of the way. It was clear that something was putting obstacles in the way of their pursuer. She still didn't open the incoming message. There was a crash behind them as the maintenance droid was kicked into a vertical vent. 'Where are we going?' Torricone demanded.

'Just keep moving!' This wasn't the time for him to question her orders. The three rounds she'd taken in her back really hurt when she remembered but they were nothing life threatening.

The downward slope of the air vent they were in was getting steeper and steeper. More hypersonic screaming echoed through the vents. Miska's ear filters cut out the worst excesses of the noise. There was an explosion of blood from her left leg and it gave out under her. She was sliding down the smooth metal of the air vent now, leaving a trail of red behind her. She screamed out as she hit Torricone and he landed on her, jarring her wounded leg. Sparks flew off the metal as the chasing contractor fired again. She was having less fun now.

The two of them were sliding towards another hatch, picking up speed. Miska knew that when they hit the closed hatch the contractor would be able to take careful aim and put a burst through the top of each of their heads. Then the hatch opened, they flew through and dropped eight foot onto the metal grid over the rock that passed for flooring. Torricone landed on top of her, really making her scream this time. She was faintly aware of the hatch clicking shut on its servos above them.

'Get off me,' Miska howled, pushing Torricone away. She tried to get up but her leg gave way again. 'Ow, fuck!' EM-driven bullets tore through the air vent hatch, powdering stone, tearing through metal and ripping into the wrapped pallets of raw material stacked throughout the room. At least they were where Miska wanted to be. Torricone helped her to her feet. 'That way!' she pointed deeper into what appeared to be a storeroom. Torricone dragged her through a passage made of the stacked and wrapped pallets. It opened out into another cavernous chamber formed of the asteroid's rock. In front of them was a huge machine that looked not unlike an ancient printing press. The asteroid's 3D printer, which she knew was capable of manufacturing weapons. *If only I knew how to work it*, she thought, but it was already working. The small conveyor was moving slowly, churning out two matte-black, carbon fibre AK-47s, along with magazines for the archaic assault rifles.

'C'mon, c'mon,' Miska muttered, looking between the conveyor and the hatch to the air vent. Her augmented hearing picked up the sound of something rattling down the vent. 'Get down!' She grabbed Torricone and practically fell into him, pushing him into the sides of one of the pallets, finding herself crushed against him as the high explosive grenade went off. The hatch flew past them, hitting the wall behind the conveyor hard enough to embed itself in the rock. 'Fuck this,' Miska muttered. She saw the fear on Torricone's face but he was still moving, reacting, he was dealing. She limped across to the conveyor and pulled one of the AK-47s out of the printer. The weapon's carbon fibre was still hot, tacky to the touch. She threw it to Torricone and then grabbed the second for herself. She watched the magazines being printed. It was like listening to a clock tick.

'There'll be a stun grenade, look away, close your eyes, it'll still fuck you up, do what you can,' she told Torricone. The magazines were out. She heard a grenade rattling down the air vent. She grabbed a magazine and threw it to Torricone. He caught it, closed his eyes and looked away as he slid the magazine home. Miska grabbed the other magazine. She closed her eyes. There was a really bright light. Her eyes polarised but it still shone through her closed eyelids and she went momentarily deaf as her audio filters fought to compensate for the thunder of the stun grenade. Eyes still closed she limped to where she knew the edge of the pallets were as she slid the magazine into the AK-47, racked a round and switched the sticky weapon's selector to single shot. She hoped that the weapon worked. She opened her eyes. She was still seeing afterglow.

The contractor slid out of the airvent. Miska fired. It went high as he fell to the ground but the round exploded in the air above him. She adjusted but he was rolling behind the pallets closest to the vent. Torricone chased him around the corner with a three-round burst.

'I can't see for shit,' Torricone hissed as her hearing returned. She wanted to tell him to be quiet, as the contractor could probably hear him. In the quick glimpse she'd caught of the contractor she had noticed that he was wearing his helmet, his face covered as well. There were bulbous lenses over his eyes, adding increased protection from stun grenades, and possibly providing thermographic vision as well. She guessed he was less worried about his hair compared to his fellow contractors, one of whom would still be alive if he'd worn his helmet. Chances were he knew where they were. She glanced at the blast door to the printer chamber. It remained closed. She knew there were two Wraiths on guard on the other side of the door, assuming they hadn't moved or been killed. *If wishes were horses*, she thought. She had to focus. Deal with the situation with the resources they had. He might know where they were if he had thermographics but he could only shoot one way at any given time. She caught Torricone's eye and hand-signalled her plan to him. He nodded and turned, heading away from her.

The printer was still chuntering away producing more ammunition for the AK-47s as Miska turned and limped in the opposite direction to Torricone. She heard the distinctive pop of a grenade being fired and tried to jam herself between two tightly packed pallets. The grenade exploded against the back wall over the printer. The force of the blast battered her and she felt shrapnel tear into the pallets, something rip open the other side of her face. She was pretty sure that she heard Torricone cry out in pain.

'You okay?' she subvocalised over a private comms link.

'Got hit in the back, I'm bleeding ...' Even over the link she could hear his pain.

'Can you move?' she asked. There was no answer, then she heard a grunt of pain.

'Yeah, I think so ...' he subvocalised. Miska moved cautiously out of her hiding place, checking around before turning back to Torricone. He was lying on his back on the ground. She started to ask him another question but saw his eyes go wide. Miska threw herself forward as EM-driven bullets tore apart the pallets next to where she had been stood the moment before. Torricone was firing the AK-47 on full automatic, the gunfire accompanied by the multiple explosions rolling into one long thunderous roar. Miska rolled onto her back. Pain shot through it as the dart-shaped bullets lodged in her dermal armour were pushed in deeper. The contractor was behind her, at the corner of the pallets, disappearing behind them in a hail of buffeting micro-explosions.

'Cease fire!' Miska subvocalised across the link. Torricone must have fired off half his magazine. 'Flank him, get into the pallets behind him.' She was on her feet, the AK-47 at the ready as she limped as fast as she could towards the corner, going wide, finger curled round the trigger, the weapon's rudimentary smartlink superimposing a crosshair on her IVD where the bullet should land. She was aware of Torricone back on his feet behind her, moving into the central corridor between the pallets. Frightened or not, he was up, moving, and prepared to walk into a gun. Doing his job.

'First lateral corridor,' Torricone announced across the link.

Then came the sound of more hypersonic screaming. Miska moved around into the second lateral corridor. The contractor was about halfway down, firing away from her. He had her back to him. She started to squeeze the trigger but suddenly the air was filled with micro-explosions, sending her staggering behind the second row of pallets. Torricone had popped around the opposite corner, staying low, and risked a three-round burst at the contractor. Now the contractor realised there was someone behind him. He fired a long burst at Torricone, sending him scuttling for cover, suppressing him and then turned towards Miska. She moved further back as the EM-driven rounds chewed away at the pallet-load of raw materials she was hiding behind. She heard another three-round burst and accompanying explosions from Torricone's AK-47. She edged round the corner to see the contractor staggering backwards. It was clear, however, that they didn't have anything that would penetrate his armour. She needed to find a weak point. She leaned into the AK-47 and fired, once. The recoil kicked back into her shoulder as the gun bucked. The round hit him on the back of his helmet and exploded. It didn't have anything like the penetration required to go through the helmet but it must have rung his bell. It also allowed her to judge the accuracy of the smartlink. The round had dropped in just a little lower than the crosshair. Most importantly, though, it had let the contractor know where she was.

'Cease fire,' she told Torricone as the contractor turned towards her. The crosshair was just on the brim of his helmet. She squeezed the trigger again. He was knocked back, his face shrouded in the fire of the micro explosion for a moment, clearing to show the helmet's broken facemask and the bloodied face underneath. Miska squeezed the trigger a third time. The face disappeared, the helmet flipped off as though on a hinge hanging at the side of the contractor's head, which was missing from the mouth up. The contractor collapsed to the ground. Torricone stared down at the dead man, appalled. Then he looked up at Miska.

'Did I shoot at you?' he asked.

'Little bit,' she told him. 'My own fault, I walked into your field of fire.' *Because you're distracted and getting sloppy*, she told herself. She advanced on the body, the AK-47 still levelled at it. Even if he had been augmented with Martian nanotech that wasn't growing back any time soon.

She was pleased that she didn't have to tell Torricone to get back on the clock. The car thief had his weapon at the ready, though it couldn't have much ammunition left in the magazine, and he was checking all around them. As he turned back towards the central corridor Miska heard movement behind her. She whirled around bringing the AK-47 up, but a bulky figure batted it aside with surprising force, tearing it from her grip. Powerful, clammy hands wrapped around her throat and she was lifted up into the air and rammed into the side of the pallets.

Oh c'mon! she wanted to scream but the powerful fingers were starting to crush the dermal armour protecting her throat. She found herself looking down at Chanar, the huge shift boss. *Torricone's going to shoot him in the head any second now*, she thought. She felt a cracking sensation in her throat. She was small enough and his arms were long enough that she managed to bring her leg up and start stamping on his face but there was no real power behind it.

'Let her down,' Torricone said putting the barrel of his AK-47 against the side of Chanar's head. The shift boss was just staring up at her, nostrils flaring. He looked really angry. 'I

252

don't want to kill you but if you don't let her down I will pull the trigger,' he told Chanar. There was no indication that the shift boss was paying him the slightest bit of attention. Torricone stabbed Chanar in the side of the head with the barrel. 'Now!'

Oh just fucking shoot him, you insufferable hippy! she thought. She was trying to compose a text to send him with those very sentiments when a stack of pallets was pushed over and there was another, much larger figure in the row with them. The Wraith grabbed Chanar and tore him off his feet, forcing him to drop Miska. The power armour then slammed the miner into the rock wall.

'Hi boss,' Mass said.

Miska was glaring at Torricone as she rubbed her neck. They were stood by the printer now. Mass was holding one of the L-39 anti-tank rifles in one hand, his Retributor clipped to his back. He was also holding down a struggling Chanar by standing on him with one foot. The blast door was open, and just outside she could see Hangman-Two-Three standing guard with the other L-39. Hangman-Two-Four's Wraith was on the other side of the door. Miska turned towards Mass's Wraith.

'How'd you open the door?' Miska asked.

'We've been in negotiations with someone calling themselves Che Guevara. I think you need to answer your comms,' Mass told her. She looked at the flashing icon in her IVD and opened the link.

'Hello, Corporal Corbin.' She recognised the sentient virus's voice. 'I need to get you up to speed quickly. I'm reinstating your access to the station's lenses.' Windows started opening in her IVD. She saw the assault shuttle at the docks. A thick square of metal lay on the rock floor, the molten edges where it had been cut out of the airlock still glowing. There were two squads of eight contractors, each backed by two operators in Martian Military Industries Machimoi power armour suits, at each blast door exit from the docks. Miska was reasonably sure that the 20mm Dory railguns the Machimoi were carrying, improved versions of the venerable Retributors, weren't adapted for firing rubber bullets. The contractors were attaching thermite frame charges to the blast doors. It would take a while but the thermite would burn through the door and they would gain access to the rest of the station.

Miska had dragged the contractor's corpse around to the printer with her. His weapons were code protected. She was running cracking programs to try and gain access to them but it would take time. Other than the PDW and the contractor's sidearm the only things they had that would beat the Martian body armour were the two L-39s. This was the first bad news.

She expanded the lens feed from the ops centre. The prisoners locked in there with Cartwright were all dead. That was to be expected. The female contractor, the hacker, was lying on the same couch that Merrill had been on and was tranced in. That was also to be expected.

Next she checked the net feed. Triple-S's ship, the *Excelsior*, looked like a tall ship, if said sailing vessel had been made out of the latest material that science could grow. It was a sleek and ultramodern racing yacht enlarged for war and crossed with a stealth bomber. The *Excelsior*'s net presence was off the coast of Faigroe Station's pirate port and was bombarding it with black fire and neon lightning attack programs. Faigroe Station's returning electronic warfare looked like cannon fire from the hilltop colonial fort. Meanwhile intrusion countermeasures that looked like drowned pirates made of liquid black mirror oozed from the calm, reflective sea and attempted to clamber up the side of the ship, only to be met by the contractors' own intrusion countermeasures in the shape of faceless, black-clad humanoid figures. This at least looked like a standoff.

Then she checked the external sensor feed, which used a mixture of external lens footage and information from the sensors to make a three-dimensional image of the tactical situation. The *Excelsior* was standing off for the time being, ready to intercept the *Hangman's Daughter* if it got any closer, and waiting for the two TCC light cruisers, which were about twenty minutes away from effective weapons range with the *Hangman's Daughter*. If they closed then it was all over. The *Daughter* was a larger ship than both the cruisers put together but while the prison barge could defend itself reasonably well, even on autopilot, both the cruisers were dedicated warships. They were faster and more heavily armed and armoured than the *Daughter*. This was not good.

'Well?' Torricone asked.

'All-in-all, I'd say we're pretty fucked,' she said, smiling. Torricone stared at her. Mass's Wraith's head turned to look at her as well.

'I was thinking of something a little bit more constructive,' Che said. Miska shared the comms feed from the virus with Mass and Torricone.

'Okay, first things first,' she said, kneeling down, with some difficulty, next to the contractor she'd killed. She searched through the pouches on his webbing. 'Where's Joshua?' she asked Che. The virus made her aware of his position. 'Does Cartwright know where Joshua's being held?'

'I believe so,' the virus answered. She saw the net feed rewinding, shifting position. It started playing again and Miska saw

255

an icon that looked like the female contractor with Cartwright if she'd been made out of riveted iron plate. As she watched, the iron figure became transparent and finally disappeared, just leaving the odd visual distortion in the air. She was good. 'It was one of the first pieces of information she went looking for.'

After she'd found his whereabouts Miska guessed that the contractor's hacker had scouted the pirate port for the heavier guns on the ship, a bit like a forward observer calling in a danger close artillery strike. *That takes a pair of ovaries*, Miska reflected. It was a race. Cartwright was arrogant, perhaps over-confident, and had underestimated them, but she didn't think he was stupid. He would send some of his people and at least one of the Machimoi after Joshua. She did a few quick calculations about how long it would take them to cut through the intervening blast doors. She didn't like the numbers. Unless …

'Che, I'm right in thinking that you have complete control of the interior of the station, correct?' she asked as she found the contractor's medkit and straightened up.

'With the exception of the external airlocks, or I would have flushed these assholes out into space already,' the virus answered. Miska didn't like that the electronic war was going so badly that Che had already lost control of the airlocks. On the other hand it was one of the first things any attacking force in space-borne combat went for. At least Che was in charge of all the interior doors. That would make things easier.

She smeared flesh accelerant gel into her leg wound. Fortunately it was a through-and-through. The round had been too high velocity to lodge in her leg, it had taken some meat with it but not hit anything too vital.

'All the prisoners are still in lockdown?' Miska asked.

'For their own safety, but I wish to move them,' Che told her.

It made sense to have the prisoners, particularly the children, as far away from the contractors as possible. They'd just get in the way. She picked up the flesh-knitter and, gritting her teeth, ran it down the wound to seal it.

'Are you still in charge of the station's weapons?' she asked. This was another system that tended to be targeted first in any assault, for obvious reasons. It was less of an issue because the contractors already had people on board.

'Barely,' the virus told her. It was still what passed for good news around these parts.

'You,' she said to Chanar, still underneath Mass's Wraith's foot. He just glared at her. 'Look, entertain all the revenge fantasies about me you want, but if you want your people to live then you have to take charge because Uboka's dead.'

'I will—' he started.

'If it's not helping then you're risking lives,' she told him. He shut up and then nodded. 'Okay, good. Let him up,' she told Mass. The Wraith's foot came off the shift leader, who struggled to his feet.

'Mass, who's your best shooter?' Miska tried walking around. Her right leg felt weak but it was holding her weight. It would have to do.

'I am,' Mass told her.

'We don't have time for ego, Mass,' she said, the warning carried in her voice. 'You're in a position of command now. I'm going to need you well back from the action making decisions calmly, understand me?' She was taking off her armoured jacket now, and pulling up the back of her T-shirt to expose three bloodied wounds. The penetrators were still lodged in her dermal armour.

'Shit,' Torricone said. He'd been using the flesh-knitter on his own wounds. She knew it looked worse than it was.

'You,' she said to Chanar. 'Take the medgels from the kit and apply them to each of the wounds.' He hesitated for a moment but then knelt down and removed three of the medgels.

'Don't you need to take the bullets out?' Torricone asked.

Miska shook her head. 'The gels will suck them out, break them down, clean and then seal the wound,' she told him. *In time*, she added silently. Chanar straightened up and started applying them to her back. 'Mass, best shot?'

'Chan. Hangman-Two-Five,' he told her somewhat reluctantly.

'Okay, good. Che, put me through to Reg in the crèche,' she told the virus. The comms icon blinked and then Reg answered. 'Hey Reg, it's Miska.' If she was expecting a tirade of abuse then she was disappointed. Instead all she heard was a dry chuckle.

'I'm guessing you need something,' he said.

'No bullshitting. If you get your weapons back how many of your people have got ordnance that will beat milspec Martian Military Industries body armour?' she asked.

'MMI? The hard plates over and inertial suit, and I'm guessing they've got decent dermal armour?' he asked.

'Good guess,' Miska told him. The comms link was quiet for longer than she liked.

'About a quarter of us,' he finally replied. 'But y'know, we're mercenaries, so what's in it for us?'

'I'm in this because the contractors who came to relieve us ordered me to execute you all, and I said no,' she told him. Torricone, hearing this barefaced lie, stared at her. 'You guys're fighting for your lives. If any of us live then I'm sure the miners will be happy to honour your contract.' There was more silence across the comms link.

'You make a compelling argument,' Reg finally answered. She added him to the group comms and asked Che to open a link to the *Hangman's Daughter*. Again it took longer than she would have liked, presumably because of the ongoing electronic war in the net. She was very aware of the seconds ticking away but her dad finally answered.

'Hangman-Actual to Hangman-One-Actual, where the fuck have you been?' he demanded. He was clearly worried because he rarely swore within her hearing.

'I don't have the time, Dad,' she told the ghost of her father.

'You want the QRF?' he asked, meaning the Quick Reaction Force.

'Negative, they've got nothing that would touch the contractors. But it's okay, I've got a plan.' She told him what it was.

'I've heard better plans,' he said, a grim expression on his face. 'To be honest, I've heard better plans for martyrdom.' She tried not to roll her eyes. She really needed him to back her up right now.

'If you've got a better one …' she said. He just shook his head.

Miska opened the comms link up to everybody on the group link: 'Okay, this is what we're going to do.'

CHAPTER 17

The Wraiths scrambled over the rough rock of the asteroid's exterior. Torricone had all but taken apart one of the airlock lock mechanisms to open it. Both Che and Miska had supported him in the net, fighting to take control of that particular system from the contractors. Miska was in Hangman-Two-Three's Wraith and carrying one of the L-39s. She was pretty sure that the power armour suit had a leak in it. Not that the power armour suits had been set up for vacuum operation anyway, though they were supposed to be hermetically sealed and pressurised. She suspected the upper atmosphere transfer to the fuel scoop drones had been too much for the ageing armour. It was cold in the power armour, she could hear an ominous hiss and she was feeling a little light-headed. At first she thought it might be psychosomatic until a warning icon appeared flashing in her IVD. She wasn't worried about running out of oxygen so much as passing out due to the lack of air pressure, and then running out of oxygen.

'It looks like you're venting gas,' Torricone said over the

comms link from Hangman-Two-Four's Wraith. He was carrying the cumbersome mining laser the assault team had captured earlier. After brief consideration they had dumped both the Wraiths' modified railguns. The EM-driven rubber bullets would give the Triple-S contractors a bit of a battering but they were probably augmented and armoured to the degree that it wouldn't inhibit their combat effectiveness too much.

'Yep,' Miska agreed. The Wraiths were scrabbling on all fours, trusting ageing molecular hooks on the palms and feet of the power armour to keep them adhered to the asteroid. Miska didn't really like how they felt either. 'Seems that the guards didn't keep the Wraiths maintained to vacuum-capable standard. Who knew?'

Joshua was being kept in a cell in the security offices on the other side of the ops centre. They could have made a run for it through the rec area and into the admin area where the ops centre was, but the contractors would be coming the same way. If the contractors won the war in the net then they could free Cartwright, which could trap them between two groups of enemy combatants. Miska couldn't take the risk. So she decided to do something that she hoped they wouldn't suspect. Torricone pointed out that they wouldn't suspect it because it was stupid but he still agreed to come along.

'You told them that you changed sides when the TCC decided to kill all the prisoners,' Torricone said over the comms link. *Oh, here we go*, Miska thought. 'You were prepared to hand them over to be killed if the contractors hadn't turned on you.'

'You want to talk about this now?' she asked, wondering what it was with the males in her life and their piss-poor timing. She half-leaped over a crater in the side of the asteroid mine, grabbed an outcrop and scrambled over it. Proxima G was to her back. Out here even the storm fronts far below seemed peaceful.

'Yes,' he said.

She wondered if he was just trying to take his mind off his own fear. After all, he'd grown up on a planet, he wasn't used to being just an inch or so of sealed armoured plate away from a pretty unpleasant death. Not to mention all the action they'd seen today, though he'd handled himself well, suspiciously so.

'You remember the explosive collar around your neck? What's it going to take for you to realise that I'm not a nice person?' She gave this a few more moments' thought. 'I'm not evil, or a psycho or anything, I just don't—'

'Care?' he interrupted. 'Extreme moral relativity, I get that. And we're not nice people, I get that too. If I squint funny I can even see you justifying to yourself going after the miners, after all they picked up the guns, they made a decision ...'

'That's the thing, I don't have to justify anything to myself—' Miska started, her voice a little slurred. Her feet were cold in the Wraith's control slippers. Her fingers, in the control gloves, were numb as well.

'But kids?'

They were crawling up a mostly flat bit of rock. It felt a little like scrambling up a cliff. Nearby, one of the station's missile batteries was moving around on its mount, searching for targets. There was just a moment of trepidation, through the light-headedness, that the contractors had taken control of the station's weapon systems and it was about to open fire on them.

'You have to compartmentalise these things ...'

'You know what I think?' he asked.

'That comms silence is for other people? That rhetorical questions are cool?'

'I think that you knew they were going to betray you the moment they told you to execute everyone, but you had to play it out so it looks like you tried to complete the contract. Make it clear that it was them that broke it.'

That only works if we get out of here alive, she thought. She missed a handhold and her feet slipped, both of them coming away from the rock. Between the control slippers, the gloves and the wireless connection to her brain, the Wraith effectively was her body. As she fought to drag her feet back down and connect with the rock, she felt cold, shivery and was having to fight for breath.

'Miska?' Torricone asked. He had stopped and turned to look at her.

'Keep going,' she managed. 'Tell me about your mum.'

'What?' he asked. He sounded surprised. 'Maybe you should conserve your air,' he suggested. It seemed clear that he didn't want to talk about this.

'I will, if you talk to me.' *I don't sound too needy*, she told herself but she was fighting for every breath now in the thinning air, struggling to feel her extremities as it got colder. 'You said she taught you to fight, that she was a priest ...'

'Yeah,' he said and that was it.

Miska took another cold, painful breath. 'She still alive?'

'Yeah,' again, more hesitant.

'Sure?' He didn't answer. 'My mom's dead.' He still didn't answer. 'Where'd she learn to fight?' she managed.

'I don't know. I guess she did some stuff beforehand, maybe military, something like that. She never talked about it much. I always got the feeling that being a priest was somehow penance and don't ask, I don't know what for. Something bad, I guess. She really wanted the best for me ...'

Even oxygen-hungry the paranoid tradecraft part of her brain was telling her the vagueness was part of poorly constructed, hurried legend. It was a cover story. He was one of the shooters who killed her dad. Except that she heard something in his voice: regret, even shame. She opened her mouth to try another question but the *Excelsior* hove into view subjectively above them, its blunt nose pointed down at the gas giant, manoeuvring thrusters burning as the frigate fought gravity.

She was glad that Che didn't hesitate. Every single weapon system on that side of the station opened up. Lasers scorched and railguns pitted the frigate's armour. Missiles launched at near point-blank range. Suddenly Miska was warm again as the exhaust from the nearby missile batteries bathed the two Wraiths in fire. She was concentrating on climbing. The rock felt soft to the touch, heated by the missiles' engines. She was aware of explosions from the various lens feeds in her IVD. She knew, and could have checked the station's external lens feed to see, that the *Hangman's Daughter* was on hard burn, engaging the *Excelsior* from long range with its laser cannons. Waves of force battered them against the rock as the *Excelsior* launched a missile and the station's laser point defence system destroyed it in mid-flight. It was a spectacular waste of the station's defences and it was designed to do one thing: keep the *Excelsior* off their backs long enough for them to reach the admin area's emergency airlock.

Blood-red light stabbed down from the *Excelsior* as it banked and fled. The laser superheated the cold rock of the asteroid, making it explode. Miska was battered into the side of the station once again, feeling woozy. Silently, and seemingly in slow motion, Torricone was ripped off the side of the rock. He started spinning away. Miska let go of the rock with her hands and stood up straight amid the force and light and stretched out, reaching for Torricone. The steel fingers of her enlarged armoured form brushed against the other Wraith's leg and then closed.

'I've got you,' she told him. She could see the *Hangman's Daughter* over the distant curve of the planet, engines burning bright, fingers of red, destructive light reaching out for the *Excelsior*. She watched the contractor's frigate flee behind the station through the lens feed in her IVD. The *Excelsior* was systematically destroying every one of the station's weapon systems but their purpose had been served, it had bought them enough time for the *Daughter* to close and protect them. The prison barge would have to flee when the TCC's cruisers were in range in – Miska groggily checked the countdown in her IVD – just over eleven minutes. She pulled Torricone back down onto the rock. She noticed that the comms link had gone quiet. As they continued their way towards the airlock, the surrounding landscape transformed by the recent exchange of fire, she hoped he hadn't soiled himself.

Between the adrenalin and her lung implants Miska managed to make it to the emergency airlock. She was standing over it swaying, her vision tunnelling, bathed in the strobing red light of the laser torch as Torricone used it to cut through the airlock. The molten-edged cuts in the metal met and Torricone stamped on it, sending the rectangle of metal floating down into the airlock's interior. A flashing red light warned them of the airlock's violation as Torricone climbed into it. Miska bent down to pull herself in. The strobing red light returned as Torricone started to cut through the interior. Things went dark for a moment. Miska came to holding onto the molten edge of the cut in the emergency airlock's exterior door. The flashing warnings on the inside of the airlock were becoming quite insistent now.

'Get in here,' Torricone told her over the comms link. Some inane part of her oxygen-starved mind wanted to tell him that she gave the orders. 'Decompression will tear you off the asteroid.' He stopped cutting.

Don't do that, she thought, *time!*

He reached up to grab her armour, and with some difficulty in the cramped confines he managed to drag her in. She bounced around a little, Torricone using a boot to move her out of the way. She was falling towards what felt like a vertical wall but would actually be the floor inside the station, as the artificial gravity was stronger in the airlock. The hellish light started again as Torricone resumed cutting. She could see gas escaping through the cut he'd made with the torch. Suddenly a rectangle of molten-edged metal tore itself out of the interior airlock door and battered into them. A moment later she was flying around the inside of the airlock, bouncing off the walls as air and anything else that wasn't secured poured out. Then it got dark again.

'Pop the seal, Miska, pop the seal!' The voice swam through the darkness to her.

'Stop shouting,' she mumbled.

It took a moment for her to work out the meaning of all the red warning icons in her IVD. With a thought she opened the front of her armour and sucked in air. She was sitting in yet another corridor cut out of the rock and illuminated in red, as befit an emergency. The airlock was to her back. The emergency shutters had come down, sealing the breach and rendering the airlock unusable. The surrounding area was a mess from the debris dragged there by the decompression.

'You okay?' Torricone asked; he was out of his power armour, kneeling down next to her own.

'Wooo!' Miska said. 'That was a rush! Tell me you didn't feel that?'

Torricone rocked back on his heels. 'A rush?' he asked quietly. 'A fucking rush! A warship just shot at us!'

'I know, right? Intense!' Miska was wondering if she was still a bit light-headed from the lack of atmosphere. She felt unsteady on her feet, a little dazed but otherwise okay. Her 'ware was feeding her system oxygenated blood at an artificially high rate, which probably contributed to her feeling a little high. At least that was her excuse and she was sticking to it. She pushed herself forward, half out of her Wraith, grabbed Torricone and pulled herself to him, kissing him, her mind screaming at her to stop.

He tensed initially and then relaxed, returning the kiss and then suddenly he pushed her away. She fell back into the power armour's cradle. He scuttled back, staring at her. She was trying to make out the expression on his face. Fear? Shame? Disgust?

'No,' he said, shaking his head. 'Just no.' Then he was angry. 'How fucking dare you when I'm wearing this!' He tugged at his collar. 'How sick are you?' He may as well have slapped her.

'Take it easy, *chico*, I was just a little bit light-headed, okay? I got excited with the ship shooting at us.' She was checking around them now, they'd made a lot of noise and it meant that she didn't have to look at him.

'Look, I'm sorry, that sounded harsher than I meant,' he told her as she slid back into her Wraith.

She wanted to scream the word 'coward' at him. Instead: 'Whatever, we're still working.' She opened a comms link. 'Hangman-One-Actual to Hangman-Actual,' she said not looking at Torricone, putting the hurt she felt down to the recent lack of oxygen, trying to remember who and what he was to her.

She sealed the Wraith and pushed herself to her feet. Torricone climbed into his Wraith.

'Hangman-Actual to Hangman-One-Actual, received, over.' She could hear tension in her dad's voice. *If he asks me one more time if I'm okay, I'm going to punch him the next time I see him*, she decided, as irrational as punching a VR simulation might be.

'Sitrep,' she said, asking for a situational report.

'She feels like she's about to shake herself apart,' her dad told her. *Feels?* she wondered.

'Can you do it?'

'She'll hold together,' he said. He didn't sound all that convincing. 'Are you all r—' She severed the comms link.

She took a moment to look at the windows from the various feeds to check the tactical situation. Doing her best to find a reason not to look at Torricone, to ignore the sudden awkwardness. Chanar and a number of the newly released mercenaries were shepherding the miners and their children through the corridors of the admin area towards the stores. The miners who had already reached the stores area were arming themselves with the printed AK-47s, for all the good they would do. It looked like they were going to use the main blast doors leading to the stores as a killing ground. They were closing the blast doors that led to admin and the commercial area, trying to funnel the contractors down the widened main passage from the docks. As Miska watched, the miners were moving the two remaining mining mechs into position on either side of the door. She watched as mine engineers, carrying improvised explosive devices made from mining charges, crawled into the vents to lay the IEDs. The remaining Wraiths were providing cover. Miska was pleased to see that Mass was staying well back in one of the storerooms issuing commands. Reg, next to him, was doing the same for his mercenaries. Arguably it was a waste of a Wraith having Mass stay back, but the sad fact of it was the miners had very little that could penetrate the contractors' superior body armour, let along damage the Machimoi power armour they had with them.

In the rec area Chan, Herbert, a chartered accountant serving twenty years for two counts of second-degree murder after killing his husband and his husband's lover, was on one knee. Mass's best shooter, he had the other L-39 at the ready, covering the tail-end of the miners making for the stores. Reg's mercenaries, the ones carrying weapons they reckoned could beat the contractors' power armour, were there as well.

Miska checked on the whereabouts of the contractors. There was a squad of eight making their way down the main tunnel from the dock towards the stores. They presumably knew it was a trap and didn't care. The two Machimoi with them were on point. Ahead of them two rotor drones led the way. The Machimoi signalled a halt as a rotor drone stopped three quarters of the way down the corridor. The rotor drone backed away from an air vent and one of the power-armoured contractors lifted his Dory railgun and triggered its under-barrel microwave projector. The focused microwaves detonated an IED in the air vent, spewing the mangled remains of the two engineers who'd been trying to set it out into the main tunnel. Moments later low-powered lasers, presumably carried by some of Reg's mercenaries, turned the corridor a hellish red and the rotor drones tumbled to the floor as glowing smoking debris.

The Machimois responded by firing short bursts from their railguns, suppressing the laser wielders as they launched four more of the tiny rotor drones from the holders on their backs. Even with only eight contractors and the two Machimoi, Miska knew it was going to be a massacre.

There was a patrol of four contractors and one Machimoi making their way carefully through the rec area. One of them jerked back as a round from a powerful slug-throwing sniper rifle with a gauss-kiss on it caught him in the face. A sniper who was one of Reg's crew had fired the shot. Another one was picked up off the ground and his body seemed to cave in on itself as Chan's L-39 caught him dead-centre. Miska watched the lens feed as the sniper picked up her weapon and ran. She cursed as she watched Chan shift aim.

'No, Goddammit, fire and manoeuvre, fire and manoeuvre!' she said as Torricone and herself moved quickly through the passages cut into the asteroid's rock. She could hear Mass shouting at Chan. Chan had decided to try his luck with the Machimoi, the exact thing they had told him not to do. He fired once, staggering the Martian-made power armour, then again. The rounds were hitting the large armoured humanoid shape but not going through the armour. Another shot. Then the Machimoi managed to bring his Dory to bear. The first burst tore through Chan's Wraith. It was clear he was dead. The Machimoi put two more into the Wraith just to be on the safe side.

'Shit!'

The two remaining contractors were advancing, laying down fire, filling the air with hypersonic needle-shaped armour-piercing rounds. She saw the woman with the shotgun who'd threatened her in the Revolution Will Be Televised cut down.

The gunman in the duster was backing towards the exit, custom-printed large calibre gauss pistols in each hand, firing round after round. Another contractor was rapidly firing a 25mm automatic grenade launcher, laying down thermal smoke, High Explosive and fragmentation grenades to cover his comrades' retreat. The explosions battered the contractors around a bit but they kept on advancing, firing, cutting down more of the mercs.

She checked the ops centre. There was a hole cut in the door. The hacker was still lying in one of the couches, tranced in, but Cartwright was gone.

And then Nyukuti, covered in his own blood, was standing over the hacker. Miska couldn't believe he wasn't dead. He'd taken a lot of rounds. He looked as though he could barely stand. He raised his boomer-sword. The contractor's eyes flickered open. She'd performed an emergency dump from the net, but Miska knew from experience it took a moment or two to work out where you were and what was going on. The hacker reached for the stand-over man but he brought the boomer-sword down and made her a head shorter. Miska spent just a moment wondering what it said about her life that this passed for good news. Nyukuti collapsed to the ground. She hoped he wasn't dead. She was left with one burning question, though:

'Che, where's Cartwright?' she asked as they reached a wide T-junction that led to the security offices. Joshua was in one of the cells on the other side of a door on the right, about three quarters of the way down the corridor. She knew that there was another T-junction at the end of the hundred-foot-long corridor.

Che showed her feed from a series of security lenses being burned out by focused microwaves. It was Cartwright with a patrol of four of the contractors and one of the Machimoi.

Miska thought he looked angry. The trail ended in the corridor that led to the T-junction opposite. She had no time but one advantage: as yet they didn't know where she was.

'Torricone, give me the laser torch. The Wraith's useless against their weapons and its hands are too big for you to fire the PDW we took from the contractor. I need you to get out of the Wraith and provide suppressing fire, use me for as much cover as you can. When they fire grenades you take cover in one of the rooms? Understand?' She was all business now, desperately trying to forget the kiss. *The kiss or his rejection?*

Torricone hesitated. *I don't have time for an argument,* she thought, but he handed over the laser torch and she slung the bulky tool across her back.

'Don't mess with the power armour, leave that to me, understood?' she asked as the front of Torricone's Wraith slid open and he stepped out. He was wearing the MMI body armour they'd taken from the contractor they'd killed in the printer room. He nodded, the PDW at the ready.

'Che, any help much appreciated,' she told the computer virus.

'I think you should move now,' he told her. She took a momentary glance at the battle in the stock area. One of the mining mechs had a Machimoi on the ground. The machine looked exactly like a predatory insect, its spinning drill maw cutting through the armour. The second Machimoi had braced itself against the wall, its foot keeping the other mech back as it put burst after burst into it from the railgun. The contractor's power armour was wreathed in explosions as the miners, the Wraiths and the remaining mercs fired everything they could at the Machimoi and the contractors, who were using the lip of the blast door for cover. The contractors, for their part, were taking their time, and almost casually cutting down the miners and their allies, one after another, every so often firing a grenade that would send broken bodies spinning into the air. The remaining contractors and the other Machimoi who'd made their way through the rec area were at one of the other entrances to the stores, affixing a thermite frame charge to the closed blast door. When they were through they'd be able to flank the miners.

'Ready?' she asked Torricone. He looked shit-scared and she couldn't blame him, but he nodded. They turned the corner, Miska going first, bringing up the L-39. Moving quickly, knowing that stealth in a situation like this with ancient power armour was basically nonsense. She didn't much like the L-39's homemade smartlink either. It seemed glitchy. She had the 20mm anti-tank weapon up at her shoulder like a regular rifle. Ten feet, twenty feet and then, ahead of her, the Machimoi turned into the corridor from her left. She squeezed the trigger on the L-39. Two contractors appeared from her right, one standing, the other kneeling. The gauss-kiss-assisted round hit the Machimoi, staggering it. She fired again. Heard the hypersonic scream as controlled, disciplined three-round burst after three-round burst hit her Wraith. Next generation Martian technology met the hundred-year-old design. The Wraith should have protected her against small arms fire but her power armour was feeding her IVD warnings about structural integrity. Their rounds were literally chewing her Wraith apart. Thirty feet, forty feet. Another two rounds from the L-39, keeping the Machimoi off balance. The occasional hypervelocity penetrator chipping away at the weapon, if they destroyed that then she was dead; but they'd been well trained and were going for the centre mass every time. Torricone made his presence known, firing a long burst down the corridor towards the two contractors, the rounds biting away at the rock. Tagging one of them, sending him staggering back out of sight. Fifty, sixty feet, moving fast but not so fast that she lost Torricone. Another two rounds. Every time the Machimoi tried to get its balance she hit it again. Four more left in the box.

The doors on either side of the corridor opened as they passed them, thanks to Che. One of the contractors poked his PDW around the corner and fired the grenade launcher blindly. Torricone threw himself into one of the rooms. Che closed the door behind him. The grenade exploded, knocking Miska's Wraith into the wall, armour sparking off rock. The Machimoi almost recovered. Miska squeezed the trigger. The L-39 kicked back hard against the Wraith's shoulder. The Machimoi hit the wall at the end of the corridor. Three rounds left.

'Reloading,' Torricone told her over the comms link. *Good*, she thought, he was holding it together. The contractors were back. The front of her Wraith was covered in pitted holes. She could feel them coming through now, though they'd lost most of their power penetrating the Wraith's armour. She tried to ignore the pain of multiple hits, her armoured clothing hardening to stop them reaching her flesh. She fired again. Eighty foot. Two rounds left. She fired again, slamming the Machimoi into the wall. Ninety feet. One round. *Okay*, she thought, *you've got all the gear but can you brawl?* The Machimoi pushed itself off the wall. Miska dropped the L-39 and kicked the other power-armoured suit as hard as she could. Then followed that with a punch and grabbed its Dory railgun and squeezed, almost snapping it in two. The two contractors were just machine gunning her in the side now. The Wraith couldn't take too much more of this kind of abuse.

'Grenade,' Torricone told her.

She heard the pop. The contractors moved away from the corner. The explosion rocked Miska's power armour but the Machimoi hadn't been expecting it. Miska swept the Machimoi's legs out from underneath it. She was already reaching for the mining laser. She stamped down on the Machimoi, slamming it into the ground. It was surprising how few power armour jockeys had first-hand experience of hand-to-hand in their suits but Miska had been in some really dirty fights. She switched on the laser torch before she brought it to bear on the Machimoi. The strobing red light cut a smoking line through the rock. One of the contractors, dazed by Torricone's grenade, walked into the beam. His bisected body collapsed to the ground. Miska stamped down on the Machimoi again and then all but stabbed it with the laser torch, raking it up through its chest area where the pilot's head would be. The powerful laser cut through the composite armour as though it was paper and the Machimoi went still.

The first HEAP grenade hit Miska's Wraith in the head. It was the sensor area for her power armour. Her own head was further down in the armour's chest. The detonation still battered her around hard enough to make her IVD jump and leave her dazed, nauseous and seeing lights. The second grenade decapitated her Wraith and almost caused her to black out. Somehow she had the presence of mind to trigger the emergency release. Explosive bolts blew off the front of her armour. Miska all but slithered to the ground. This, and the fact she was shorter than most people expected operators to be, meant that the burst aimed at her head went high. She had the gauss pistol she'd taken from the dead contractor in her hand. It was second nature. Three contractors left. One too many. A three-round burst from the pistol and one of the contractor's facemasks was replaced with a red mess. Shift, aim, fire. Another contractor falling back, face-shot, a spray of red in the air but she knew the third contractor had her.

Except he was dancing backwards as round after round hit him. Martian armour versus armour-piercing, electromagnetically driven, Martian hypervelocity rounds. The latter wins. There was a red mist behind the contractor. *Too many rounds*. Something nagging her at the back of her dazed and battered mind. The contractor fell to the ground and Torricone was standing over her reloading his PDW. *Good teamwork, poor fire control*, she thought. Something was still bothering her. More hypersonic screaming. Then it was Torricone dancing backwards and falling. She felt like screaming. Cartwright was standing over her, PDW levelled at her, and Miska knew she was dead.

CHAPTER 18

'Eject the magazine and toss the gun to me and the magazine down the corridor,' Cartwright told her.

Miska, sitting at the feet of her headless Wraith, was wondering why he didn't just shoot her but complying meant a few moments more life, and life meant hope. She took the mag out of the stolen gauss pistol and tossed it before tossing the weapon past Cartwright.

'You've got a pouch with four extra mags, chuck them as well.'

She unclipped the pouch from the webbing on the front of her jacket and chucked that too. Never taking her eyes off Cartwright. He still looked angry. She wondered if he wanted her alive for some reason. Gobbin? It seemed unlikely that the bounty the FBI and the marshal service had put on her head would stipulate alive. 'You carrying any other weapons?' he asked.

'Can't think of a good reason to answer that,' she told them. 'And whatever I tell you, you're still going to have to check.'

She was carrying Joshua's concealed backup pistol but she suspected that even if she used it against Cartwright's bare skin his dermal armour would stop the round dead. That left her with the folding knife she'd also taken from Joshua. She'd inspected it, it looked like a good knife, but nothing like a match for the titanium-bladed, diamond-edged combat knife she'd lost in the ops centre.

'I could shoot you,' he suggested.

'And you're not gonna?' she asked, a little confused. He wasn't behaving like a professional. Maybe he was infused with just a little too much Small Gods' tech and it had affected his ego. *Give a little, get a little*, she decided. She reached into the small of her back and removed the pistol's holster and tossed it past Cartwright. The two spare mags went down the corridor. Then the major did two things that she didn't expect. He grinned, and then he removed the magazine from the PDW and placed the weapon behind him and tossed the magazine down the corridor.

'What are you doing?' she asked.

'I don't need guns to kill you,' he said.

'Well no, but they make things a lot easier,' she pointed out. *Cyberpsychosis?* she wondered.

'You know, you're the human equivalent of that fucking virus. Seventeen successful ops and I've never lost a single man,' he spat.

Control freak, she decided. 'Because you pick easy jobs, soft targets.'

'You've lost me my bonus.' *Greedy control freak*, she amended. It was clear he wasn't paying her the slightest bit of attention and enjoyed the sound of his own voice. 'So you're going to suffer.'

278

'Do you think you're a supervillain?' Miska asked as she struggled to her feet. She was having difficulty focusing due to the ringing in her head and the omnipresent nausea. She really didn't want to get hit in the head again.

'I'm not the villain!' he screamed at her. Miska just raised an eyebrow.

'This is idiotic. You should have just shot me,' she told him. She couldn't help herself, though she noticed that he still had a sidearm. 'I'm going to beat your ass for being stupid.'

'I've already won this fight. I'm effectively the next step in human evolution—'

Miska kicked him in the head. It was a foolish thing to do. Kicks that high were too slow and he was too fast but he must have been distracted by his own human-plus soliloquy because she connected. Then he made her pay for her own foolishness. He caught her leg and delivered his own kick to her back, a kick that would have broken a non-reinforced spine. Instead it bounced her face-first off the rock wall. He grabbed her by the hair and pulled her back. Instead of resisting, Miska let him yank her. She threw herself into a clumsy hand-flip – it had been a while – that sent her booted feet running up the wall, helping her with the momentum. She landed on her feet. Cartwright was looking at a clump of her hair in his fist. Her scalp hurt so she punched him. Then again. Leaped into the air and elbowed him in the head, sending him staggering. A punch, another elbow, stamped down on one knee, putting him down on the other. Bringing her own up into the bottom of his jaw. *Martian superman my ass*, she thought.

'Enough,' he said, standing up and hooking a punch into her stomach that lifted her up off her feet and slammed her into the rock ceiling. She fell to the ground. Even with her boosted physiology her diaphragm was struggling to draw in air. *The fucking hair again!* she thought as he lifted her up. She lost more hair tearing herself free again and elbowed backwards, catching him in the face. She was pretty sure the rock had more give. He punched her in the kidneys. It felt like they'd exploded. The pain sent her to her knees. She knew he'd cracked her dermal armour. Miska tried to kick back out at him but he caught her ankle. *Dumb*, she had a moment to decide, as he stepped into the T-junction and spun her round, throwing her at the decapitated Wraith. She knocked the Wraith into the fallen Machimoi and ended up in a heap with the two destroyed power armours. She started to get up, but instead felt him grab her and yank her to her feet. She swung at him, he blocked, punched her in the stomach. The air exploded out of her again and she sank down to one knee. She held up a hand.

'A moment,' she managed between gasping for breath.

'Have you had enou—' he started. She put everything she had into the uppercut to his groin. He screamed and stumbled back. She managed to stagger to her feet. He looked really angry so she laughed at him. Cartwright grabbed her and slammed her against the rock wall. Suddenly he had the knife her dad had given her in his hand and nothing was funny any more.

'Give me my knife back,' she managed, drooling blood down herself. Miska knew she wasn't thinking straight, the pain, nausea and not least the anger, but she had remembered the one weapon she had left. Her left side was to him, concealing her right hand as it reached for the folding knife she had taken from Joshua in the ore shuttle.

'Oh you'll get it back but first—' The knife snicked open and she rammed it into his open mouth. His screaming sounded like that of an animal. His eyes widened, pain and fury warring on his face. Fury won as he spun her around and threw her into the corridor. She crawled away from him. Glanced behind her. He was waving his hands around in front of his mouth as though he didn't know what to do with the knife sticking out of it. Then he realised what she was trying to do and came after her. Miska reached the L-39 where she'd dropped it, grabbed the weapon and rolled onto her back as Cartwright reached for her. She squeezed the trigger at near point-blank range. She screamed out as the recoil dislocated her shoulder and sent her sliding along the floor. The round caught Cartwright, sending him flying backwards. At the same time she heard a pop. The 25mm HEAP grenade caught him in mid-air and he exploded. His head spun off as though she'd just triggered a lowjack. She slumped back to the ground, her shoulder and many other parts of her body competing for agonised attention. She glanced over at the bloodied, badly injured Torricone, the under-barrel grenade launcher on his PDW still smoking. He slumped back to the ground. She wanted to do the same. Unconsciousness seemed a beautiful thing but she couldn't risk it. The miners were about to get flanked and torn to pieces and the TCC cruisers were nearly upon them. She forced herself to her feet and went looking for a few things.

'Get up, soldier!' she shouted at Torricone. She couldn't bring herself to call him a marine, though he'd certainly been working for a living today.

'Fucking kidding me,' he mumbled through a mouthful of blood.

Miska all but dragged Torricone down the corridor towards the security offices cellblock. He was leaving a trail of blood behind him but she didn't have the time to deal with that right now.

She was watching countdowns in her IVD. The miners had been flanked and they, along with the mercs and the remaining Wraiths, had pulled back into the actual stores themselves. Two of the Wraiths had been destroyed, and there was some wreckage scattered about that might have once been a third. She also saw the remains of the two mining mechs. All that was left was for the contractors to hunt down the rest of the miners and their allies.

The door to the small cellblock was open. There was a barred door inside that slid open. Joshua was in the first cell. She left Torricone leaning against the rock, trying to hold his blood in. He would need medical attention soon. Joshua stared up at the bloodied mess that was Miska, appalled.

'You,' he managed. Che opened the barred sliding door to his cell. Miska wasn't sure that was a great idea, she didn't think that she was capable of dealing with him if it came to a fight.

'I need your backdoor into the *Excelsior*,' she told him.

'I don't have one,' he told her.

'That's your fucking plan?' Torricone spat, drooling more blood. 'I got shot for this bullshit!'

He didn't understand. Every hacker she knew, whenever they came into long-term contact with any kind of net architecture, added their own backdoors, their own failsafes. It was part good practice, part pride, but mostly self-protection. You never knew when a deal could turn bad or when an employer could turn on you. She'd set up backdoors herself on numerous occasions.

'I wasn't on the *Excelsior* long enough,' he told her. He was looking past Miska. She suspected he was trying to see if Nyukuti was with them.

'You're not a very good liar,' she told him.

He crossed his arms. 'But you don't have the time to break me, so you may as well surrender.'

Torricone's laughter sounded like a wet cough.

'Your friends have made it pretty clear that they're not going to accept a surrender,' he told Joshua. Miska watched the hacker blanch.

'I don't have my stand-over man with me,' she said and transferred what she was just about managing to carry with her dislocated right hand into her left. 'All I've got is this.' She threw Cartwright's head, Joshua's knife still rammed in his mouth, onto his bunk. Joshua pushed himself away from it, staring, horrified. He looked between it and Miska.

'You people are fucking bastards,' he managed.

'And you're a coward, and we know that.' She drew her own knife and showed it to him. 'Live or die, it's that simple.'

He sent her access to the backdoors into the *Excelsior*'s system and she forwarded them to Che just as Torricone slid to the ground.

It didn't look like anything had happened with the frigate. She checked the external lens feed. The *Excelsior* was still holding off the station as the TCC cruisers came into close firing range, taking position over the station.

Checking the feed from the stores room she saw that the two remaining Machimoi were completely still. That was the thing about the contractors with Cartwright. They were too confident in their unassailable Martian technology. All their vehicles had integrated comms, unlike the antiquated Wraiths her crew had been using. Even so, she was impressed to the point of horror at the power of the Che virus.

'This is Excelsior-One-Actual to all Excelsior call signs. You will lay down your weapons and offer an unconditional surrender immediately. You will not be harmed but any refusal to do so will result in an immediate termination of contract, unpaid.' It was the Che virus but it sounded like Cartwright, right down to the cadence and rhythm of his speech. They were too professional to disobey on an op but each of the squad and fire team leaders queried the order and made it clear that they were winning. She could hear the anger, the frustration in the contractors' voices. The Che virus just told them that the situation had changed.

Miska locked Joshua back in his cell and was seeing to Torricone's injuries, applying medgel to the entry and exit wounds. It was difficult with only one arm working properly. At the same time she made contact with Reg and Chanar and told them that the contractors were about to surrender. They took some convincing. In fact they had to see it to believe it. Then she contacted Mass. She told him what was happening.

'Make yourself in charge of disarming them, steal as much as you can, get the Machimoi if possible.'

Mass chuckled over the comms link. 'Will do, boss,' he told her.

Miska checked the window for the net feed in her IVD, expanding it. The war between the *Excelsior* and the pirate port, with its cannons and neon lightning, certainly seemed to be ongoing but she was pretty sure it was all just for show. In the net the two TCC cruisers looked like proud, tall sailing ships of a type called East Indiamen, according to the info on them. They were sailing through the still-calm black glass ocean, the net's representation of space, around the headland that protected the port. Presumably they were about to join in the electronic war.

She glanced at the last remaining countdown. Che had opened the comms link between the *Excelsior* and the two cruisers to her. The virus had cut out the human crew and, as he'd done with Cartwright, was spoofing their comms, sending false signals to the TCC cruisers, letting them think the contractors were still in control. Miska smiled as she imagined the panic on board the frigate. The smile left her as she thought about what the Che virus had done. Admittedly it had effectively had an invitation into every system that it had invaded, but even so it was too powerful.

Joshua was sat on his bed, hugging his legs, face-down, dealing with his choice of life over loyalty. Getting killed for a corporate contract was a lot to ask, to be fair.

She checked the last remaining countdown in her IVD. It had almost reached zero. She enlarged the external lens feed window again. It looked like the *Excelsior* was sporing. The frigate ejected crystalline sand to confuse the TCC cruisers' lidar and chaff, small pieces of aluminium foil, to confuse their radars. A quick glance in the electronic world saw both the net representations of the *Excelsior* and the colonial fort turn their attention on the East Indiamen, as the two copies of the Che virus electronically attacked the TCC cruisers. She opened a comms link.

'Hangman-One-Actual, to Hangman-Actual, how are you doing Dad?' she asked.

'Hangman-Actual to Hangman-One-Actual, I hate this.' The reply had been audio only. Her dad, like any ground-pounder, hated fleet actions. Few things made an infantryman feel more helpless, more divorced from control of their own destiny. He might have been nominally in charge of the *Hangman's Daughter* but ultimately he was at the mercy of the ship's advanced, borderline-AI autopilot. 'But we'll be there,' he assured her.

'Solid copy, Hangman-Actual.' She killed the comms link and looked at the feed from the station's external lenses. In real space the *Excelsior* blossomed ordnance targeting the closest cruiser. The frigate launched multiple heat-seeking missiles. Lasers, rail-guns and the frigate's large spinal particle beam weapon lit up space. A frigate picking a fight with a cruiser would be suicidal under normal circumstances but the TCC's ships had thought they were dealing with an ally. The frigate was too close for the cruisers' counter measures to be truly effective. The TCC ships' point defence lasers managed to destroy some of the incoming missiles, but not enough. Plasma fire rolled across the closest cruiser. Between the plasma eating through the cruiser's armour plate and the beams of high-energy particles disrupting the ship's molecular structure, it never stood a chance. Its back broken, the ship started to come apart.

The other cruiser's manoeuvring thrusters were burning brightly as it shot away from the asteroid mine, trying to keep the wreckage of its sister ship between itself and the turncoat *Excelsior*. The *Hangman's Daughter*, having completed a full orbit of the gas giant, accelerating all the while, sped by underneath the asteroid and the cruiser, the prison barge's approach having been hidden from the TCC ships by the chaff and sand. It was little more than a strafing run. Red fingers of angry light reached out from the prison barge's laser cannons. The missile batteries emptied their payload but the remaining cruiser's point defences intercepted the majority of them, their detonating warheads filling space with silent force and light. The cruiser's engines were burning bright as it tried to leave orbit. It launched missiles and lasers stabbed down at the *Daughter*. The prison barge's own point defences took care of the missiles, though some of its armour plate took a scorching from the lasers.

Miska only saw it because she was looking for it. The *Daughter* all but ejected one of the shuttles. The craft flipped over and burned hard to bleed off speed, skimming off the very edge of Proxima G's atmosphere, aerobraking to further slow down.

The *Hangman's Daughter* was rapidly disappearing from view but its attack had only ever been meant as a distraction, giving the frigate time to manoeuvre and refill the missile cradles in its batteries. It came up from behind the asteroid mine firing again. This time it had to be more measured. They couldn't rely on surprise, though the second cruiser was still off balance, the fire from the missile that had made it through still rolling across the hull.

Lasers and railguns targeted the cruiser's point defences, trying to clear paths for the missiles as the particle beam cannon fired again and again. The cruiser fired its own weapons as it turned. The frigate's point defences reached out to destroy the incoming missiles. Hits from the cruiser's railguns powdered parts of the *Excelsior*'s armour, lasers superheated parts of the hull until they exploded, but the remaining TCC ship was running and could not bring its bigger, more powerful weapons to bear. The frigate helped it on its way with lasers and particle beams, the cruiser leaving a smoke-like trail of disrupted matter in its wake. The *Excelsior* did not follow. Miska reckoned the cruiser would get far enough out and then accelerate to faster-than-light and head back to Proxima E. She knew it would be back later, returning mob-handed. They didn't have much time.

'Okay, we need to get going,' she told Torricone. He nodded. He looked pale, shaky and pained but he was still functioning.

'You too,' she told Joshua, and the cell door slid open. She didn't want to leave a hacker loose and wandering around.

She was also trying to work out how to profit from this. The funds from the black credit chip that Cartwright had given her wouldn't even begin to cover the cost of the missiles that the *Hangman's Daughter* had just fired.

Joshua looked up at her from the bunk. His expression was difficult to make out but Miska estimated it was two parts self-loathing and one part hatred of her. Then his eyes rolled up into his head and he fell back onto the bed, his body racked by violent spasms. Torricone turned to look at her.

'I didn't do anything!' she protested.

'Shouldn't we help him?' the car thief asked. Joshua was throwing himself around the bed with some vigour. 'Hold him down, make sure he doesn't hurt himself?'

'He could be faking,' Miska said, not really believing that as Joshua spasmed so hard he ended up on the floor of the tiny cell, his back arcing painfully. She knew she should be helping him but frankly she was wondering why nothing was ever simple. She knelt down, letting out a scream as she jarred her dislocated right arm. She reached for Joshua's legs with her left. Torricone, his teeth gritted through the pain, was trying to move past the thrashing Joshua to hold his arms down when the hacker suddenly become still. His eyes flickered open. There was something very different about the expression on his face.

'Joshua?' Torricone asked.

'No,' apparently-not-Joshua answered. Miska did not like where this was going. Joshua pushed himself up into a sitting position and then stood up, looking down at his hands. A really bad idea had occurred to Miska.

'Che?' she asked. Torricone stared at her. Joshua looked up.

'It's not my name, but yes,' he told her. 'Joshua wasn't a very nice person and he was weak.' Miska stared at him.

'He's possessed?' Torricone demanded. Electronic possession was the story for about a million vizzes, she thought. The Che virus had meat-hacked Joshua.

'You're not meant to be able to do that,' Miska said. 'There are safeguards.' There were documented cases of it happening but not for a very long time, thanks to better technology and, more importantly, the Small Gods becoming manifest and moving out of the net. 'Are you one of the Small Gods?' she asked. Che/Joshua shook his head.

'This is not their technology,' he told her.

'This is sequestration, this is bad shit,' Torricone said. He'd held it together through the gunfights, despite the fear, but now he sounded really scared. Che/Joshua turned his head to look at Torricone.

'Is it any different to what she's done to you?' he asked.

'She's hardly a role model!' Torricone cried. 'And I thought you were all about breaking the yoke of slavery ...'

'By any means necessary,' Che/Joshua told him and turned to Miska.

'Are you here to kill me? Because that's not worked out for anyone yet today.' Of course, most of her fighting had been done before she'd dislocated her arm. It was only due to implanted pain-management systems she was still able to function at the level she was. It still hurt like a bastard.

Che/Joshua didn't answer immediately. She'd retrieved the hacked gauss pistol but she wasn't much of a shot with her left hand.

'No,' he finally said. 'Well, not today. What you have done is not right.'

'So what, you want to release six thousand criminals, most of them violent, on the colonies?' she asked. 'They're not nice people, I mean Torricone's okay, but the rest of them ...' She shook her head.

Again there was a long pause as Che seemed to consider this, studying her at the same time.

'No, and I know about your killswitch,' he told her. Miska went cold but did her best not to betray any reaction. 'Tamper with it and it sets off their collars. A very impressive bit of programming, even by my standards.'

'Are you going to make me ask you what you want again?'

'You know that the TCC are going to be back mob-handed,' Che/Joshua said.

'Uh huh,' Miska said as she checked the external feed in her IVD again. She could see the prison shuttle that the *Hangman's Daughter* had dropped off making its way towards the station. She knew the Quick Reaction Force her dad had assembled was on board.

'Now, I'm guessing that your intention is to cut your losses and leave the system, abandon the miners to their fate.'

'Something like that,' Miska said. She ignored Torricone staring at her.

'I think you could get the TCC off the miners' backs,' Che/Joshua told her.

'Possibly, but why would I do that?'

'Because it's the right thing to do,' Torricone suggested. Miska continued to ignore him.

'I don't think what you're doing is right. Eventually I will take an interest but if you try your best to work on the side of angels then I'll leave you and your people alone, for the time being.'

'Thanks,' Torricone muttered.

Miska tried to cross her arms, forgetting the dislocation for a moment. The pain reminded her.

290

'Who are you?' Miska demanded. 'You working alone?' Che/Joshua just looked at her, saying nothing. 'You want us to work on the side of angels, you use all your vast net power and get some money to hire us with. In the meantime we're still mercenaries, remember?'

'You're a mercenary. I'm a slave,' Torricone pointed out.

'Hush now,' Miska said, then returned her attention to the meat puppet. 'If you don't waste too much more of my time, I might be able to hit the TCC where it hurts, keep them off the miners' backs,' Miska told him at the same time as she composed a text and sent it to the Che virus: *You want this over with, find out who killed my dad and why.* He narrowed his eyes and then nodded. He'd received and understood the message. *But I want something in return,* she added by text.

'What?' Che/Joshua asked out loud. Miska just smiled.

CHAPTER 19

'I got shot,' Torricone said as Miska tried her best to drag him through the admin area towards the docks. Her right shoulder was agony and each staggering step sent more pain lancing through it.

'Yes, you did,' Miska said. They passed a number of people, mostly miners but Mass had sent one of the Wraiths with a sack to harvest what weapons and ammunition he could from the fire team that she and Torricone had fought. The miners either ignored her or glared at her angrily. *Some people just don't have any gratitude,* she thought.

'Why am I still alive?' he asked.

Through the internal lenses, which the Che virus controlling the station was still allowing her access to, she had seen the shuttle from the *Daughter* dock. The QRF had debussed to 'help' secure the asteroid.

'Luck, I guess,' Miska told him, not really paying attention as they approached the corridor that led to the ops centre.

She had no idea where Che/Joshua was. He'd picked up one

of the contractors' sidearms, seemingly instantly hacked it, taken some ammunition and gone his own way. Miska hadn't been sad to see him go. She found the possessing entity more than a little disconcerting.

'I mean it,' he said.

She gave it a little more thought. 'The PDWs fire four-point-seven millimetre penetrators, armour-piercing. They're shaped like needles, well actually more like thorns, but they'll just fly straight through you. I guess they didn't hit anything too crucial. It's why Dad's teaching you all failure drill.'

'Two in the chest, one in the head?'

'Yeah, the contractors would've done it if they'd had the time. Seriously though, it's why I like a laser, or a larger calibre slugthrower with a gauss-kiss. I like people to fall over when I shoot them.'

They staggered around the corner and she could see Mass's Wraith. He was standing just outside the ops centre with Reg and an angry-looking Chanar. All three of them turned to look at her as she approached.

'Let me guess, you're going to run away and leave us unarmed, after you used us as cannon fodder?' Chanar demanded.

'Your guys are stealing all the contractors' gear,' Reg started angrily.

'Why the fuck is the QRF all Bethlehem Milliners?' Mass demanded, the Wraith's loudspeaker cutting through the hubbub. This last got her attention. That wasn't supposed to happen. Gangs were supposed to be broken up, not go out at double platoon-strength.

'We need something to deal with Martian armour when Triple-S come back,' Reg persisted.

'That motherfucker Teramoto's in charge, what were you thinking ...?' Mass continued.

'More than half my people dead—'

'It's spitting in the face—'

'Shut up!' she shouted. *Oh, great leadership*, she admonished herself, but the three of them were quiet.

'Can I sit down, please?' Torricone asked. This she could do at least. She let go of him and he half fell, half slid down the rock wall to sit on the ground. Miska noticed Mass's Wraith's head turning to look at the car thief. Reg and Chanar both towered over her, Mass's power armour even more so. They all seemed to be looming towards her. Conscious of time, she was looking for a way to shortcut the inevitable arguments.

'Right!' she pointed with her left hand at Chanar. 'You still in contact with Che?' He glared at her for a moment and then nodded.

'Okay, he's effectively hired me to handle the TCC, but I need to get going.'

'What's he paying with?' Reg asked. She could hear the suspicion in her fellow mercenary leader's voice. He was watching one of the Wraiths walk by carrying a sack of weapons, ammunition and gear taken from the contractors. The Wraith had an L-39 over one shoulder and was carrying a Dory railgun, and had its backpack ammunition drum awkwardly in the other hand. 'We saw your people loading up the undamaged Machimois.'

'That's our fee,' Miska confirmed. 'That and the frigate.'

'So you'll leave us absolutely undefended?' Chanar demanded. He shifted towards her. Miska was pretty sure he would have cheerfully crushed the life out of her if he thought he could have got away with it.

'Easy there, pal,' Mass growled. 'She said we'll take care of it. You're just going to have to trust us.' Miska was pretty sure that Mass was assuming that she was just going to abandon the miners to their fate. Chanar didn't look convinced either.

'Kind of difficult to do that when you've already betrayed us once,' Chanar pointed out.

'Strictly speaking it was a successful infiltration, rather than a betrayal,' Miska explained. 'But I can see why you'd feel that way. Look, talk to Che, he'll explain it, because the longer I have to spend discussing it with you the longer it gives the TCC to react.'

Chanar glared at her and then leaned towards her. 'Never come back here. You understand me?'

She didn't like being threatened. She thought about telling him that if she ever did come back it would be for a contract. Instead she just nodded, Chanar stormed into the ops centre and she turned towards Mass. Reg grabbed her arm. The dislocated one. She did some screaming and then turned to face him. Something in her face made him back up, hands in the air. She didn't like being manhandled at the best of times, least of all when hurting. Mass was reaching for him but she held up her left hand, signalling for him to stop.

'Sorry,' Reg said. 'But we're mercenaries as well.'

'And you've got a contract with him,' she said nodding towards where Chanar was stood in the ops centre, his lips moving as he subvocalised. He was presumably in communication with Che. He didn't look happy. 'We didn't kill you. What more do you want?'

'A share of the spoils of war.'

'You say spoils of war, I say my pay.'

'The TCC send Triple-S back in here and we don't have

295

much that can touch them. Strikes me that you're profiting from my people's risk and their deaths.' Again she opened her mouth to tell him that her people had been right there with them but as she did she felt someone touch her leg. She looked down to see Torricone looking up at her, shaking his head. She sighed. *He's really getting too big for his boots,* she decided.

'Okay, we'll come to some agreement over the PDWs, see if we can find something that will help you deal with power armour,' she told the mercenary leader. *Christ, having to be diplomatic is difficult,* she decided, *why can't everyone just do what I tell them to?* 'Also you've got the Triple-S prisoners. Ransom them back to the company. They'll all have kidnap insurance, so you shouldn't have a problem getting paid.' Triple-S's insurance premiums were going to go through the roof, which at least made her smile.

Reg considered this for a moment and then nodded and walked over to speak to Chanar in the ops centre. Miska turned and looked up at the big, armoured form that was Mass's Wraith.

'You look like shit, boss,' Mass pointed out, his voice booming out of the Wraith's PA.

'Good work,' she told him. The Wraith made an expansive gesture.

'It's just another street, boss. I'm enjoying fleecing those contractor assholes, feels like old times.'

The Mafia, she thought, *best asset strippers ever.* 'If you ever question my orders in front of outsiders again, I won't blow your collar. I'll just take my knife and skull-fuck you, understand me?' It was strange watching a Wraith bristle.

'Teramoto killed one of my peop—' Mass started over the comms link.

'You don't have any people,' Miska said.

'Well, he certainly seems to,' Mass spat and Miska had to admit he had a point.

'The murderer was dealt with—' Miska started.

'We know that Teramoto ordered it, just to make a fucking—'

'That's enough,' she snapped and pointed at him, again with her left. 'Leave your street shit back in the street, understand me?' She received a curt nod from the power armour. She wasn't particularly happy about it either. She wanted to know what her dad had been thinking. 'Now grip my right shoulder.' She yelped as the power armour's hand took hold of her. 'Hold it tight.' She wrenched her shoulder back into its socket. Suddenly everyone nearby was looking her way as she did some more screaming.

'We've got a doc in there,' Mass told her. Miska blinked. Let the pain subside and then looked into the ops centre. There were corpses all over the floor. Nyukuti was lying on a blood-stained couch, the doc-turned-serial-killer her dad had sent with the QRF tending to the stand-over man's wounds. The doc was the most nondescript man she'd ever seen. She wondered if his nondescriptness had anything to do with the reason behind the sixty-plus dead patients he'd been convicted of killing.

'He going to live?' she asked. Torricone half fell over trying to turn around and look into the ops centre. She glanced down and saw the car thief look at Merrill's body, and then Gleave's. The doctor looked up at her, clearly irritated with the interruption, but nodded curtly. Whatever else Nyukuti was, he was certainly tough.

'What about him?' Mass asked, his Wraith nodding down at Torricone. 'Did he fight?'

'He fought,' Miska said. *Maybe a little too well*. Torricone pushed himself back into a sitting position and looked up at Mass's Wraith but didn't say anything.

'The *Excelsior*'s just docked,' Mass told her a little later. She checked the dock's lens feed to confirm. A platoon's worth of the QRF were covering the airlock, supported by six Wraiths.

'I need to go,' she told Mass. 'I'm taking the contractors' assault shuttle back to the *Daughter*. The Che virus is going to bring the frigate to the *Daughter* once all the contractors are off. Take everything from them, leave a quarter of the PDWs and heavy weapons, anything that could hurt a Machimoi, for Reg and his guys. Load all of our people and everything that isn't in the frigate onto our shuttle and get back to the *Daughter* as quickly as possible.'

'Understood.'

Miska turned and strode away from the ops centre, making for the docks. She contacted Teramoto and told him that Mass had some orders for him. She hoped this would go some way to putting Teramoto in his place and to smooth Mass's ruffled feathers. She received a curt acknowledgement from the Yakuza lieutenant.

At the dock she was impressed by Mass's thoroughness. The few living contractors left from the initial assault had been stripped down to their underwear. Everything else had been stolen. They were on their knees, hands cabled behind their backs, being watched over by armed members of the QRF.

The airlock that the *Excelsior* had docked with was open. Contractors and flight crew were emerging into the waiting hands of the QRF, being put down on the ground, any armour or gear they were wearing removed and their hands cabled as well. As Miska walked by, exchanging a nod with Teramoto, she had to admit that the Yakuza lieutenant was running a tight crew, and his *bōsōzoku* henchmen almost looked like real soldiers. It was as though they had something to prove.

The assault shuttle handled much better than the prison shuttles and it felt good to be connected to a piece of military machinery, especially a state of the art Martian-built Pegasus like this one. As she dropped away from the asteroid, however, triggering just a long enough burn to make for a lower orbit, she realised that after flying the *Little Jimmy* the assault shuttle still handled like a brick. This made her smile. Some things never changed.

Checking the feed from the lens mounted along the bottom of the Pegasus she saw the *Hangman's Daughter* below her in a low orbit over Proxima G. The huge prison barge was going much slower than when she'd last seen it. Aerobraking, skimming off the gas giant's atmosphere, had considerably slowed her down and saved on fuel by doing so. This whole operation had been a disaster in terms of resource expenditure but Miska had to give the upgraded autopilot its credit, it had certainly earned its pay on this job. She opened an AV comms link to the *Daughter*. Her dad's image appeared holographically superimposed over the windscreen.

'Hangman-One ... Dad, what the actual fuck!'

'What have I told you about that kind of language?' her dad asked, but crucially he didn't sound angry.

'Teramoto and all his *bōsōzoku* junior-Yak buddies? What were you thinking? We don't do that, and you're rewarding bad behaviour.'

'You left me in charge, Miska, and it sounded like things were going bad. I sent them because I knew they could work as

299

a cohesive team.' And from what little she'd seen on the dock it looked as though her father was right. More to the point she had, indeed, left him in charge. It wasn't fair to second-guess his decisions now.

'I'm just worried that it's set a precedent,' she said.

'We set the precedents,' he told her. *Sometimes it doesn't feel that way.* She thought back to the deal she'd made with Vido. 'Torricone?' he asked.

'Someone taught him how to fight, to shoot as it happens, but all his experience was in the street. He told me it was his mum. This was the first time he'd seen real combat and he was shit-scared. The people who came for you were real drink-blood-from-a-hollowed-out skull types, hard-core, pipe-hitting carnivores.' The comms link went quiet. 'Plus Vido said he knew him back on Barney's Prime.'

'That just means the LCN could have been involved, and he's covering.' LCN was a law enforcement/intelligence community acronym for la Cosa Nostra, the Mafia.

'Is that what you think?' she asked.

She watched her father's weathered, craggy face consider it. She wondered if having him around helped or not. She was self-critical enough, in a positive way, to suspect it didn't, but not worried enough to do anything about it just yet.

'No,' he finally said. 'I don't get the meat-eating, apex-predator feel from him. He's a smarter than the average street punk, and someone's taught him some skills. That's about it. He probably should have joined the marines.'

Miska chuckled. 'You think everyone should have joined the marines.'

'It'd be good for them.'

'Pretty crowded Corps.'

'Give the next alien-invading mother— race a fright, though,' he told her. 'I'd like to meet his mum.' The change of subject left Miska a little confused.

'Who's?'

'Torricone's.' He was grinning at her.

'Dad!'

'Hey, I'm old not dead. Well, I am dead but you know what I mean.'

She stared at him for a moment, appalled, and then burst out laughing.

'How'd it go?' her dad finally asked.

'We won,' she told him. *At a cost.* She hadn't even seen the butcher's bill yet. She didn't know how many and who they'd lost.

'Until the TCC return with Triple-S and make an example of everyone on the station?'

'I'm dealing with that. Besides which, we need to teach everyone an object lesson about what happens when people screw us over.'

'How?'

Her dad's face appeared on the screen on the pillar she was walking towards. She was up on cellblock six. The ghost blue light from the gel-filled tanks seemed peaceful today, but perhaps that was just in comparison with all the recent violence.

'I don't think this is a good idea,' her dad told her as she walked by. His image appeared on the next screen. 'Miska, I don't think you've thought this through.' She walked past that image and he appeared on the next pillar. 'He pretty much ignores any training. We don't even know if he's got any sense of self-preservation. He could just ignore the collar.' *Then he'll lose his head*, Miska thought. 'And you're going to let a prisoner know about *Little Jimmy*?' That was the part of her plan that made her feel the most uncomfortable. She reached the end of the cellblock and her father appeared six stories tall on the big screen against the back wall. 'You know this is wrong, don't you?'

She knew he wanted to add: *Answer me, young lady!* and was thankful that he knew enough not to. The thing was, he was right. Just the idea of what she was about to do sent a thrill of excitement running through her. She felt like a kid playing with fireworks.

With a thought she had the ship lower the arm that held solitary from the roof.

The *Little Jimmy* wasn't any faster travelling at superluminal speeds than other similarly capable ships that the TCC and Triple-S would send. She had seen the taskforce being assembled in orbit as she'd approached Proxima E. There were more than enough ships there to obliterate the asteroid but she suspected that they would try an assault anyway. She wondered if they were already doing PR damage control. Was she being blamed for whatever bad thing was about to happen? Were the Triple-S already being put forward as heroes trying to save the asteroid from her pirates? Perhaps the miners were now little more than hostages, happy workers, grateful to the TCC, but oh dear, Miska and her army of criminals have massacred them all. It didn't matter, she'd collected more than enough documentary evidence of what had been happening as she went along. She'd put it all on the net when they were finished. Not that it mattered. People believed what they wanted to anyway.

The *Little Jimmy* was buttoned up tight. The manoeuvres had been done far out, the heat already bled off, all unessential systems shut down to minimise EM signature, and she'd hit the atmosphere as far away from the spoke and TCC's HQ arcology as she could. If they'd noticed her entry she was hoping that they'd assume it was just one of the common meteors out of Proxima's nearby debris ring.

She wove *Little Jimmy* through the strip-mined trenches eaten out of the planet's pitted, meteor-blasted surface, following the paths of the huge, worm-like robot mining machines. It wasn't flying through artificial canyons towards the city-sized planetary headquarters of a powerful hypercorp whose nose she'd bloodied that was making her nervous, however. It was her silent passenger sitting in the bucket seat behind her. Absurdly, she felt like she was on a first date.

She found what she was looking for, a box-like, hardened plastic and composite shack covered in various aerials. It was a comms relay/booster shack designed to help the operators communicate with the huge machine worms in the canyons through Proxima E's corrosive atmosphere.

She was relying on *Little Jimmy*'s reactive camouflage, an exuded, liquid crystal thinscreen that showed synchronised footage of the surrounding terrain and/or sky to blend in with it, to keep her hidden. Her eyes were closed. Her body was the ship-turned-aircraft, her senses the sensors. She manoeuvred *Little Jimmy* until it was vertical, perpendicular to the cliff, just under the comms shack. She extended the landing gear, moving the stealth ship closer and closer to the canyon wall. The caustic wind was kicking her around, trying to ditch her wing-first into the smoothed-down rock but she held it and felt the landing gear touch the wall, the molecular hooks adhering to the surface. Miska realised that even tranced in to the ship, she'd been holding her breath.

Her icon appeared as a hologram standing on the ship's control panel in front of her tranced form.

'There's an Hostile Environment Suit, a climber, and weapons by the airlock. Signal me when you're in position,' her holographic icon self told him. He nodded and unbuckled his seatbelt and climbed up through the ship towards the airlock. The hologram disappeared.

In the skull of the metallic raven that was the *Little Jimmy*'s net representation, Miska was watching feed from one of the ship's external lenses through a floating window. One of the huge worm-like mining machines was making its way past the ship. Its segmented body was a series of armoured skirts. Its maw was a mass of different shaped, different sized, very powerful drills that it used to pull itself through the planet's rock flesh like a maggot in an apple. Inside its body the ore was refined, the various minerals extracted, the crushed by-products used as raw material for construction printers. With a thought she sent the *Little Jimmy*'s tendrils wriggling out to bury their way into the relay shack. When she checked how the mining machines looked in the net she wasn't surprised to see that they were monstrous worms.

She was aware of the airlock opening and then closing. She noticed that he hadn't taken the HES suit or any of the weapons.

The TCC's electronic security had given her more than a little trouble. It had taken some time to sneak and then spoof their systems as comprehensively as she needed to. She was pretty sure that even with her skills she wouldn't have been able to do it without the hardlink to their comms, the software in *Little Jimmy*, and the NSA backdoor library it contained in its memory. Still, apparently it had given him enough time to cover the distance from the comms relay shack, through the graveyards of skeletal, wind-corroded, abandoned machinery, to the arcology itself. She had received his signal. Then it had been a matter of waiting as she watched the real world through the lens feed, waiting and timing.

Miska watched as Laura Gobbin and her two bodyguards walked into a dark office. The floor to ceiling windows that made up two sides of her corner office were completely opaque, the lights out.

'Lights,' the HR executive ordered. The lights didn't come on. One of her windows became a screen, however. Cartoon Miska looked out at her from the arcology's netscape. Both the arcology and the nearby spoke had been designed in what Miska could only describe as industrial-feudal-Japanese-chic. The arcology itself looked as though someone had mixed a castle from Japan's Tokogawa Shogunate era with an oil refinery. She didn't think the TCC were getting past their pollution aesthetics any time soon.

'Hi!' Miska said, with cheeriness she didn't quite feel. Her various injuries and fatigue were catching up with her. To Gobbin's credit she showed no sign of surprise. 'Sorry about the lights, it's a real fucker when things don't do what they're supposed to, isn't it?'

'Do you have a point?' Gobbin asked. She was standing in the light from the open door. Her bodyguards were on either side of her, both of them mostly in darkness, but Miska could see enough of them to know that they were paying attention to their surroundings, demonstrating situational awareness. They weren't watching her on the screen, or looking at their boss. They were checking all around, looking for real world threats.

Okay, now we find out if it's all hype, she thought. Gobbin sneered and said, 'I'm late for a meeting.'

Miska almost missed it but it looked as though one of the bodyguards had been yanked, no sucked, into the darkness. Gobbin hadn't even noticed. *Holy fuck! Who is this guy?* She couldn't have done that. Not in those circumstances, not without someone else in the room noticing. She wasn't sure she knew any operators who could. She knew she should have been frightened. Instead she felt excited.

'Would that be to discuss Faigroe Station's independence?' she asked.

Gobbin said nothing. She just stared at the screen.

'They're to be left alone. The station is theirs now. You don't go back there, no blockades, no bullshit financial, propaganda, or psychological warfare, and no hacking. Just leave them in peace, let them trade with the free ports and indies.'

Gobbin laughed. It contained no trace of humour whatsoever. 'Or what, Corporal Corbin?' the HR exec demanded.

'Or we come back.' It had taken her a moment to respond. The other bodyguard had gone as well! She hadn't even seen that and Gobbin still hadn't noticed.

'Are you trying to frighten me?' Gobbin asked, a cold smile on her lips now.

'I think you misunderstand,' Miska said. In the net three monstrous, leathery worms with multi-segmented mouths reared up over the netscape. '*You* are the message. Your bosses had better understand.' The windows became transparent just in time for Gobbin to watch the three huge machine worms bite into the bottom of the arcology. It was like an earthquake hitting. Gobbin staggered. The Ultra was there to catch her. He looked like the marble statue of a god come to life. His prison uniform had mostly been corroded away by Proxima E's winds, and was now little more than rags. He held a bloodied scalpel in his left hand. The two bodyguards were lain out on the floor, shaken from their repose by the impact, blood forming a puddle underneath them.

Gobbin, to her credit, looked more angry than afraid. 'You people really are bastards.'

CHAPTER 20

The *Little Jimmy* slowly circled the arcology, which was being rapidly evacuated as the three huge, worm-like mining robots chewed their way into the lower levels. The hardest thing had been spoofing their controllers into believing the huge machines were somewhere else as they approached the arcology. There must have been panic when they were first spotted. There would still be panic, though Miska noted that they hadn't been hit with orbital weapons. She assumed there was an ongoing and rapid cost analysis comparing the damage they were doing against how much the robots cost and how much revenue they would lose if they were destroyed. If the war in the net to take control of the robots wasn't won before the scales tipped against the machine worms, then they'd be destroyed. And that had been the purpose of the message. There was no point in threatening a company. It wasn't good, or evil; it was an amoral construct designed to generate profit for its shareholders. Miska knew she had to disrupt said profit to such an extent that it simply wasn't worth defying her. She was optimistic that she'd done that but she only had so much hope for the miners. They'd chosen a hard road. The worst part, however, had been having to use *Little Jimmy*, her ace-in-the-hole.

The reactive camouflage was still on and she was still moving slowly to allow it to adapt. The TCC might have had other things to worry about right now, what with their arcology being eaten into like a rotten apple, but she was sure that they would be looking for the cause of this catastrophic breach. The Ultra had sent another signal, requesting to be picked up. She was almost surprised that she'd heard back from him.

He was standing out on top of one of the arcology's buttresses, the rags of his prison uniform blowing in the wind, as she banked the *Little Jimmy* around one of the building's corners. She noticed that he no longer had the scalpel. She had no idea where the blade had come from, which was something else she should probably be worried about. Despite the reactive camouflage he seemed to be watching the ship as she brought it in to land. The molecular hooks on the landing gear held the ship fast in the face of the howling wind. She tranced out and undid the straps on her bucket seat, making her way back towards the airlock, telling herself that she wanted to check his collar, make sure that it hadn't corroded in any way. And then he was standing there in the airlock's inner doorway looking at her as though he was somehow old and wise enough to know everything.

'Why?' she asked him. In a way she was disappointed that he had done what she had told him to. She'd half expected him to refuse, maybe even escape the collar. She had wanted him, somehow, to be above it all, not just another member of her slave legion. She wasn't sure why she felt this way.

'I respect the collar,' he told her, his voice a deep musical bass. She tried to tell herself that this was artifice. He was a designed person. Not real. It didn't matter. Then she reached out and laid a hand on him. His skin was warm marble that burned to the touch.

It took every bit of her fatigued patience to take the time to sneak out of Proxima E's atmosphere and space. To get far enough away from the planet to set sail rimward. Passive scans and the stealth ship's long-range lenses told her that the task force was still in orbit. She'd also picked up the coronal display of a particle beam weapon being fired from one of the defence platforms into the atmosphere. It looked like at least one of the robot mining machines had died by violence. She extended the *Little Jimmy*'s gossamer wings and let the ship accelerate to FTL. She decided to stay in the net for the duration. The Ultra's presence was making her feel awkward. She kept an eye on him via the lenses in the ship's cabin. For security reasons, of course.

Decelerating, she sent a message to a net dead letter drop that she knew Rafael would access eventually. She let the CIA case officer know about the Martian tech that Triple-S had used, including 'ware that looked suspiciously close to Small Gods tech. Again this made her smile. It would make life difficult for the security contractors if they had dealings with the US government, or anyone else who'd outlawed the too-easily abused tech.

When she was close enough and slow enough for the lag not to irritate her she opened an AV comms link to the *Daughter*.

'Hey Dad,' she said, far too tired for comms discipline. 'Mission was a success.' He looked sceptical but didn't say anything. 'How're things your end?'

'They're back and unloading,' he told her.

'What's the bill?'

'Gleave and Merrill from your team. Six Wraiths from Mass's, including the one you killed. I'm reviewing some of the footage coming in. It looks like it was pretty hairy. Frankly, it could've been worse.'

Six Wraiths. Six dead prisoners. Halliwell had committed suicide as far as she was concerned. He was no loss. Chan had also got himself killed, but was more of a loss. His death was an excellent example of why her prisoners should listen to those who knew more than they did about actual combat.

She had liked Gleave despite his total lack of backbone. Except he had given the worst possible people the worst possible information at the worst possible time. It wasn't quite as clear-cut as her death leading to the detonation of all the collars, there were failsafes, but there was no good reason to tell the prisoners that. She had assumed that they had enough self-preservation not to tell the enemy. In Gleave's case she'd hugely underestimated the power of cowardliness. Also she'd needed a distraction, and few things distracted like an explosive decapitation. It was only then she remembered that their deaths meant they'd lost five of their precious Wraith power armours. She was pretty sure that Gleave, Merrill, Chan and Halliwell weren't the killers, no skills, or at least not the right ones. She'd review the footage from the other Wraith jockeys, but unless any of them were showing uncharacteristically high-end talent, and a great deal of self-preservation, which given that they were dead seemed unlikely, then they probably weren't the killers either.

'How are the wounded?' she asked.

'Well, they're all going to make it, Nyukuti is still on his back but he's awake. Apparently he took nine rounds. Doc's got no idea how or why he's alive.'

She nodded. She was pleased that the strange stand-over man was still with them. 'Okay, make sure all the weapons are stowed and there's enough droids on duty but break into the guards' beer stash.'

'QRF as well?'

'No, just those who saw combat.' She was still pissed off about Teramoto's apparently successful power play.

'Whereabouts?'

'Hangar deck.' It wasn't the cellblocks so it wouldn't drive home their incarceration so much, but it was also a wide-open space where the automated guns could more easily back up the guard droids.

'Understood.'

'I'm nearly home,' she told him and wondered for a moment when she'd started thinking of the *Daughter* in that way. Then she broke the link.

Beer. It wasn't much but they'd earned it. *When did you start to like them?* she wondered.

The *Hangman's Daughter* looked more ungainly than ever with the *Excelsior*, the assault shuttle and both the prison shuttles plugged into each of its four docks. Her engines were burning brightly as she sought to escape Proxima G's gravity well. Piggybacking the frigate was going to cost them a lot of fuel. Miska knew, however, that between the frigate, the cache of Martian tech, and the money that Cartwright had paid her they would come out ahead. They would strip the *Excelsior* of anything they could use and then sell it. The deal she had made with Che had included the virus evacuating itself from the ship's and the shuttle's systems, as well as any gear they had taken from the contractors. Not that she wouldn't be checking.

Feeling somewhat trance fatigued, Miska came back to the real world and brought *Little Jimmy* in manually. It was good to continually practise these skills, but as soon as she was back in the real world real fatigue hit her like a wave and suddenly the wounds in her legs, face and back hurt. Her shoulder was still very tender and she felt every inch of the beating that she'd taken at Cartwright's hands. *Before I killed the fucker.*

'Would you like me to bring the ship in?'

Suddenly her eyes were open again. The *Hangman's Daughter* was filling the windscreen at an odd angle and it was coming towards them too quickly. She'd fallen asleep. The Ultra's question had woken her. He'd been so quiet, so still, that she'd forgotten that he was there. She righted the ship, used the manoeuvring jets to bleed off speed and took the ship in a long arc around the conning tower and, staying clear of the big engines and their exhaust plume, under the ship. Slowing right down and inverting the ship she took it into the infrastructure. Adhering it to the hull she extruded the tendrils again. She was very conscious of baring all to the Ultra.

Four of the guard droids were waiting for the Ultra on the other side of the airlock. As they put the restraints on him she suddenly couldn't shake the feeling that with him the droids, the collar, her armed presence – none of it was enough if he truly wanted to do something. The guard droids started to lead him away but he stopped. Two of the droids moved to subdue him.

'Hold!' she told them. The Ultra turned to look at her. Miska decided that she was just going to shoot herself if she actually blushed. *Try and remember you're a fucking marine, a Devil Dog*, she admonished herself.

'Thank you, I enjoyed myself,' he told her. *He really is making this sound like a date.* 'You are a very resourceful person.' Then he let the guard droids lead him away. She was watching his nearly naked, perfect porcelain back trying not to grin like one of the sillier girls she'd known at school. She had to remind herself that what she was looking at wasn't so much a person as a weapon.

Teramoto and the QRF, all of them either members of the Bethlehem Milliners *bōsōzoku* gang or low echelon Yakuza, were all stood to attention in neat parade rows as Miska approached the prison shuttle dock where the infiltration and assault teams were sat around on crates enjoying the guards' beer. Miska wasn't sure if she was supposed to think of it as tribute, an apparent acknowledgement of her authority, or a demonstration of their discipline, but she saw it as a message. Teramoto was letting her know who was really in charge of the men in the QRF. She wondered if Mass was getting the same message. If he didn't then Vido would when the button man told the *consigliere* about it. The problem with the little display was she couldn't appear too churlish about it.

'Thank you, Teramoto,' she told him, trying not to speak through gritted teeth. The Yakuza lieutenant was looking at her, studying her, though his expression remained impassive. 'You did good work,' she forced herself to tell him. He nodded in thanks. 'Get your battle dress uniforms stored and head back to the pods.'

His curt nod was almost a bow. He issued orders and the QRF turned as one and jogged away across the hangar deck accompanied by guard droids. She felt herself relax more as they left.

'You don't like them much, do you?' Mass said from atop his crate.

That wasn't good. She couldn't afford to be seen to be playing favourites. Besides, if she was honest with herself then what she most disliked about Teramoto was that he seemed to be outsmarting her from a position of weakness. *If you were being really honest then there's an argument Uncle Vido is as well.* She suspected that one of the talents of the successful criminal was the ability to exploit a given situation. She grabbed a beer and went and sat in the rough circle of crates that the two teams who'd been on the sharp end had made. Including her there were nine of them in total, nine out of the seventeen who'd gone. In some ways they'd done very well against the odds they'd faced. She'd thrown rookies with horribly out-dated equipment against professionals armed with the best technology could provide. It still wasn't good enough.

'I don't like any of you, Mass. You're all criminals, really bad people,' she said and smiled. There was some laughter around the circle. She was trying hard not to look at Torricone. She convinced herself she could feel his eyes on her, however. The thought of the kiss still embarrassed her. The rational part of her mind told her that his rejection was what she had deserved, and more importantly what she had needed.

On a fucking op! What were you thinking? She could only imagine what her dad would have said had he known about it.

'See, we like you because you're the biggest criminal of all,' Mass said. 'You get that I'm Italian, right? I mean, of Italian descent.'

Now Miska laughed.

'Massimo? Really? You surprise me.'

315

'Yeah, well you heard of the Roman Empire?' he asked. She nodded. 'Well they were Italians—'

'From Rome?' one of the Wraith jockeys asked. There was some more laughter.

The man, little more than a boy really, looked like he was pretending to have a good time, but there was a haunted expression in his eyes and Miska noticed that his hands were shaking. *Better after than during*, she thought.

'Yeah, very funny, there's a clue in the name, right? But these guys were hard-core. I mean, one Italian city and they ruled the world. But they had penal legions ...'

'Legions of penises?' Miska asked. There was more laughter.

'No, it means ...'

'I know what it means.'

'We're like those guys, we're *volones*,' he said, smiling, leaning back on the crate and taking another sip of his beer, a look of pride on his face.

'Would that make me Gracchus facing Hannibal?' she asked. Mass's eyes narrowed. What was interesting was that the button man knew what she was talking about.

'Maybe,' he said.

She looked around the circle. Some of the remaining Wraith jockeys seemed as easy with it all as Mass. She guessed they'd been on the sharp end of their own criminal endeavours. One of them was staring into space, his beer untouched. She followed his eyes. The body bags containing the eight they'd lost were lying on the hangar deck behind her. *That could have been done better*, she decided.

Torricone's face was slack. He looked changed, somehow. He was stripped to his waist, medgels patched across his wounds. He was taking sips from his beer, watching her.

'Are we running before the TCC hit the miners?' he asked.

'We're leaving the system but I think they've got a lot more to worry about than Faigroe Station,' Miska told him. She suspected he was trying to decide whether or not he believed her.

Torricone nodded. 'I'm glad you made the right decision, in the end,' he finally said. She decided to let him believe what he wanted to believe.

She glanced over at Nyukuti. The stand-over man was lying on a stretcher laid out between two crates but he had propped himself up on an elbow and was drinking. She had no real idea how he was still alive. He raised a beer to her.

'We dreamed red dreams,' he told her. She just smiled. She had no idea what he was talking about. She took a sip of her beer and then looked down at the scarred and pitted floor of the hangar deck.

'You did good,' she said and then looked up at them. 'I'm proud of you.'

They finished the beers, told a few war stories, Miska tried not to fall asleep and then the guard droids came to escort them back to their pods. Mass was the second last to leave.

'It was a kick, you know,' he said draining the dregs of his beer and putting it down on the crate. Then he looked her straight in the eyes. 'That doesn't mean we've forgotten what you've done to us.' Any trace of warmth, camaraderie, humour was all gone. She met his hard stare and just nodded. Then he smiled again as the droids marched him away. She turned to watch. If anything she was thankful for the reminder.

She looked up and saw Torricone still watching her. Mass nodded to him as he passed. Torricone didn't say anything. He just turned his back to her and let the droids escort him away, leaving her there on her own.

*

Two days later, most of which she'd slept through, her body was beginning to look less like one big bruise. She was tranced in wearing her naturalistic icon, sat atop the command bunker underneath the tower in Camp Reisman. Net versions of the two Pegasus assault shuttles they'd inherited went screaming overhead, banking sharply out over the woodland terrain. One of them covered the other as its ramp opened and flight-capable Machimoi leaped out of the shuttle and into the air. Then the empty shuttle covered the other as it delivered its own power-armoured troops. All over the camp, and in the terrain beyond, various training exercises were taking place under the watchful eye of her dead father's many icons.

'You played a dangerous game,' her dad said from behind her. She looked back at him.

'Either you're sneakier than I thought, or you just spontaneously appeared up here in a way we said we wouldn't do because it threatens the verisimilitude of the simulation,' she said suspiciously. He just smiled and sat down next to her.

'You knew they were going to burn you but you had to play the game as long as possible so other potential customers think you're a good little—'

'Girl?' she asked, teasing him. He narrowed his eyes.

'I was going to say mercenary.'

'Fine, but less of the little. And now any potential customers know that we'll try and fulfil our contract ...'

'And the consequences of betraying us. Would you have really let them kill those miners?' he asked.

'Is it any worse than what I'm doing here?'

He nodded out over the parade ground where one of his alter egos was screaming at a platoon of marching criminals.

'Cause and effect. These guys made some bad choices, hurt people.'

'That isn't a legitimate effect to the cause, and now they just hurt people for me.'

'Second thoughts?' he asked.

She knew that what they were doing had never sat well with him, regardless of the reasons, but he had chosen to back her.

'I don't really care, about them, the miners, any of it,' she told him and then, after a moment: 'You don't trust me, do you? My judgement.'

'Do you?'

The question was like ice water thrown in her face. Miska knew she'd done some questionable things throughout: Torricone, the Ultra, the insane tactics, little more than stunts that had paid off. *No, you got lucky*, she told herself.

'You don't fight like me. You're either some crazy tactical genius or ...'

'Or just crazy?'

He laughed. 'I'm not sure I agree with any of this, particularly not your reasons. I meant what I said when I told you it wasn't worth it. You don't let me go it'll chew you up and you won't like what it spits out.' Miska looked down at the pitted concrete on top of the command bunker. 'But there's enough of me left to know to trust you, to back your play.' She looked up at the electronic ghost of her dad, blinking. 'So I'll trust you if you will.' She grabbed him, hugging him fiercely. 'Woah!' Hugging him as though he was still alive.

'They were going to throw me out,' she told him a little while later, after she'd let him go.

'Who?' The wrinkles in his face practically turned into crevices as his brow furrowed.

'The Raider Regiment, Dad, the marines. The CIA came along at just the right time.' She looked up at him. 'I think I'm just a killer.'

The construct was good enough that she could see the sadness in his eyes. She looked away.

'See, I like it on the sharp end,' she said. 'Drop me into a shooting war, danger close RT strikes, hell, a fucking frigate shot at me and I loved it – admittedly I was starved of oxygen at the time – but that's why I do this stuff, what I live for.'

'You don't like killing, you like action. There's a difference.'

'Not if it's the same end result. See, I never bought into all that patriotic, serving a higher purpose bullshit ...'

'That I did?'

She turned to look at him. 'Sorry.' He just smiled.

'That higher purpose isn't our greedy, venal politicians. There's some good ones, on all sides, but most of them I wouldn't piss on if they were on fire. It's not psychotic corporate interests either. That higher purpose is people, Miska, just people. That's what the oath's about.' He shrugged. 'To me, anyway.'

She looked down. 'Yeah, well, I don't think I'm wired up properly Dad.' She gestured out over the camp. 'I mean, look what I've done.'

'Remorse?'

'No. Well yes ... maybe.'

'Starting to like them?' he asked. She gave this a lot of thought.

'Yes,' she finally said.

'That's inevitable with command.'

'But these are bad people. I mean, they've caused a lot of pain ...'

'Liking them is inevitable, but you can't be their friend.' He seemed to be telling her something. For a moment she felt a guilty thrill as she remembered kissing Torricone. 'Because you're going to get a lot of them killed. You do, however, need to learn to respect them.' He stood up and looked out over the camp.

'Respect them? You think they're all scum.'

'I think everyone I train is scum, until they're not. I reviewed some of the footage from the fighting on Faigroe Station. This lot have got a long way to go yet. As for the rest of it, do what you've gotta do, don't hesitate, but try and make sure you're doing the least amount of harm.'

'Least amount of harm, huh?' she asked, smiling.

'I've known you too long to suggest you try and do good.' She laughed. It was like he'd never died. Perhaps it was a bit too much like that. 'Where to next?'

'The Sirius System,' she told him. The concern was back on his face.

'You know you can't go home, right?' he asked and Miska nodded.

'We need to do some buying and some selling,' she told him. 'Look for our next job.' The message she had left for Rafael in an electronic dead letterbox had told the spook to go on ahead of them to scout for work.

'The Dog's Teeth?' he asked referring to the densely packed asteroid belt between Sirius A and B. 'That's Crimson Sisterhood territory.' Miska nodded, the Sisterhood were a highly organised network of pirates operating out of the Teeth. 'You know we've got some of their menfolk on board, right?'

'Them and everybody else. Still one of the best black markets for ships in the colonies.' Her dad raised an eyebrow but said nothing. 'Oh, and I've thought of a name,' she told him. 'Though I had some help.' She was thinking about Gobbin's last words.

'Yeah, what are we going to be called?'

'The Bastard Legion,' she told him proudly. His face fell.

'Miska, you know I don't like it when you use that kind of language.'

ABOUT GOLLANCZ

Gollancz is the oldest SF publishing imprint in the world. Since being founded in 1927 Gollancz has continued to publish a focused selection of bestselling and award-winning authors. The front-list includes **Ben Aaronovitch**, **Joe Abercrombie**, **Charlaine Harris**, **Joanne Harris**, **Joe Hill**, **Alastair Reynolds**, **Patrick Rothfuss**, **Nalini Singh** and **Brandon Sanderson**.

As one of the largest Science Fiction and Fantasy imprints in the UK it is no surprise we have one of the most extensive backlists in the world. Find high quality SF on Gateway written by such authors as **Philip K. Dick**, **Ursula Le Guin**, **Connie Willis**, **Sir Arthur C. Clarke**, **Pat Cadigan**, **Michael Moorcock** and **George R.R. Martin**.

We also have a strand of publishing in translation, which includes French, Polish and Russian authors. Gollancz is home to more award-winning authors than any other imprint, with names including **Aliette de Bodard**, **M. John Harrison**, **Paul McAuley**, **Sarah Pinborough**, **Pierre Pevel**, **Justina Robson** and many more.

The SF Gateway
More than 3,000 classic, rare and previously out-of-print SF novels at your fingertips.
www.sfgateway.com

The Gollancz Blog
Bringing you news from our worlds to yours. Stories, interviews, articles and exclusive extracts just for you!
www.gollancz.co.uk

GOLLANCZ
LONDON